MW01505723

Happy reading!

Books by Josh Clark

The McGurney Chronicles Series

The Legend of Paul McGurney

Devil's Playground

Infinity

The Ends of the Earth

Ten Thousand Strong (Coming Soon!)

Other Works

Dakota Divided

Available online and in bookstores everywhere.
Also available in all eBook formats.

josh
clark

the mcgurney chronicles

book four

the ends of the earth

Published by White Feather Press. (www.whitefeatherpress.com)

ISBN 978-1-61808-026-4

Printed in the United States of America

Cover design created by Ron Bell of AdVision Design Group
(www.advisiondesigngroup.com)

White Feather Press

Reaffirming Faith in God, Family, and Country!

for my friends and family

The McGurney Chronicles: The Ends of the Earth begins right where *Infinity* left off. If you have not read *Infinity*, or any of the other books in the series, I strongly encourage you to put this book down and read the first three before coming back to this one. If you've read the first three books and need a little refresher on what went down at the end of *Infinity*, I have included the last few chapters to bring you up to speed. It is my hope that you enjoy reading this book as much as I enjoyed writing it.

Happy reading,

Josh

WHAT HAS COME BEFORE...

A *new stranger!*
Todd woke up with a start, drenched in sweat, not having any idea where he was.

"A new stranger! A new stranger!"

His throat was dry and his head felt heavy—like a thirty-pound dumbbell had been lodged in his skull. He found himself in a dull grey room, the smell of a sterile environment all around him: bandages and an unmistakable floor polish. Where was he besides trapped in a dark, cage-like room, trapped and unable to move his right arm?

And then it all came back to him like a flood—the horrific injury, the revelation that the Opposition was dead and that a new threat loomed large over Zak, Jordan and Andrea. He was in the hospital in Toledo, sleeping away the night while the others in Infinity needed him. There was a monster on the loose, one without a face or a name, and Todd had to warn the others. He had to get the message out by any means necessary.

Todd heard a rustle coming from the darkened corner of the small room, and immediately is heart leaped into his throat.

He's here! The stranger is here!

"Stay away!" Todd shouted to the corner. He jerked spastically in the bed, clawing to get as far away from the terrifying rustle as possible but found his right arm immovable and shooting with sharp darts of sizzling pain. When he heard his mother's voice respond, a wave of immense relief washed over him.

He's not here! The stranger is not here! But that means he could be in Infinity!

"Todd? Honey, what's wrong?" His mother rushed over to the bed, flicking on a small lamp near the headboard in the process. The new light caused Todd to wince, and he felt his mother touching his face.

"Todd! Todd! What's the matter? Are you OK? Are you in pain?"

The complexity of the circumstances didn't fail to amaze him. How had everything gotten to this point? How had the entire long and winding road starting with last summer in Colorado gotten him here in a hospital bed in Toledo when his brother and cousins were at home possibly getting stalked by a vicious new murderer without a name? How had this all happened? It seemed like only yesterday that he had been a normal kid with normal worries—the occasional zit and algebra test, wondering what to buy in the a la carte lunch line. Now it was life and death. For all the marbles. Now he was playing for keeps, and with only one good arm.

Todd's eyes finally adjusted to the light, and he squinted up at the weary, worried face of his mother, his nerves tense and on edge, like a thin plate of ice ready to shatter into a billion pieces.

"Where's Dad?"

"I sent him home. He didn't want to go, but there was no reason we both needed to be here. One of us might as well go to work in the morning."

Todd realized that he had no time for idle chatter. What was the old saying: idleness is the devil's workshop?

At least it wasn't Devil's Playground!

"Mom! I need to talk to Jordan!"

His mother looked at him like he was deranged. "It's 12:45 in the morning! Whatever you have to tell him can wait until tomorrow afternoon."

"No! You don't understand! I need to talk to him now! Where's your cell phone?"

"Todd!" His mother whispered forcefully, trying to calm him down. "You need to quiet down. Other patients are sleeping."

"Your cell phone?" Todd asked, only minutely subdued.

"They don't allow cell phones in hospitals."

"Then I need to go—we need to go! Right now!" Todd made an attempt to sit up in bed in order to rip out his IV, but his mother grasped his good arm.

"Todd! What on earth is the matter with you? Do I need to call a nurse? You're acting crazy!"

"I'm not crazy, Mom," Todd said, struggling to free himself from his mother's grasp. "Jordan and the others are in trouble!"

"It's the medication," Todd's mother mumbled, a revelation to herself more than to Todd.

"What? No, I'm fine! I just need to talk to Jordan."

Todd's mother reached to the red page button at the side of the bed and pushed it.

"A nurse will be on the way, honey. I don't know what kind of medication they gave you, but it's making you delirious."

"What? No! No nurse! I'm fine!"

"No you're not. Now just lie back down and keep your voice down, for crying out loud!"

Todd sat up as far as he could, his mother still gripping his left arm tightly. He looked straight into his mother's eyes, purposefully, deeply, trying to let her see that he wasn't cuckoo.

"Mom," he said as evenly as he could. "I'm fine. I can think straight, I can reason OK, and now you have to listen to me. Call the police—just do something if you aren't going to let me talk to Jordan myself. They can't be home alone—tonight—at all. There is a crazy killer out to get them."

A wave of hope swept over him as his mother's eyes took on nervousness around the edges. For a moment, Todd could see that his mother was seriously weighing whether or not to believe her son. But the look only lasted for a moment, her vulnerability was gone when she brushed off the statement with her hand, and put back on the hard exterior shell of disbelief.

"The only thing crazy here is the amount of meds they gave you! Good night! You'd think that you were suffering from multiple personality disorder with all of the stuff they've got you hopped up on!"

Todd's heart sank. So that was it. There was no way he was going to relay a message to the others. They were completely and utterly alone and clueless to the fact that the enemy they thought they were protecting themselves against was long gone, replaced with a brand new fiend, one who could take the shape of anyone at any time because he was faceless as of yet. Nameless. Shapeless. The stranger could be anybody. The stranger could be anywhere.

A thin, middle-aged nurse rushed into the room, alarm on her gaunt, sharp face.

"Is everything all right in here?"

"Yes!" Todd whispered ferociously, crazy with worry for Jordan and the others.

"No, no, it's not," his mother said, talking over her struggling son to the nurse. "I think the medication is making him delusional."

"I'll get a doctor," the nurse said, turning around. "Are you OK here?"

"Yeah—yeah I think so," Todd heard his mother say.

As the nurse exited the room, Todd realized that he was fighting a losing battle. He sank back down onto his back, defeated, all hope for getting the message out gone. His surgically repaired right arm throbbed, but he couldn't care less about the pain. Pain was secondary now. He didn't care if his arm fell off as long as he was able to get the message out that he needed to. And that wasn't going to happen. In a minute, a doctor would be coming in and would probably give him a sedative shot. And that meant he would be out cold, or at least subdued to the point of losing his instincts, and that would not be good. Without his inhibitions he wouldn't be able to get the message out about the new stranger. And if he couldn't get his message out, Jordan and the others could be in a world of hurt. It could be too late when the drug wore off.

He threw his good hand to his face and couldn't hold back the tears.

"The Opposition's dead and there's a stranger on the loose!" He said it over and over again to no avail. His mother just shook her head at his bedside and blamed the medication.

"Why? Why won't you believe me?"

And he rocked with sobs as the doctor bustled into the room and prepped him for his sedative shot.

m-m-m

After Zak finished praying, he opened his eyes and looked up at Andrea and Jordan. How small they looked, how frail and childish. In all reality, they were no match for the Opposition. And Zak knew he was no match, as well. He would die like the other two if it came to hand-to-hand combat. He was nothing special physically, no forced to be reckoned with.

And what of his mother? Here she was sleeping under a marked roof, with marked prey sitting on the floor of a small bedroom no less than twenty-five feet and two walls away. Would the Opposition kill her, too, if he attacked tonight?

We're just kids! Children! What harm could we possibly be to the Opposition and his Master?

And just then as he looked first at Jordan and then at Andrea, his perspective changed. Yes, there was no doubt that they were all three mere children, physically weak and susceptible to a large assassin if it came to blows. But what Zak realized in that moment was that he and the others were more than just children when it came to all things eternal. They possessed a belief that was greater than all principalities and evil of the world, greater than all forces of death and hate. What they possessed trumped the physical and sent Satan to his knees. Yes, what they lacked in physical strength they made up for in a Power that knew no limits. As Jesus had told him when the two had met so intimately in Paul McGurney's house, he was special—*they* were special. Jesus was working in them and had plans for their lives that would not sour and spoil, but blossom into fruit—abundant, breathing fruit. Jesus had said He was always working for the good in those he loved, and He loved Zak, Jordan and Andrea. They were His and He was theirs. They were mutually joined at the hip, heirs to the same kingdom. Jesus was alive and living within them; why should they fear?

Zak's eyes met Jordan's, and Zak didn't have to say anything, because both somehow knew. A tranquility settled over the room and time seemed to suspend and hover. Peace reverberated off the walls, off the dresser and bed, and ricocheted back to the children. Andrea's lip stopped trembling, and the three just allowed themselves to rest in the presence of One they couldn't see but knew was there nonetheless. Were there battles to fight? Perhaps. Could they fall victim to the blade of a madman? Maybe. But in that moment, as silence enveloped the room and a hush swept over their souls, they all realized that to live was Christ, and to die was Him, as well. They were being caressed by an unseen, ever-present hand, lulled into the lullaby of grace. And it felt so amazing, as grace never fails to feel.

m-m-m

Jordan felt the rush of fear leave him, felt a peace beyond his understanding grab hold of him. He felt his eyes close, his lids heavy with sleep. And he slept more peacefully than he ever had in his entire life.

m-m-m

Andrea couldn't place the new feeling. Not the overwhelming sense of peace and security that seemed to blanket the room like heavy snow after a snowstorm. It wasn't the way the she felt so light, as if all her fears were spoken for, as if someone was experiencing them in her stead. It wasn't that. It was something else.

She looked over at Jordan and saw that his eyes were closed and he was breathing heavily, his head leaned back against the wall and his mouth partially open in what could only be described as a blissful smile. She saw that Zak was also beginning to settle in and allow sleep to sweep over him as his head bobbed once and finally stayed down against his chest. Her own eyelids were heavy, and she wanted nothing more than to enter into a deep sleep like the other two, but something kept happening with the room. Maybe it was her eyes, or maybe she was dizzy, but it kept seeming as though the room was swaying back and forth. She clenched her eyes shut once and opened them again to see the room swaying back and forth like a porch swing.

What in the world?

The room continued to sway, but now it threatened to overtake itself, to upend and become gravity's opposite.

This can't be right! Something is definitely going on—

And then the room completely turned upside down, and Andrea found herself sitting on the ceiling—or was it still technically the floor? Whatever the case, this was most definitely not normal.

Um—am I dreaming? Or is there something I need to know about?

And then the room instantly went black.

m-m-m

Andrea's eyes were just getting adjusted to the dense blackness when all of a sudden the darkness exploded into an intense light—a familiar light.

Where am I?

Andrea looked around her new surroundings, and found that what she saw was completely familiar and strangely time-altering. Andrea realized that she was standing on the golden road of her dream world from last summer, the same golden road that led her to the majestic mansion on the hill of encrusted gemstones. This was the world from which she had retrieved a pearl from the silver wheat field and heard the Voice a little under a year ago. This was the dream world which had been the starting point for the adventure she and the others were still a part of, the story that was still being written.

How amazing! It's all the same!

Andrea looked down and saw that a tiny stream of water was flowing between her feet, precise and straight, cutting the golden road like butter. The trees all around her clinked their golden leaves in the perfumed breeze, and a bird of an exotic orange and red perched atop one of their golden branches.

For the first time, Andrea really realized where she was.

I'm standing at the fork in the road, with my back to the path that leads to the house on the hill!

Slowly, she turned around, not wanting to disturb the perfection of the dream world or to be whisked away from it with any sudden movements. As she did, she was startled by a familiar voice.

"Hello, Andrea."

Andrea completed her turn and found herself standing face to face with Paul McGurney. The ancient man rested on his cherry cane, his transparent, veiny hands folded atop one another. His spider-webby white hair blew gently in the breeze, and his sharp, blue vacant eyes were sparkling. The old man was wearing his familiar cardigan and khaki pants. The only difference was that he was barefoot, his small feet being warmed by the polished gold of the path.

"Hello, Andrea," Paul McGurney said again, his eyes sparkling. "This is where it all began, is it not?"

"Yeah, it is," Andrea said smiling, her head filling with all kinds of questions.

"It is so good to see you again. I've missed your company," McGurney said, his smile as wide as ever.

"I was hoping that I'd get to see you again. Did you arrange this?" She indicated the golden surroundings with an open palm.

"Ah, no," McGurney said, shaking his head. "As you know, I am but a messenger. A humble servant for a Greater cause. I had no knowledge that I would meet you again until I was given it, but I had hoped that I would have the pleasure of making your acquaintance again."

"Where have you been this past year," Andrea asked, dispensing one of the million and one questions that fought to leap from her mouth at the same time.

Paul McGurney chuckled. "Some things are not necessary to reveal, or cannot be until the appointed time. Let's just say that I have been here and there."

Now it was Andrea's turn to laugh. "I didn't realize how much I missed the way you talk in riddles sometimes."

"Sometimes riddles are the best form of communication, for they require the listener to really hear what the speaker is saying."

"I guess you're right," Andrea said, all smiles.

"And I bet I am right to assume that you are wondering what you are doing here again," Paul McGurney said, taking a hand off of his cane and pointing to the golden landscape.

"Well—yeah," Andrea said. Did it really matter *why* she was here? Wasn't it enough just to *be* here?

"I have come to tell you something important, something serious and vital that you must relay to the other children."

Paul McGurney's face became solemn, and Andrea knew that when the old man's face took on that look, it meant business and possible peril.

"I don't know if I like the sound of this," Andrea said, trying to giggle but only managing a weak squeak.

"Sometimes things we don't like hearing must be said in order to quicken the process of restoration," Paul McGurney, his eyes narrowing but holding their gleam.

"I guess you're right."

"Before I tell you what it is I am sent here to say, let me assure you that you are in good hands. He who began a good work in you will be faithful to complete it, but sometimes the road of faith is full of bumps and potholes. You must hold on, Andrea. You must hold onto the faith you found last summer, to the faith that called you home."

"I know, Mr. McGurney, but it's so hard sometimes," Andrea said, fighting back the urge to cry.

"I know, dear one. Faith never guaranteed a peaceful path through life. You are being opposed by an evil that wants to destroy the fruit you have already begun to bear. You must hold fast and realize that where you are fearful, there is Power." McGurney chuckled. "You must do it afraid, as I hear you have become fond of saying."

"I am afraid, Mr. McGurney. I'm scared."

"Trust, child. You must trust. The Knowledge never proves false or comes back void."

Andrea nodded, stifling the sobs that wanted to burst forth from her chest.

"And now, dear one, I must tell you what I am sent here to tell you," Paul McGurney said, his voice becoming a near whisper.

"Listen closely dear one, for life and death is held in balance, and good and evil are waiting to come to blows in a final culmination of principle forces."

m-m-m

In her Colorado cabin, Margaret Kessler locked her doors for the night, and sat down in her tiny living room in a chair that looked away from the kitchen nook and the front door. The creep Hanson guy hadn't been back to work on her phone line yet, and for that Margaret was grateful. That guy scared her something fierce.

He could be the stranger!

Margaret was convinced that something was different about the man—different enough for her to take her shotgun out of her closet upstairs to keep it handy at all times. She was taking no chances.

Margaret looked to the small window and saw that the snow the forecasters on TV 8 had predicted was now coming down steadily. Snow in May was not uncommon in the high altitudes of Colorado, but the two to four feet the meteorologists had suggested was definitely an unwelcome surprise. What made it all the worse was the distinct possibility of Margaret's being snowed in without a phone or any kind of communication to the outside world. She owned no computer and had balked at getting a cell phone when both her daughters had suggested she should last winter, after she had been snowed in for three days before finally chaining up the tires of her old Jeep and braving the slick roads when she ran out of milk and bread. Being snowed in wasn't so bad, except that now the prospect of it sent a chill up and down her spine.

He might be out there waiting for me! If I get snowed in, then I am a sitting duck!

Yes, Hanson might be the stranger—but he also might just be a creepy electrician. How was a person really supposed to know? What kind of litmus test was she supposed to make? Her gut didn't feel right about the guy, and didn't they always say that first instincts are usually right? But who were *they* anyway?

I wish I had some answers!

She looked to the crossword puzzle book, still in the same place she had left it after realizing that Paul McGurney had sent her a message via the Down clues.

"Maybe I missed something."

Bending over to reach the coffee table, she felt a cool breeze tickle the back of her neck. She sat back up.

"What in the world–"

All of a sudden, a steel hand clapped over her mouth. Her blood turned to ice when she felt the cool edge of a sharp, serrated knife to her throat.

"Silence!" a deep, distorted voice rasped. "You will listen without speaking or I will cut your throat!"

Margaret's head spun as terror seized her every muscle.

How did he get in?

"You will deliver the children to me upon their arrival!" The voice hissed. "Is that clear?"

Margaret didn't know how to respond, both because blind horror had overcome her and because the perpetrator had told her not to speak.

"Do you understand?" the voice screamed at her.

"I–" Margaret began, and she felt the hand clamp tighter over her mouth.

"It's a yes or no question, you old bag!" the voice demanded.

Margaret began to panic. She would never give up her grandchildren to whoever it was behind her; but if she answered in the negative, she was a goner.

"I don't have all night, woman!"

Margaret knew what she had to do, knew the next word that came out of her mouth could be her last. Whispering a silent prayer, she mustered up her courage and answered her attacker.

"No!"

Margaret felt the attacker's muscles go rigid as he became filled with rage.

"What did you say?"

"I said no!" Margaret spat, as the knife at her neck now began to draw blood.

"You made a poor choice, you old bag!" The voice screamed. "A poor, poor choice!"

As her heart pounded, Margaret prayed that the children would somehow hear the voice inside her head screaming for them to stay home.

The Stranger had come.

And now...

the story

continues

the ends

of the

earth

and then they were scattered

The Stranger

Chapter One

*T*here was a thick silence as Andrea readied herself for whatever bombshell Paul McGurney was about to deliver. She shuddered as she played what he had just said over in her mind.

"Listen closely, dear one, for life and death is held in balance, and good and evil are waiting to come to blows in a final culmination of unseen forces."

Andrea was frightened by the fervent intensity in Paul McGurney's piercing blue eyes. Though vacant and void of sight, they had the ability to become startlingly animated and alive whenever he imparted information of importance, causing Andrea's stomach to roil and cool pricks of electricity to run up and down her spine. She knew these eyes, knew the *look* of Mr. McGurney's solemn urgency, and she shuddered as she waited for whatever potentially terrifying bits of information he would dispense. The first time she had seen the *look* had been last summer. The old man's eyes had narrowed, his brow had furrowed in ardent concentration as he had evenly revealed to her family foursome that an evil assassin was hot on their trail—the Opposition—and that he wanted to destroy all of the Knowledge she and the others had gained, all of the glorious insight and intimacy they had found in Jesus. Now there was something new, something else Mr. McGurney was about to say, and Andrea could tell it was going to go down as smoothly as broken glass. She licked her lips, her heart pattering loudly, and addressed Paul McGurney.

"W—What are you saying, Mr. McGurney? Are you talking about the Opposition coming to attack us? Is he coming tonight?"

Paul McGurney's eyes softened momentarily, compassion and love present where sight was not. He smiled gently.

"My child, I sense your fear. It is not my intention to make you fearful. It is only my intention as a dear friend and messenger to make you aware." He reached out an ancient hand and touched the top of Andrea's head, ruffling her hair gently in a grandfatherly way.

Andrea felt her eyes puddle with warm tears. Mr. McGurney was one of the most sincere, true friends she had ever had. She knew it was not his intention to cripple her with fear, nor was it his motive to lead her into harm. After all, it had been Paul McGurney who had confronted the Opposition at Devil's Playground, and Paul McGurney who had introduced her and the others to Jesus. Mr. McGurney was kind and compassionate, yet straightforward and forthright. Being a messenger for a Higher Purpose, it was his duty to fulfill his mission and impart his message to the children. He was only doing his job. But was she ready for this—old enough to be the one to bear such an important message? Why couldn't Todd have been the one to receive this news?

She steadied her resolve and sniffled back her frightened emotions. She was here and that was all there was to it. If Todd were supposed to be here, he would've been sent, too, instead of being cooped up on a hospital bed with a broken arm and dislocated shoulder. She would have to be the conduit through which important information was passed.

Be strong. I am here for a reason.

Mr. McGurney removed his aged hand from Andrea's head, his eyes reassuming their concentrated fervor.

"You are being hunted, dear one, by a fiend set on your destruction."

Andrea felt the warm, perfumed breeze pick up and rustle the golden leaves on the golden tree branches. As she pulled stray strands of hair from her face and tucked them behind her ears, she wondered why Mr. McGurney was telling her something she already knew. This seemed like yesterday's news—so—*last year*. It seemed like the Opposition had been a shadow lurking in the corner for eons now, stalking and plotting to kill her and the others last summer in Colorado, and now coming back to get revenge in Ohio a year after being defeated at Devil's Playground. There had been a definite year-long reprieve from the Opposition's torturous prowling, but somehow the events of Colorado and Infinity, Ohio, meshed themselves together in Andrea's head. This time around, as opposed to Colorado, the Opposition had been literally within breathing distance of killing the children.

The Opposition had taken the form of Andrea's fictitious Uncle Phil, had infiltrated her mother's house and had literally slept feet away from Andrea in a bedroom adjacent to hers. She had had a sickening feeling—a queasy discernment that Uncle Phil was not who he said he was. And by the time she and the others had pieced the jigsaw puzzle together, he had taken flight, realizing he had been found out. But now he was back. Waiting—hunting. His assignment was to kill the four children, and he knew three of them were leaving for Colorado in a little over twenty-four hours. If the Opposition was going to make a move, it was going to be tonight. But she knew all that, didn't she? Why was Mr. McGurney telling her something she already knew?

"Mr. McGurney, we know we're being hunted. The Opposition is after us and--" she stopped abruptly when she saw the old man

3

shaking his head gently, his eyes sparkling somberly.

"No, child. You do not understand. The Opposition is no more."

"What—what do you mean? The Opposition is—what? Dead?" Andrea's head was reeling. Could it really be? Could the Opposition be dead? But what did that mean? Was Paul McGurney telling her what she thought he was telling her?

"He has expired, dear one."

"Mr. McGurney—in English, please!"

Paul McGurney smiled lightly. "Yes, child. The Opposition is dead."

Andrea felt lightheaded with happiness. Her feet wanted to dance a jig—her arms wanted to wrap around Mr. McGurney in a hug of triumph. Somewhere in her head she was hearing *Ding-dong, the witch is dead*! The elation she felt, the alleviation of an anchor around her neck, it was all too much.

"You can't be serious! He's dead! He's really *dead*!?" And she did throw her arms around Paul McGurney, making the old man stumble ever-so-slightly.

"Andrea, dear one, there is something else," Paul McGurney began as Andrea hugged him again and jumped up and down on the smooth, golden street.

"We're free! We're free!" Andrea continued, spinning around and taking in the gorgeous golden surroundings, allowing the fragrant breeze to whip her hair into a frenzy. Paul McGurney put out a hand to calm her, gently squeezing her shoulder to get her to calm down for a moment. When Andrea felt McGurney's hand, she stopped spinning and turned to face him. When she did, she wished she hadn't, for the old man's face was solemn again, and his eyes told a story Andrea knew she didn't want to hear. Her smile faded at once, and she felt her stomach tighten.

"What is it, Mr. McGurney? The Opposition is dead—it can't be *that* bad, can it?"

"You have nothing to fear, for fear is not your God," Paul

McGurney began, echoing something he had told the children last summer.

Andrea knew he was setting her up for something not-so-good. It was true that fear was not her God, but sometimes fear served as a warning. And sometimes it spiraled out of control. Andrea knew Mr. McGurney was speaking to the latter, but somehow his words didn't seem all that comforting when she knew there was more he was going to say.

"I know, Mr. McGurney. But what is it? What could be worse than the Opposition?"

Paul McGurney studied her for a moment as though he could actually see her earnestness and desperation. He cleared his throat and continued.

"The Opposition will no longer harm you. But there is another who has risen up to take his place."

"Another?" Andrea's eyebrows shot up and cool prickles of sweat picked at her forehead despite the warmness of the golden world.

"Yes, child. Another predator more powerful than the first is now tracking your every move. This person is powerful and fiendish, yet still subservient to the one true God. Greater is He Who is in you than he who is in the world, Andrea. Never forget that."

Andrea felt the blood drain from her face. " A new predator? A new Opposition?"

Paul McGurney nodded. "A new opposing force. A Stranger stalking in the night."

"But what do we do? What do I tell the others?" Andrea was nearly hysterical with panic. Her breath became short and she felt herself on the verge of hyperventilating.

Paul McGurney raised a wrinkled, tremulous hand. "Do not lose heart, dear one. You are more powerful than any force of evil, fiercer than a double-edged sword when you possess the Knowledge of Christ."

5

Andrea felt herself tearing up again, but warred with her emotions to dam the flood. "I know, Mr. McGurney. I know. But sometimes it's so hard being strong."

"Strength is a byproduct of faith, child," McGurney began as the breeze made a few of his wispy white hairs dance. "Where there is faith, there is courage and steadfast resolve. You must never lose sight of the fact that you have already won. When Jesus Christ died for you, He defeated death and sin once and for all and gave you access to eternal life. All you had to do is accept His free gift, and you have, Andrea. To live is Christ and to die is gain."

"I like the living part a lot better," Andrea said, picking up a golden leaf that had fallen on the golden path. She scratched at its pristine golden veins with her fingernail.

"Life is full of obstacles, Andrea. Some are physical, and others are spiritual. You must understand that every obstacle and opposing force is light troubles compared to what is in store for you for all eternity."

"But what about now? What do we do *now,* while we're still alive, Mr. McGurney?"

"Watch and pray, child. Be vigilant and alert, on your guard at all times. The Word says that the Evil One prowls around like a ravenous lion, stalking and waiting for those he can devour. The Evil One is the Stranger's master, and he wants only to steal, kill and destroy the Knowledge you have obtained." The old man paused, allowing the leaves to chime in the breeze. "Take heart. Have faith. You are loved."

With that, Andrea's surroundings became fuzzy. The golden path seemed to sway back and forth, and then it completely traded places with the sky.

"Mr. McGurney, when will I see you again--" But before she could finish her question, the dream world vanished and she found herself back in Zak's room.

6

Chapter Two

*D*eep in the bowels of the earth, an emergency meeting was taking place. Around the monstrous cherry table in the middle of a candlelit conference room sat the top-ranking Fiends, the movers and shakers of hell itself. The conglomerate of ancient oppressors and soul-snatchers, the principalities of the land and air, the demonic generals of Lucifer's vast infantry, sat with the grimmest of expressions as their lord took the floor. Ghastly shadows danced on the earthy walls, and gnarled roots jutted from the crumbling structure. This was definitely not a meeting for the weak at heart. Fear was thick in the room, morale was low. The Fiends knew why they were here. They had been thwarted one too many times.

Lucifer—the Prince of the Air, the Father of Lies—stood from the head of the table and glared at his emissaries. Cloaked in a cloud of sulfurous smoke, his feral eyes were the only part of his massive being that could be seen. Yellow and terrifying, they chilled even the most indomitable of the Fiends.

"You have failed me," Lucifer said in an icy voice. He peered at his Fiends, pierced them to the core with his deathly eyes. "You have failed me in ways I cannot fathom. My tangible assassin, Sorak, known to the children as the Opposition, failed me because *you* failed *him*!" Lucifer slammed his fists onto the table and the dark hole of a bunker seemed to tremble.

"What is it you do, exactly?" Lucifer continued, his sizeable person seeming to prowl the ground at the head of the table. "Aren't you supposed to pave the way for my will to be done? Aren't you supposed to destroy hope and character? Faith itself? Aren't you supposed to instill fear and incite panic? Aren't you the best of the best? Don't you command legions of my disciples into battle?" His voice rose with every rhetorical question, and the Fiends shivered in his presence. The Master's anger was legendary.

"The Opposition had to die because he failed. He failed because you failed him. I have another tangible assassin commissioned to destroy the children, one more ruthless, more cunning than the Opposition ever was. But my new agent of death needs assistance in order to succeed." Lucifer stopped and spoke with the directness of fiery darts. "And *you* must allow my new killer to succeed. These children, this disease, must be annihilated."

Lucifer paused to let his words sink in. The Fiends fidgeted, knowing that should they fail, they would be sentenced to a death more terrifying than they could ever imagine, one worse than their present state of lightless, hopeless chaos.

Lucifer continued, his voice razor-edge sharp, his eyes balls of fire. "You must go before my assassin and kill the children's spirits. You must twist their minds to believe lies, you must torture their resolve so they will doubt the abominable Knowledge. You must break the grandmother's heart so she will fall from grace." He pounded the table to emphasize his last point. "And you must *not*, under any circumstance, allow the children to hold conference with Paul McGurney. Is that clear?"

The Fiends trembled. Only one, a scaly, decaying general named Tor, had the courage to answer.

"Yes, my lord. We will do as you say."

Lucifer's eyes blazed. "Then get it done!"

8

Chapter Three

Margaret Kessler sat trembling on her sofa, holding a Kleenex to her slightly bleeding neck. Outside, the snow was coming down in thick paper sheets, and the wind was howling and wailing in the deep, lonely blackness of the night. All was still at the moment, too dreadfully still inside her small mountain home. Margaret looked timidly to her cabin door, where only five minutes earlier, the Stranger had exited into the frigid darkness. A tear streaked down her cheek, and she couldn't keep her teeth from chattering together.

How am I alive? How am I still here?

The fact that she was still breathing and her heart was able to beat at seemingly seventy-eight million beats per minute was a miracle. An intruder—the Stranger, she was sure of it—had broken into her cozy little cabin and demanded that she turn over her grandchildren upon their arrival in Colorado in a little over twenty-four hours. The Stranger had held her from behind, a heavily serrated knife to her throat, so she had not been able to get a good look at him. He had been gruff and violent, his voice raspy and course. Threatening her life, he had demanded repeatedly that she give up her grandchildren to him, and she had refused. This had infuriated the intruder, and she had thought he would take her life right there in her living room. But he hadn't; he had thrown her down on the ground—she had the already-forming bruises on the heels of her hands to prove it—and demanded that she not turn around until he left, threatening to bloody her and worse if she did. She had obliged, and he had left the cabin with an unsettling slam of the door, but not before vowing that he would return. After waiting a few fear-drenched minutes, Margaret had gotten up from the floor and quickly locked the cabin door. Not satisfied with the flimsy standard door lock, she piled heavy books—dictionaries, dusty old encyclopedias, the Kessler family Bible—in front of the oak door. She moved an end table and love seat beside the books, wedging them as tightly as she could in order to obstruct entrance and ease her mind. She knew she was vulnerable through the windows of the cabin, but for some reason the door being barricaded made her heart and tremors slow down and her breathing normalize. Just the knowledge that no one could possibly break through the door without her knowing it soothed her, and she now rested her head on the back of the couch, being sure not to look out the big picture window behind her into the black night.

"I can't believe I've almost died *twice* in the last year!" Margaret said to the empty room. She chuckled nervously, the tension thick in her voice. She raised a hand to the back of her head, to where she had a permanent knot from last summer, compliments of the butt of the Opposition's nasty gun. The Opposition had kidnapped her in order to bait the children into following him up the Pike's Peak trail to Devil's Playground, where his plan had been to throw the children off a cliff one by one. His plan had been thwarted by Paul McGurney and the Knowledge, and he himself had ended up taking a tumble from the treacherous overhang. Or so everyone had thought. Unbeknownst to Margaret, the Opposition had survived the fall by getting his army-issue belt loop caught on a jutting rock, and had come back to torment the children in Ohio. But now there was something—someone new hunting the children. *The Stranger*.

Margaret Kessler had had a few run ins with the supernatural, but none had been more surprising and out of the blue than finding a message from Paul McGurney concerning the coming of the Stranger in the DOWN clues of a crossword puzzle. She had been on edge then, hand-wringing nervous because her grandchildren were supposed to be flying into Denver three days from the afternoon she had gotten Paul McGurney's message and her power had gone out. With no access to a phone—her cabin was twelve miles from any other sign of civilization—and it beginning to snow something fierce, she had no way of warning the children to stay put in Ohio; that a trek to Colorado might end up being a trek to their graves. And to make matters worse, the electrician from Divide sent to fix her phone—which was *still* not fixed—gave her the creeps. His last name was Hansen, and Margaret had not ruled out the possibility that he was the Stranger. A big man, round and girthy, with thick arms and broad shoulders, Hansen, in Margaret's intuitive opinion, was public enemy number one at the moment for lack of more suspects. The Stranger could be the Opposition. Margaret saw no reason why he couldn't be. But something about the Stranger's voice had been different, more gruff. Where the Opposition had had a mission to kill the four children, the Stranger seemed like a wild card; a crazed murderer who would kill anything in his path. But who really knew? Margaret wished she could speak to Paul McGurney. He would know what madness was ensuing. She also wished she could make contact with the children before they walked into a trap. So much drama. So many unanswered questions.

And that brought her up to the present, sitting on her sofa with a Kleenex to the small cut the Stranger's knife blade had left on her neck, wondering how it was possible she had survived *two* attacks in less than a year.

"I just wish I could warn them before it's too late," Margaret whispered to the stillness. "Just stay home. Please stay home."

Margaret sighed, taking the Kleenex off her neck. Her cut

was no longer bleeding, and she stood up from the sofa. Crossing the small living room to the kitchen, she prepared to boil water to make herself a cup of green tea. As she was filling the kettle with tap water, her hand trembling from shock, she threw up a silent prayer to the God she had come to know and love since last summer's fiasco.

Jesus, keep us safe!

Chapter Four

"Um—guys? We have a situation," Andrea said as the surroundings of Zak's room became clear. She glanced to the four corners of the small bedroom to make sure everything was still barricaded—Zak's desk in front of the door, the bed in front of the desk, books piled high atop Zak's desk chair to seal off the only window in the room. All was still in place. But that didn't make her feel any better.

"Hey, guys. Wake up!" Andrea nudged her brother and he snorted softly once and wiped at a strand of drool on his chin with the back of his hand. Jordan startled awake beside him, both boys now completely aware of their surroundings and the terror that had forced them to seal themselves off from the outside world.

"What? What is it? Is everything OK?" Zak's eyes darted around the room, making sure the Opposition wasn't trying to break through the door or squeeze through the window. Andrea touched his hand gently to center him again and to reassure him that all was safe at the present moment. She hated to calm him down only to rile him up again with the devastating news she had received from Paul McGurney. The past week had been a trying one to say the least, and the effects of constant fright and looking over their shoulders had visibly worn on both boys—and her. Andrea wanted more than anything to keep the information to herself, to pass it off as a fantastical dream, but she knew better. She knew enough now from a year of experience with such matters as time travel and dream worlds to know what she had just seen and felt and heard had been as legit as the rug she was sitting on and the soft smell of lavender air freshener in Zak's room. She had to tell and it was going to be hard.

"What is it, Andrea?" Jordan whispered fervently, his deep brown eyes wide and filled with trepidation.

"I—I just had a dream," Andrea began. She never really knew how to explain her experiences in the dream world to anyone—it wasn't something particularly *normal*-- so she clumsily started over. "I just had a dream—I mean—a dream that wasn't a dream—and Mr. McGurney was there."

Instantly the two boys leaned forward intently, as if their lives clung to every word Andrea was about to speak. She realized quickly that she need not be embarrassed to speak of her dream, nor did she have to completely find the right words. She was looking back at her brother and cousin, both of whom had had experiences like hers, though theirs were also uniquely their own. So she took a deep breath and just let it flow.

"The Opposition is dead," Andrea blurted. This was not particularly how she wanted to start, but she'd have to go with it. It would bring a few seconds of false hope and then a crash, like coming down from a sugar high.

Both boys looked at each other, their faces lighting up like florescent bulbs, smiles spreading wide across their cheeks.

"The Opposition's dead! Are you serious? This is *awesome*!" Zak exclaimed. He remembered his mother sleeping in the room next door and he visibly tried to bring down the volume of his ecstatic voice, but the news was too much. "We're free! Jordan—can you believe it? It's over!" Zak grabbed Jordan and smothered him in a seated bear hug. Releasing him, Zak jumped to his feet and danced around the room.

Jordan beamed at Andrea. "For real? Is this for real? Because if it is, then I'm gonna get up and dance with him!" He searched Andrea's face for a jubilant moment and then his smile slowly faded when he saw Andrea's expression was grim and fearful. Zak continued to dance in he background, oblivious to Jordan's revelation.

"What? What is it? There's more isn't there? Zak—stop dancing and just settle down for a minute!" Jordan grabbed his cousin's leg, but Zak shook him off.

"I can't stop dancing, man! We're free! We're fr--"

"There's someone new," Andrea said over him. "The Opposition's dead, but there's someone rising up to take his place."

Zak immediately stopped dancing. "Whoa, whoa, whoa. Hold on a sec. Tell me you didn't say what I think you just said!"

When Andrea didn't say anything, Zak plopped down beside her and his eyes pleaded with hers.

"What do you mean, there's someone else? The Opposition II? What? *Who*?"

"Mr. McGurney called him a stranger—*The* Stranger. He said this one's more powerful than the Opposition."

Zak's hands went to his hair and he all but pulled a blonde clump out by its roots. "No, no, no, no, no, no, *no*. No! This isn't supposed to be happening! Not now! Not ever! Not when we're about to leave for the summer!" He was frantic now, teetering on the edge of hyperventilation. "What else did he say? *What else did he say*?"

"Zak, just calm down, man--" Jordan said, putting a hand on Zak's shoulder. Zak shrugged it off hastily as if it were searing lava.

"I want to know what Mr. McGurney said! What else did he say?"

"He said to be on our guard. To watch and pray and that greater is He Who is in us than he who is in the world.'

15

Zak threw up his hands, sweat now beading on his forehead. He looked around the room, his eyes alive and aflame with hysteria. "You mean like *now*? You mean to watch and pray like now? To be on our guard more than we already are? The Terminator couldn't get through the door right now, and we're supposed to be *more* prepared?"

Jordan stood up, trying to reason with Zak by holding his shoulders gently, trying to make eye contact while Zak's head darted this way and that.

"Zak, come on, just sit down--" Zak threw off Jordan's hands and shoved him away. Stunned, Jordan fell harmlessly onto Zak's bed, his face an O of disbelief.

"It's the same old thing," Zak said, his breath coming in short gasps. " ' Be on your guard,' 'watch and pray.' Well, maybe I don't want to do that anymore! Maybe I want a tank and a bazooka and some serious ammo! It's one thing to say to be on your guard, but it's another thing to do it, and I'm sick of living like this!" He collapsed on the floor, the sobs now coming. "I sometimes wish I'd never met Jesus!"

Jordan and Andrea were silent. The only noise that could be heard in the room was Zak's sniffles and sobs. Andrea didn't know what to think. His outburst shocked her, not necessarily because of what he had said, but because it had been *him*. He was the leader now with Todd indisposed, and he had been doing such a good job at staying strong for her and Jordan. But now he was a mess, crumpled on the floor like a slumped ragdoll, defeated and afraid of the world.

But maybe that's one quality of a good leader, Andrea thought suddenly. *Maybe a good leader isn't afraid to be vulnerable—to be scared. Wasn't Jesus afraid that night He prayed for the cup to be passed from Him literally moments before He was arrested?*

When the words spewed from his mouth, Zak knew he hadn't meant them. Not in the slightest. After all, it had been only a few hours and some change since he had had an amazingly intimate moment with Jesus, where Jesus had reassured Zak of His love and reaffirmed that His call on Zak's life was true and thriving. As Andrea came over and sat down beside him, Zak shook with sobs and tried to rationalize why he had said what he had said at all.

Because sometimes it would be so much easier to just do my own thing without worrying about getting killed for it.

Zak sniffled and wiped away the tears that now only trickled down his cheeks. "Guys, I'm sorry. I—I didn't mean it."

Andrea rubbed his back in small circles. "We know, Zak. We know you didn't mean it. We all feel that way sometimes."

Jordan sat down on the floor beside the two and hugged his knees to his chest. "Yeah, man. I struggle with this one a lot. Especially since we didn't have to barricade ourselves in your bedroom or worry about getting slashed to death if we walk down the wrong street at the wrong time before—before all this," Jordan scratched the back of his neck and sighed. "I feel like that sometimes and I don't like it, either. But I think it's natural."

Zak looked at Jordan and met his cousin's deep amber eyes. "I wish Todd was here. I don't think I like being the oldest." He mustered a laugh and swiped at his nose. "Look at me, I'm such a baby."

"Sometimes a good cry is the best thing," Jordan said with a smile.

"Look at me, I do it all the time!" Andrea said, clapping Zak on the back.

Zak and Jordan laughed together, knowing Andrea wasn't admitting anything all too secret. With a sniffle, Zak felt his stomach muscles clench and his face become sober again. He looked at Jordan.

"I know what you're thinking," Jordan said, the same solemn

countenance on his face. "We're still in a huge mess. A new predator presents all kinds of problems."

"Like—how do we even know what this guy looks like?" Andrea asked, feeling the tension thickening in the room. "Is he gonna look like the Opposition?"

Zak considered her question for a moment—all of their questions, really. Not one of them had any idea what to expect from crazy killer number two. He squeezed the bridge of his nose gently, the first throbs of a stress headache drumming somewhere deep in the back of his skull.

"There's really no way to know," Zak said finally. "We can't know until--"

"He attacks us," Jordan finished grimly. Zak saw a little tremor run through his cousin's arm, ending at his hand, making his fingertips twitch slightly.

"I think we could potentially have two things going for us," Zak said, trying to muster up as much bravado as he could. If he was going to be the leader, then he was going to have to start thinking and speaking like one.

"What could we possibly have going for us?" Andrea asked bleakly. Zak could see the well of tears in her eyes waiting to splash free from the dam of her fleeting resolve.

"Well, let's think about this," Zak began, making invisible bullet points on an invisible outline on his bedroom floor. "Number one, we have the whole separation factor. With Todd in the hospital in Toledo, the Stranger can't get us all at once. There's no way he can be two places at the same time, so there is the potential that we are sitting ok."

"At what cost?" Jordan asked defensively. Zak realized right away that what he had said could seem like he meant the children in Infinity would be ok as long as the Stranger was working on eliminating Todd. Jordan continued with narrowed eyes before Zak could jump in and make the necessary correction. "So basically you're saying we're ok here because the psycho is slitting

Todd's throat as we speak?"

Zak put up his hands. "Whoa, man. Just a second. That's not what I'm saying at all. What I'm saying is that distance and separation can ultimately work to the advantage of everyone. Think about it, Jordan. What kind of stealth assassin is going to try to take Todd out in a crowded hospital? For that matter, does the Stranger even know of Todd's injury?"

"Which brings us right back to square one," Jordan said, the defensiveness now gone and replaced with apprehension. "If the Stranger doesn't know about Todd's injury, then where do you think he's coming?"

"Right here," Andrea whispered softly.

"We need to get on that plane to Colorado *now*!" Jordan said, running his fingers through his hair.

"But that does no good. The Opposition knew we were going to Colorado. The Stranger could be waiting for us there. We could potentially be the same sitting ducks there as we are here," Zak said.

"But he also knew Todd was staying back," Andrea pitched in.

"True. So that creates another problem. The guy can't be in two places at once, so where's he gonna be?" Zak's stomach was now turning upside down, flipping over and over like pancakes on a griddle.

Jordan wiped away this line of disturbing conversation. "So what's the second thing we have going for us?"

"The fact that we've been tipped off. Mr. McGurney told Andrea, and I doubt the enemy knows that. So, that's most definitely in our favor."

Jordan shook his head and bit at his lower lip. "Why doesn't Mr. McGurney give us the whole picture? If he knows about the Stranger, he has to know more than he's telling us."

"I don't think so," said Andrea. "Remember, he says he's just a messenger. And messengers report what they've been told.

Plus, Mr. McGurney loves us. He wouldn't keep important stuff from us just to watch us squirm."

"You're right," Jordan said, studying the bedpost intently. Zak loved watching Jordan think. His intuition was remarkable and his insight poignant and above his age level.

"So basically we're back to being sitting ducks," Andrea said, her eyes still welled with tears. "I don't like being a sitting duck."

Zak smiled and hugged her close. "Neither do I. But look on the bright side: tomorrow's the last day of school."

Andrea could hold her tears back no longer. She pursed her lips and grimly said, "It could be the last day of everything."

Chapter Five

*T*he Master had spoken. There was no time for stagnation. In the deepest places of the earth, the loathsome emissaries of evil, the highest-ranking Fiends, outlined their plan of attack. Target: four children, one old woman. How difficult could this be?

"This will be a tougher assignment than you think," one demon general told his legions of minions. "The children you are to assault are rooted in the Knowledge. The Truth is in them, and the Truth has set them free. Be warned, the children are equipped with the Word and they *will* use It against you. The old woman is also not as feeble as she appears. She is growing in the Knowledge at a sickening pace. Consider her armed and dangerous." The Fiend general, a scaly, wolf-faced anomaly, paced before his battalion of evil spirits. He stopped to address them with his most pertinent information.

"You spirits, you cunning, ruthless, breeders of lies and discord—*you* are vital to Master Lucifer's mission to defeat these wretched brats and their disgusting grandmother. You are to pave the way for Lucifer's tangible assassin to work. Where Sorak failed, this assassin must succeed. If the assassin succeeds, *you* succeed. You must hover about the children and their grandmother, feed on them like leeches. They will not be able to see you, but they *will* be able to discern your presence. Be wary of this discernment; it is a gift given by the Knowledge and is particularly strong in the boy they call Jordan. It is important that you fill them with lies, doubt, fear. You are to divide them, harass them and suck away their hope. It is our mission to destroy them, and you have been chosen by the one true lord, Lucifer, to be the vehicle to do so." The Fiend unsheathed a large sword and held it high.

"For Lucifer and his dominion!"

The battalion answered the Fiend general by raising swords of their own in a cry that shook the earth.

The war had begun.

Chapter Six

*T*here was light coming from somewhere. Piercing, sharp, probing light. Even through Todd's closed eyelids the light was extremely bright. He opened his eyes and immediately his pupils were assaulted by a spotlight of white.

What in the world?

Trying to turn away from the incredible light, Todd felt his right arm pull back against him, a sharp pain sizzling up into his shoulder and back down through his elbow.

"Ouch! What's going on?" He struggled frantically for a moment, trying to disentangle himself from whatever was impeding his movement. He felt like a helpless fly tangled in the sticky goo of a spider web.

"Todd. Honey, are you alright?"

Todd stopped fighting the pull on his arm when he heard his mother's voice. And then everything became clear. The light, the tug on his arm-- he was waking up from a deep, drug-induced sleep after surgery and was facing the small window in his sterile hospital room, the partially open blinds allowing the piercing light of morning to come beaming in on him. He turned toward his mother's voice the best he could. She sat in a chair at the foot of his bed, a green blanket up over her shoulders, her eyes weary and puffy with a night of uncomfortable sleep.

"Yeah, Mom. I'm OK. Just—didn't know where I was for a second. Are you ok?'

His mother brought her arms out from under the blanket and repositioned herself in the chair. "I didn't sleep very well, but I'll live. This chair is lumpier than my mashed potatoes." She stopped fidgeting and settled herself. "How does your arm feel?" Todd looked at his right arm. A cast had been put over his elbow so his arm stood straight out from his body. He realized he must look like Frankenstein when the monster stood sideways.

Great. I look like the walking dead!

As he adjusted his position on the bed, he felt a dull burning in his shoulder and remembered how cockeyed and awful his arm had been mangled when he had slid into third base. The shoulder had popped way out of socket, and apparently it had been reset, because his arm was being supported by a sling. When two and two were put together, Todd didn't like the equation. This was going to be a long, slow recovery.

"The doctor said we can take you home if you can keep some food down this morning. The sling is just temporary. Your shoulder wasn't as badly out of place as they had initially thought. Your elbow is what's going to keep you held up for awhile."

"How long's awhile?" Todd asked, not really wanting to know the answer.

"Four to six weeks with the cast. And then physical therapy."

Todd sighed.

Great. Perfect.

"Do you want me to go see about getting you some breakfast?" his mother asked, standing up and stretching her stiff muscles.

Todd felt his stomach rumble at the mention of food. "Yeah, that sounds good."

"OK, I'll be right back." His mother exited his hospital room and Todd sighed.

I can't believe this is happening! I can't believe I won't be able to play football next fall!

Todd felt hot tears well in his eyes. It wasn't fair. Not only was he not going to be able to play football next fall, but he was stuck in the hospital on the last day of school. And Jen was at school. How could he miss the last day when his new girlfriend would be leaving him for the summer to Colorado Springs?

Colorado...Paul McGurney...

All of a sudden Todd's face broke out in a cold sweat.

Paul McGurney told me the Opposition's dead and there's a new stranger out to get us! The doctor came in and gave me a sedative shot before I could get the word to the others!

"I can't stay here!" Todd exclaimed to the empty room. "I have to go and get help! The others need me!"

He sat up straight in the bed, his arm protesting with sharps streaks of pain. He thought for a moment about paging a nurse and telling her to call the Infinity Police Department to send help to Zak and the others, but quickly realized his reasoning behind wanting to do this would sound delusional to the nurse.

"Then I'm just going to have to leave myself!" Todd threw his legs over the bed, forgetting he was only clothed in a hospital gown and that he was in Toledo, over an hour away from the others. He was just about to rip the IV out of the back of his hand when his mother walked in with a tray of hospital food.

"Todd! What on earth are you doing?" His mother set the tray down on the bedside table and rushed to Todd, who had nearly succeeded in extracting the IV tube from his hand.

"Todd! Stop! You're going to hurt yourself! What are you *doing*?"

"I have to get to the others! They need me!" Todd struggled against his mother, who was trying to pin him to the bed.

"Todd! You're scaring me! I'm going to page a nurse!"

"No! No, you have to listen to me!" Todd said, giving up the struggle. He lay back against his pillow, his breath coming in heavy pants. His eyes filled with tears. "Mom, you've gotta believe me. You've just gotta." Before he knew it, he was blubbering like a baby.

"Ssh, ssh. It's OK," his mother said soothingly as she stroked his forehead. "It's the pain medication that's got you a little loopy. Why don't you just rest some more."

Todd knew he had no choice but to obey. What else could he do? If he protested any more he was likely to get sent to the loony bin. His only option was to keep quiet and trust that the others were safe.

"Can you at least call Aunt Patty's to make sure Zak and the others are OK? It would make me feel a lot better."

His mother looked at him thoughtfully for a moment and then nodded. "I'll call Patty right now if you'll just rest."

Todd sniffled. "OK."

"I'll be right back, then. Don't you go trying to rip that IV out while I'm gone, you hear me?" Todd's mother kissed his forehead and walked out of the room.

"Jesus, keep them safe!" Todd whispered to the empty room.

Chapter Seven

*T*he Stranger gazes up the hill to Paul McGurney's de-
crepit, rundown house. The night is chill, the moon
peeking through wispy cotton-strip clouds as snow
falls heavy and wet. The rooster weather vane at the peak of
the house spins madly, although the wind is but a shrill breeze.
The Stranger gazes and trembles, rage and terror combining with
the cold to make the house all the more detestable. This is no
ordinary rundown home. This is the house of Glimpses, a dangerous sanctuary and portal to the Knowledge. This is a house
the Stranger loathes.

The Stranger steps forward and is now at the base of the
hill. The snow on the hill glistens like a thousand crystals in the
moonlight. The children will be here soon, the Stranger knows.
The children will walk this very hill and enter this very house
in a matter of days. It is the Stranger's mission to make sure
the children never make it here. Their deaths must come before
they are filled with any more of the Knowledge. Any more of the
Knowledge could be catastrophic. The Master has spoken these
very words.

The Stranger gazes up the hill and watches a cloud slip over
the moon. There is blackness now. It is morning in Ohio, but
blackness still reigns in Colorado. The Stranger smiles. A plan

is formed in the darkness. The children and the old lady must die in the darkness. They must never be allowed to see a Colorado morning.

The Stranger smiles into the blackness as the snow continues to fall.

Death is on the way.

Chapter Eight

*J*ordan woke with a start.

The Stranger! The Stranger's here!

He quickly jumped to his feet and stood in the middle of the small bedroom like a deer in headlights. On the floor, Zak moaned once and rolled onto his back. Andrea was curled into a ball, a blanket tucked around her body. Jordan rubbed his eyes and realized the room was bathed in soft morning light.

"We're alive," he said aloud. He ran his fingers through his hair and looked to the barricaded door and laughed. "We're alive!"

Zak moaned again and covered his eyes with the back of his arm. Jordan gently kicked him in the side.

"Wake up, Zak! It's morning! And we're still here!"

Zak took his arm from his eyes and squinted at Jordan, his morning-groggy brain trying to process what his cousin had just said. Finally, it dawned on him. Zak stood up and yawned.

"We made it, man," Jordan said, patting Zak on the back. Zak grinned back, his hair shooting in all different directions.

"It's good to still be here," Zak said, his voice deep with the coating of sleep. "Let's get this stuff away from the door. I don't think the Stranger would be dumb enough to attack in the daylight. Plus I have to go to the bathroom."

Jordan and Zak worked to move the obstacles away from the door as Andrea slept soundly on the floor. When they had successfully de-barricaded the room, Jordan looked to Zak.

"Now what?"

Zak's eyes darted to the digital alarm clock. It read 6:07.

"Now we get ready for school. And now I get to go to the bathroom. Better get Andrea up. She'll show you where the cereal bowls are. Mom has to be to work by six, so we usually get around in the morning on our own." With that, Zak exited the bedroom.

Jordan went to Andrea and shook her awake. After a groggy moment of displacement, Andrea's eyes popped open and she was on her feet in a matter of seconds.

"We made it!" she said, nearly bouncing up and down.

"It's great, isn't it?" Jordan said. He felt his stomach rumble. "How's 'bout some breakfast?"

Jordan sat in his last class of the school year and stared out the window as the late May sunshine sprayed the schoolyard with a shower of its hopeful light. He had finished his history exam within the first thirty minutes of class and now had to wait for the bell's chime to signal his release for the summer. As he watched a squirrel scurry across the lawn outside, he realized the spring sunshine was slowly rejuvenating his hopes of making it through the next few hours alive. Maybe the Stranger wasn't going to attack. Maybe he and the others would board the plane to Colorado safe and sound without a glitch.

Maybe everything will be OK…

Hope was what he needed, something to distract him from the terrifying reality he was living. What would happen in Colorado without Todd's being there to function as the leader of the foursome? Would Jordan have to step out of his comfort zone and lead with Zak in order to keep Andrea's fears at bay? Jordan nibbled the eraser end of his mechanical pencil and sighed.

So many questions, God. Why does it have to be this hard?

Jordan realized that life had become even harder since he had decided to accept Christ as his personal Savior. Jordan inwardly chuckled when he thought how some people had the notion that once you accepted Christ into your life everything instantly became peaches and cream and a bed of roses. In Jordan's experience, this was certainly not the case. There was the obvious physical fear; he and his family were being hunted by a maniacal assassin. Not every Christian was hunted by a maniacal assassin, Jordan knew. In fact, he was willing to bet close to none were. For some reason the forces of darkness had chosen to come after him and the others in a tangible way, and Jordan knew he had no choice but to accept the fact. He chose to bear the Name of Christ, therefore he would be hunted in some form or another. There was a verse in the Bible that described Satan as a prowling lion who sought those he could devour. It came with the Name.

But the day-to-day things had become more difficult as well. When you possessed the Knowledge of Christ and professed His Name, you had to live up to His Name on a daily basis. Sure, the Holy Spirit was able to give counsel and help when things got hard. But it was ultimately the Christian's choice how to act in certain situations. God was a God of choice; He didn't create humans to be robots. And when you professed yourself to be a Christian, choices were sometimes more difficult.

But it's worth it. It's all worth it.

Jordan could barely sit still any longer. A whole summer's worth of adventures awaited him, and he couldn't wait to see how they played out.

Hopefully with me still alive…

Chapter nine

Margaret Kessler opened the garage door and was immediately assaulted by an icy breeze. Snow lathered the driveway, and more was falling to add to its thick coating.

I thought the summer was just around the corner?

Grabbing a snow shovel, she proceeded to sweep away the mound of snow that had deposited itself at the base of her garage door.

The children shouldn't be coming. They should stay at home—far away from Colorado. Far away from...

A chill washed over her, adding to the frigid cold of the biting air.

I shouldn't even be out here! He could be anywhere, waiting to attack! I wish the phone would work so I could warn the children!

Margaret felt an unspeakable panic vibrate through her body. Here she was with her garage door open, its innards and herself exposed to a freakish late-spring blizzard and a stealthy homicidal stranger. With a level of dread so pronounced she shuddered, Margaret realized it was too late in the game for the children to be warned. They would be boarding the airplane and flying to Colorado and there was nothing she could do about it. It was all now in God's hands. She was afraid, but she had to trust that all would be OK. Faith was all she had at this point.

"Might as well put the chains on the Jeep tires," Margaret said to herself as she looked out over her snow-covered driveway. "It's going to be an adventure trying to get down this mountain tomorrow morning."

She went to work putting the chains on her tires, all the while glancing over her shoulder to make sure she wasn't being stalked by a crazed Stranger. When her fear was too great to bear, she closed the garage door.

He's out there---He's watching and waiting...

Chapter Ten

From deep in the snow-covered forest the Stranger watches the old woman shoveling snow away from her open garage door. She is fretful, on edge because she senses danger but does not know where it lurks and when it will strike again. The Stranger smiles. Yes, death is coming. Death is coming to the old woman just as it will come to the four children. She has dabbled in the Knowledge and now she will pay the ultimate price.

The Stranger sees a chipmunk scurry over the snow and dart up a nearby tree. The snow is so heavy the chipmunk doesn't leave any tracks.

Just like that, the Stranger thinks. I will strike the old woman and obliterate the children without leaving any tracks. Where the Opposition failed, I will be successful. The Master will praise my killing abilities and elevate me to a seat of glory as he promised.

The Stranger watches as the old woman chains the tires of her Jeep, a precaution that will only delay her demise for one more day. She will know the end tomorrow.

The Stranger waits, watches and schemes as the snow continues to fall.

Chapter Eleven

"I called your Aunt Patty and told her to tell the others you're feeling better," Todd's mother said as a nurse exchanged Todd's pillow for a fresh one.

"When do I get to go home?" Todd asked, still slightly groggy from the sedative he'd been administered.

"You can leave when you can keep food and drink down," the nurse answered as she adjusted the tilt on his bed.

"But I ate an hour ago," Todd said, knowing he was fighting a losing battle.

"We have to give it some more time," the nurse said kindly, although the twitch at the corners of her lips betrayed her tone. Todd realized she probably had patients just like him on a daily basis who fought for an early discharge despite the doctor's orders. He could understand her exasperation, but still, he wanted *out*.

Todd looked to his mother, trying a new line of persuasion. "They're leaving soon and I didn't get to say goodbye."

"Honey, you can call when you get home. I'm sure they'll understand. Besides, they're most likely aboard the plane by now."

Todd glanced at the wall clock. 6:42. The plane was scheduled to depart at 6:02. Barring a flight delay, Zak and the others were on their way to Colorado---on their way to almost certain death. Todd felt a lump rise in his throat.

"I'm too late," he whispered.

His mother misunderstood his statement.

"You can call them when you get home," she repeated. "By that time they should be in Colorado."

Todd's eyes filled with tears. He hadn't even heard what his mother had said.

"I'm too late," he whispered again. Then the tears fell.

Chapter Twelve

Zak's ears popped as the plane gained altitude. Beside him, Andrea stared out the window as the plane's wings sliced through the cotton candy clouds set in an immaculate blue sky. The seat to his right was occupied by a charcoal-suited businessman who had zonked out even before the plane had begun its taxi on the runway.

"Well, we're in the air," Jordan said through the crack between seats. Jordan's mother had been unable to purchase three seats in a row, so Jordan had volunteered to be the odd-man-out. He had the window seat behind Andrea and shared a row with a young mother and her fussy toddler.

"That doesn't necessarily mean anything good," Zak said as he thumbed through the airline's lackluster selection of magazines from a pocket attached to the seat in front of him.

"Just trying to be positive," Jordan said, though not defensively. He, too, knew safety was not a guarantee upon arriving in Colorado.

"I hear ya," Zak said with a sigh. He sat back in his seat. "I just wish Todd could be here."

"I know. Your mom said Todd seemed to be doing well. It's too bad I didn't at least get to talk to him."

"We'll call him first thing," Zak said. "I think it's important we stay in constant communication all summer."

"I think you're right," Jordan said, talking a little louder because the toddler beside him had erupted into a tantrum.

"It's weird we haven't heard from Grandma," Zak said.

"You don't think---" Jordan said, the panic evident in his voice.

"I'm not saying that," Zak said. "All I'm saying is that it's weird we haven't heard from Grandma. I mean, she loves to call us. She likes to talk in general, you know that."

Andrea turned from the window and looked at Zak. Her eyes conveyed a fear that broke Zak's heart. "I hope she's OK."

Zak took a deep breath—a leader's breath. He had to be calm for Jordan and Andrea's sake.

"Everything will be OK. We just need to have faith."

Andrea put her head on Zak's shoulder, and he felt the weight of the entire situation crashing down on him.

How am I supposed to keep everybody safe when I'm scared myself?

The plane's engine was a hypnotic drone that had lolled many of the passengers to sleep. Zak knew he and the others would never shut their eyes. They were on high alert, their brains running on overdrive.

We're flying into a den of lions, Zak thought as he watched the clouds outside the window. *Hopefully we don't get eaten alive.*

Chapter Thirteen

Margaret Kessler made her way to the baggage claim and visored her eyes with her hand. She was looking for her three grandchildren, the pit of her stomach roiling not only from her hazardous trek down the ice-slicked roads coming out of Divide, but also from the constant twinge of terror that throbbed her insides to nausea. She knew she was picking her grandchildren up from the airport only to drive them back to Divide—back to the den of lions waiting to devour them. In all reality, the airport was probably the safest place in Colorado they could be. But she knew she couldn't hole her grandchildren up in the airport forever. First, it was implausible. Second, if evil wanted so desperately to hunt them, an airport would only serve as a sanctuary for so long.

Margaret scanned the crowd of travel-weary passengers who sluggishly waited for their luggage to materialize on the large conveyer belt. She did not see her grandchildren among the neatly dressed businessmen and iPod-eared other passengers. To her right, a mother was chiding a fussy toddler who wanted to take a ride on the conveyer belt. A knot tightened in Margaret's gut.

What if the Stranger snatched them away the moment they got off the plane! I don't know what he looks like! They'll be gone forever!

"Grandma?"

Margaret turned and saw Andrea grinning at her, a pink duffel bag slung over her granddaughter's shoulder. Margaret's fears immediately evaporated and were replaced with joy only a grandmother could understand at the sight of her grandchild.

"Oh, my word! How you've grown since last summer!" Margaret exclaimed. She drew Andrea into an embrace. "Did you bring the others with you?"

They separated from their embrace and Andrea repositioned her bag on her shoulder. "Yeah. They're over there. Their bags haven't come through yet." Andrea pointed to where Jordan and Zak stood by the conveyer belt. Both waved and Margaret's heart was warmed.

Andrea's face suddenly dropped its smile.

"Grandma, I have something to tell you--" She couldn't finish because she was knocked backwards by a bustling man with an enormous black duffel slung over his shoulder. The man didn't bother to apologize as he breezed his way to the exit.

"Some people are so rude," Margaret tsked. "Are you OK?"

"I'm fine," Andrea said, regaining her footing.

"That dude just lowered his shoulder on you, sister!" Zak said, making his way to where Margaret and Andrea were standing. Jordan trailed behind him wheeling a suitcase.

"Zak and Jordan! Come here and give your grandma a hug!" Margaret exclaimed, throwing her arms wide. "I've missed you so!"

First Zak and then Jordan hugged Margaret as the airport announcement about not parking in restricted areas blared over the loud-speaker.

"I'm so happy to see that you've made it here safe," Margaret said, an unintended inflection of relief in her voice.

Zak looked to Jordan, whose expression turned grim.

"Believe me when I say we're *more* than happy to have made it here alive."

Margaret felt all the blood drain from her face.

"Oh, no. Oh, no! You, too!"

Now it was Jordan's turn to blanche. "What—what are you talking about, Grandma? What do you mean by 'you, too'?"

But Margaret's pulse was racing too fast to answer Jordan's question. She felt she might be sick as little blips of light pulsed at the sides of her eyeballs.

"I had no idea—I just thought I was in trouble here in Colorado. My crossword--the electrician—I thought it was just me! But I was wrong!" Margaret felt like the world was spinning at breakneck speed.

Zak clenched his jaw and swallowed hard.

"Grandma, are you talking about--"

"The Stranger," Margaret finished for him in an uncharacteristically tremulous voice.

Zak and Jordan looked at each other, fear stamped on their faces. Andrea's lower lip began to tremble.

"Tell us everything," Zak said.

Margaret managed a weak laugh as her insides twisted into a sailor's knot.

"I see we won't have any trouble finding conversation for the ride home."

Chapter Fourteen

*T*odd's cell phone chirped as he raised himself the best he could with his left arm. His head swam with pain medication, and for a moment Todd considered letting the call go to voicemail. With a sigh, he decided against missing the call and reached to the coffee table and grabbed his phone. He flipped it open and tried to focus his eyes on the screen so the room would stop spinning.

"Hello?"

"Todd? Hi! It's Jen!"

Todd immediately felt better. Medicated or not, talking to his new girlfriend snapped him out of his funk.

"Jen! I finally get to talk to you!"

"I know, right?" Jen laughed. "I'm just calling to tell you I made it safe and sound to Colorado."

Todd felt his stomach somersault when Jen said the phrase "safe and sound." He and the others were *anything but* with the Stranger on the prowl.

Todd toyed with a tag on one of his mother's legion of throw pillows. "Glad to hear you made it to Colorado Springs. How's your uncle?"

Jen was staying with her uncle for the summer, and once again Todd felt a twinge of jealousy that she was in Colorado and he wasn't. Despite the gnawing fear that kept his insides in a constant state of mush, Todd wanted more than anything to be able to spend time with Jen away from Infinity and its Midwestern monotony. Colorado Springs was less than an hour from Divide, and Todd could only imagine how amazing it would be to spend time with Jen in such a beautiful locale.

"He's doing well. I'd be lying if I said I didn't miss you, Todd. We'd be close enough that we could hang out on the weekends."

Todd sighed. "I know; it stinks that I'm cooped up here."

Jen's voice grew concerned. "Is something wrong, Todd? You sound like something—I don't know—bad has happened."

Todd looked at the orange pill bottle mocking him from the coffee table, felt his shoulder shriek with pain. He chuckled and shook his heavily-medicated head. "I've had quite the last twenty-four hours."

"What? What happened—are you OK?"

Todd looked at his heavily-casted arm. "Uh—I sorta broke myself."

Jen gasped and Todd recounted the tale of his ill-fated slide into third base.

"I got to come home a little over two hours ago. Now I'm all cooped up here on the couch with nothing but the TV remote and a pack of beef jerky."

Jen sighed, clearly affected by his predicament. "I'm so sorry, Todd. That sounds so terrible."

"It kind of is. Dad's at work and Mom decided to go to the office for a few hours. But don't worry about me. I'll be fine. Probably'll sleep off some of this medication."

"Well, if there's anything I can do, just let me know," Jen said.

Todd chuckled. "I guess I could use a few prayers."

To Todd's surprise, Jen snorted. "Yeah. Like that'll do anything. I mean if you need anything *practical*, let me know."

Todd didn't know how to respond. What Jen had said about

43

prayer threw him for a loop. Prayer was what was getting him through every painful hour with the prospect of a madman wanting him dead. Over the past year, prayer had been a vital part of his existence, his growth in Christ. If Jen didn't believe in the power of prayer, that meant Jen didn't believe in the existence of God.

"Todd, you there?" Jen asked.

Todd hadn't realized he'd let his end of the conversation go dead. But what Jen had said really messed with his head.

"Earth to Todd!" Jen giggled. "Am I still talking to my boyfriend?"

Todd shrugged off his concern with what Jen has said. Better to not get into a religious discussion when Jen was so far away. He'd come back to it later. In the meantime, he had Jen on the line and that was all that mattered.

"I'm still here," Todd said.

"I'm glad. Man, Todd! I miss you!" Jen groaned. "I just want to hop a plane back to Ohio and feed you chicken noodle soup."

Todd laughed. "I'd be all for that. But you need to have fun. Get out—explore a little for me."

"I'll try," Jen said grudgingly. Todd heard a voice in the background. "Well, I have to get going. We're setting up for a barbecue tonight. Some of my uncle's work buddies."

"Have fun," Todd said.

"Sounds like a blast," Jen said in a sarcastic whisper. Todd could see her rolling her eyes on the other end of the line.

"Hope you feel better," Jen said. "Hey! Skype me if you can. I've got my laptop here."

"Never thought of that," Todd said. "Will do. Text me your info."

The two exchanged goodbyes and Todd flipped his phone shut with an empty ache in his chest. Not only was he doomed to spend the entire summer away from Jen, but a crazy new Stranger

44

was stalking around somewhere waiting for the right moment to take him out. And not just him; Zak, Jordan, Andrea and his grandmother were also in his line of fire.

This stinks! The totally stinks! I'm helpless here!

Restless, Todd grabbed his phone again. He sent a fleet-fingered message to Zak: Call me when u get there.

Todd leaned back against the couch cushion and thought of Paul McGurney and all the ancient texts the man had sent the children warning them about the Stranger. That all seemed like a million years ago, when in reality it had only been a few days. Could the Stranger be in two places at once? Were there two Strangers, one in Colorado and one in Infinity? If the latter were true, then Todd was nothing more than a sitting duck. His right arm—his dominant one—was useless. What would be do if an insane murderer attacked? Claw the assassin's eyes out with his left hand?

Thinking about the possibility of two Strangers elevated Todd's fear level to the stratospheric realm.

What's going to happen to me? What's going to happen to the others?

Todd sighed and grabbed the remote control. Flipping through the channels, he came to *ESPN*. A tennis tournament was on, but Todd saw none of it. All he could think of was the fact that he and the others were doomed.

Chapter Fifteen

*T*he Stranger stands in Margaret Kessler's kitchen. Admittance to the cabin was simple; the woman had punched a numerical code in order to close the garage door after she had shoveled the snow away from the door. The Stranger has keen eyes, sharp and wild. Even from a distance the Stranger had been able to see the woman's bony fingers punch the numbers.

It is all so simple.

The Stranger looks around the cabin, soaking in every beam and floorboard, every nook and cranny. The cabin is quaint, tidy. Just enough space for a woman who lives alone.

The Stranger moves to the living room and steps in front of the sofa. The smell of the old woman is strong. The Stranger's assassin nose is trained to sniff out prey. In a few hours the cabin will be filled with the scent of three children. That is, unless death finds them first.

The Stranger walks through a downstairs bedroom, scheming a way to make death known to the children and to the old woman. The death must be perfect. It must fit the crime of seeking the despicable Knowledge. There must be fear. There must be a loss of hope. There must be a loss of faith.

The Stranger is back in the cabin's living room. Snow continues to fall beyond a small window.

I will petrify them first. I will terrify them. I will make them doubt everything they have believed in. And it starts right now.

The Stranger grins. The grin is vile, pure evil. The Stranger walks into the kitchen and unsheathes a knife from the old woman's knife block. There is work to be done now. The children and the wretched woman must know who they are dealing with.

The Stranger begins the work, the knife slicing swift and deep. The cabin is defiled—degraded by the knife's blade. The Stranger knows the work is offensive to the Knowledge. The Stranger knows to the core that the Knowledge sees all, judges all—will judge all.

But the Stranger pays no mind to the future. The present presents the possibility—the inevitability—of blood. The Knowledge is rooted in Blood, and blood the Knowledge will get.

The work is done. Sweat glistens on the Stranger's brow.

This will destroy their resolve. They will think the Knowledge abandoned them.

The Stranger takes one last look at the knife's work before thrusting the knife into the center of the kitchen table. It doesn't even wobble, rather stands tall and true like a boastful demon. The Stranger smiles a smile of pure evil and slips out of the cabin's front door.

Chapter Sixteen

*S*ilence, like the snow on the narrow roadway, had drifted over the Jeep. It hung in the stale air of the Jeep like an ax about to fall, like a bomb about to explode. The children had recounted the events from Infinity, including the Opposition posing as Zak's and Andrea's uncle Phil and his subsequent demise from an unknown source. Jordan saw that his grandmother has been particularly terrified when they recounted how Andrea had been tipped off by Paul McGurney about another foe picking up where the Opposition had left off. With a tremulous voice, Margaret told her grandchildren of the strange crossword puzzle message she had gotten from McGurney and of the husky electrician, Hanson, whom she feared might be the new stranger. She finished by telling the children of the terrifying experience of getting threatened at knifepoint and how she had refused to hand the children over to the stranger upon their arrival in Colorado. As the puzzle pieces began to fall into place, Jordan felt his stomach tighten and his muscles turn into limp noodles. How could the foursome possibly complete with a new stranger, especially without Todd? The news of Todd's baseball injury and following surgery had unnerved his grandmother, less because Todd's football season was in jeopardy, more because Todd was a sitting duck in Infinity.

Jordan broke the thick silence and asked the question all three Ohioans wanted to know but refused to ask.

"What did the Stranger look like?"

Jordan's grandmother's jaw tightened, and he saw her knuckles grow white as gripped the steering wheel in remembrance.

"I didn't get a chance to look at him," Margaret said. "He came in and sneaked up behind me as I was sitting in my chair. You know how my chair doesn't face the door. Well, all I felt was a cold piece of steel at my neck and—and—I never got to see what he looked like. It happened so quickly." Margaret swallowed and Jordan couldn't imagine what that must have felt like for his grandmother. Last summer she had been abducted and held at gunpoint by the Opposition, and now she had been threatened by an unseen foe.

"What did he sound like, Grandma? Did he sound like the Opposition?" Zak asked as he looked over from the passenger seat.

Margaret thought for a moment. Jordan looked to Andrea, who sat directly behind her grandmother. Andrea's eyes were locked on the rearview mirror, where she could watch her grandmother as Margaret recounted the horrific episode.

"He didn't sound like the Opposition," Margaret remembered. "He sounded—gruffer. Yeah, that's a good word for it. His voice was deeper, grainier than the Opposition's. Almost like a smoker's voice, you know, all sandpapery? His voice was so low it almost sounded synthetic—robotic."

Jordan suppressed a shudder. He could almost hear the voice his grandmother was describing. He imagined the inhumanly deep voice announcers used as the beginning of horror movie trailers, and allowed the shudder to overtake him as he put himself in his grandmother's position.

"So we don't even know what the guy looks like," Andrea said as the Jeep bounced over a fallen branch. "We don't even have a face to have nightmares about."

"Somehow that's worse," Jordan heard Zak mutter. His cousin folded his arms, and Jordan saw in the side mirror that Zak's eyes were fearful.

"We have to see Paul McGurney—today!" Andrea exclaimed.

"I don't think that's a possibility," Margaret said. "You think it's snowing here, wait until we climb up the mountain. Even if Paul McGurney's road decides to actually show itself, there's no way I'm taking the Jeep down it. We'd get stuck in five seconds and then we'd be up a creek without a paddle."

"We can walk," Andrea offered.

Margaret shook her head. "You kids aren't dressed for the snow. You don't even have jackets on. What kind of grandmother would I be if I let you trek to Paul McGurney's the way you're dressed?"

"We can get changed at the cabin first," Zak said, the hope evident in his voice. "Besides, you're coming with us. We can't get lost if you're with us."

Margaret held up two bony fingers. "Two things, kids. One, you have to remember that I've never been to Mr. McGurney's house. I don't know what I'm even looking for. Two, I don't mean to burst your bubbles, but the road wasn't there when I came down the mountain. And you have to remember that the Colorado wilderness is nothing to mess around in when the weather's throwing fits. Even the most experienced hikers have found themselves in life-threatening jams when they thought they could beat Mother Nature."

"That was three things," Zak said with a tired smile. "I know you're right, Grandma. I don't *want* you to be right, but even if the road is there, it might be more dangerous for us to try to hike it. Besides, if the weather up the mountain is as bad as you say it is, we're probably safest in the cabin anyway. There's no way the Stranger is going to brave blizzard conditions."

"You can't know that," Andrea said, sitting back in her seat.

She toyed with her seatbelt and went silent.

"We have to try tomorrow," Jordan said. "No matter what, we have to get to Paul McGurney. He can help us figure out what the next step should be."

Jordan's comment was met with silence. Everyone in the Jeep knew he was right. Getting to Paul McGurney's house on the hill was of the highest importance.

I just hope Zak's right about the Stranger not attacking us tonight…

"We're going to have to stop once we get to the base of the mountain and throw those chains on the tires. I'm not even going to try to climb a slick incline without them," Margaret said. The children all agreed they'd help with the task.

All of sudden, Zak started from the front seat.

"Hey! I got a text from Todd!"

Jordan and Andrea eagerly leaned forward to see what the text would say. Keeping in contact with Todd the entire summer would be vital, especially as the danger started to intensify.

"What does it say?" Jordan asked impatiently.

"It says to call him as soon as we get there—I mean here," Zak said.

"Well—call him!" Jordan and Andrea said at the same time.

"OK, OK. Just a sec," Zak said, thumbing through his contacts. "I need to remember to move Todd's number to the VIP list." Why Zak hadn't just pushed the call button when he'd read Todd's text, Jordan didn't know. He'd show Zak the shortcut later.

Zak made the call, waited for it to catch, and didn't have to wait long for Todd to pick up. Jordan could only hear Zak's side of the conversation, and he became alarmed when his cousin's face turned as white as the blowing snow. Zak hung up, shaken.

"What? What is it?" Jordan exclaimed.

Zak swallowed hard once, twice.

"Is something wrong?" Margaret asked.

Zak exhaled. "Todd thinks there might be two Strangers. One here and one in Infinity."

Jordan felt like he had taken a cannonball to the gut.

Game over.

Chapter Seventeen

Margaret Kessler was more than nervous. He heart pounded as she commandeered the Jeep around the winding mountain roads. The children had fallen into petrified silence, each one staring out the window with a gaze Margaret knew well. It was a gaze of deep thought, of deep terror. The beautiful Colorado scenery rushed by and the children saw none of it.

It shouldn't be like this. My grandchildren shouldn't be petrified to come see me.

Margaret thought back over the course of the last year. Things had changed so much for her. After the whole ordeal last summer, she had found hope in a God she never known she had been seeking. Finding Jesus had been the best thing that had ever happened to her. It still was. Waking up every morning and knowing she had a purpose again, something and Someone to look forward to, is what kept Margaret from the gloominess and isolation of her wilderness cabin. After her husband had died, Margaret had found herself slowly growing into a shell of a woman. All sense of purpose had died with him, and there had been days when Margaret had seriously contemplated the worth of her lonely existence. If it hadn't been for her grandchildren, Margaret often wondered if she wouldn't have offed herself to find some semblance of peace. But there would have been less peace in such a death, Margaret knew now. She had not yet met Jesus, and she shuddered to think what would have become of her had she decided to take her own life.

But then she had found Jesus, had experienced His love and grace through her grandchildren. She had never met Him face to face as her grandchildren had, but Margaret knew Him in an intimate way because she sought and found Him on a daily basis. Sometimes He was a gentle whisper to her heart and sometimes He was in her laughter and tears. Whenever she found Him, she knew He was the hope and purpose she had been seeking all along.

But why does this have to be so hard?

Margaret pulled up to a stop sign and glanced in her rearview mirror. In the back seat, Jordan and Andrea still stared out the window as though in a fog.

Why? Why is this happening, Jesus?

Margaret accelerated again and realized that if she lived through the summer she would move back to the Midwest. She had been thinking about moving to Infinity for quite some time. There was no reason to be in Divide any longer. That season of her life, the lonely wilderness period, was over, and her grandchildren needed her in Infinity. And she needed her grandchildren as well. There was no reason to stay holed-up like a hermit in Divide when her real purpose was to live and love her grandchildren like Christ loved her. She would find a realtor, put her cabin up for sale and move to Infinity in the fall.

"We're getting close," Zak said, startling Margaret from her thoughts. "The snow is picking up. Should we chain the tires?"

"I think that'd be a wise decision."

As Margaret pulled off the road, a sudden terror gripped her.

I'm leading them back to my cabin—but for what? To get slaughtered?

Margaret looked to her grandchildren and wondered if they

54

were thinking the same thing.

There is another option...

Margaret opened her door and was immediately met with a blast of icy Colorado wind.

"The chains are in the back," Margaret called as she popped the Jeep's hatch.

There is another option. I won't say anything now, but I'll think on it. But it seems to make the most sense...

Chapter Eighteen

*T*odd knew he needed to be in Colorado. He felt it in his bones, sensed that his presence was necessary. In Ohio, his entire summer would be spent around the house. He'd mosey back and forth from the refrigerator to the TV in hopes that one or the other would provide a temporary euphoria. He wouldn't be able to procure a summer job. A one-armed teenager couldn't line baseball fields for the town's summer recreational facilities, nor could a hobbled teen mow lawns for pocket change. If he didn't think he was too old, he might consider a paper route. But even at that, he might not be able to chuck the rolled-up papers with his left arm. All in all, he was jobless and in somber spirits.

But it wasn't the fact that he was all but useless in Ohio that made Todd want to go to Colorado. It wasn't even that Jen was there as well, although that added to his desire to be in Colorado. It was the fact that he felt like he was *supposed* to be there, that he'd be missing something if he were to stay in Ohio for the summer. Set the Stranger and the maybe-getting-killed stuff aside. Todd felt *pulled* to Colorado, lured by something that wanted him there.

I've got nothing tying me here. Football's over for me this year. I wonder...

Todd adjusted the couch cushion and had an epiphany.

Why can't I go? Why can't I hop a plane and spend the summer with the others?

Todd was excited. He had been moping on the sofa for hours, and now he had something worth thinking about that wasn't impending death or his longing to see Jen. He knew he had shaken Zak up when he had told his cousin he feared there might be two Strangers. Todd regretted the statement, partly because he didn't know if it was true and partly because he didn't want the others to fret. They had enough to worry about.

I have to be there…

Todd did some mental math. He had enough in his savings account to buy a roundtrip ticket. That wasn't the problem. The problem was convincing his parents to allow him to go. They weren't ones to make quick decisions. He would have to give them space and time, allow them to think it through. Pushiness would not work with his parents. Slow and steady often won the race.

Todd smiled.

"I'm going to get to go to Colorado this summer after all," he said to the empty living room.

Chapter Nineteen

*J*ordan was antsy as his grandmother trekked up the familiar steep mountain road with her Jeep. The incline was lathered with snow, the white stuff thick and drifting like icing on top of a wedding cake. Not only was the snow hazardous to travel upon, but the prospect that the road to Paul McGurney's house might not be there set Jordan on edge. The trip back from the airport had been devastating at best, each occupant of the Jeep knowing full well the gravity of the reality they were all a part of. It would a blessing and a half if Paul McGurney's road would be unforested and *there*. The foursome definitely needed something to perk their spirits, and Jordan prayed McGurney's road would be it.

"That's the fork up there!" Andrea exclaimed. She had taken off her seatbelt and was now perched between the Jeep's two front seats. Despite the obvious safety hazards, Margaret didn't say anything. Jordan knew that she, too, was eager to see if the road had materialized.

"I've never seen this vanishing road," Margaret said as the Jeep plowed through the thick snow. "I hope you kids are right about it's being there this time."

The Jeep approached the fork in the road and Jordan thought

his heart would burst out of his chest. He realized he hadn't wanted something this badly in a long time. Should the road not be there, he would be utterly crushed.

"I see it! It's there!" Andrea shouted. "Mr. McGurney's road—it's there!"

When Jordan saw that Andrea was right, he could have wept. "I knew it," he said, laughing. "I knew it'd be there!"

"Well, I'll be jarred," Margaret said as she looked out the passenger window and saw a road she had never seen before appear from the snowy foliage. "There's a road running plumb through those trees. I've been here all these years and I've never…" Her words trailed off and Jordan laughed as she shook her head in disbelief.

"Believe it, Grandma! We're going to get to see Mr. McGurney!" Zak exclaimed.

"Let's go now!" Andrea begged. "The chains are on the tires--we can make it!"

Margaret shook her head. "Now hold on just a minute. I thought we talked about this. We can't just go high-tailing it down a snow-covered road as night is falling. That wouldn't be smart. For one, if I slow down to make a turn, I doubt we'd get started up again. The snow is deep and it's not wise to stop until we get to the cabin. This weather is dangerous. Let's see what tomorrow looks like."

Jordan was just as anxious to see Paul McGurney as Andrea was, but he knew his grandmother was right. It'd be foolish to try to make it to McGurney's and back with night setting in. The children would have to wait until tomorrow to see their ancient friend.

"I agree with Grandma," Zak said. "Plus, I'm starving."

"You're always starving," Andrea said as the Jeep rumbled past the road to Paul McGurney's house on the hill.

"I hope you kids are hungry," Margaret said. "I loaded up the deep-freezer with bacon when I heard you were coming."

What else would it be besides bacon? Jordan thought with a smile.

And for a moment, all was right with the world.

The moment of rightness passed as quickly as it had come. Jordan knew something was wrong the moment the Jeep pulled into the garage. He sensed it—felt it creeping on the back of his neck. He had been blessed with the gift of discernment, a gift that had proved to be more than valuable over the past year. Now he felt like the garage was suffocating him, like an evil had recently passed through the cabin. Adrenaline coursed through his veins, making the sides of his eyeballs strobe with the first impulses of panic.

"Whew! We made it!" Maragret said as she opened the driver's side door. "We'll worry about the chains later. Right now I want to go inside and start supper. You kids scuttle inside before you catch cold!"

"It feels like we never left," Andrea said as she climbed out of the Jeep and stretched her legs. Her teeth chattered as she was met by the garage's frigid air. "It's freezing for late spring!"

"The garage is still clean," Zak said, looking around the orderly space. "Way to go, Grandma!"

"It better still be clean," Margaret said as she popped the Jeep's hatch. "I spent long enough cleaning it last summer."

The foursome gathered their luggage from the back of the Jeep and made for the tiny cabin's door. Jordan felt an inexplicable foreboding as he hauled his luggage to the cabin door, like something had been set in motion that he couldn't stop. Something vile—something evil.

Something is not right! We are walking into something terrible!

"You kids go put your luggage in your rooms and freshen up

for supper," Margaret said as she began to open the door. "I'll get the bacon crackling while you settle in. How does that sound---" She swung open the door and was struck mute. Jordan was horrified to see his grandmother's face drain of all its color.

"Grandma, what wrong?" Jordan asked, his voice shaky. He watched his grandmother take a step into her cabin and throw her hand to her chest. For a terrifying moment, Jordan thought his grandmother might pass out.

Andrea moved around Jordan and followed her grandmother into the cabin and Zak and Jordan looked at each other, their non-verbals saying everything.

Whatever is in the cabin is bad! Whatever Grandma is seeing is so bad we need to leave now!

"What is it, Grandma?" Andrea asked, turning on the cabin lights.

Jordan felt his heart splatter on the garage floor when he heard his cousin's bloodcurling scream.

Chapter Twenty

*T*he Stranger hunches in the snow outside the tiny cabin. No inclement weather is enough to keep this assassin away. Besides, the snow is falling thick, and within ten minutes all traces of the killer's presence will be covered. The Stranger is more than pleased—exuberant, even—at the terror brought about by the heavy knife about to be discovered by the Knowledge-seekers. First will come the terror, then the loss of hope. And then death will find the abominable Paul McGurney and his merry band of posers.

The Stranger watches as the old woman parks her Jeep inside the garage. The assassin knows death could have come quickly to the foursome, especially in the thick and slippery snow. An obstruction could have been placed in the Jeep's path forcing all its inhabitants to leave the vehicle to move it. The Stranger could have ambushed them then and made them bleed out onto the snow. But where is the fun in that? No, making them lose hope, taking them to the edge of their faith and then pushing them over is the key. Slow and steady brings death. Meticulous planning and scheming brings about demise. Once McGurney is out of the way it will be child's play.

The garage door closes and the Stranger knows the realization of the knife's handiwork will come quickly. A few seconds *pass and the Stranger can no longer stand the suspense. The kill calls, but terror must come first.*

A bloodcurling scream sounds inside the cabin. To the assassin the sound is a concerto, a symphony of success. It reverberates off the trees of the forest and into the Stranger's sound-sensative ears. The cabin walls do not muffle the sweetness of the scream. It is a sweet, sweet sound.

The terror has begun. The scream begins the death knell. The rest will fall like dominos until the moment of the kill.

The Stranger hunches in the snow unseen, unheard but felt. The terror inside the cabin is enormous. And death waits in the shadows.

Chapter Twenty-one

*T*odd's mother walked into the living room and set the mail on the coffee table.

"Bills, bills and more bills," Donna Lawrence said as she cleaned her glasses with the bottom of her blouse. "Some things never change. How are you feeling, honey?"

Todd hoisted himself up with his left arm and clicked off the TV.

"Mom, I've got an idea," Todd started, wanting to get his whole plan out before his mother could interrupt him. He'd been scheming for over half an hour and could barely contain his excitement at the possibility of going to Colorado. "By the way, I feel fine."

His mother sipped a cup of tea she'd been nursing and nodded.

"That's good, honey. Now what's your idea?"

"OK. So you know how I'm sort of—well—broken right now?" He tapped his sling in case his mother had forgotten.

"Yes, I can see you are a little—incapacitated—at the moment," his mother answered with a grin. "What are you getting at, Todd?"

"Well, I was just thinking that since I can't play football next year, and seeing how I can't really lift or work out--"

His mother beat him to the punch. She shook her head and set her mug down on an end table.

"No, Todd. Absolutely not. In your condition I don't want you traipsing around the mountains."

How did she know what I was going to say? I barely know what I want to say!

"But, Mom," Todd started, fighting to keep his voice from elevating to a whiny elementary-aged octave. "I'll pay for the plane ticket. I'll cover all the expenses. I'll—I'll even do my laundry for a year if you'll just let me go!"

His mother raised a sarcastic eyebrow. "You'll do your laundry for a year? Where do I sign?"

"But, Mom," Todd began again, "this could be the last summer I get a chance to go to Grandma's!"

"Yes, and what about your driving classes?"

I forgot about those!

Todd swallowed. He was at a crossroads. He wanted to drive as much as he wanted to play baseball in college. If he went to Colorado he'd forfeit the chance to take the driver's education classes currently offered at his school and would have to wait another half year to begin.

But it's hard to drive with a bum arm!

"Mom, I can't get behind the wheel of a car anyway," Todd said. "I'm going to have to catch the classes the next time around anyway."

Plus, if the Stranger kills us all it's a moot point.

Todd's mother was in deep thought. He had her where he wanted her.

"I guess you can say I have other priorities right now," Todd offered, using a phrase his mother liked to use when she was reminding him about the importance of getting homework done in a timely fashion. "I just want to spend as much time as I can with Jordan and the others. You know we'll never get this time back."

Todd's mother blinked. She was a softy for sentiment. Todd had skillfully struck the right nerve.

"Your father will agree with me when he gets home. You're in no condition to go to Colorado, Todd. It's admirable that you'd drop everything and go to Colorado to spend the summer with your brother and cousins. But it just doesn't make sense."

Todd sighed.

That's OK for now. At least I planted the seed.

Todd pretended to brood as he clicked on the TV again.

I'll be in Colorado before you know it.

Inside, he was smiling.

Chapter Twenty-two

Margaret Kessler's breath caught in her throat. Her brain felt underwater, her limbs tingled with the pins of constricted blood flow. She had to clutch the doorframe to keep from passing out.

"Grandma—w-what is this?" Andrea breathed, sheer horror in her voice. To Margaret, her youngest grandchild's voice seemed a dimension away, as though Andrea were speaking into a drinking glass.

"Oh—oh…" Jordan said as he stepped in front of Margaret into the kitchen. "No! No!"

Margaret felt another body scooting around hers, and for a moment she felt panicked by the fact that she could not urge her limbs to move to clear a path.

"Jordan, what's--" And then Zak saw and his voice caught in his throat, a clicking sound that sent an extra wave of nausea over Margaret.

"I—I need to sit down," she heard herself saying. "Boys— Zak, Jordan—please take me to the recliner." She felt her grandsons take her arms and allowed herself to be guided to the living room. Without bracing herself at all, she a fell into the recliner and heard the tired springs pop and squeak under her backside.

"Water—someone get me water," Margaret said through a

mouth as dry as sand. She swiped at the damp, cold sweat that had come to her forehead.

"Zak, will you go?" Andrea asked in a small voice. "I don't think I can."

"Yeah—yeah, I'll get it," Zak said, his voice trembling as well.

Margaret felt a hand on her shoulder and raised her head to see Jordan's sad brown eyes looking into hers.

"Grandma, I'm so sorry," Jordan said in a whisper. His voice broke and Margaret saw a tear trickle down his cheek.

"I can't believe it," Margaret answered, her eyes sweeping over the kitchen. "I can't believe someone would do such a thing—would *write* such terrible phrases!"

The nausea came back as she surveyed her destroyed kitchen. Phrases—awful, vulgar, obscene and blasphemous phrases—had been carved into the cabin's support beams and handcrafted ash cupboards. Vicious scrawls, deep and derogatory, covered the cutout around the refrigerator. Horrific, unprintable words and ungodly phrases scarred every square inch of the wood floor. The kitchen was destroyed, defiled by a hand of evil who sent a clear message with every deep cut. As Margaret's eyes filled with tears, she saw the knife that had been used to carve up her kitchen. It had been cruelly jabbed into the kitchen table, the same kitchen table her husband had been spent hours in the garage making. It had been his last project before he died. Now it was destroyed. Margaret didn't even have to stand from the recliner to see that the worst of the messages—the most heinous threats and gloating curses—were carved onto the tabletop.

The carved taunts screamed at her; the phrases jumped from the wood and filled Margaret's mind with raspy shouts. They mixed together and slammed against the insides of her skull: *God is dead! Curse God and die! I am your god! Lucifer was here! McGurney is a false prophet! Eternal destruction! Forsake your hope! God is hate! I'm coming for you!* And many more vile phrases clashed in her mind. Margaret broke into tears.

"The tabletop—it's destroyed, too," Zak said softly. Margaret could only nod through a film of tears.

It all is. It is all destroyed—defiled. This isn't my home anymore.

Andrea was shaking, on the verge of hyperventilation. "Is he still here? Could he be here?"

"He could be anywhere," Jordan said, tracing his finger over a deep scar on the pantry door. "That's just it—he could be anywhere."

"Grandma," Andrea said, taking Margaret's face in her hands, "Grandma, we have to go Mr. McGurney's. Even if we have to crawl, we have to go!" Andrea's brown eyes pleaded through a torrent of tears. Margaret clenched her jaw and tried to regain her composure.

I have to stay strong! If I don't stay strong the kids won't stay strong!

Margaret took Andrea's hands in her own. By this time, Jordan and Zak had come to her recliner, awaiting the verdict. Would they trek to Paul McGurney's house or not?

"We can't go tonight," Margaret said, swallowing the lump in her throat. She wanted to leave the house more than any of them, to displace herself from the horrific scene that had stolen her cabin's security and concept of *home*. Margaret knew she would never feel the same way about the place again. She had been violated, her cabin had been robbed of its domesticity. But she also knew to hike through a blizzard to Paul McGurney's house in the dark would be a death sentence.

"What do you mean?" Andrea countered, the tears streaming down her cheeks. "We can't stay here! He could come back! He could be *here*!"

Margaret cleared her throat and shook her head. "We have to stay here tonight. We have no other option. We're fortunate the Jeep made it up the mountain. We're snowed in and have to wait it out." She looked at her three grandchildren, made eye contact with each one. "We have to be strong. We have to be brave. We have to live our lives without succumbing to fear. There's four of us and we are strong in the Lord. I would hate to come against us all at one time!" This made Jordan and Zak chuckle. Andrea just sniffled.

"We are going to ignore all this," Margaret continued, sweeping her hand over the Stranger's handiwork. "I'm going to fry some bacon, grill some burgers on the stove insert, and we'll have some bacon cheeseburgers for supper. I'll get my shotgun from upstairs and it will be within arm's reach at all times. OK?" Margaret's eyes met her grandchildren's again. Jordan and Zak nodded, and Andrea whimpered an OK.

Margaret nodded. "Good. But first we're going to pray."

Chapter Twenty-three

Zak found early on that putting on a front of normalcy made the situation even more disconcerting. The five inhabitants of Margaret Kessler's desecrated cabin ate their bacon cheeseburgers atop plates that wobbled due to the scarred and slashed tabletop they sat upon. They all tried to look somewhere—anywhere---but at the mess of jagged blasphemies and taunts left by a faceless, nameless Stranger, but they found they had to look. Their eyes were compelled to take in the carnage as a passerby is transfixed by a wreck on the side of the interstate. Zak saw the others's furtive glances, the fear that seemed to swim atop their pupils. His grandmother had taken her glasses off with a trembling hand to "rest her eyes," but Zak knew it was because she didn't want to see the reality of the cabin's destruction any longer.

"We need to buck up," his grandmother said, addressing the elephant in the room. She wadded her napkin, put it on her plate and folded her hands on the destroyed table. She sighed.

"I know this is bad, guys. I know what you all are thinking, because I'm thinking it, too. But we have to stay positive. We have to have faith." She glanced to the ground, where her shotgun rested at her feet. "And we have to realize we're protected. Both from above and by this baby." She nodded toward the shotgun. "I've got enough shells for this thing to last a lifetime."

"We have to see Mr. McGurney," Andrea said. "We have to get to his house and see what he has to say about all this."

Margaret nodded, considering Andrea's statement. "All in due time, Andrea. The snow'll let up soon enough. We'll get to go visit Mr. McGurney when it's safe to do so. For now, I think we need to talk about sleeping arrangements and such. I realize, Andrea, that you'd probably like to stay in the boys's room."

"Yeah," Zak said. "It's cool with me if you want to. You can have Todd's bed."

Andrea surprised Zak by shaking her head. "I think I'll sleep in my room," she said, indicating the bedroom across the living room from the boys'. "If I'm going to have faith that everything is going to be OK, I've gotta start living it."

Zak was floored. Andrea had always wanted to stay in the boys' room, even when the Opposition and the Stranger were nothing but figments of the imagination.

"Uh—OK," Jordan said, taking one last drink of his ice water. "If you're sure you're OK with that."

Andrea nodded. "Really, I am."

"I'm going to sleep on the living room couch," Margaret said. "I'll just feel safer knowing I'm down here with you guys."

With your gun, Zak thought with a chuckle.

"I think I'd feel safer, too," Andrea said looking around the kitchen.

"Well, that's settled, then," Margaret said, standing up. "Why don't you all go unpack. I'll take care of the dishes while you call your parents. They need to know you got here safe."

Zak stood up from the table and surveyed the ruined kitchen one last time.

Yeah, we got here safe. But staying safe now that we're here is the problem.

Chapter Twenty-four

*T*hree ugly Fiends hovered about Margaret Kessler's destroyed kitchen. The four Knowledge-bearers were eating dinner and trying desperately not to talk about the carnage of the kitchen. It was the Fiends' job to remind them.

"You heard what the general said," one drooling, fly-faced demon said as he floated above the scarred kitchen table. "We have to take away their hope. We have to crush their spirits."

"Hope-sucking is my specialty!" said another hairy, mosquito-faced spirit.

"Let's get to work!" a horse-bodied demon rasped.

Three of the spirits flew close to the children and their grandmother and began whispering lies into their ears, while the mosquito-faced demon used his proboscis to leech onto the children one by one.

"An unseen attack," the horse-bodied spirit said to himself with a chuckle. He continued his work of spreading lies and discord.

Chapter Twenty-five

Margaret Kessler rinsed off the dinner plates and placed them in the dishwasher. As she applied a little elbow grease to a spot of dried barbecue sauce, an overwhelming sense of despair washed over her.

What's the use of being strong? Why lie to yourself—to them?

Margaret felt tears well in her eyes. She looked at her kitchen cupboard, saw the scrawled obscenities, and felt the utter hopelessness of it all.

I might as well give up. What do I have to live for? My husband's dead, my family lives two thousand miles away—I might as well let the Stranger do his work.

Margaret shook her head and scolded herself softly so the children wouldn't hear her from their bedrooms.

"That's foolish talk and you know it. The children need you to be strong. You have *them* to think about."

But do they really care about me? I mean, really. They only see me twice a year at the most. Can they possibly care about my measly little life?

A tear fell from Margaret's eye and she didn't bother to wipe it away. The hopelessness was too strong. She let herself cry it out.

❦ ❦ ❦

Above Margaret's head, the horse-demon hovered, whispering in her ear about the hopelessness of the situation and about how her life was worthless and void of anything for which to live.

"Your grandchildren don't even care about you," he whispered, a sick grin on his horse-face. He loved seeing his victims cry.

As Andrea unpacked her bags in the room across from the boys', an overwhelming sense of dread seized her. The feeling rose from her feet like an acidic tide and sizzled her spine with terror. Why had she decided to get brave and volunteer to sleep in a room by herself? Because the Stranger had already been inside the cabin and he knew the layout of the house, Andrea should have stayed in the boys' room where three-against-one odds were a lot less dismal than what she might face alone and vulnerable in a dark bedroom. She closed her suitcase and sat on her mattress. Placing her head in her hands, she tried to hold back tears that desperately wanted to cascade down her cheeks. The enormity of the hopelessness struck her like a sucker punch, and she had an awful certainty that she would never live to see the end of the summer.

This is it! We're doomed! The cards are stacked too high against us! We'll never make it out of this alive!

The tears came, the dam of whatever resolve she had left bursting like her hopes for a future.

I don't want to die yet!

Slithering around Andrea's ankles, the fly-faced demon whispered of hopelessness and impending doom. The girl was trying to hold on, struggling to keep faith alive. But her tears were threatening to ruin all that.

"The spirit is willing, but the flesh is so, so weak!" the fly-faced demon laughed to himself. He continued to whisper of the utter doom that awaited the children this summer.

"Not even Paul McGurney can save you from death…"

The girl's resolve broke. Tears came.

Chalk one up for Lucifer.

§§§

"Man, I don't know how we're gonna make it," Jordan said, flopping down on his bed. He put his chin in his hands and watched Zak unpack his socks to place them in an antique dresser. Zak turned to him, socks in hand.

"I've been thinking the same thing. It feels like, I don't know, like we've got no chance this time. Like we're walking right into an ambush we'll never escape." He tossed the socks onto his bed and sighed.

"The Stranger's gotta be that Hanson guy Grandma was talking about," Jordan said, nibbling his lower lip.

"I hope you're wrong," Zak said, sitting on the edge of his mattress. "Grandma said that dude was huge."

"It'd make sense, though. An electrician who happens to be huge showing up right when Grandma was going to see Paul McGurney? Doesn't smell right." Jordan sat up and leaned against the wall.

"But he could've taken her out then and there," Zak said. "Instead, he got her a pack of frozen peas for her head. That's pretty nice for an assassin."

"He couldn't kill her," Jordan said, looking to the ceiling. "If he did, then we would never have come."

"That's where you're wrong," Zak pointed out. "Remember? Grandma's phone was out---still out. We came regardless. He could have killed her and we would've found her body--"

"OK. Let's not talk about that," Jordan said with a grimace. "I see your point, though. That Hanson guy can all but be ruled out."

Zak shrugged. "Maybe. But I'm not ruling out anybody."

"And Grandma's convinced Hanson is the Stranger."

"He's coming back sometime. He has to fix the phone line and some other electrical stuff. We have to make sure Grandma doesn't shoot first and ask questions later."

Both boys chuckled. A heavy silence pervaded the room.

"It still feels hopeless," Jordan finally said, his eyes still to the ceiling. "I can't shake that."

"I know what you mean," Zak answered, studying the floor. "It's like it sticks to you, you know?"

Jordan didn't have to say anything to confirm his cousin's observation.

"Jordan?" Zak asked after another moment of silence.

"Yeah?"

"I'm terrified."

Jordan swallowed hard. He knew the feeling.

"Me, too."

$$\text{\SSS}$$

The mosquito-faced demon used his proboscis to suck the hope from the boys while the horse-faced spirit, fresh from his assault on the old woman, whispered fear into their ears. Horse-face smiled a sick, evil smile.

"They are terrified."

Mosquito-face returned the evil grin.

"Don't you love how easy it is?"

Chapter Twenty-six

Night turned into morning in the Colorado wilderness. When Jordan opened his eyes, the first thing he saw from the window was that the snow had stopped falling and the sky was a rich, cloudless blue. As he sat up in his bed, a wash of hope swept over him.

We get to see Mr. McGurney today!

But the feeling of hope immediately gave way to an oppressive emotion of fear. Jordan ran his fingers through his bedheaded hair as he recalled the harrowing dreams he'd had last night. Violent and terrifying, they had woken Jordan at least three times in the dead of the night convinced the Stranger was outside his bedroom door. The Stranger had chased him through his dreamworld wielding a vicious knife and a smile of pure evil. Although Jordan couldn't recollect the Stranger's face, he'd never forget the assassin's cruel, cold eyes. Calculating eyes. Demonic eyes.

Jordan shuddered as he looked at Zak's bed. His cousin lay on his back with his arm slung over his head, mouth open with a thin spindle of drool icicling onto his pillow. As Jordan swung his feet onto the cold floor, he wondered whether Zak had been tormented by terrible dreams as well.

Jordan stretched and stood from the bed, his knees popping

from a night of rest. Walking to the window, he peered out into the mountainous countryside. The snow sparkled in the new sunlight, millions of diamonds twinkling in the morning. Although the snow was thick, Jordan judged by the early morning sunlight that much of it would melt away by late afternoon. In the distance, the purple summit of Pike's Peak stood sentinel over the land, an awesome yet chilling reminder of last summer's adventures. Jordan touched the window with his fingertips.

Somewhere out there… Somewhere out there you are hiding—waiting…

"Did it stop snowing?"

Jordan turned at Zak's sleep-slurred voice. His cousin hadn't risen from bed, but he squinted out of slitted eyes like a patient coming out of anesthesia.

"Yeah, it stopped. Looks like it's gonna be a pretty nice day."

Zak wiped the drool from his cheek and sighed.

"I had quite the dream, let me tell you."

Jordan returned to his bed and sat down. "You, too, huh?"

Zak sat up, stretching his arms over his head. "Yeah, man. The Stranger—he had me tied to one of Grandma's chairs and he was standing over me with a knife. Freaky stuff. You have a similar dream?"

Jordan shrugged. "He was chasing me with that knife you were talking about."

Zak nodded. "I can only imagine what kind of dreams Andrea had."

"No doubt."

Outside their door, the boys heard the clank of a skillet being placed on the stovetop.

"Grandma's up. Bacon time," Jordan said, slapping his knees and standing.

Zak yawned and threw the covers from his legs. "Well, at least we get to see Mr. McGurney today."

Yeah, if we don't get chopped into pieces first!

Jordan looked at Zak, and he didn't have to say what he was thinking to know they were both on the same wavelength.

$$\text{❦❦❦}$$

"It was awful," Andrea said, absently toying with some shredded hash browns with her fork. "I probably slept like three hours tops. I kept thinking I heard the Stranger coming into the cabin. And it's so dark in my room…"

"You wouldn't have had to worry about the Stranger coming to get you," Margaret said, taking a sip of her strong coffee. "I had my shotgun locked and loaded."

But I didn't sleep a wink! Margaret thought.

The night had been unruly. The wind had howled and the tree braches had scratched the roof like fingernails along drywall. As Margaret tossed and turned on her surprisingly uncomfortable couch, she couldn't shake the feeling that she had been violated by an insane killer. Her cabin and her privacy had been destroyed by the assassin's ugly knife, and her peace of mind had been ripped away. What is more, she had a strong hunch as to the true identity of the Stranger, and that terrified her.

It has to be the electrician, Hanson! And if it's him, he's huge!

Margaret tried to shake the abysmal feelings as she sopped up the last of her runny egg yolk with a piece of whole grain toast. Her plate wobbled on the scarred table, and for a moment she thought the feelings of defeat would etch themselves into her heart as the assassin's blade had the tabletop. Thankfully, Andrea changed the subject to something a little more hopeful.

"When are we leaving for Mr. McGurney's?"

"I vote right after breakfast. We can all shower fast and be on the road in an hour or so," Zak offered, pushing his plate away.

"I'm with him," Jordan said, sipping his orange juice. "The

sooner the better. The snow's stopped and the sun's out. The roads have to be better than yesterday."

"We'll go as soon as we get things cleaned up here," Margaret said acting as grandmotherly as possible. Inside, she wanted to get to Paul McGurney's just as badly as the rest of them.

"Cool," Zak said. "I call not doing dishes."

Margaret smiled. "I think you just volunteered yourself, young Zachary."

🐍🐍🐍

Above the heads of the cabin's inhabitants, the three Fiends scowled and swore.

"I hate that McGurney!" Fly-face rasped. "If those brats and the old bag make it to his house, we'll have lost ground!"

"I hope the master has a plan! McGurney will speak of the Knowledge, and we'll be thwarted!" Horse-face said.

"No way I'm going into the old man's house!" Mosquito-face grimaced. "That's too much Truth in one place for me!"

"Then we must afflict them now!" Fly-face said, hovering over the boy called Jordan. "We must scare them---destroy their confidence—make them doubt their safety!"

Horse-face smiled as he caught a glimpse of movement outside the cabin's window. The smile became larger and more menacing as he saw who was approaching.

"It looks like our work just got easier!"

The other two Fiends looked to the window, and then cackled in agreement as they watched the figure approach the cabin.

Chapter Twenty-seven

*T*odd knew he was the only student from Infinity High School taking his finals in the comfort of his own home. But comfort was relative; his right arm shot with laser blips of pain, and he found it increasingly difficult to concentrate on his Algebra II exam. He was on summer vacation and had missed his exams due to his hospital stay. Now Mrs. Tankersly, the media center supervisor and bus route coordinator, sat across from Todd in his mother's favorite loveseat. The frizzy-haired fifty-something flipped through the *People* magazine she had brought, while occasionally eyeballing him to make sure he wasn't using a cheat sheet. Todd knew the school had to send a proctor to his house to make sure he wasn't copying formulas from his textbook, but he found Mrs. Tankersly's presence to be woefully annoying. She flipped her magazine pages like a bullwhip and popped her gum like a valley girl. Needless to say, Todd's concentration was shot.

I've got other things to deal with right now!

"Todd? Are you finished?" Mrs. Tankersly looked over the top of her magazine at him as if he had just stolen a cookie from the cookie jar. He hadn't realized he had spaced out.

"Uh—yeah. I'm not sure about this last one. Might as well call it a day." He put down his pencil and leaned back into the couch.

Mrs. Tankersly closed her magazine and picked up his exam. Eyeing him once more as if he'd stolen government property, she nodded and stood up.

"Well, Todd. I hope you recover quickly from your injury." She made to leave and Todd didn't try to stop her.

"Thanks. I hope so, too." He stood up and walked to the door, not wishing to continue the going-nowhere banter.

"Have a great summer," Mrs. Tankersly said as she opened the door.

If I make it through alive I'll be more than satisfied!

"You, too."

When Mrs. Tankersly was finally gone, Todd set his laptop on the coffee table and booted it up. He had a Skype date with Jen, and he was going to be late. When her face appeared on his screen, Todd remembered again why she had the ability to make his heart flutter. With her deep brown eyes and acorn hair to match a smile that made her face glow, Jen was the epitome of a good catch.

"So are you coming to hang out with me or not?" Jen asked with a heart-melting smile. She sat in what appeared to be her uncle's den. A wall of books loomed behind her, their spines displaying such names as Stephen King and Brad Meltzer. Todd thought for a moment and answered cryptically.

"I wouldn't put it past me yet."

Jen laughed. "That's what I like to hear."

Todd smiled back and then remembered he wanted to ask her about a comment she had made about religion and faith. She had laughed scornfully when Todd had mentioned he was praying that everything would be OK concerning his arm. But now, broaching the topic seemed excruciatingly awkward.

But it's bothering me. I need to see where she stands.

"Does your uncle go to church somewhere in Colorado Springs?" Todd asked. It was a weak opening, a feeble attempt to steer the conversation the direction he wanted it to go. Still, he had to see what she said.

Jen's smile faded to a snarky smirk. "Church? Why would he want to go to church?

Todd felt his tongue take on an extra four pounds.

"Well—I just—I don't—I just wondered."

"If he was going to make me go to church while I'm out here I would have stayed in Ohio," Jen said, brushing her bangs from her forehead. "Besides, Sunday is for sleeping in late and eating omelets for brunch."

Todd didn't know how to respond, so he didn't. Jen continued despite Todd's reluctance to speak.

"Don't get me wrong, my uncle's super spiritual. I know he flies to New York twice a year to attend some type of soul-cleansing ceremony where they rub your body with crystals or something. If you ask me, it's pretty weird."

Todd decided her last sentence provided him a way back into the conversation.

"Yeah, that sounds pretty whacked out."

Jen shrugged. "If you ask me, the whole concept of religion is pretty lame. I mean, think about it: why do you and I have to answer to some silent being in the sky? How can some ghost—and why *should* some ghost—forgive us for our sins?" Jen threw finger quotes around her last five words and laughed.

Todd felt his heart pounding. He'd read somewhere in the Bible that a believer was to be ready to give a testimony as to the Hope they possessed. But right now Todd wanted nothing more than to hide under the couch.

"So—you don't believe in anything?"

Jen thought for a second. "I don't know about that. I don't believe I have to answer to anybody. My own decisions dictate the way I live my life. If I make poor choices, it's my own fault. If I make good ones, more power to me. I just don't think I need some Jesus or Buddha grading me on my performance. It doesn't

84

seem fair."

Todd nodded, not out of agreement, but because it bought him time to collect his thoughts. He sighed.

Here goes nothing!

"Jen, there's something you have to know about me," he started.

"You're not going to tell me you're some serial killer or something," Jen interrupted with a feigned horrified expression. "Because I am totally *not* cool with that."

Todd laughed, thankful to expel some of his nervous energy.

"No, it's nothing like that. It's just—a year ago my life changed. A lot."

Jen nodded and urged him to continue.

"Well, I used to be skeptical about everything. I thought what I read in my science book was absolute truth and there was no deviating from that truth." Todd paused and wetted his lips. "That was until I *met* Absolute Truth."

Jen threw up her hands.

"OK, OK. Hold it right there. You're not going to hit me with the whole "born again" thing, are you? Because I would much prefer you tell me you're a serial killer."

Ouch! Why so hostile?

Todd took a deep breath and fumbled with his cell phone.

"I—actually—yeah. I met Jesus last summer."

Jen shook her head, and for the first time Todd saw flashes of anger in her eyes.

"Let's get one thing straight, Todd. If we're going to be together, we don't talk about sappy Jesus stuff, OK? You don't try to force it on me and I won't question your beliefs, however naïve I think they are."

Todd felt a jolt of anger in his own chest at her choice of words, but he suppressed it as best he could.

"Jen, I just thought it's important you know where I stand--"

"And now I do," Jen interrupted. "You're in the Jesus camp.

That's cool for you, I guess. But, please—leave me out of it. I don't want to drink that particular Kool-Aid."

Todd felt backed into a corner.

"Jen, I--"

Jen silenced him with a raised palm.

"I need to go, Todd. My uncle's gone and I have to shovel the front walks. We'll talk later when you're over your moment."

Todd didn't know what to say.

"Jen, please--"

"Adios, for now," Jen said. And then she signed out.

Todd stared at his computer screen unable to believe what had just transpired.

What was that? Why was she so adamantly opposed to my talking about Jesus?

But the computer screen didn't answer, nor did God's voice suddenly speak into the silence of the room. Todd was left to wonder what he should do about Jen, abide by her wishes and not speak about Jesus, or try again later.

How do I get myself into these situations?

Chapter Twenty-eight

Margaret wanted to waste no time in getting to Paul McGurney's house. Too much was at stake, too much uncertainty ruled the moment. The sense of hopelessness, the gnawing urge to throw in the towel because it was all too hard, crept over her again as she literally threw her dish towel on the kitchen counter.

"Why don't you get ready to go," Margaret said to Zak.

Zak placed the last plate in the dishwasher and nodded.

"OK. We need to get there as fast as we can."

Margaret sighed and pinched the bridge of her nose with her fingers.

"I know, Zak. We'll get there as quickly as we can--"

Three thunderous knocks on the cabin door jolted the rest of her words from her mouth. Margaret looked at Zak and saw him pale. Jordan and Andrea ran into the kitchen from the boys' bedroom and stood behind the scarred dinner table, looking toward the door in obvious fear.

Margaret swallowed, trying to find an elusive composure.

He's here! The Stranger came back!

Margaret found her voice and was alarmed by how quivery and unsure it sounded.

"Everything's OK. I don't know who could possibly be at

the door, but it most certainly isn't the Stranger. He wouldn't knock."

It's the perfect trap! If he knocks, I simply let him in to kill us all!

"Grandma—I--" Jordan started. His eyes moved from the door to Margaret in rapid succession.

"Hush. It's fine."

And as if to prove it really was "fine," Margaret felt her feet moving toward the door. Her brain screamed at her, her entire being revolted against the idea of opening the cabin door, but in some ludicrous way, she knew she had to take the chance. She knew she had to be strong for the children and exemplify faith at all costs. But faith was hard when you didn't believe everything would be OK.

Three more knocks shook the small cabin as Margaret reached for the doorknob. She flinched, her stomach falling and her jaw trembling. Still, she reached for the knob and unlocked the door.

I should have brought the shotgun with me! What was I thinking?

Now, nothing stood in the way of the Stranger and his destruction should opening the door reveal the assassin.

I'm inviting him in! I'm letting him inside my home!

Margaret's hand was on the knob, and she swallowed hard one last time. She opened the door, prepared to scream—prepared to die.

☙☙☙

The Fiends hovered over the kitchen island, barely able to contain themselves. What was about to transpire would be priceless entertainment. The ugly demons had done their part instilling fear and doubt into the minds of the cabin's inhabitants. Now they would see the fruits of their labor.

🐍🐍🐍

Margaret opened the door and felt the weight of death press upon her chest. When she saw who was standing on her doorstep, all the air left her lungs and her head began to swim with blips of yellow light. For a moment she thought she might have a heart attack.

"No—no!" Margaret heard herself gasp. Instinctively she flinched back from the monstrosity before her, and she knew the children would be following her example.

Run! Run, kids! It's him!

"Ma'am?" the hulking man said, reaching out his hand to touch Margaret's shoulder. In that moment, Margaret realized she had made a grave mistake in not bringing the shotgun to the door with her.

"Don't touch me!" Margaret shrieked, falling back against the wall. Margaret heard the shotgun cock and stole a glance at the children. Zak stood with the loaded shotgun pointed dead-red at Jason Hanson, the man who *claimed* to be an electrician.

Jason Hanson heard the cock of the gun and his face went pale. He put up two huge hands and pleaded with Zak not to shoot. Margaret saw the fear in the man's eyes, but still, she was convinced that this man—the man who had come a few days prior to fix her wiring behind the refrigerator—was the Stranger.

Shoot him, Zak!

"No! Please! Don't—put the gun down!"

Margaret scooted behind the kitchen island and grabbed a butcher knife from the knife rack. She looked at Zak who swallowed hard. His finger twitched on the trigger.

"Not after what you did to my house—to my family!" Margaret spat, thrusting the knife in Hanson/the Stranger's general direction.

Hanson flinched as Zak moved his trigger hand from the gun and wiped his palm on his jeans. The huge man vigorously shook his head.

"No! You-you have me confused with someone else! I—I'm just here to work on your wiring!"

"Grandma?" Zak asked, gun still pointed at Hanson/the Stranger's chest.

"How can I trust you?" Margaret screamed. "Look at my house! See how terrified we are!"

Hanson's eyes swept over the scarred kitchen and then locked back on Zak and the gun. He licked his lips and swallowed hard.

"I—I helped you the last time I was here," Hanson offered. "Y—you fainted when I came to the door and I got you something to put on your head. W-why would I want to hurt you? You must have me confused with someone else."

Margaret clenched her jaw. Jason Hanson hadn't hurt her the first time he had come over. He had given her a bag of frozen peas to prevent her head from swelling. He really *hadn't* been violent at all.

But it could be a trap! It could all be an elaborate set-up!

"Put the gun down, Zak," Jordan said softly. Margaret looked at the children and was horrified to see Jordan stepping to Zak's side.

"Not until Grandma tells me to," Zak said, the gun still locked on Hanson's chest.

"He's not the Stranger," Jordan said, gently touching the barrel of the gun. "Lower it, Zak."

Hanson, visibly glad to finally have an ally, picked up where Jordan left off.

"I think I'm just in the wrong place at the wrong time. I'm no stranger. Just your friendly neighborhood electrician." He laughed nervously and swallowed again.

"Grandma?" Zak asked, looking to Margaret.

Margaret's brain screamed at her to not believe the big man. He was the Stranger! He was the reason for all the fear! But something inside of her was fighting to get to the forefront of her emotions.

He's not the Stranger. He's just an electrician.

Jordan walked over to Margaret and put his hand on her shoulder. With his other hand he touched her tense forearm and gently applied pressure.

"You don't need a knife, Grandma. We don't need a gun, either. He's just an electrician. He isn't the Stranger. I can feel it."

Margaret slowly allowed her forearm to fall. She dropped the knife to the countertop with a clatter. Jordan had a deep intuition. Discernment was one of his gifts. If he said Hanson wasn't the Stranger, then Hanson wasn't the Stranger.

"Grandma?" Zak asked again.

Margaret looked at Hanson and then looked at Jordan. Jordan nodded.

"It's OK, Zak," Margaret said, "you can put the gun down."

Zak hesitated for a moment and then clicked the gun to safety and propped it against the kitchen counter.

"Thank you!" Hanson said, still standing with his big hands raised. "This is not the way I like to start a morning."

Jordan walked around the island and put out his hand toward Hanson. Margaret's muscles tensed as she waited to see what would happen.

"Jordan Lawrence," Jordan said.

"Jason Hanson, electrician," Hanson said as he smiled and shook Jordan's hand. Margaret saw the color return to the big man's face, and her own heart began to slow to its normal rate.

"Whew! I'm glad we got that cleared up!" Hanson said. He nervously laughed and stepped into the cabin.

Chapter Twenty-nine

*T*odd felt the tiny hairs on the back of his neck stand on end. His flesh became a topographical map of goose-bumps, and from his place on the couch, Todd was certain he was being watched.

He's here—the Stranger—he's here!

Todd didn't want to move, for fear of alerting the Stranger to his location. He quickly realized that if the Stranger was watching him as he thought he was, then the assassin already had Todd's location marked. With a sinking feeling, Todd knew he was a sitting duck.

If he's here, I'm toast.

Todd's cell phone chirped an incoming text message alert and Todd nearly toppled from the couch. He picked up his phone, grateful to have something to distract him from the constricting feeling of the living room. To his surprise, the text was from Jen:

Sorry for overreacting. Miss you.—JeN

Todd smiled despite feeling like a firefly trapped in a Mason jar. At least he and Jen were back on good terms. At least that was going right.

But it doesn't matter if I get axed here.

Todd quickly thumbed a cheerful response and closed his phone. Looking toward the window, he saw no dark shadow lurking with large knife. He listened for a moment and heard no creaks or floorboard groans that signified an attack.

So why do I feel like I'm being watched?

Todd sighed and grabbed the TV remote. Flipping through the channels, he settled on an *Everybody Loves Raymond* rerun and tried to ignore the roiling in his stomach.

Three nasty Fiends hovered above the couch where Todd sat watching television. They had been sent by Horse-face and Mosquito-face to damage Todd's spirit. They had spent the last fifteen minutes whispering horrendous things in his ear— things about an impending attack and about how hopeless life was. They whispered about God's cruelty at causing Todd to go through season-ending arm troubles and about how God had all but abandoned him as he sat, broken, in Infinity. The Fiends swirled around the sofa and hurled insults and curses and watched Todd's face and shoulders fall under the weight of it all.

It was too easy.

Chapter Thirty

Margaret studied Jason Hanson as he set out his gear on the kitchen island. The man was not the Stranger. He couldn't be. The way he had been so gentle with her when she had passed out, the way he joked with the children about being in the wrong place at the wrong time was all very normal. And nice. As Hanson adjusted his tool belt on his sizable hips, Margaret wondered what had gotten into her to make her think this jovially overweight electrician could possibly be an insane murder.

I'm just on edge, is all. I don't know how long we can stay here. There's always the option I've been thinking about...

"Looks like someone went to town on your woodwork in here," Jason Hanson said, knocking her from her thoughts.

"Uh--yeah. We had some--some vandals come through," Margaret said, knowing the explanation sounded more than lame.

Jason Hanson studied the vicious scrawls that covered the once-beautiful wood.

"Seems like some pretty hateful vandals. Did you report this to the police?"

Margaret fumbled for words. "We--we prefer not to get the authorities involved. They have other criminals to catch."

Hanson studied her for a moment and then shrugged.

"You don't mind if I pull your refrigerator out again to take a look at those pesky wires, do you?"

"Uh—no. Go ahead, do what you have to do. I can't wait to get my phone up and running again."

"You and the rest of the mountain," Hanson said, grabbing the side of the refrigerator. The big man pushed it aside as though it were an empty cardboard box. Studying the mess of wires, he shook his head. "This one looks like it might take awhile."

Maragret chuckled, feeling her nervousness drain into normalcy. "That's OK. We were just going to step out for awhile, weren't we kids?" The children confirmed her statement with head nods.

"Well, you don't mind if I set up shop here while you're gone?" Hanson asked, adjusting his tool belt again.

Margaret looked at Jordan and Zak and then back at Hanson. *He isn't the Stranger. He's just an electrician doing his job.*

"I think that will be fine."

Jason Hanson smiled. "Well, just know its me in here when you get back. I don't want to be staring down the barrel of that thing again." He nodded to the shotgun.

Margaret picked it up and made sure it was unloaded. She smiled back.

"Deal. I'll take it with me so it doesn't spook you while you work."

The big man nodded. "That'd be great. You folks have a good step-out. Be careful out there. It's still a little slippery."

Margaret heard her chuckle come out in a nervous spurt.

"We'll be careful. If you need anything to drink, feel free to check the fridge." She looked to the children. "What do you say we hit the road?"

The trek down the mountain to the fork in the road proved hazardous. Ice slicked the road, and more than once Andrea saw her grandmother tense behind the wheel. The foursome had left the chains on the tires, so at least Andrea could muster a bit of security in them. But as the Jeep got closer to the fork, Andrea's stomach was in knots.

How long can we keep this up? How long can we run from danger before we lose our minds?

At least she was going to get to see Paul McGurney. Maybe the old man could bring some comfort to an otherwise uncomfortable situation.

I hope he can help us. We need all the help we can get!

"Well, I'll be jarred," Margaret said as she came to the fork in the road. "I don't know what I was expecting, but I'm still surprised this road is here. Forgive my amazement."

"We've been there," Zak said. "I remember it like it was yesterday."

Margaret turned onto the road that led to McGurney's enchanted house.

"Now, come on, young Zachary! You sound like an old geezer like me!"

Andrea laughed. It felt good to laugh. Laughing was a lot better than crying.

🐚🐚🐚

The three ugly Fiends floated above the Jeep. Mosquito-face insisted they should be whispering fear and doubt into the children's ears, but Fly-face told him to hold back.

"There will be time for more. They are going to seek the Knowledge with that old kook."

Horse-face let out a raspy growl. "I hate the Knowledge! He always is one step ahead of us!"

Mosquito-face cursed and snarled. "The old woman was set

up to blow a hole through Hanson's fat body! And now—they aren't even afraid of him! That was supposed to be one of the best cards we could play—make the brats and the old bag fear Hanson as the Stranger! But we've been thwarted!"

"These brats must be important to the Knowledge," Fly-face said. "Otherwise this would all be over."

"We'll get them yet," Mosquito-face rasped.

"We might get them, but I'm not going into McGurney's place. Too much Knowledge for me," Horse-face said.

The other two concurred. They would follow the Jeep and stalk the children, but they would not enter the house on the hill. It was too risky; could be too painful.

"They'll be dead soon enough," Mosquito-face said. "The master always gets his man."

Chapter Thirty-One

"*W*elcome, children!" Paul McGurney said as he beckoned the children to the back of the elegant room with a wave of his timeless hand. "I have missed you!"

Jordan couldn't help but feel a twinge of nostalgia for the previous summer as he walked by the lavish cherry table and rich, woody furnishings. It had only been a year ago that he and the others had literally seen McGurney's dark and foreboding house transform into one of grandeur and antiquated luxury. He remembered the way the musty, dark room had erupted into brilliant light in a flash, and how all the drab weariness had been replaced with splendors they had never seen before. He just wished Todd could be here now to experience it all again. For a moment, Jordan forgot about the terror facing the children and simply relished in the moment, taking in the mansion as if he were seeing it for the first time.

"Come, children! I have much to tell you!" Paul McGurney said as the children approached the cozy living area in front of the enormous fireplace. McGurney sat in his leather arm chair, his waxy hands crossed on his lap. A broad smile shone on his face, and his vacant blue eyes were alive with firefly sparkles. Jordan stopped before the old man and patted him on the shoulder.

"It's good to be back, Mr. McGurney!" The old man gazed up at him sightlessly, the thin wisps of his white hair slightly askew.

"It is wonderful to have you back, Jordan," He touched Jordan's arm gently.

"Mr. McGurney!" Andrea shouted, brushing past Jordan and stooping to hug McGurney.

"Oh, Andrea, it has been too long," Paul McGurney said with a chuckle. "And Zak! I have missed you as well!"

"Tell me about it," Zak said, stooping to hug the old man after Andrea let him go. "I wish we had never left."

Paul McGurney straightened from his hug with Zak and looked to Margaret, who stood behind the children with an expression of wonder.

"And it is good to see you again, Margaret." Jordan saw the old man's eyes sparkle. The first and only time McGurney had met Jordan's grandmother had been under perilous circumstances at Devil's Playground.

Margaret hugged the old man and continued to gape at her surroundings. "I just—forgive me for being so googly-eyed. It's just—I've lived on this mountain for what seems like a lifetime and I never expected—well—*this*!"

McGurney chuckled and studied the air above Margaret's head. "I am so happy to have you all here. Even though we can't see tomorrow, God is faithful and just. He has brought us here for a reason and a specific purpose. Our God is faithful."

Jordan couldn't disagree with Paul McGurney's statement, although he wondered how God could make all things come together for the good when things were going so, so badly.

"Come, children Do sit. We have much to discuss and much to experience." McGurney motioned with the wave of his age-spotted hand to the leather sofa across from his chair. "The lemonade is as fresh as the morning."

Jordan and the others took a seat on the leather sofa, a sweating pitcher of lemonade and three glasses before them on a coffee table. Zak poured Andrea and Jordan a glass and finished with one for himself. Jordan couldn't help but feel the touch of sadness as he looked to Todd's customary place on the sofa and saw it empty.

"I do wish Todd could be here with us," Paul McGurney said somberly, as if reading Jordan's thoughts. "I pray his recovery is fast and thorough."

"It was pretty nasty," Zak said, taking a gulp of his lemonade. "Pretty much grossed me out."

Paul McGurney chuckled and Jordan appraised the old man. McGurney wore his patented Mr. Rogers zip-up blue cardigan with white khaki pants. Fuzzy blue slippers peeked out from underneath the cuffs of his pants.

Hasn't changed a bit!

"Mr. McGurney," Andrea blurted, "what is going on? Who is the Stranger? Why is he after us?"

Jordan felt his stomach muscles clench. For a moment, being in Paul McGurney's enchanted house had made him forget the dangers that threatened the children. Now the reality of the situation was setting in, and he felt the panic rise within him like floodwater.

Paul McGurney's amiable face turned serious. "It is unfortunate that we have to meet under such perilous circumstances. But your enemy is always on the prowl."

"But *who* is the enemy, Mr. McGurney?" Andrea asked, her voice trembling.

Paul McGurney sighed and seemed to study the air above the children's heads with his sightless eyes.

"Some things are not revealed to me, dear one," he said softly. "I am but a messenger sent to fulfill the purpose my Father has set for me. As you glimpse the past through my window, so do I only glimpse the bits and pieces deemed necessary to impart to you."

"But that's so unfair!" Andrea said, throwing up her hands.

100

She crossed her arms and exhaled in exasperation.

"It's like God is just messing with us," Zak said softly. Jordan wasn't all that shocked to realize he felt the same way. Why would God toy with them like this? Why couldn't He just be *specific*?

Paul McGurney's expression turned thoughtful. "You know, children, I have often felt the way you do now."

Jordan felt his eyes grow wide. This was not something he expected Paul McGurney, of all people, to say. "What do you mean, Mr. McGurney? *You* feel this way sometimes?"

McGurney chuckled once more and folded his hands on his lap. "It is only natural, Jordan, to question the ways of a Superior. Do you ever question the judgment of your parents?"

"Uh—yeah. I mean, sometimes they do things that don't make sense."

"But do you trust they have your best interests in mind? That they love you and only want to make decisions that benefit you and not harm you?" McGurney asked. Jordan could see where he was going

"I guess so."

"And if your parents have the best in mind for you when they make decisions you don't agree with, then isn't your heavenly Father the same?" Paul McGurney smiled.

"I see what you mean, but it's so hard," Zak said, sipping his lemonade. "I mean, even *you* said you have the same feelings from time to time!"

"I am no different from any one of you, Zak. I do not always see the direction my Father wishes for me. Sometimes the direction seems downright painful and completely unsafe. But I still *trust* and *know* that He is who He says He is and that He will never lead me through fire I will get scorched by. It is the trust that is the hard part. When you accepted Jesus as your Lord, you gave your life over to him. Never did He say life after acceptance was easy. But He did say that if you would only trust that his ways are absolute and that He works for the good of the ones He loves, He will never leave you in your time of peril."

The children took a moment to let all Paul McGurney had just said soak through the walls of their resistance. Jordan wanted more than anything to believe that Jesus knew what was best for him. He wanted to believe more than anything that Jesus would make things all right. But fear got in the way. Fear of pain, of torture, of death at the hands of an unseen madman. The Opposition had been bad enough, but at least the children had known who he was. But this new Stranger—this new Stranger could be *anybody*!

"I just wish it could be easier," Jordan said with a sigh.

"I know, Jordan. But we must trust that God's ways are best. He will see you through no matter what." Paul McGurney smiled and his eyes twinkled again. "Remember, dear one, that we are co-heirs with Christ."

Jordan saw Andrea scrunch her nose. "Cores?"

Paul McGurney laughed, his blue eyes shimmering. "Not cores, child, co-heirs. This simply means that we get from the Father what Jesus gets from the Father. When we accepted Him as our Savior, we became brothers and sisters of Christ. Think about it, children: we inherit from the Father what Jesus does. Heaven—eternity—a place of honor in the eyes of God."

Jordan nodded as the implications of what Paul McGurney was saying sunk in.

"So, you're saying we get what Christ gets. Does that mean we get His power?"

McGurney laughed. "An excellent question, Jordan. In short, yes. The same Spirit Who dwells within Christ dwells within You. Jesus Himself promised His disciples that they would do even greater things than He did while He was on earth."

"Awesome," Zak breathed.

"Yes, Zak, it is awesome. If Christians truly understood how much power they have in Christ, the world would be a very different place," Paul McGurney said.

"I wish we could see Jesus again," Zak said, wistfully.

"Mr. McGurney—can we go somewhere?" Andrea asked, suddenly excited. Jordan felt his own heart skip a beat when he realized what Andrea was asking.

The Glimpses!

Paul McGurney laughed and reached for his cherry cane. "The time has come for such Glimpses. There is much to see and much to experience!" McGurney painstakingly stood from his seat and looked at the children with a renewed vigor.

"Come, children! To the window!"

The Fiends hovered outside Paul McGurney's house. They didn't enter. So much Knowledge would be painful. Instead, they waited and plotted. More chaos was to come.

Chapter Thirty-two

*T*odd could stand it no longer. He was cooped up, terrified and sensed something awful was about to happen. At any minute, the Stranger could pop through the door—or the window—or through the attic vent---and it would be game over for Todd. Horrible thoughts swam through his mind.

Where is God in all this? I thought He works for the good of those He loves.

Shudders overtook him, trembles that shook Todd to the core.

We're never going to make it an entire summer. Who am I kidding; we're as good as dead.

He warred with tears as, like Macbeth, every noise appalled him.

I need to be in Colorado. But for what? To get slaughtered?

The tears came and Todd hated himself for them. He wasn't supposed to cry. He was supposed to be the strong one, the one who faced the giants and won because he was *supposed* to. Now, he felt like a withered leaf just clinging to life.

Jesus—if You are listening, I need some help here.

🐍🐍🐍

Three nameless Fiends knew they had the one called Todd on the ropes. Here was the leader of the pack of brats, and he was vulnerable and broken and tired. They continued to whisper lies and deceit and chaos as the plan for Todd seemed to be in perfect alliance with the master's. It was clockwork; destroy his spirit and then destroy his body.

Chapter Thirty-three

*T*he vortex of time swirled about the children, years upon decades upon centuries flying by in a matter of seconds. Margaret felt her heart thundering in her chest, and her eyes darted from one section of the swirling blackness to another. She had never been one for rollercoasters or spinning carnival rides, and now this whole *time travel* thing raised her level of trepidation about sixty notches. She looked at Zak, who had a broad smile on his face.

"W-we're going to be OK, right? This is entirely safe?"

Zak laughed, his eyes shining. "We've made it back how many times now without a glitch? Just hold tight, Grandma. You're in for something awesome."

Margaret felt her hand tremble as she steadied herself on Zak's shoulder.

"I hope you're right—I just—I just never thought I'd ever—oh, boy!"

Andrea laughed and grabbed her other hand. "Trust us, Grandma. These adventures are the best part!"

"Yeah," Jordan said. "I was afraid the first time, but now—man, I'm stoked!"

Margaret swallowed hard and tried to smile. "I don't know if 'stoked' is the word I'd use to describe the way I feel. More like terrified, petrified or I'm too old for this."

" 'I'm too old for this' is five words," Zak pointed out. "And look, the ride's almost over. What happens now is the blackness starts to wash out and a picture starts to come into focus. It's kinda fuzzy at first, like when you're looking through a microscope and trying to make the slide come in crystal clear. Well—look—you see what I mean. It's happening now."

Margaret did see what Zak was saying. All around her, the blackness had vanished and a distorted picture was struggling into focus. Margaret had a flash thought that the Stranger might be lurking behind the distortion with his degrading knife, ready to inflict immense pain. He had sure carved up her kitchen. Why wouldn't he do the same to Margaret and her grandchildren?

Get a grip, old lady! If the children aren't afraid, you shouldn't be, either!

"I wonder where we are?" Andrea asked, the excitement heavy in her voice.

"We're about to see," Jordan said, straining to make sense out of the distorted picture before him.

And then everything was clear. Margaret gasped for good measure as the fuzziness dissolved and the picture before her came into focus.

"We're inside," Margaret said, taking in the dimly lit space she and the children had been deposited into. "It's--it's a barely furnished room."

"It's the upper room," Zak breathed, the awe thick in his voice. "I mean, I think I know where we are."

"The upper room?" Andrea asked, looking around. "You mean like the one where Jesus and His disciples ate the Last Supper?"

"My heart's not burning," Jordan said. "I don't think Jesus is here. And this room is pretty big." Jordan's eyes widened for a moment. Margaret turned her head to where Jordan was looking and saw a circle of about twenty people seated on the dirt floor.

One man was talking while the others listened intently. Margaret looked to Jordan with equally wide eyes.

"Why don't they sit at the table?" Margaret said. She realized her voice had come out in a whisper, and for the first time she wondered whether the people seated on the floor could see and hear her and the children.

"Can they see us?"

Zak shook his head. "I don't think so. They would have noticed us by now."

"Who are they?" Margaret asked, her eyes sweeping over the men and women of the circle. As she counted the men, fifteen in all, she saw that they wore simple robes and even simpler sandals. The women of the group had coverings for their heads, but their robes were as simple as the men's.

"Peter is talking," Jordan said. "I wonder what he's saying."

Margaret thought she had heard wrong. "Peter? You mean, Peter the disciple of Jesus?"

Andrea laughed. "Isn't it cool?"

"Incredible," Margaret breathed, shaking her head.

Margaret saw that Zak was grinning. "I think I know where we are and what's going to happen this time. Just wait for it."

"Wait for what?" Margaret asked, taking in the small room that held nothing but a battered table and some large water jugs in the corner. Course material hung over the windows, and weak light cast its beams on a simple dirt floor.

"Come on!" Andrea said, pulling at Zak's hand. "Let's get closer. We're here for a reason, aren't we?"

Margaret looked to Zak. "You mean--we're going to go over to them--this is incredible."

Zak laughed. "You'll get used to it. It's a lot to take in at first. I'm coming, Andrea."

Margaret followed on Zak's heels as he allowed himself to be led by the exuberant Andrea. As Margaret got closer to the cluster of robed ancients, Peter's rich baritone voice became clearer;

108

and Margaret watched as he absently pulled at his beard while he spoke to his listeners.

"Wait a second," Margaret said when the foursome stopped before the seated group. "I can understand what he's saying. How can I understand what he's saying?"

"Sshh," Andrea said, putting a hand to her lips. Margaret leaned to Zak, who was visibly captivated by what the fisherman-disciple was saying.

"How's he speaking English?" Margaret whispered.

Zak didn't take his eyes off Peter. "I don't think he is. I mean--I think they hear him in their native tongue, and we hear him in English."

Well, I'll be jarred!

Margaret couldn't believe her ears as she heard Peter speaking fluent English. But, Zak had to be right. There was no way Peter's listeners would be understanding the fisherman-disciple if he spoke English to them. No, Peter must be speaking in a tongue they understood. The revelation excited Margaret, and she stepped closer to the cluster of seated believers so she could hear what Peter was saying.

"They are coming from all corners of the world," Peter was saying. "I worry there will not be enough space for them here in Jerusalem. What do you think, James?"

Peter looked across the circle to a young, barefaced man in a red robe.

"Well, this house is filled to capacity. We are upstairs while hundreds of believers are packed into the downstairs residence. And these are all new believers."

Peter nodded and stroked his beard. "John, do you think our new brothers and sisters in Christ will be persecuted for their beliefs in the cross?"

A dark-haired disciple in a green and black robe answered, "I fear it. Did the Master not warn us of such things before He left? There are a lot of God-fearing Jews in the city right now, as it is

Shavu'ot. One can only hope they will be amicable."

"But will they rise to violence?" a silver-haired man asked.

"We cannot be certain, Matthias," Peter answered. "We can be certain that the number of brothers and sisters in Christ is growing rapidly, and there will be backlash. Caiaphas is more than angry at being made to look like a fool. We must instruct the believers to keep their heads should they be challenged by Jew, Greek or Gentile."

"May I say something?" a woman's voice said from the circle. Margaret looked to her right and saw a tiny woman in a blue cloak flanked by another woman on her left and one on her right raise her hand to address the group. Margaret's breath caught in her throat.

It can't be!

"Certainly, Mother," John said with a nod.

It is! She's--she's Mary! Jesus' mother!

"I think it is important to remember that we cannot keep this message to ourselves," Mary said. "Jesus instructed us to go and make disciples of all nations. I am as fearful as the rest of you about persecution. I was-- I *am*--His mother, after all. My Son said that as the world hates him, so they will hate us. But I ask you, brothers and sisters, is our safety more important than the souls of those who walk the streets of Jerusalem and Judea? We must be persistent with our message, as Jesus was persistent with His."

The cluster of believers murmured their agreement, John reaching over one of the women to squeeze Mary's shoulder.

"She is right," Peter said. "The message of the cross cannot be kept to ourselves. We must prepare our hearts and minds to go forth to give testimony to what we have seen."

"But the majority of us are mere fishermen. I, myself, used to be a tax collector. The rest of us come from equally frowned-upon and uneducated backgrounds. What if they will not listen?" a middle-aged man in a brown robe said.

Peter nodded. "I understand your concern, Matthew. But we must remember we are speaking of our former occupations. Remember, the old is gone and the new has come. Jesus Christ Himself chose us to convey His message of hope to the world. If He had wanted to reach the world through educated and well-respected men, He would have called them from their trades and they would have become His first disciples." Peter's eyes scanned the circle.

"Remember, dear brothers and sisters, that the Messiah Himself was from Nazareth. Isn't the old saying 'what good can come from Nazareth?' What is more, He was a carpenter's apprentice, not a high-ranking government official or a teacher of the law. His beginnings were the same as ours. And if God the Father found it fit to send His Son to Nazareth to build things out of wood and to be raised up at the appointed time, He surely will give us the words and respect needed to convey His message to the world."

"You have spoken well, Peter," John said. "I think it is best to seek the Lord in prayer. We must know His will and how we should go about expanding His Kingdom. It is not by our strength that we will tell the world, for our flesh is weak. It is by the grace and power given to us by the Lord Jesus Christ."

"Let us pray," Peter said. And with that the cluster of believers sought the Lord.

"This is incredible," Margaret whispered, even though she knew the praying circle could not see or hear her. She saw Zak was grinning.

"Just wait. It's about to get better."

"What do you know that we don't?" Andrea asked, moving closer to Zak as Matthew prayed for protection and courage.

Zak laughed. "I don't want to spoil it for you. Believe me, you'll know when it happens." He nodded his head toward the praying believers. "They're going to be surprised, too."

All of a sudden, Margaret felt a fire in her chest. She rubbed

111

her sternum and cleared her throat.

"Are you OK?" Jordan asked, concern in his intuitive face.

"Just a little heartburn is all," Margaret said. "Must've been the bacon at breakfast."

Without warning, Andrea burst into a fit of giggles. She, too, rubbed her chest.

"It's not bacon, Grandma! I feel it, too!"

Jordan's eyes ignited into jubilance. "I feel it! I feel it, too!"

Zak laughed and nodded. "I told you! I told you! He's coming!"

Margaret continued to rub her chest, feeling the fire within her turning into a deep, pleasant burn. It was almost as if her heart wished to leap from her chest cavity.

"Would someone please tell me what's going on? This isn't a heart attack, is it?"

Andrea couldn't contain her giggles. She was now jumping up and down.

"No, Grandma! It's--"

But Andrea could not finish her statement, for all of a sudden the room began to shake.

"It's happening!" Zak shouted as the material over the curtains fell away, and a violent wind swept through the room.

"What's happening?" Margaret shouted over the roaring of the wind. But it was no use. Her words were lost in the incredible vortex. It might have been a tornado, or it might have been an earthquake and a tornado combined. Whatever it was, it was *loud*. The ground beneath her trembled, and Margaret leaned against the wall for support.

The cluster of believers had ceased praying, and now their robes and hair were being tossed and tangled in the fierce wind. Margaret saw they were trying to speak, but as her words had been lost in the uproar, so were theirs.

Margaret felt Andrea tugging on her arm. Margaret looked down and saw her granddaughter's black hair blowing straight back, as though an industrial hair dryer were only inches from her face. The girl was trying to say something while pointing to the far window. Margaret couldn't decipher what Andrea was saying, but she looked at the window and her eyes widened as her heart nearly leapt from her chest.

This is incredible!

As Margaret watched in wonder, what appeared to be tongues of fire floated from the windows and came to rest above the heads of the startled believers. Not extinguished by the violent wind, the licks of flame seemed to burn straight up and down, as though fed by an unseen source.

I know this story! The Holy Spirit has come upon them!

Margaret watched as a tongue of fire came to rest above the head of each member of the circle. Peter had a large smile on his face as he looked up and watched his lick of flame burn bright orange. Mary laughed and pointed to the flames above the heads of the women she sat beside, and they looked up and shared hallelujahs.

All of a sudden, an unseen plug was pulled: the violent wind stopped, and the tongues of fire vanished as quickly as they had come. The room no longer trembled; and, for a moment, no one said anything, each trying to process what had just occurred. The room was completely quiet, as though the incredible wind and the tremors of the earth had not occurred. But the silence didn't last long. All at once, the believers started speaking again, but Margaret didn't hear them in just English.

"They're speaking in all kinds of languages!" Zak said, reading the look on Margaret's face. "The Holy Spirit--God's very Spirit--has just filled them!"

"Look at them!" Jordan said. "They're so excited they look like they could burst!"

"They're so loud!" Andrea said, watching as the believers hugged each other. Peter ran to the window and looked out, speaking in a tongue Margaret couldn't place, but yet understood in her spirit. In absolute exuberance, he raised his arms and let out a proclamation in the foreign tongue.

Margaret and the children followed Peter to the window, and Margaret saw people had stopped on the street and were staring up at the joyous Peter.

"You're drunk!" one man shouted. He shifted a basket of fruit he was carrying and nodded to another man, who held a rope attached to a small calf. "That man's had too much wine!"

Margaret heard a commotion to her left, and when she turned, she saw that the other believers had burst through a door Margaret had not noticed and now stood on a balcony overlooking the street. Laughing and shouting and speaking in all different languages, the believers caused quite a scene.

"The city streets are so busy," Andrea said. "Look at all the people stopping. They have no idea what's going on."

Margaret saw that Andrea was right. As the sun was still low in the sky, Margaret guessed it to be about eight or nine in the morning. This particular street in Jerusalem was packed with people on their way to buy and sell and celebrate the Jewish holy day with their families.

"You are all drunk!" Someone shouted. "Learn to hold your alcohol!"

"How is it I can understand them?" one women asked another. "I'm from Egypt. There's no way these men and women are speaking my language."

"Wait a minute," another said. "These men and women are speaking your native tongue? That's impossible. They are speaking my language. I am from Phrygia."

"And I'm an Elamite!" another man said. "They are speaking *my* language."

"They can't be!" another man answered. "I'm from Mesopotamia. They are speaking the language I grew up with!"

As the streets became engorged with people, a bustle worked through the crowd

"What does this mean?" the city-goers asked each other. "They are declaring the wonders of God in our own tongues!"

Peter rushed from the window and joined the others on the balcony. Pushing his way to the front, he put up his hands to quiet the crowd as Margaret and the children watched from the window he had vacated.

"Fellow Jews and all of Jerusalem, let me explain this to you; listen carefully to what I say. These people are not drunk, as you suppose. It's only nine in the morning! No, this is what was spoken by the prophet Joel: 'In the last days, God says, I will pour out my Spirit on all people. Your sons and daughters will prophesy, your young men will see visions, your old men will dream dreams. Even on my servants, both men and women, I will pour out my Spirit in those days, and they will prophesy. I will show wonders in the heavens above and signs on the earth below, blood and fire and billows of smoke. The sun will be turned to darkness and the moon to blood before the coming of the great and glorious day of the Lord. And everyone who calls on the name of the Lord will be saved."

A murmur worked its way through the crowd, and Margaret smiled.

Thank you, Jesus, for allowing me to see this.

Peter held up his hands. He had more to say:

"Fellow Israelites, listen to this: Jesus of Nazareth was a man accredited by God to you by miracles, wonders and signs, which God did among you through Him, as you yourselves know. This man was handed over to you by God's deliberate plan and foreknowledge; and you, with the help of wicked men, put Him to death by nailing Him to the cross. But God raised Him from the dead, freeing Him from the agony of death, because it was impossible for death to keep its hold on Him. David said about Him: 'I saw the Lord always before me. Because He is at my right hand, I will not be shaken. Therefore my heart is glad and my tongue rejoices; my body also will rest in hope, because You will not abandon me to the realm of the dead, You will not let your holy one see decay. You have made known to me the paths of life; You will fill me with joy in Your presence.'"

The crowd murmured again, captivated by what Peter was saying. He continued:

"Fellow Israelites, I can tell you confidently that the patriarch David died and was buried, and his tomb is here to this day. But he was a prophet and knew that God had promised him an oath that He would place one of his descendents on his throne. Seeing what was to come, he spoke of the resurrection of the Messiah, that He was not abandoned to the realm of the dead, nor did His body see decay. God raised this Jesus to life, and we are all witnesses of it. Exalted to the right hand of God, He has received from the Father the promised Holy Spirit and has poured out what you now see and hear. Therefore let all Israel be assured of this: God has made this Jesus, Whom you crucified, both Lord and Messiah."

Another peal of chatter worked its way through the crowd, and Margaret realized the enormity of what Peter had just done. Not only had he boldly preached the message of the cross to the people of Jerusalem and the various nations represented therein, he had unashamedly proclaimed to the crowd that Jesus was, indeed, the long-awaited Messiah. Margaret knew from reading the rest of the New Testament that those very words would set into motion an amazing time of harvest and persecution for Peter and the early Church.

"What do we have to do to be saved?" one man called.

Peter smiled. "Repent and be baptized, every one of you, in the name of Jesus Christ for the forgiveness of your sins. And you will receive the Holy Spirit. The promise is for you and your children and for all who are far off--for all whom the Lord our God will call."

"Amen," Margaret said. All of a sudden, her surroundings became fuzzy.

"We're going back," Zak said.

Margaret felt Andrea take her hand. She gave it a little squeeze.

"I will never forget this," Margaret said as ancient world faded to black. "Thank you, Lord, for allowing me to witness such a pivotal moment in history."

And the foursome was sucked into the vortex of time.

Chapter Thirty-four

Jordan again sat with his cousins and grandmother in the cozy living area before Paul McGurney's large fireplace. The old man sat in his leather recliner, ancient hands folded atop his stomach, a smile playing at his lips. His vacant blue eyes sparkled.

"Three thousand were converted that day," the old man said. "When Peter addressed the crowd, the Holy Spirit moved the hearts and minds of those listening. His proclamation that Jesus was and is the Messiah was revolutionary. It also caused many to hate the early church."

"I figured as much," Margaret said, sipping a mug of steaming green tea. "I knew I was witnessing a changing point. Some would love the message of the cross and others would hate it."

Paul McGurney nodded. "Yes, and the majority of those you saw in the room that day died as martyrs for the cause of Christ."

"Even Peter?" Andrea asked.

McGurney pressed his lips together and nodded again. "Yes, dear one. Even Peter. He was crucified upside down because he found himself unworthy to die in the same manner as the Savior."

Jordan remembered the way Peter had absently stroked his

beard as he had conversed with his fellow believers, remembered how exuberant he had been the day Jesus had made his triumphant entry into Jerusalem. He remembered how Todd had spoken of Peter walking upon the turbulent sea in order to reach Jesus, how the fisherman-disciple had stood and boldly addressed the crowd at Pentecost. Peter had come a long way, from a fisherman to a fisher of men. It saddened Jordan to think the man had died in such a torturous fashion. But Jordan suspected Peter had known the day he had addressed the crowd in Jerusalem that once the Spirit's words had flowed from his mouth, there was no turning back, and that where the Spirit told him to go, he would go, regardless of the cost. As the apostle Paul would later write, 'to live is Christ and to die is gain.' Jordan smiled to himself. Yes, Peter had won.

"The peril you are facing now is great," Paul McGurney continued. "But you have God's Spirit to guide and direct you. Just as for Peter and James and John, the Spirit is ready and willing to lead you. The moment you accepted Christ's free gift, the Holy Spirit--God's Spirit--was sent to be your comforter and intercessor."

"Which is why the tongues of fire didn't settle over us," Jordan said, working Paul McGurney's words over in his mind. "We had already accepted Christ in the present before we were transported into the past."

"Excellent insight, Jordan," McGurney said, beaming. He tapped his chest. "The Spirit is our deposit, our guarantee. Through Christ and by His Spirit, we have access to the throne room of God."

"I like the sound of that," Zak said, scooting forward on the couch.

"But what about now?" Jordan asked. "I get that the Holy Spirit is our guarantee, but what about the situation we're in? What about the Stranger and the threats and all that?"

Paul McGurney took a deep breath and let it out in a long

exhale.

"You are not just battling a tangible assassin, dear ones, you are battling a host of principalities set on your destruction. The evil you see is but a glimpse of what is really going on. If you could peel back the layers of the physical world, you would see that there is a dimension where good and evil battle for the souls of men. This dimension crawls with fiends and demons ready to take you down."

Zak threw up his hands. "So, how do you counter that? I thought the whole getting-hunted-by-a-masked-assassin thing was bad enough! It seems a little hopeless when you put it that way!"

Paul McGurney gave a half smile. "I know it seems as though the world is out to get you. When you see with the eyes of your heart, you realize not everything can be taken at face value. For every bit of good in this world, there is an evil trying to counter it. But, Zak, you can take heart in the fact that, as you are a co-heir with Christ, you have the authority in His name to make demons tremble."

"It all comes back to the co-heir thing again," Zak said.

"Yes, it does. If you truly believe in all of Christ's teachings and not just parts, you will see that everything Jesus gets, we get, as promised by the Father. Just as Jesus was able to cast out demons, so can we. But we first must be able to recognize evil."

"I've heard people say there's no such thing as demons and a devil," Andrea said.

Paul McGurney nodded. "And that is just what Satan wants people to believe. When we are ignorant to the reality of evil, evil can do its greatest work. Either you believe all of God's Word, or none of it."

Jordan squinted his eyes in concentration, trying to piece together all McGurney was saying.

"So, we have authority in His name, I get that. But you're saying that even Christians are assaulted by princiwhaties?"

Paul McGurney chuckled softly. "Principalities. And, yes, Jordan. Christians especially. Who better for the forces of evil to make out as hypocrites, liars and stumbling blocks? If the forces of evil can sway a Christian to act in a way that is against the teachings they know to be true, then what a victory! You know that, as Christians, you are supposed to be bearing fruit. Others see that fruit and are drawn to God's heart through the way you approach life. When Christians do not bear fruit, the enemy wins."

"That's scary," Margaret said, setting down her mug.

Paul McGurney nodded. "Yes, but it is reality. For a believer to be unaware of what is truly happening in the spiritual realm is dangerous."

"It's a process, isn't it?" Jordan asked. "You learn these things as you become more in tune with Christ."

"Yes, Jordan. And when you know these things, you realize that you have a guarantee in Christ. In the spiritual battles of life, God's presence is greater than your fear."

"I like that," Margaret said. "It's sounds powerful."

"It *is* powerful," McGurney said with a chuckle.

"But when will the fear go away?" Andrea asked. "It seems like there's always something to be afraid of."

"Advancing God's kingdom usually requires a tough battle. And this battle usually rages for years, not days. Look in the Old Testament at the story of Joshua. Read the apostle Paul's letters in the New Testament and see what he went through to advance the kingdom of Christ. Opposition will always be there. Evil will always be ready to pounce on the unguarded heart."

"How do you avoid having an unguarded heart?" Zak asked. "It's easy to let your guard down when things get tough."

McGurney nodded. "One way to remain in the Spirit is to never fall victim to becoming a borderline Christian where you fail to recognize the ungodly influences of the world. It goes back to producing fruit. Either you are producing it or you aren't. There's no in between. Half-rotten pieces of fruit are discarded."

Jordan saw Zak nod.

"I know it is a lot to take in," Paul McGurney said with a smile. "But just know you are never alone. The Spirit intercedes with groans when you don't know what to pray. Your Father loves you, so much so that when He begins a good work in you, He's faithful to complete it."

Margaret leaned forward in the loveseat. "Mr. McGurney, can we pray? I'm feeling bogged down by it all."

Paul McGurney's eyes sparkled. "Of course, dear one. Of course."

Chapter Thirty-five

Margaret and the children made it back to the cozy wilderness cabin without any problems. After spending a good hour in prayer, Margaret and Paul McGurney had gotten to know each other while Zak, Andrea and Jordan had explored McGurney's enormous mansion. Zak had been only a little discouraged to find the upstairs vacant. There were five bedrooms and two full bathrooms on the second level, but no furniture or decorations of any kind could be seen. Zak had thought for sure that the rest of McGurney's house had to be as amazing and magical as the big downstairs level. In reality, it was nothing more than an airy, somewhat outdated mansion. The only thing that had made the children curious was that Paul McGurney had no personal items, nothing to indicate he used any other part of the house besides the sitting area in front of the fireplace. Zak had wanted to ask the old man about it, but Jordan had insisted that even an ancient prophet was entitled to some privacy.

It was around four o'clock in the afternoon when the foursome arrived back at Margaret's scarred and desecrated cabin. Walking into the cabin had been difficult. The knowledge that the Stranger had been in the house once already frightened them all. But after a sweep of the house with the trusty shotgun revealed no ferocious predator, the children were able to rest easy and discuss the things they had seen and experienced at Paul McGurney's house. Jordan had immediately called Todd and filled him in on the goings on, and reported back to the others that Todd felt cooped up and disheartened. He hadn't told Margaret, but Todd was secretly scheming a way to get to Colorado. He had all but promised Jordan he would be arriving shortly.

The electrician, Jason Hanson, had left a note on the scarred countertop stating that he'd need to come back tomorrow to finish the job. Zak was grateful the large man was coming back. Having another body in the cabin was one more body the Stranger would have to deal with, should the assassin choose to attack.

And he'll attack. It's just a matter of when...

When it was time for supper, Margaret whipped up some mashed potatoes and stuck a frozen meatloaf in the oven. As the children ate, they talked excitedly about what the next day might bring.

"I can't wait to go back," Andrea said, shoveling a spoonful of mashed potatoes into her mouth. "It's like we never left."

Margaret took a drink of her ice water and motioned to Andrea. "Honey, don't talk with your mouth full. But, yes, I agree. I can't wait to go on another one of those time travel things."

"I can't imagine where Mr. McGurney will send us next," Zak said. "I hope it's somewhere we can see Jesus."

Supper went on, with more excited conversation. The wind beat upon the cabin's windows, and at every sound and strange bump, each person's eyes darted to the shotgun resting at Margaret's feet. Even in the joy of seeing Paul McGurney again, Zak felt the fear hanging in the cabin air as thick as wood smoke. The inevitable attack would come soon enough. Zak could only imagine what form it would take.

The Fiends swarmed around the dinner table, whispering doubts and terror into the ears of the children and their old bat of a grandmother. The master had sent word that "something big" was about to happen, so they were to work ceaselessly at destroying the foursome's feelings of safety. Horse-face could tell that the intuitive brat--the one called Jordan--was scared out of his mind. The way the boy played with his food instead of eating, the way he kept glancing at the door and the windows, gave him away. Mosquito-face wasted no time in burying his proboscis in the boy's neck and injecting him with a venom of self-doubt and creeping fear.

"I'll take the old woman," Horse-face said. "You all work on the others. We must prepare the way."

"With pleasure," Fly-face said.

And the Fiends went to work, preparing the way for what was to come.

Chapter Thirty-six

*A*ndrea pulled the covers up to her chin and glanced at the window. The night was black, and a little trickle of fear slid down her spine.

No. I can't give in to fear. I can't let it rule my life. Besides, Grandma is sleeping on the couch right outside my door--with a shotgun, no less. I just need to have faith that everything is going to work out for the good.

Andrea thought back on the day, how she and the others had been whisked away to the ancient world and had seen the Holy Spirit come like fire. Who else could say they had seen something so amazing? God was revealing Himself to her in so many incredible ways, and all Andrea could think to do was to praise Him for His revelations.

Andrea heard her grandmother roll over on the couch. She knew the sleeping arrangement had to be terrible for her grandmother, especially since the latter's nice, warm bed was just upstairs. Andrea had offered to sleep on the couch, but her grandmother would have none of it. She was going to protect the children, no matter what might come through the front doors or windows.

Not the best thought to fall asleep with...

Andrea rolled onto her side and prayed that everyone would be safe, and that everything would work out for the best.

Please, God, keep us safe...

Chapter Thirty-seven

Margaret Kessler tossed and turned on the living room couch, wondering when it had gotten so lumpy. The shotgun was on the ground directly below where she lay. Should Margaret hear or see anything out of the ordinary, it would be in her hands and ready to fire.

I pray that doesn't happen. I need to ask Mr. McGurney about what I've been thinking...

For Margaret, the travel through time had been more than incredible, it had been downright awesome. The fact that she had actually seen the disciples and had witnessed the Holy Spirit come at Pentecost was amazing. Before she had turned out the light, she had read Acts chapter two one more time, just to make sure she hadn't been dreaming. She hadn't. The whole of what she and the others had experienced was recorded in black and white on the pages of her Bible.

Thank you, Lord, for allowing me to see You--to physically see Your glory come down from heaven. You've been so good to me, so steadfast through my years of wandering. Thank You, Jesus. My words will never be enough.

Margaret drifted off to sleep with a smile spread across her face. If today's adventure had been this miraculous, what would tomorrow's bring?

Scattered

Chapter Thirty-eight

*T*he Stranger enters the bedroom with a stealth only the deadliest of assassins can manage. The door does not creak on its old hinges, the floor does not protest under the killer's lithe movements. The Stranger has done this before. Knowing how to move about when silence is paramount is nothing new. Death has struck this way many times and in many eras. This will also be the way Paul McGurney shakes hands with death.

But first...

The Stranger waits at the foot of the bed, reveling in the cloak of darkness the night has provided. No moonbeam slices through the darkness and rests on the bedspread, no trace of yellow light perches on the windowsill. All is black. Black as dried blood.

The girl murmurs something in her sleep and turns over onto her side. The assassin's eyes are attuned to the darkness; the Stranger can see even the stray hairs resting on the girl's pillow. The silence of night provides for perfect hearing. The girl's heartbeat—slow and steady, slow and steady—taps its own death knell in the killer's ears. The Stranger smiles at the irony. The Knowledge has infiltrated the girl's heart and poisoned her with the Truth. Now the assassin will extinguish the beating of her heart. The Truth will not set her free.

But this is all in due time, of course. This is after the Plan has run its course, after the wretched old man is dealt with in a merciless fashion. And there must be a witness to his demise. Someone must give testimony to what meddling with the Knowledge will bring.

The Stranger stalks around the bed and now stands before the sleeping girl. The rise and fall of her breathing is hypnotic, and for a moment the Stranger's mind wonders to the times before the killing, to the times when the assassin's life's purpose was not vicious murder and squelching those who possessed the Knowledge. Yes, there was a time long ago—in the ancient days—when blood and death and loyalty to the Prince of the Air were not necessary to survive, when the Truth was not something to be feared. But that was long ago—so long ago that the memories are numb and distant.

The Stranger unsheathes a heavily serrated knife. The girl murmurs again in her sleep, her head gently stirring on her pillow. A strand of hair falls over her forehead, out of the elastic band that holds the rest in place. Outside the cabin wall, a pile of heavy snow falls off the roof with a dull thud, the sound penetrating the thick darkness of the bedroom like a thunderclap. The Stranger freezes, the vicious knife at the killer's side. Should the girl wake at the noise, death will pierce her heart and McGurney will live to see another day. She cannot wake or the Plan will need revision. The girl only coughs gently and continues to sleep.

The Stranger crouches over the girl, so close the assassin's muggy breath makes a few hairs on the girl's forehead dance. The killer raises the demonic knife to the girl's forehead and moves the hair back into place with its deadly tip. The Stranger is a master with the knife, brushing away the strands with an eerie gentleness. Applying any more pressure would break the girl's skin and she would awake. If she wakes, she must die.

The assassin stands to full height and turns the wicked knife over so the handle points up. Unscrewing a plastic cap from the knife's bottom, the assassin uncovers a vicious needle, a syringe filled with serum used in a hundred abductions such as this. The liquid inside the needle induces paralysis of the body's muscular system except heartbeat and breathing while leaving the abduct-ee awake and aware of what is transpiring around her. The vocal chords are incapacitated while the brain is left fully-functioning. In essence, the Stranger's prey can sense her surroundings but is helpless to interact with them.

Chapter Thirty-nine

*A*ndrea was in sheer panic mode. Her mind raced with adrenaline and terror, her brain working triple-time to process the horror of what was happening. The fleeting hope that her abduction had been just a dream had vanished when the biting, dry air of the Colorado night had stung her eyeballs—the only part of her body she could move at will. And that was the absolute most horrific part of the ordeal: her body was useless, her limbs failed to respond when her brain sent the appropriate signals, her body was numb from head to foot. But she could see it all—*process* the nightmarish reality of being carried like a sack of potatoes through the hellishly black wilderness over the shoulder of an unnamed assailant. She could not move her neck, and her eyes were able to take in only the cloudy white of the snow and the dark outlines of the kidnapper's heavy boots. She could hear the crunch of the snow and the snap of twigs, the heavy breathing of her captor as he ran at a surprisingly fast pace through the blackness to a destination unknown. As the reality of the situation began to sink in, Andrea was pummeled with the first waves of hopelessness—the first premonitions that the unknown destination would be the last she would ever see.

Please, God! Warn the others!

As her captor bounded through the snow, Andrea's body

bouncing on his shoulder like a rag doll, Andrea desperately prayed that her death would be quick and painless. Her kidnapper was obviously the Stranger, and when he had spoken in her bedroom and her eyes had snapped open as he had covered her mouth, she had known her time was short.

Quick and painless! Let it be quick and painless!

The Stranger's voice had been deep and gravelly, like tires on a stone driveway. Andrea's grandmother had been right; the Stranger's voice had also had a robotic quality, as if were being amplified with an effect through a hot microphone. His face had been masked in black, only his wild eyes had penetrated the dark room. And they had been terrifying.

I wish I could tell the others! I wish there was some way I could warn them!

Andrea remembered the sharp pain of the assassin's needle as it had plunged into her neck. The wasp-sting of the long needle had lasted only a moment, and then Andrea had felt nothing at all. Whatever the Stranger had shot into her veins had paralyzed everything but her fear.

"How are you doing back there?" The Stranger's gritty voice rocked her from her thoughts. Andrea tried to move her lips to respond, but found she could not bring them to life. The Stranger mocked her.

"I know you can't answer me, but I know you can hear me." His words came out in short, derisive spurts as he bounded through the blackness. "How does it feel, little one? How does it feel to know you are going to witness death—and then experience it yourself?"

Andrea's brain exploded in warning signals.

Witness a death!? What does that mean!? Has he taken the others, too!?

The Stranger sensed Andrea's fear and used it against her.

"Just wait, little one! Just wait and see what meddling in the Knowledge brings! You and your Knowledge-varmints will

133

be exterminated, and Lucifer will set up his kingdom on your ashes!"

No! You know you lose in the end! Jesus wins!

Andrea wanted to scream at the Stranger, to go down with an argument. How naïve was this guy? Hadn't he read Revelation?

"You opened a can of demons when you chose the Knowledge," the Stranger continued, jumping over a snow-covered boulder. "Oh, how they would love to tear you apart. I am privileged to be the one to destroy you!"

Jesus, help me!

"I can't wait to see the look in your eyes when you realize where we're going!" the Stranger said. "I can't wait to see your faith drain from you when you realize God is cruel, that he will not intervene to stop my knife from slicing your flesh!"

Andrea wished she could plug her ears. The Stranger's voice hit her brain like acid, flashing horrific images of her impending death to the forefront of her chaotic thoughts. Pain. Blood. Death. And the cruelty of God—even though Andrea knew in the core of her that God is love and life—flooded her mind like a tidal wave. The Stranger had planted a seed, a lie, and the lie was clawing her mind like a rabid cougar.

Will God save me? Will God save all of us?

The Stranger continued to run through the blackness, his boots beating down on the snow, his breath coming in spurts. Andrea bounced up and down on his shoulder, a worthless nothing tossed about like an old rag.

You're not cruel, God—please be with us!

Chapter Forty

*T*odd awoke in a cold sweat. His shoulder was throbbing, but the pain seemed to be far away. He was too terrified to feel it. Bolting upright, he threw the covers off his legs and swiped his forehead. Outside his window, the Ohio night was black as death.

What a dream!

Todd placed his hand over his chest and felt his thundering heart. Already the dream was fading, as dreams do in the first seconds of waking. But there was something that gnawed at him, something that scratched the back of his mind like fingernails on a chalkboard.

He's taken her...he's running...

Todd slowly stood and walked to the window. The eerie green glow of his alarm clock cast its pale emerald light on the carpet, giving his room the ambience of an extraterrestrial spacecraft. Outside his window, blackness ruled the night. The moon was shrouded by clouds, and the massive oak outside his window loomed like a monster poised to wrap its tentacle-limbs around the house. All was quiet—too quiet. Todd felt the silence like an icy hand on his neck, his tiny hairs prickling under the touch. Just standing at the window looking out into blackness, Todd could sense the stirring of evil as it churned in realm of the unseen.

Our battle is not with flesh and blood...

Todd shivered. Somewhere out there was a killer bent on his destruction. Possibly *two* assassins. Somehow being stalked as prey had become par for the course. First the Opposition, and now the Stranger. Choosing Jesus had put a target on his back, and he could all but feel the sniper's laser honing in for the kill.

He's got her... she's not safe...

Todd stepped away from the window, his arms and hands beginning to tremble. He shook his head to clear the last remnants of his dream, but for some reason he could not get rid of the last crumbles that seemed to stick to his brain like metal dust particles to a magnet. And it was these particles that made his body quake.

The Stranger...Andrea...he's taken her...

Todd could no longer stand. The muscles in his legs had become gelatinous globules of weak tissue, cold sweat seeping from every pore on his body. A wave of nausea swept over him as he stumbled back to his bed. For a moment he thought he might be sick on his bed sheets.

He's drugged her...he's taken her...Andrea...she's not safe...

The room seemed to spin, as if the glow of his alarm clock was inebriating. The blackness of the night, the violence and evil that lurked behind the curtain of reality, was so palpable, so thick Todd thought he actually saw the through the scrim of this dimension and into the realm of the supernatural.

Get rid of them, Todd...you have work to do...

Another wave of nausea hit him like a wrecking ball to the stomach. Todd doubled over, clutching his gut. Now he was sure of it; he was not alone in the room.

Get rid of them, Todd. You must tell the others...

Todd's brain swirled through images from his dream. The Stranger. The assassin running through the wilderness. The killer carrying something...some*one* over his shoulder...Another jolt of sickness hit him, and he clutched his stomach as sweat

136

poured from his forehead.

Todd...GET RID OF THEM...

And then Todd understood. It came to him in an instant. He fought the pains in his stomach and sat up.

Call the others...warn them...

"I hear you, Lord. Speak," Todd said into the blackness.

A searing heat tore at his insides, and he fought to keep his mind clear.

Get rid of them, son. Take authority and be done with them...

Todd swallowed hard and wiped the sweat from his brow. His eyes frantically searched the room. Although it appeared empty, he was anything but alone.

In an instant, he became enraged. Standing up on his wobbly legs, he spoke into the darkness with a vicious whisper coming through clenched teeth.

"How dare you, cowards!? You have no authority here and you know it! You've already lost—it's over, done! In the Name of Jesus, get out of my room! In the Name of Jesus, *get out*!"

🐍🐍🐍

The Fiends were thrown back against the wall, pain screaming through their bodies like flaming bullets.

"No! Stop! Anything but that *Name*!" Fly-face wailed as a torrent of burning pain streaked through his body.

But the one called Todd wasn't done. He insisted on the authority of Christ, demanding the Fiends to leave. One by one they fell from the air, shot out of the sky by a Force more powerful.

"I can't stand it any longer!" one grotesque demon groaned. He clutched his chest as though he'd been mortally wounded.

"I'm getting out of here!" another agreed.

A chorus of the same filled the room, as Fiends rolled on the floor in agony.

The kid meant business. Their authority was gone.

It was time to flee.

🐍🐍🐍

Todd felt the nausea vanish as quickly as it had come. He stood heaving in the middle of his bedroom, his fist raised in authority, his body dripping with sweat. It was over. Jesus had won.

Todd wiped the sweat away and prayed for clarity. He had a job to do. But what?

The Stranger has taken her…warn the others!

In an instant, Todd knew. His dream came back to him, and images reeled through his mind like a motion picture.

The Stranger had abducted Andrea. He had drugged her. And he was taking her…

Warn the others…

Todd bounded to his desk and grabbed his phone. His heart thundered in his chest as the urgency of the situation washed over him. He needed to call Jordan and do it fast. He thumbed the correct buttons and prayed his brother would answer his phone.

One ring, two.

"Come on, Jordan! Pick up!" Todd was frantic. In his dream, he had seen it all, from Andrea's abduction to the Stranger's final destination. The latter was the part that chilled him to the core.

Three rings, four. The call would go to voicemail unless Jordan picked up—

"Hello? Todd?" Jordan's voice showed no signs of sleep. He was awake and alert with the dread a phone call in the middle of the night brings.

"Jordan! You have to hurry! He's taken Andrea!"

And without waiting for Jordan to respond, Todd breathlessly recounted his dream. It was when he told Jordan where the Stranger was taking Andrea and why, Jordan panicked. Todd heard him burst through his bedroom door and bound through the kitchen to Andrea's room.

"She's not here! Todd—Andrea's not here!"

Todd's heart fell into his stomach.

"You know where to find her. Now go!"

As Jordan ended the call, Todd prayed it wouldn't be too late.

Chapter Forty-one

*T*he Stranger sees the destination. The snow is still thick, but the assassin's legs are in top physical condition, and the girl called Andrea doesn't weigh enough to hinder the Plan. Everything is moving forward swimmingly.

The Stranger hopes the girl has taken it all in: the surroundings, the darkness, the hints that will spell her final doom. The assassin has been waiting for this moment. To crush the children's hope is to crush them. When they find the girl called Andrea has gone missing, and when they piece together the entire puzzle involving her disappearance, they will be too late. One of the four brats will be dead, and Paul McGurney will be helpless to stop the remaining dominos from toppling.

The Stranger is close now. The ground begins to incline and a final burst of strength and adrenaline allows the assassin to reach the destination. Without breaking stride, the killer kicks in the door and barrels into Paul McGurney's earthly home.

Chapter Forty-two

*J*ordan was on the verge of hyperventilating. He'd ended his phone call with Todd and had sprung into action, waking first his grandmother and then Zak. After Margaret and Zak confirmed Andrea's disappearance, they all threw on warmer clothes and prepared to head out into the night to find her.

"I'll kill him!" Zak shouted as he stuffed his arms into his heavy coat. "I'll rip his throat out!"

Jordan had never seen his cousin so enraged. Zak's face was red, and all his muscles seemed clenched as if ready for combat. Jordan knew Zak had every right to be full of rage; after all, it was his sister who had been kidnapped by the Stranger. But Jordan also knew they should all set their emotions to simmer so clarity of thought could prevail. Jordan desperately wished he could practice what his brain was preaching, but he found himself tremulous with anger and nearly paralyzed by fear.

How did this happen? How did he get in with Grandma sleeping on the living room couch?

"I can't believe he came in the front door," Margaret said, still visibly numb with shock. "I can't believe he walked right past me!"

But the Stranger had been crafty. It must have taken him

painstakingly quiet minutes to remove the door plate and the door knob. Both lay on the porch, screws and all neatly arranged atop the snow as though the assassin had wished to leave a housewarming gift. But the Stranger was no kindly neighbor, and the labor of his systematic dismantling of the doorknob definitely not a warm pecan pie. His intent was murder, and he had simply reached through the hole he had created by removing the doorknob and unlocked the door. Jordan could deduce the rest. The killer had squeezed his body through the ever-so-slightly opened door and had shut it soundlessly and quickly to keep the cold night air from disturbing the cabin's inhabitants. He had lithely crept right past Margaret to Andrea's bedroom and had repeated his steps in reverse--with Andrea in tow-- to escape into the wilderness night. Todd had said she had been drugged, and Jordan believed Todd's dream to be accurate. If it weren't Andrea would still be sleeping safely in her cozy bedroom instead of being dragged by a crazed assassin to Paul McGurney's house.

"Let's go, kids!" Margaret said as she grabbed a box of ammunition for her shotgun. For a moment, the sight of his grandmother going all Rambo and packing heat with ammo to spare seemed absurd and incredibly out of this world. That was until Jordan saw her veined hands were trembling and could read the terror on her face. Although she hadn't said it, Jordan knew his grandmother had to be blaming herself for Andrea's abduction. It was only natural for her to feel responsible when she had been the one sleeping in the living room, shotgun locked and loaded. But Jordan didn't blame his grandmother. She could easily have been disposed of, could have been the Stranger's first victim. For some reason he had ignored her and taken Andrea instead, and Jordan couldn't put a finger on why.

He theoretically could have killed all of us. Why didn't he?

"He has to have made tracks," Jordan said, trying to keep his voice from shaking. "The snow's deep and it's stopped coming down."

"Why do we need to track him?" Zak snapped. "We know where he's going." He clenched his jaw, his eyes aflame. "Grandma—I hope you're a good shot. Because if not, I'm taking over."

In any other circumstance, Jordan knew his grandmother would have reproached Zak for spouting off. But now his anger was fueling him. An angry Zak, although not as level-headed as Jordan would have preferred, would come in handy against an armed assassin. Right now the slightly scrawny, average-height boy was bubbling with adrenaline, and adrenaline brought strength and the ability to fight.

"I've never had to shoot this thing, Zak," Margaret said, indicating the shotgun. "But believe you me, son, if I have to, I will." She nodded to Jordan. "Get the flashlights. We need to go."

Jordan was one step ahead of her. He held up three flashlights.

"Let's go." He couldn't hide the quake in his voice.

It was 3:42 in the morning.

Chapter forty-three

*A*ndrea immediately knew where she was. The sense of hopelessness, the weight of impending doom, crushed her as the Stranger kicked in the door to Paul McGurney's house on the hill. Although her eyes perceived only the rich, mahogany floorboards, Andrea knew the Stranger had come to kill Paul McGurney. And after he was done with Mr. McGurney...

"I want you to watch this," the Stranger hissed. All of a sudden Andrea's lifeless body was airborne. She hit the cherry dining room tabletop and bounced twice before skidding to a stop. For a brief moment, Andrea was thankful she could feel nothing, for she guessed her knees and elbows would be screaming in agony, should her pain receptors be properly functioning. The Stranger grabbed her and roughly manhandled her onto her side, her temple now resting on the tabletop. For the first time since her abduction, Andrea had full view of something other than the ground. And she didn't like the scene before her eyes.

The Stranger stood over her, masked in black with nothing but his wild blue eyes showing through the material's thin slits. Andrea was surprised by the man's stature; he couldn't be over five and a half feet tall, and his build was slight and unassuming. The terror standing before her was definitely no hulking

Opposition. But the fact that he had successfully kidnapped her and had run with her through the snowy mountain trails proved he had inhuman strength. That, in itself, made him even more terrifying than the Opposition.

"You get to watch the whole thing unfold," the Stranger jeered. His gloved hand swiped Andrea's bangs off her eyes. The Stranger backed away from the table and surveyed Paul McGurney's elegant house for a moment. Andrea could tell he wasn't admiring the rare artwork or immaculately detailed wall carvings. He was a hunter, and he was seeking out his prey.

"Where are you, old man!" the Stranger roared. He ran to the wall, ripped off one of the priceless paintings and broke it over his knee. "Come out and face me, old man!" Unsheathing his vicious knife, he made a jagged X through another painting.

Don't come out, Mr. McGurney! Please—get away from here!

The Stranger became more enraged every time he called McGurney's name. The assassin's knife bit into more artwork, drew a jagged scar along the wall, and carved into an ornate end table. Bent on destruction, as he was, Andrea knew nothing but the death of Paul McGurney would quench his bloodlust.

Stay away! Run, Mr. McGurney!

But Paul McGurney couldn't hear Andrea's thoughts. The ancient old man answered the Stranger in a calm, clear voice.

"I'm right here, Stranger. Leave the child be."

And with that, the old man rose from his leather chair. He must have been sitting too low for both Andrea and the Stranger to see, as the back of his chair was facing the two and his stature was slight and had been enveloped by soft leather.

The Stranger froze, his eyes burning. He pulled his knife from the wall where he had used it to scar the priceless wood paneling and laughed with acidic contempt.

"You come out of hiding at last!"

"Leave the child be," Paul McGurney repeated as he leaned

145

against his chair. Andrea's heart sank even lower as the old man turned around and began to shuffle toward the assassin.

"You know I can't do that, old man! You know why I'm here and how easy it will be to accomplish my task." The Stranger took a step forward. A space of fifteen feet separated Paul McGurney from certain death at the hands of the crazed killer.

"Yes, I know why you're here," McGurney said, his voice not wavering from its calm. "I know you are here doing your master's work, just as I am doing mine."

The Stranger laughed, taking another step forward. "And where is your Master now? Will he save you from my knife? Or will he let you and the child be sacrificed to my blade."

"You know nothing of sacrifice," McGurney answered, his cane before him as his slippered feet made progress on the smooth wood floor. "True sacrifice means one must give up something in order for a greater cause to be achieved."

"You don't think I've had to give things up?" the Stranger snapped, his eyes smoldering. "You don't think I've had to leave my life behind to follow the Plan?"

Paul McGurney stopped for a moment, his vacant blue eyes sparkling in the dimly lighted room. "Your sacrifice is built upon lies. You've been tricked into believing you are serving a just cause."

"Shut up, old man!" the Stranger shouted thrusting his knife into the space between them. "You are the one who has been deceived! You foolishly believe your God—your *cruel* God—will deliver you from death!"

"He already has," McGurney replied, steadfast in his resolve.

"Lies!" The Stranger roared. "You speak like a man who is about to achieve victory! Don't you know what I can do to you?"

"I know full well what you can do to me," Paul McGurney said, his speckled hands folded atop his cane. "But it's all life."

146

"What are you saying, you old kook!?" the Stranger shouted, specks of spittle flying from his lips. His voice had risen higher, and Andrea was all the more unnerved by the way he seemed to teeter on the edge of derangement.

"I said 'it's all life.' To live is Christ and to die is gain," McGurney said in his gentle baritone.

The Stranger cursed and laughed, derision heavy in his voice. "What about to suffer? What about to bleed? What about to feel my blade bite through your flesh and divide muscle and bone? Is that life? *Is that life?*"

"'Blessed are the persecuted, for theirs is the kingdom of heaven'," McGurney said, a smile playing at his lips. "You see, Stranger, it's all life."

The Stranger let out a guttural scream. He waved his knife in a crazed frenzy.

"Don't quote Scripture at me, you kook! Don't you *dare* throw that trash in my face!" The assassin shot forward and Andrea tried to scream. Paul McGurney didn't move.

The impact was excruciating. The Stranger's shoulder barreled into the elderly McGurney's stomach and the old man's slender, fragile body was hit with the impact full force. McGurney's cane clattered the floor as the old man was lifted off the ground for a horrendous moment before crashing to the hardwood floor with a sickening thud. McGurney's head took the brunt of the impact, and for a moment he appeared to have been knocked out from the fall. The Stranger straddled the old man's helpless body, seething vicious curses through clenched teeth. The killer was past deranged, and Andrea knew it would all be over fast.

No! Please! Don't hurt him!

Paul McGurney came to as the Stranger heaved atop his chest. McGurney's breath came in choked spurts, and a pool of blood formed under his ancient skull.

"Now we end this, old man!" the Stranger breathed. His eyes smoldered; his gloved hand creaked as he clenched the angry knife at his side.

Paul McGurney swallowed once and spoke through labored breath. "You can take my life, Stranger. But let the child go."

The Stranger raised the knife and Andrea's heart fell.

"We've been over this. You know I can't do that."

Paul McGurney turned his head and sought Andrea's eyes with his deep blue ones. For a heart-wrenching moment, Andrea could have promised the old man's eyes had their sight, for they welled with tears and peered into her own.

"I love you, child," McGurney said. "Our reward awaits us. Have no fear."

The last bit of hope Andrea carried was extinguished. Paul McGurney would die here. And she would, too.

The Stranger roared with triumphant laughter.

"Fear is all you have left, old man!" He moved the knife over McGurney's heart. With one swift motion, it would all be over.

No! No!

"You're finished!" the Stranger screamed.

With that, he plunged the knife toward Paul McGurney's heart

The Fiends who hovered overhead cackled and whooped. It was finished! The old man was dead!

Chapter forty-four

*T*he first explosion obliterated the end table closet to the Stranger, sending splintered wood and lamp shrapnel raining down over the assassin and the prostrate Paul McGurney. The Stranger froze, abruptly halting his knife millimeters above Paul McGurney's chest. Andrea heard the cock of a gun and saw the Stranger's eyes go wide with terror-laden disbelief. The second explosion blew a hole in the wood paneling five feet to the Stranger's left.

"No!" the Stranger shouted, springing to his feet. The gun cocked and the Stranger leapt behind the stairwell. Another explosion vaporized the stairwell's railing and created a bowling-ball-sized crater in a framed piece of art on the wall. Dust and debris clouded the room, creating a grey haze of destroyed furnishings.

Andrea's heart thundered as her brain tried to process what was transpiring. She could not see the new shooter; the gun blasts cannoned behind her and she was still paralyzed by the Stranger's serum. But whoever it was had the Stranger on the run.

"Stay back, kids!"

At the sound of her grandmother's voice Andrea's deflated hope was renewed. She wanted to shout—to run to her grandmother's side—to get Paul McGurney out of harm's way—but she was helpless to do anything but wait the battle out. A sense of urgency overwhelmed her, and she could do nothing but remain inert and lifeless.

"Grandma—Mr. McGurney! He's hurt!" Jordan's voice shouted.

"Stay back!" Margaret Kessler warned through the falling debris. "Just stay back, Jordan!"

Andrea heard the gun cock. She waited for another explosion to shake the house, but it didn't come. Instead, an eerie silence filled the large space, and Andrea felt the first twinges of panic coming back.

"Andrea?" her grandmother called from the doorway. "Are you OK?"

No! I'm not OK! Get me out of here!

"She's drugged—she has to be!" Zak shouted, his voice thick with urgency.

"Andrea—I don't know if you can hear me," Margaret Kessler called. "We're behind you. What weapons does the Stranger have?"

A knife! He has a knife! That's all, I think!

Andrea was desperate for her voice to return. It made sense for her grandmother to be cautious; she had no idea what kind of weaponry the Stranger had on his person and she, therefore, could not advance into the room to retrieve her from the table. She looked to Paul McGurney, who coughed and tried to blink away the effects of his fall.

"He has a knife," McGurney said. He coughed and tried to raise himself. Andrea was shocked at the amount of blood that had pooled under his head.

"Are you OK, Mr. McGurney?" Jordan asked. Andrea heard her grandmother scold him to get behind her.

"I'm afraid I can't get up," McGurney said, collapsing back to the floor. "Get the child. The Stranger carries no other weapon than a knife."

150

"Shut up, old man!" the Stranger hissed from behind the stairwell. A shot blew a hole in the ground before the stairs. More dust filled the air, sending Paul McGurney into a coughing fit.

"Stay back!" Margaret yelled. "I've got plenty of ammo and I *will* use it!"

"I'll kill you! I'll kill *all* of you!" the Stranger yelled.

"Kinda tough when you're hiding behind the stairs!" Zak taunted.

"Just wait! Your insolence will be rewarded by my knife!" the Stranger shouted. He peeked his head around the stairwell and Andrea heard her grandmother cock the shotgun again.

"Are you gonna come out, or are you gonna make me come in there and get you!" Margaret said.

"I dare you to come after me, woman! I dare you to come get me!" the Stranger retorted. He shook the knife defiantly, and Margaret Kessler let fly with the shotgun. The newest blast took off the first two steps, the dust and debris creating a momentary haze.

And that was all the Stranger needed. Before Andrea knew what had happened, the Stranger violently grabbed her from the table and held her lifeless body out in front of himself. The dust began to settle, and Andrea's head lolled to her chest, her neck muscles useless to fulfill their duties. The Stranger snapped her head back up and balled a portion of her hair in his fist so her head would not fall again. Andrea's hopelessness returned as the Stranger held her before him like a human shield.

"Now you'll think twice about firing your weapon!" the Stranger shouted. The dust settled and Andrea saw her grandmother standing just inside the doorway, her shotgun at her shoulder, a horrified expression washing over her face.

"What's going on--" Jordan asked, peeking in from outside.

"Get back!" Margaret shouted. Jordan's head popped back out of sight.

"Drop your weapon," the Stranger said in a vicious growl.

"Put her down or I'll blow a hole in you big enough to drive my Jeep through!" Margaret said, not lowering the shotgun.

The Stranger laughed. "Then you'll also blow a hole through this worthless brat!" He shook Andrea.

"Margaret," Paul McGurney coughed. "Don't shoot."

The Stranger's voice lost all its laughter. "Listen to the old man. Drop the weapon or I *will* kill her."

Leave me! Get the Stranger!

Margaret swallowed and looked to the doorway. Both Jordan and Zak were now standing in the doorframe, their pallor betraying their bravado.

"I said *drop your weapon!*" the Stranger shouted, his voice booming in Andrea's ear.

"Grandma--" Zak started.

"*Do it now!*" the Stranger roared.

Margaret lowered the gun from her shoulder, her finger still wrapped around the trigger.

"Put the gun on the ground!" the Stranger demanded.

Margaret swallowed hard again and looked to Paul McGurney. Andrea could not see him, but she heard the old man cough and try to speak.

"Keep quiet, old man!" the Stranger said.

"Grandma—do what he says!" Jordan pleaded.

"No! He's bluffing! Go in there and shoot him!" Zak shouted.

"*Put the gun on the ground!*"

"Give me the gun," Zak said, reaching for the shotgun. "I'll take him out!"

The Stranger's voice was manic. He swore. "If you don't drop the weapon right now I'll slit her throat!"

"Grandma!" Jordan panicked.

Margaret nodded and put one hand in the air. She slowly began to lower the shotgun to the floor.

"Grandma! Let me--" Zak began to reach for the weapon.

"No!" Margaret shouted. "Please, Zak—stay back!"

"Margaret," Paul McGurney managed. "God will make a way. Do as the Stranger says."

The Stranger's head snapped to Paul McGurney. "Rhetoric won't save them, old man! Biblical clichés are useless!"

Andrea watched as her grandmother took the opportunity afforded her by the Stranger's addressing Paul McGurney to unload the shotgun. She thumbed the safety and continued to lower the weapon. The Stranger's head snapped back to Margaret, and Andrea could almost feel his triumphant sneer.

"That's good," the Stranger coached. "That's a good old bag. Faster now. Drop the weapon."

Margaret dropped the shotgun to the floor. Its muffled thud signified Andrea's last hope shattering to pieces.

"OK. I put down the weapon. Let her go."

Andrea couldn't see the Stranger, but she knew he wore a sickening smile.

"Kick it this way," the Stranger instructed.

Margaret slowly inched her foot forward, hooked her shoe under the gun's barrel and kicked it toward the assassin. Andrea, dangling like a ragdoll, wanted nothing more than to be able to kick her way out of the Stranger's grasp and grab the gun before he could. But it wasn't going to happen. The Stranger simply walked to the gun, adjusted Andrea to his left arm and picked the gun off the floor.

"I saw you eject the shells," the Stranger said as he threw the gun on the table behind him. "Good form, I'll give you that."

"Let her go," Margaret said. A pleading quality had entered her voice, a desperation that unnerved Andrea to the core.

This is not going to be OK!

The Stranger laughed. "You are a brainless woman. An ignorant fool!"

"Let her go!" Zak shouted, his fists balled, his muscles rigid. "If I ever get a hold of you--"

"Your bravado is admirable," the Stranger admonished. "What is it you say? 'The spirit is willing but the flesh is so weak'? You don't have the chops to face me, small one! You'd be better off to jump from a cliff then to face off with the likes of me!"

Zak swallowed hard, the fear in his eyes seeping through the blind rage.

Grabbing the empty shotgun from the table, the Stranger began to move toward Paul McGurney's large window, the window that had been the portal to many of the children's adventures the previous summer. Andrea dangled in front of him like a limp noodle.

"Now, if you'll excuse me, I must be going," the Stranger said as he faced the elegant window. "But be advised: I don't intend to be gone long." His deranged eyes swept around the room. "I'll be back to kill you all. And this time you won't stop me." He held up Andrea as a hunter would his prized kill. "I'm taking her as a down payment."

Andrea's brain exploded with the Stranger's statement.

No! You can't take me!

"Come after me at your own risk," the Stranger sneered.

And with that he stepped into the window, and he and Andrea disappeared into the void of time.

Chapter forty-five

*P*aul McGurney held a pack of ice wrapped in a towel to the back of his head. The wound had stopped bleeding, and Margaret was grateful to see that what had been such a bloody mess had only turned out to be a minor laceration. A considerable bump had formed, and Margaret had retrieved an ice pack from McGurney's mammoth kitchen. Although she was grateful Paul McGurney was only minimally harmed, her hands trembled when she thought of where—and *when*—the Stranger had taken her granddaughter. Zak and Jordan felt the same way.

"Where is she? Where has he taken her?" Zak was frantic. He paced in front of the leather couch where Margaret and Jordan sat, numb.

"Why don't you have a seat, son," McGurney said in his gentle baritone. "We must realize we cannot do anything rash. We must think out our next course of action."

Margaret saw Zak's nostrils flare. He stopped pacing and looked at Paul McGurney.

"Who is he? Who is that monster? You have to know!"

Paul McGurney's blue eyes scanned the space behind Zak's head. Margaret felt a ball bearing lodge in her throat when the old man shook his wounded head.

"I'm afraid not, Zak. I am as much at a loss as to the Stranger's identity as you are. I have not been granted that knowledge."

Zak threw his hands up in frustration and sat down hard next to Margaret.

"Then—what? We sit back and wait for him to come back?"

Jordan cleared his throat and leaned forward. Margaret saw that he was trembling, and she placed her hand on his knee.

"He wants us to follow him," Jordan said in a small voice.

"And we should!" Zak said, his jaw twitching. Margaret saw how hard his fingers were clenched into fists and realized she felt the same violent rage as her grandson.

"But think about it," Jordan continued, finding his voice. "If we follow him, we'll be on his turf. He'll be able to control the situation."

"So, like I said, we should just *wait for him to bring her back?* She could be *dead* by the time he comes back for us!" Zak fought back tears, and Margaret wished she had a tissue handy. The war of emotions, the violent, vengeful spirit that was simmering inside of her battled with the urge to hole up and cry. She was over seventy years old; Zak was barely fifteen. She couldn't imagine what was going on inside of him.

"Will he come back through the window?" Jordan asked. "I mean, we did last summer. If he's coming back through the window we can just wait for him."

Paul McGurney nodded and sighed. "These things are not absolute, Jordan. Remember, you did not need the aid of the window to transport to other times and places when you were in Ohio."

"Mr. McGurney," Zak pleaded. "where did he take her? You have to know something?"

Paul McGurney sighed and lowered the ice pack from his head. He thought for a moment before answering.

"While I cannot be certain, I would imagine the Stranger has her hidden somewhere in the ancients."

"The ancients?" Jordan asked.

156

"Yes, Jordan. I believe he has hidden her where he has the greatest advantage. You are correct in your assessment of the situation; should you go after her, you risk walking into a trap." He paused, considering his next words. "But should you choose to wait for him to come back, Zak could be proven right. The assassin plays by no rules. His master is ruthless, as you are well aware. The stakes are raised considerably from last summer. The Stranger wants nothing more than to kill all of you in an attempt to squelch the Knowledge from working in and through you. He has cause, and he has justification. The Opposition failed, and he must succeed according to his master's wishes."

"So where does that leave us?" Margaret asked. "What should we do?"

Paul McGurney smiled, his eyes conveying a hope Margaret didn't feel.

"We pray for clarity. We ask for our Creator to move another mountain. If our God is for us, who can be against us?"

Margaret heard Zak stifle a sob. She turned to her grandson and saw that his eyes were welled with tears. He was looking intently at Paul McGurney with a longing in his eyes that broke her heart.

"God is still for us, right, Mr. McGurney? I mean—He's—He's still watching over us?"

McGurney leaned forward and touched Zak's knee.

"Sometimes the Cross is hard to carry, son. Sometimes it feels as if God is silent; as if He is hiding behind a black cloud and allowing bad things to happen for no reason. But take heart, dear one. Your God loves you and He has promised you life abundant. He will never leave you in your time of need, nor will he take back His enduring promise."

Zak was crying now, the tears streaming down his cheeks in unashamed emotion. Margaret couldn't hold them back herself, and neither could Jordan.

"You are co-heirs with Christ, dear ones," Paul McGurney

continued. "The glories promised Him are your own. Believe that. Hold fast to that promise. Yes, Zak. Your God is for you because He loves you as He loves Jesus."

Margaret saw that even Paul McGurney had tears running down his cheeks.

"And I love you all," he said to Margaret and the boys. "I will fight beside you until my time here is through." He smiled and his eyes sparkled.

"Now, let's pray."

Chapter forty-six

*T*odd got off the phone with Jordan and felt his entire body go numb. The Stranger had taken Andrea into the ancients, had stepped behind the present reality and hidden her somewhere in the past. The notion that she could be anywhere and any*when* made Todd dizzy. He sat down on his bed and tried hard not to tremble.

I can't believe this is happening! I have to get to Colorado!

Todd felt trapped in Ohio, caged by the miles upon miles that separated him from the others. His mother had been adamant that he would not be going to Colorado with his arm in a sling. But his mother had no idea of the absolute terror the children had become entrenched in. Todd sighed.

It's time to tell them the whole story...

Jordan looked to the elegant window and wondered how far away Andrea truly was. It wasn't miles that separated her from safety, but millennia. And Paul McGurney had said the Glimpses into ancient times didn't come with a set of rules. There was no instruction manual for the portal-window, no dots to connect that would form a clear picture of what they were dealing with.

Now, with Andrea gone and the future looking bleaker than ever, it was all blind faith. For the first time since he had accepted the Knowledge, Jordan would have to completely and wholeheartedly walk the talk. It was past the point of being stalked and hunted, past the point of being threatened and assaulted. What he was dealing with now was reality peeled back to its raw tissue: when all hope is lost is there still a Hope to believe in?

"We can't sit around and wait," Zak said a few minutes after Paul McGurney got through praying. "I'll go crazy if we sit around and wait."

"We don't know how the portal works, Zak," Margaret reminded him. "We could be walking right into an ambush should we follow the Stranger into the ancients."

"But we don't know how it works until we try it," Zak said, looking at the window. "I'll volunteer if no one else wants to."

Jordan shook his head and tried not to think about being ambushed thousands of years away from home.

"It's not that we don't want to go, Zak. It's just—we might need some more firepower. And I'm not just talking weapons. I'm talking people."

Zak took a moment to process this before turning to Paul McGurney.

"OK. So we don't know where the portal will take us. But how did you know where we would go last summer? I mean, you were pretty specific when it came to our destination."

Paul McGurney chuckled and folded his hands in his lap.

"I am but a messenger, dear one. I am only sent to do my Master's will. He orchestrated your divine appointments and I merely assisted in the process."

Zak nodded and ran his fingers through his hair.

"It's just—it all isn't adding up. I feel like there's a puzzle piece missing. Like—like something needs to happen for us to know what to do."

"A sign," Jordan said, squinting.

160

"Yeah, a sign. I can almost feel it. Like there's something about to go down. But it's not with me. It's—I don't know—I can't describe it."

Paul McGurney studied the air above Zak's head.

"I think you are feeling something, son. Though the answer lingers, wait for it."

"It's so hard to wait--" Zak started.

A hard rapping at the door silenced him.

Jordan looked at Margaret who looked at Paul McGurney.

"The again, some answers are found with a simple knock of the door," McGurney said. "Please, help me up. I believe our answer is here."

Chapter forty-seven

Zak heard the knock at the door and felt his entire body freeze. It was one of those moments that felt unreal, like when you look at yourself in the mirror for too long and your face melts into oblivion, or when you first come out of anesthesia and feel the lightness and absurdity of the world around you. The knocking at the door had that effect on Zak; it should not be happening at this *precise* time and in this *precise* circumstance. It was all too theatrical, all too on cue.

"Who do you think--" Jordan started, but dropped his question as Margaret put up a hand.

Paul McGurney was already shuffling to the door, his slippered feet making a swishing sound against the hardwood.

"Is this a good idea?" Margaret asked. Another knock at the door made her visibly apprehensive. "Do you think it could be the Stranger?"

"We'll never know until we open the door," Zak said, jogging to Paul McGurney in order to help the old man traverse his destroyed dining hall. When he reached McGurney, the old man's eyes were sparkling with a hope that calmed Zak's frayed nerves.

"This is your answer, Zak," Paul McGurney said as the pair maneuvered around a piece of broken banister. "I believe the

Lord has sent us a bridge."

Three more raps sounded at the heavy mahogany door, and Jordan took up a position on Zak's left. His grandmother trailed the threesome as Zak guided McGurney around more debris.

"A bridge," Jordan breathed, obviously in awe at who could be behind the door.

"Our way to the ancients," Zak said. McGurney chuckled.

As the battle-weary yet hopeful party came within a few feet of the door, Zak wondered who was responsible for the rapping. He remembered Edgar Allan Poe's famous poem, "The Raven," from English class, and could relate to the speaker's nervous anticipation at who could be tapping at his chamber door.

Todd! It has to be Todd!

Zak's chest swelled at the thought. Todd's presence in Colorado would boost morale and serve as a unifying force against the Stranger.

But Jordan just called Todd—it's impossible.

Yet, Zak knew the impossible was never out of the question, not when Paul McGurney was involved. Although the old man considered himself a mere messenger, whenever Paul McGurney had a hand in anything, impossibilities seemed to bend and fracture.

Another knock at the door, another few steps for Zak and his kin. Zak's heart pounded in eager anticipation.

The group stopped before the door, and three sets of eyes turned to Paul McGurney. It was his house, after all. He would be the one to open the door.

McGurney gripped the door's gold latch with his wrinkled hand. His blue eyes twinkled.

"And now for your answer," Paul McGurney said. And he opened the door.

When Zak saw who was standing on McGurney's dilapidated porch, he couldn't keep from gasping.

"But how did you--" Margaret started. She squinted, trying to

163

process what she was seeing.

Paul McGurney chuckled.

"Do come in," he said to the visitor standing on the porch. "I'm sure you'll have plenty of questions to answer. And some to ask, yourself."

Chapter forty-eight

*T*odd shut his phone and ran his good hand through his hair. Calling Andrea's cell had been a futile effort, one he had taken up as a last attempt to see if she was safe. He was now completely and utterly helpless in Ohio.

I have to tell Mom and Dad. Aunt Patty has to know, too. We have to get to Colorado—fast!

Todd looked at the clock. His mother would be coming home for lunch in about ten minutes. He would tell her then. And he would tell her *everything*.

Chapter forty-nine

So many things swirled through Andrea's head that she thought her brain might short out. The ominous void of time and space that accompanied the trip into the ancients disoriented her, and the churning vortex of generations long gone enveloped and pressed upon her like a lead blanket.

And she was in the void with a killer.

Like being trapped in a dark cellar with a rabid raccoon, Andrea's mind was on fire with uncertainty and sheer terror.

"I was beginning to think we weren't going to make it," the Stranger said in his metal-grating voice. If Andrea could have moved, she would have shuddered.

We? I'm not a monster like you!

"This part always makes me think of the finality of death," the Stranger continued, referring to the blackness surrounding the two. Andrea was slung over his shoulder like a sack of potatoes, and all she could see was the debilitating darkness that seemed to suck her hope into its black hole.

Stop talking! I hate the sound of your voice!

"I'm sure you're wondering where we are going," the Stranger said in a chillingly conversational tone. "And I'm also willing to bet you're wondering how long the muscle relaxant will last."

So--I won't be like this forever! A spark of hope ignited inside of her but was immediately extinguished by the Stranger's next words.

"We're going deep. We're going to one of the darkest places you can imagine. In your nightmares you haven't come close to experiencing the horrors you are about to see."

Horrors?

"As for the serum I injected into you, it will wear off in due time. Who knows, if you're a good little brat I just might consider leaving you with the ability to move."

The swirling blackness began to crack, and light began to peek through the dense pocket of nothingness. Andrea thanked God for light.

"I think we're here," the Stranger said. "Now, don't you dare think about trying anything brave."

How can I? I can't move!

"I'm serious about you being a good little maggot. If you misbehave, I'll have to cut your throat."

The assassin yanked her from his shoulder and now held her in his arms as Superman would a helpless victim. Andrea was most definitely a helpless victim, but the Stranger was no Superman. He had an evil streak that would put even Lex Luther to shame.

The blackness gave way to a fuzzy scene as the ancient world struggled to come into focus. Andrea couldn't begin to imagine where she was—she didn't want to. All she knew was that it would take a miracle for her to get back to Colorado. The assassin had said he was stowing her away somewhere worse than even her nightmares. As her surroundings began to come into focus, Andrea could only pray the Stranger was lying. She knew how terrifying her nightmares were. She didn't want to imagine what the Stranger's concept of terrifying was.

"Welcome to Babylon," the Stranger said with an acidic chuckle.

Andrea's surroundings came into sharp focus. It was dusk, and the streets of the seemingly large city were scant with people. A group of women carried jars of water down a road leading away from where the Stranger stood cradling Andrea. A teenage boy held up vegetables he carried in a large basket, eager to sell his wares to the disinterested passersby. Night was soon to fall on the city, and the dusty streets would clear and she would be alone with the Stranger.

Where are we? Why are we here? This doesn't seem all that terrifying—a bunch of simple buildings in what seems to be an intersection of a large city.

"Don't get your hopes up," the Stranger said, as if reading her mind. "This isn't where you'll be staying the night. I have a much better place in mind."

As the Stranger turned to his right and began to walk down a narrow street, Andrea could only wonder what "better" meant.

Chapter fifty

"You've got to be kidding," Zak said as he saw who was standing in Paul McGurney's entryway. "Tell me how this is possible. I don't get it."

Zak looked to the others and found the rest, save the old man, to be in complete disbelief at the sight of Jason Hanson—the man Margaret Kessler had once pegged as the Stranger—standing with an awed expression beside McGurney's ornate, gold coat hooks. Paul McGurney wore a broad smile, and his eyes glittered with new excitement.

"Welcome, sir. Please, make yourself at home."

Hanson cleared his throat and licked his lips. Putting his hands to his sizeable hips, he looked as if he were about to say something but then stopped himself. His hazel eyes worked around the large house, surveying both the luxurious furnishings and the battle scars left by Margaret's shotgun. Zak saw the man struggling to form words.

"I—uh—I just--" But he could not finish his sentence. The man was clearly flustered, and he shook his head as though to wiggle his thoughts free.

Paul McGurney chuckled. He touched Hanson's elbow.

"Why don't we move to the fireplace. It's more comfortable in the back."

They made their way to the back of McGurney's elegant

house, traversing the shattered furnishings and broken ground with a sense of new hope and confusion. Jason Hanson walked as though he had just awoken from a brilliant dream world; his eyes moved over McGurney's grand house and the old man himself as if Hanson were seeing through the eyes of a child.

The five sat down before the fireplace, McGurney in his leather chair, and Zak, Jordan and Margaret on the couch. Hanson sat in the leather loveseat across from McGurney, his hands folded over his ample belly, his eyes still surveying his surroundings. A fire Zak had not noticed in the after-battle chaos popped and cracked beneath a big stone mantle. The air was different, and Zak could sense a change coming. He looked at Paul McGurney. The old man sat smiling, his blue eyes sparkling as he read the space above Hanson's head.

"Welcome, Jason. I am Paul McGurney."

Zak knew Paul McGurney couldn't see, but he had to wonder whether the old man had read the cursive name stitched on Hanson's blue work shirt or if he had produced it of his own accord. Zak shrugged it off. The logistics didn't matter as long as Hanson was here to help bring Andrea back from the ancients.

Jason Hanson cleared his throat and swallowed, trying to find his voice.

"Hi—um—hello, I mean," he fumbled.

Paul McGurney chuckled. "It's all right, son. We have all been in your position before. The Knowledge gets into your blood, and, when you least realize it, confronts you with His mystery in a way that can leave you feeling—a certain longing."

Hanson swallowed again and wiped at his sweaty brow.

"I—uh—I don't know about any Knowledge, but I—I don't really know how I got here, either." The big man shifted in his seat and the leather squeaked underneath him. He looked at Zak and his kin and smiled apologetically.

"What do you mean?" Margaret asked, leaning forward. "You look like you've seen a ghost."

Hanson gave a nervous laugh. "Well, ma'm, I feel like I did. It's just—the dreams. And now—this," he extended his arm to indicate Paul McGurney's mansion. "It just seems—well, it seems impossible."

"What do you mean when you say 'dreams'?" Jordan asked. "You mean you dreamed about this place?"

Hanson shook his head once again, disbelief still on his face.

"I had a couple dreams," he started. He looked at Paul McGurney as if seeking permission to proceed. When the blind man didn't nod, he seemed uncertain.

"Mr. McGurney is blind," Jordan explained, picking up on Hanson's discomfort.

"Forgive me," McGurney said, raising an ancient hand. "I should have said something."

Hanson shook his head. "It's OK, Mr. McGurney. I'm just—well—I'm just trying to piece together what's happening."

"Please, son, continue," McGurney said, folding his hands on his lap. "You had some dreams?"

Hanson nodded, then quickly caught himself. "Uh—yeah. I had a couple dreams about a golden road and—and a stream of water leading me to a field of, well, you aren't going to believe this--"

"Pearls," Jordan finished for him, a broad smile stretched across his face.

Hanson was stunned. "How—how did you know?"

"And I'm guessing the stream of water led you up a jewel-encrusted hill and to--" Zak started.

"This house," Hanson finished. He was floored, utterly baffled at how two teenagers could know his dreams. "How are you—what are you—*how do you know all this*?"

Zak's heart began to beat faster. This wasn't a mere coincidence. These things didn't just *happen*. Hanson was here for a specific purpose.

"We had the same dreams, Mr. Hanson," Jordan said.

"What? And please—call me Jason," Hanson said, his elbows now on his knees, his hands rubbing his face.

"We had the same dream as you last summer," Zak said, feeling the excitement mounting.

"*Last summer*!?"

"What did you think about the road?" Margaret chipped in, getting in on the fun.

"It came out of nowhere!" Hanson said. "The few times I've been up here it was just—trees! And then, poof! A road that led me here!"

Zak's excitement ebbed a bit when he realized how much Andrea would enjoy seeing this. She would giggle and ask Hanson a thousand questions at once. But she wasn't here. And maybe Hanson was the ticket to bringing her back.

"And—and I heard a Voice," Hanson said, his eyes dreamy. "It spoke to me—I mean the *real* me. It's like the Voice spoke to my heart and knew everything about me."

"Tell me about it!" Zak said. "The Voice was the coolest part of the dream!"

By now, Hanson was beyond floored. He looked back and forth from Paul McGurney to the threesome on the couch.

"Somebody needs to explain to me what's going on! I drove up to Mrs. Kessler's place to fix the wiring in the kitchen and on the way back down the mountain—I mean—I can't explain it— but it was like my heart was *tugging* at me to come here. And the road—I mean the one in *real life*—was there! Is there! I don't really know what I mean, but I know it wasn't there when I drove up the mountain this morning. And now—now all *this*! Am I going crazy? Are *you* all crazy? What's going on?"

Paul McGurney chuckled and leaned forward.

"You are being wooed, son. You are being pursued."

"Wooed? What? Who's following me?"

"Someone you'll want to get to know," Jordan said. He looked at Zak and then at Margaret. "Should we tell him?"

Zak didn't even need to think about it.

"From the beginning."

Hanson, still hopelessly clueless as to what was transpiring, pleaded with the foursome.

"Please—tell me! Before I come to the conclusion I've gone insane!"

Jordan nodded, and Margaret touched Zak's knee, indicating he should be the one to start the story. Zak cleared his throat.

"Well, Jason, it all started last summer…"

🐍🐍🐍

The Fiends swarmed around Paul McGurney's dilapidated porch. A hush had descended upon the ghouls, and a sense of trepidation seized even the highest-ranking of the horde. Where victory had seemed so promising a moment ago, the arrival of Jason Hanson brought a new sense of apprehension and a lot more questions.

"Why is he here?" Horse-face hissed. "This wasn't in the projections!"

"The master knows what he's doing," Fly-face said, his voice unable to hide a tremor. "If the fat Hanson man is here it is not due to the master's negligence."

"It's the Knowledge!" Mosquito-face spewed. "The Knowledge is trying to woo another to his fold!"

"Don't mention that Name!" Horse-face shrieked. "Don't panic! The master knows what he is doing. The Stranger has the one called Andrea, and things are still in line with the Plan."

"I hope you're right," Mosquito-face muttered, using his proboscis to sniff the air.

"I am right. Now—ready yourselves for when the brats exit!" Horse-face shouted.

But even he had his doubts that everything was going to be OK.

Chapter fifty-one

*J*ason Hanson ran his fingers through his hair, trying to process all he'd just been told. It had taken over forty minutes to get the entire saga out, and Jordan could only imagine what kinds of questions were running through Hanson's mind. It all had to be so wonderfully confusing, so apprehensively perfect. The entire tale, starting with the dreams and the pearls from last summer and ending with the shotgun battle that had led to the Stranger's escape to the ancients with Andrea, had been told in urgent excitement by the threesome on the couch. Paul McGurney only nodded in affirmation, and only spoke when it was necessary for him to explain to Hanson who he really was. Where Zak, Jordan and Margaret had had almost a year to process what had—and was—transpiring around them, Hanson had gotten it all in forty minutes. And it was clear his head was spinning.

Jason Hanson nibbled at his lower lip, his eyes scanning the ceiling in deep thought.

"So, OK, I think I get most of it. But—but what I'm tripped up on is the whole Knowledge part. You mean to tell me the Knowledge is—is *Jesus*?"

Jordan nodded. "Yep."

Hanson absently rubbed his cheek. "And—and you *saw*

Him?"

"On several occasions, actually," Zak said with a grin.

Hanson laughed and put up his hands. "I'm sorry, guys. But *Jesus*? The Guy who died on the cross and all? *That* Jesus?"

Margaret smiled reached over to touch Hanson's knee.

"Yes, Jason. That Jesus. If it helps you to believe, I have never seen Him in the flesh, but I know beyond a shadow of a doubt He is Who He says He is."

Hanson looked to Paul McGurney, whose nod confirmed Margaret's statement.

"I—uh—I mean, I'm not a religious man or anything. I go to church with my family every Easter, but apart from that, I make a point to stay away from those stuffy old buildings filled with 'thou shalts' and 'thou shalt nots.' I guess what I'm saying is—I'm not really the Jesus type. If the Knowledge—the Voice—really is Jesus, why would He be talking to a guy like me?"

"Religion has nothing to do with it, Jason," Paul McGurney said. "Christ's love is about a relationship. An intimate friendship between God and man—Father and son—Lover and beloved."

Hanson lowered his head and rubbed his eyes.

"You don't understand, Mr. McGurney. I've—I've done some pretty rotten things. There's no reason for Jesus to want me."

Paul McGurney's blue eyes sparkled. "You are right, Jason. There should be no reason why a perfect God puts up with His imperfect creation. But that's the beauty of Christ; when we were still mired in the filth of our sin, Jesus died for us to set us free from guilt and the oppression of our own immorality. Jason, His blood covers your faults. When he died on the cross, He had you in mind. It wasn't about religion, it was about the desperate love of Jesus Christ for *you*." Paul McGurney's vacant eyes moved to the ceiling in remembrance.

"I, too, have 'done things.' Jason, I killed a man and was sentenced to die beside the perfect Christ. But in my greatest hour of weakness, in my most desperate moment, I called out

175

to Him to save me—to set me free. And He did." The old man raised his hands.

"My chains are gone, Jason. I have been pardoned. I have been given what I did not deserve because Christ Jesus said I *deserved* it. What I saw as filthy, He saw as a priceless gem. His blood has cleansed me from my past, from my mistakes and failures, from all I did to separate myself from Him. My burden is gone! I am free!"

Tears streamed down Paul McGurney's cheeks, and Jordan saw that Hanson, too, had tears cascading down his own.

"When the Voice spoke to me," Hanson said, trying to compose himself, "when the Voice said my name, my heart wanted—no—*yearned*-- to be know Who had spoken. It was like I was in a dream within a dream. I can't describe to you what it felt like. The Voice *knew* me."

"Christ is wooing you, Jason," McGurney said softly. "All you must do is believe."

Hanson wiped his eyes with the sleeve of his work shirt.

"I want to believe. It's just—I don't think I can live up to Him. I've done so many terrible things."

Jordan saw Margaret squeeze Hanson's knee. The big man shook his head and looked at the floor. Jordan heard the squeak of leather as Paul McGurney began to stand up.

"You must see, Jason," McGurney said, reaching for his cane. "We have a window of opportunity right now. Come, all. To the window."

Chapter fifty-two

*T*he Stranger carries the one called Andrea through the streets of Babylon. Darkness is creeping over the city, and children are returning to their homes for the night as women beat out woven rugs on their doorsteps and men amble in from their respective trades. There are no stars in the sky. The moon is shrouded by an unforgiving cloud, and the air is thick and humid, the summer night choking off the breeze like an assassin a helpless victim.

The Stranger had dismantled and discarded the empty shotgun when he and the one called Andrea had first arrived. The assassin has no use for it in the ancients, and the Babylonians certainly would not be able to operate it, especially without ammunition. Taking the shotgun, although now abandoned and destroyed, had been a victory for the assassin. Now the old nut is unarmed and terrified. The Stranger can strike again before she buys a new weapon and take her and the others out without being thwarted by a firearm.

The Stranger turns onto a narrow dirt road and the simple buildings squeeze in on the killer on both sides. The Stranger knows this road is a common hangout for the most vile of Babylonian society; thieves, murderers and ladies of the night are often found clustered around an open fire, plotting their next heist or orchestrating their next kill. A few pagan teachers can usually be found in the company of the vile, and as the Stranger presses *on into the quickening night, the Stranger feels at home.*

The Stranger is no fool. Hiding out in Babylon will not further the master's plan. The Plan calls for the eradication of the Knowledge-bearers, and in order to eliminate the children, the assassin must return to Colorado. Kidnapping the one called Andrea will serve its purpose in due time. The Stranger can use her as bait to lure the others to the ancients, but the assassin is smart enough to know the abominable Paul McGurney will never allow such a risk. The one called Andrea is valuable dead or alive. When the Stranger drops her off at the intended destination, it does not matter whether she is killed or remains alive. As long as the children and the kooky old woman think Andrea is alive, the Stranger has the upper hand.

The Stranger takes a sharp right as the narrow road widens into the more lavish part of the city. The assassin knows all the twists and turns. The assassin has been here before. Andrea's final destination is not what concerns the Stranger. It is how to navigate the portal between Colorado and the ancients that is the problem. How the time travel works, the Stranger does not know. Maybe it is the master who controls the portal, or maybe it is the Stranger's mind willing a destination that makes the destination materialize. Whatever the case, the Stranger hopes the master will illuminate the correct paths. Being able to transition between the worlds is vital to the success of the mission.

And there is still one brat in Ohio…

The Stranger smiles into the darkness. Colorado can wait. The assassin has a new appointment with the one called Todd. The master will approve. The Stranger will eliminate Todd first and then go after the remaining Knowledge-bearers. With Andrea potentially dead after tonight and Todd killed at the assassin's strong hands, the remaining Knowledge-bearers will be crushed. Their hope will be destroyed and they will all but beg for death.

The Stranger laughs out loud. The end is near. And it will be all too easy.

Chapter fifty-three

*T*he vortex of time swirled around the four time travelers, and Jordan couldn't help but steal glances at Jason Hanson. The big man was beyond dumbfounded at what was transpiring around him. Like a dog riding in the front seat of a car and fascinated with his surroundings, Hanson's head and large body moved back and forth, side to side as he surveyed the black that enveloped the bunch. Hesitantly raising a pudgy finger, he touched the swirling mass of years and history that enveloped the foursome. When his finger passed right through the churning black, he pulled it back as though he had touched a hot iron.

"OK. So, if I'm not mistaken, we just stepped *through a window*," Hanson said, eyes wide as pie tins. "And we're going to see--"

"Jesus," Jordan finished. "Can't you feel your heart starting to burn?"

Hanson rubbed his chest and shook his head. "And I thought it was just the omelet I had this morning."

"Trust me, man," Zak said, "this is going to be better than an omelet."

"And we're OK?" Margaret Kessler asked. She looked more

than nervous, and Jordan realized with a start that this was his only his grandmother's second trip into the ancients. He reached out and took her hand. She gladly received it and held on tight.

"We've always come back," Jordan said. "I'm always a little nervous during this part, too."

"I can't believe I'm actually going to see Jesus," Margaret said. "I mean—to actually *see* Him!"

"When does this thing slow down?" Hanson asked, indicating the swirling mass of generations. "I feel like I'm on the Tilt-a-Whirl."

"Just wait," Zak said with a grin. "It gets better."

The foursome didn't have to wait long. As soon as Zak finished speaking, beams of fresh light pierced the darkness. Jordan felt his heart pumping fast, and he knew Jesus was close.

"My heart's going crazy!" Margaret said, holding her chest. A broad smile stretched across her face, and for a moment Jordan got a glimpse of what his grandmother must have looked like when she was a little girl.

"He's near!" Zak said, barely able to contain his own excitement. Jordan knew the last time Zak had met Jesus he and Jesus had had an intimate talk that had changed the way Zak looked at the world and himself. Jordan could only imagine how Jason Hanson would react to such a meeting.

The darkness vanished as quickly as it had come, and now the foursome's new surroundings struggled to come into focus.

"We're not going to get ambushed by the Stranger, are we?" Margaret asked as she gripped Jordan's hand even harder.

Jordan thought for a moment and shook his head. "I don't really know how all this works, but I'm positive we either skipped over wherever the Stranger is or we took a different portal."

At the mention of the Stranger, Jordan was reminded of the peril Andrea was in. The Stranger was somewhere in time, and he had Andrea in his clutches. As the minutes and hours ticked on, Andrea's safety became more of a concern.

I want to see Jesus—but Andrea's in trouble!

The fuzz at the peripherals of the new setting melted away to reveal a simple room filled with excited men and women. Light streamed in through open windows, and a warm breeze kept the stuffiness out. Jordan instantly recognized the men as Jesus' disciples and the three women as Mary, Jesus' mother, and two of His close friends. The men were nearly shouting, waving their arms to convey their emotions. The women, though more reserved, were likewise visibly excited. Something was up, and Jordan couldn't wait to find out what it was.

"I can't believe this is happening," Margaret breathed. She released Jordan's hand and watched the excitement play out in the room.

"Ditto," Hanson said, running his hand through his hair. "We just walked through a window and into—into ancient times! Look at their clothes!"

"Can they see us this time?" Zak asked Jordan. Last summer the children had been silent observers of Glimpses Paul McGurney had shown them. No one, save Jesus, had had the faintest idea they were being watched. But the game had changed, and Jordan didn't know how to respond.

"I don't know. I mean, they couldn't see us in the upper room," Jordan said.

"Good point," Zak nodded. "I'll bet they have no idea we're--"

"We have visitors!" one of the men shouted, interrupting Zak's statement. "Come, John, let's tell them the good news!"

Zak looked at Jordan and smiled. "Guess we were wrong."

Two men approached, and Jordan recognized one as Peter. He wore a green robe and his brown eyes danced with excitement. John trailed him, wearing a red robe of his own, a matching red apple in his hand.

"We were so excited we didn't see you come in," Peter apologized. "Come, sit." He indicated a place at the table and John

181

scurried to move dirty dishes out of the way. The foursome, embarrassed at being the newcomers in the room, took seats on the ground beside the rest of Jesus' disciples. Jordan counted and realized one was missing.

Judas. So this is after Jesus was crucified.

"I don't believe this. I don't believe this. I don't believe this," Hanson said as he plopped his large body onto the ground.

"Neither do I," one of the disciples said from across the table, mistaking Hanson's disbelief with his own.

"Come now, Thomas!" John scolded. "Don't start in on that again. You have to believe us."

Thomas, who wore a black robe and peeled an orange in a disinterested fashion, shook his head again. "I'm telling you-- you must be drunk on some pretty strong wine. You yourself saw Him die, John. How can you deny it?"

Peter put up his hand to silence Thomas. "Please, Thomas. Not in front of our guests."

"Well, they might as well know now," Thomas muttered, taking a bite of his orange.

"Have you traveled far?" Mary asked Margaret in a kindly voice. Jordan's grandmother looked at Jordan with wide eyes. Jordan nodded that she should respond.

"Uh—we've come from—I guess you can say we've traveled a long way," Margaret replied. She sat to the left of Jordan beside Hanson, who still shook his head in wonder.

"Then you must be road-weary," Mary said. "Martha, why don't you fetch a basin of water so our guests can wash their feet."

"No—no please don't go to the trouble," Margaret said. "We all took showers this morning."

Mary looked at Margaret with a curious expression and then glanced down at her feet.

"I see. You also have a curious choice of footwear."

"Bought mine at Foot Locker," Hanson blurted. "On sale for

182

forty bucks."

The eleven men and three women around the table simply stared at him.

"Uh—I mean—oh, boy, this is all so crazy." Hanson looked at his Nikes and shook his head as though his sneakers were the problem.

"Crazy. You can say that again," Thomas said, tossing his orange peels onto the table. He swept his hand over the table. "My friends here think Jesus is alive."

"Thomas, please!" one of the disciples said. "You must believe us! Jesus Himself said He would rebuild the Temple after three days. Well—it's been three days!"

"Well said, Bartholomew," Peter said, patting his friend on the back.

Thomas laughed and shook his head. "Are fishermen so dense? Jesus wasn't talking about *Himself*! He was talking about the Temple! If He wanted to refer to Himself, He simply would have said so!"

"He's alive," Zak said. "We've seen Him."

The room thundered with excitement. Thomas waved the statement off and crossed his arms while Peter tried to shush the room.

"You saw Him? When?"

Zak looked to Jordan who shrugged. Why not tell them the story?

"We saw Him last summer," Zak began. Jordan saw that his cousin immediately regretted his words.

"See! They saw Him *before* He died," Thomas said triumphantly.

This sent the room into chaos again, and Peter, again, shushed the men and women so he could speak.

"So, you are saying you saw Jesus *before* He was crucified.?"

"Before *and* after. He talked to us by the tomb," Jordan said.

A disciple Jordan recognized as James slapped the table. "See! He is alive!"

"Your story is full of more holes than a bad fisherman's net," Thomas said, stealing a glance Peter. "You aren't making any sense."

Zak raised himself onto his knees and spoke with his hands as he clarified the story.

"We come from another time, another place," Zak began.

"We came through the window," Hanson offered.

Zak quickly spoke over him to erase Hanson's awkward statement that, most certainly, would be taken entirely the wrong way.

"We come from the future—that's why you didn't see us enter though the door. We just--sort of showed up. Anyway, when we were in your time last summer, we saw Jesus die and rise again. It's as simple as that. If I read my Bible correctly, He should be walking through the door any minute."

The room was silent. The disciples wore stunned expressions as they hung on Zak's every word. Only one scoffed.

"Bible? *From the future*? Peter, you can't possibly believe this foolishness?" Peter stroked his beard and remained silent. Thomas laughed and continued.

"And the rest of you—why are you being so dense? Sure, Jesus did many wonderful things while He was alive. And I miss Him as much as the rest of You. But missing Him is not going to bring Him back from the dead. I'm sorry I have to be the one to tell you this, but—He's not coming back." He looked at Zak. "As for you, please take your dark magic and foolishness elsewhere. We are grieving here. Let us remember our Friend for Who He was and for what He did."

Jordan knew what was coming. He could sense it. Zak was going to play his last card now. His cousin's blue eyes sparkled as he looked into Thomas's skeptical brown ones.

"And you are Thomas, the one who doesn't believe. You

184

want to believe—you desperately want to believe—but you need proof."

Thomas was visibly shaken. "Stop—stop this at once!"

But Zak continued. "Your friends are excited because they have seen Jesus alive. But you weren't here the first time He appeared to them. You were gone, so you don't believe it actually happened."

Thomas was floored. "How did you—who told you that?"

"You need proof, don't you, Thomas?" Zak laughed. "You sound just like my brother Todd last summer. He wouldn't believe without proof. Faith was a foreign concept to him."

Thomas stood from the table and pointed at Zak.

"What is the meaning of this?" He looked to his friends. "You have put him up to this!"

Zak shook his head and slowly stood. "No, Thomas. None of these men put me up to anything. I've read your story. You say you need to touch Jesus' nail marks and put your hand in his side before you believe."

Thomas just stared at Zak for a moment. The room was silent. Zak held a captive audience.

"Thomas, it's more than that. It's about faith. It's about believing that Jesus is who He says He is."

Thomas waved Zak off. "This is crazy talk and you all are falling for it. Until I see Jesus with my eyes, until I touch His nail marks and side as the boy said, I am going to remember Him for Who He was. And I do mean *was*."

Peter rounded the table and put a hand on Thomas's shoulder.

"Thomas, please--"

Thomas shrugged him off. "No, Peter. You're being foolish. And I'm not going to participate in your foolishness any longer."

And with that, Thomas picked another orange from the fruit bowl that served as the table's centerpiece. He walked the door and turned to the others one last time.

"I'll be back when you're through with this nonsense." Shaking his head and muttering to himself, he opened the door.

Jesus stood on the doorstep.

"Ah!" Thomas shouted, dropping his orange. It rolled to a stop at Peter's feet. Jordan saw Thomas's face turn white as a sheet.

"Hello, Thomas. May I come in?"

At the sound of Jesus' voice, Jordan's heart burned something fierce.

It's Him!

Thomas was dumbfounded. He couldn't find his words, and Jordan thought for a moment that Thomas might pass out.

"A-a-ghost!" Thomas finally managed, pointing at Jesus.

"I'm not a ghost, Thomas. May I come in?"

Thomas could only nod. He clutched the wall, his eyes wide, mouth open. Jesus walked into the room and closed the door.

"Hello, friends," Jesus said as He walked to the table. Jordan heard Hanson's breath catch in his throat.

Jesus was robed in white, His beard neatly groomed, His eyes sharp and bright. Jordan looked at Jesus' feet and saw He was barefoot. He immediately saw the nasty, jagged scars in Jesus' feet. How, now, could Thomas not believe?

The room was in an uproar. The disciples jumped up to greet Jesus, and Jesus hugged each one of them as a father would a son. The women wept, and Jesus kissed their cheeks and wiped away their tears. Jesus held his mother Mary for a long moment as she rejoiced and clutched him as though He were an infant again. Jordan and the others held back, not wanting to interrupt such a reunion among old friends. They also knew that Jesus had to deal with Thomas, or, rather, Thomas's heart.

After the initial wave of celebrations died down, Jesus turned from the others to where Thomas still clutched the wall, his chest heaving in and out.

186

"Hello, Thomas," Jesus said, a warm smile spread across his face.

Thomas did not respond.

"It's all right, friend. Come and see for yourself." He spread His hands and the white robe fell away from his wrists. The red holes, frayed around the edges and a deep red color, could not be ignored.

"Come, Thomas. Place your hands on the nail marks. Touch my side. It's I."

Thomas was hesitant. Cautiously he crossed the room and stood before Jesus. The tiny place was hushed; all waited with bated breath. This was Jesus' moment with Thomas, and Thomas had a decision to make.

Tentatively and with a trembling hand, Thomas reached out and touched Jesus' hand. As his ran his fingers over the angry scars, he flinched as if feeling the nails himself. A smile played at Thomas's lips, and tears welled in his eyes.

"Feel my side and believe," Jesus said.

Jesus didn't have to lift His robe for Thomas to place his hand into the hole the Roman soldier's spear had made. Jordan watched in awe as Thomas's fingers disappeared to the knuckles as the latter examined the deep wound. When Thomas took his hand away, His face was transformed.

"My Lord! My God!" he cried and fell to his knees before Jesus, clutching His knees as a child would a father. Jesus stroked Thomas's hair and allowed him to cry.

"Why did you doubt?"

Thomas raised his head and through a film of tears responded, "I'm so sorry, Lord. You are my God and King. What was destroyed has been rebuilt in three days!"

Jesus laughed. "Stand up, son! Let me hug you!"

The two embraced and Thomas joined the rest of the disciples at the table.

"And I see we have more friends here," Jesus said, indicating the Colorado foursome.

"This is crazy," Hanson breathed. "This is absolutely nuts."

Jordan and the others stood as Jesus approached. Jordan felt as if his heart was going to leap out of his chest.

Jesus embraced Zak first.

"Zak! You've been so brave! I'm so proud of you!"

As always when Jesus spoke, finding words was difficult. Zak beamed and said thank you. Jesus turned to Jordan and swept him up in His arms.

"Jordan, how you're growing! It seems like only yesterday you getting into your mother's kitchen cupboards. I remember when you tipped over the flour. How funny!"

Although Jordan had no recollection of the moment--he had been only two--it was an indescribable feeling to know Jesus was there even before Jordan knew Him.

Jordan stepped aside and couldn't wait for the next few moments. His grandmother was physically meeting Jesus for the first time, and the awe on her face was priceless. This was his grandmother meeting her Savior.

Jesus took Margaret's hands in His own.

"Margaret, my child. I relish the time we spend together every morning. You've grown so much in the last year. I love you more than you can even fathom, and I want you to know you are never alone." Jesus pulled Margaret to Himself and Jordan saw his grandmother's eyes fill with tears.

"I'm so glad you chose Me. I had been waiting for that moment your whole life. I'm so glad you let Me love you."

"Jesus—I don't know what to say," Margaret said through her tears.

"Your heart says it all, good and faithful servant. Your heart says it all."

And Jesus held Jordan's grandmother as she wept with joy. Her heart had found her Messiah, and now her faith was confirmed by sight.

When Margaret pulled back from Jesus' embrace, her eyes were slick with tears and her face glowed. All she could do was look at Jordan and smile.

The room remained silent as Jesus approached Jason Hanson. The big man had been off a ways while Jesus had greeted the others, head down, right foot toeing the dirt floor. Jordan knew the man was battling within himself: battling the doubts and the religiosity he had grown up with, weighing his perceptions of Who Jesus was supposed to be versus Who He really was. Jordan was all too familiar with such inner battles. He, too, had had to relearn everything he thought he knew about Jesus. Looking back, Jordan was amazed at how society's perceptions of the Risen King differed greatly from Who He really was.

"Hello, Jason," Jesus said. "I have been waiting for this moment."

Hanson's eyes flashed from the floor and locked with Jesus' for an instant.

"You have?"

Jesus smiled. "Yes, Jason. I've been waiting for this moment since you were born."

Hanson's eyes moved back to the dirt. He said nothing.

Jesus took a step forward and placed a scarred hand on the big man's shoulder. Hanson seemed to crumble at His touch.

"I know your fears of inadequacy, Jason. I understand your doubts about Who I am."

Jason Hanson lifted his eyes from the floor, and Jordan saw they were rimmed in red. A desperation Jordan felt as a ball in his throat was in Hanson's eyes, a thirst that needed to be immediately quenched.

"I—I don't know what to say to You," Hanson said, his voice trembling. "I woke up this morning as an electrician, and now—this. I haven't thought about You in a long time—probably wouldn't again until I saw the first plastic nativity sets in people's yards." His eyes glistened, and Jordan could feel every one of

189

Hanson's words in the hollows of his chest, because they had once been his own.

"I'm not interested in your past, Jason. I'm interested in your present, and in your future glory."

"But—but why? That's the question I've asked myself every time Easter rolls around. Why did You do it? Why even go through all the pain? How can it be worth it?"

Jesus' eyes sparkled. "Because I love you, Jason. Because I want you to love me. Because I desire a relationship with you."

Hanson shook his head. "But the pain. The nails—I mean— look at Your hands!"

Jesus looked Hanson straight in the eyes. "I could have called ten thousand angels, Jason. I could have come down from the cross and spared Myself from death. But I *chose* to die for you, Jason. I *chose* to love you in hopes you would someday love Me. Even if you were the only one, Jason, I'd still die for you. I love you that much."

"But I've done so many things wrong! You have no idea! Even this morning I--"

Jesus held up His scarred hand to silence Hanson. The way it was positioned, Jordan could see the light from the window shining through the old wound.

"I know, and I don't care, Jason. I want you now and forever. All you have to do is repent of the old and allow Me to make you new."

Hanson was crying now. His large body rocked with sobs, and Jordan couldn't help but be overcome with the emotion of the scene. Jason Hanson was being confronted with his own mortality and the offer of a clean slate. The next few moments would be the most important of his entire life.

And then Jason Hanson broke. His knee fell to the dirt floor as Jesus' friends, both ancient and contemporary, looked on.

"Jesus—oh, Jesus!" Hanson could barely speak through the sobs. He held Jesus' scarred hand and ran his fingers over the

190

wound.

"Jesus—I believe in You! Please—please forgive me for all my sins! Take them all away! I want what the others have—I want You!" Hanson sobbed into Jesus' robe.

"And you have me, Jason Hanson. I am yours and you are Mine." Jesus gently lifted Hanson to his feet and drew him into an embrace.

"I love you, son. I love you more than you will ever know."

Jordan saw the room begin to fuzz over. The Colorado bunch was heading back, but Jordan knew Hanson would forever remember his new birth in the ancients.

"Take heart," Jesus said as the room lost all focus. "Do not be afraid. I am always with you. And I love you all."

Jesus' words rang in Jordan's ears as the foursome was swept up into the vortex of time.

I am loved. Regardless of any circumstance, I am loved. WE are loved. And that is enough.

Chapter fifty-four

*T*odd leaned back and waited for his mother's barrage of questions. He'd told her everything—literally *everything*—starting with last summer's adventure and ending with Andrea's being kidnapped by the Stranger. He expected his mother to flip out, as she was prone to do under stressful circumstances; but, instead, a silence Todd had not expected filled the living room. The only sound that pierced the silence was the tick of the antique clock beside the window, as the normally pacifying pendulum now gave off an unnerving tock that made Todd increasingly uncomfortable. He could stand it no longer.

"Mom—say something!"

Todd's mother took a deep breath and gently cleared her throat. She was equally unnerved, Todd could tell. The prospect of a terror she had not known existed frightened her to the core. But it all boiled down to the fact that Todd had inherited his mother's pragmatism; her world was run by logic and reason and had no room for meanderings on supernatural highways. Todd knew he had been a stubborn nut to crack, but his mother had decades on him. She had been attending church and was now the only family member in the house who was not yet a Christian. Todd had hope for her—she was to be attending a women's conference in the next few months with her sister—but until his mother could buy into the fact that Jesus couldn't be boxed in, she would be in a constant internal struggle.

"Mom? Are you OK?"

Donna Lawrence took another deep breath and smoothed out her black skirt.

"I don't exactly know what to say, Todd. I've always known you have a lively imagination, but this?"

Todd felt a surge of adrenaline spike in his veins. There was no time for disbelief.

"Look, Mom, I'm not making this stuff up. I'm not loopy from the medication and I'm not hopped up on some illegal substance. I'm telling you the truth. If you don't believe me, call Jordan and have him pass the phone to Grandma. We don't have time to play this game."

Todd's mother blinked and looked to the clock. Her lunch break would be over in a few minutes, and Todd needed to convince her to take action and take action now.

"Mom!" Todd shouted. "Please! We have to do something!"

His mother swallowed hard and nodded. Standing up, she smoothed down her skirt again and looked at Todd.

"Let's wait and see what your father says," she said. Her hands trembled, and Todd didn't have to look hard to see the tears forming in the corners of her eyes.

We can't wait that long!

Chapter fifty-five

"Welcome back," Paul McGurney said as the four time-travelers reemerged into the present. The old man stood with his hands folded over his cane, a large smile spread across his face. "I trust your journey was sufficiently amazing?"

Margaret could only nod. Her heart still pounded, jolts of adrenaline shot through her body and an overwhelming sense of did-that-really-just-happen? pervaded her entire being. Had she really just been in the presence of her Savior? Had she really *touched* Him? Margaret looked down and saw that her hands trembled.

Yes! Yes—it all just happened!

"Come, let us move to the fireplace," Paul McGurney said, leading the way. Zak moved to McGurney's side and guided the old man by the elbow as the five traversed the shotgun-scarred floor. Margaret stole a few glances at Jason Hanson and saw that the big man was beaming. And why wouldn't he be? He had just made the biggest and best decision of his life.

Paul McGurney plopped into his big leather armchair while the others assumed their positions on the couch and loveseat. For a moment, no one said anything. All seemed completely captivated by what they had just experienced, lost in their own thoughts and memories of Jesus' hugs and kindness. Finally, Hanson cleared his throat and leaned forward in the loveseat.

"He's real. He's more that real, He's—He's--" Hanson shrugged and shook his head. A solitary tear trickled down his cheek. "He's perfect."

Paul McGurney smiled. "You are loved, Jason. He loves you to pieces. And His love never ends."

Hanson nodded and swiped at his cheek with his sizeable hand. "Look at me—I'm blubbering like a baby!"

Margaret reached over and squeezed his knee.

"I could burst into a thousand pieces right now, too. I know how you feel. That was the first time I actually saw Him with my own two eyes, and it's all I can do to keep from bursting into tears of joy."

Hanson nodded and another tear came.

"The decision you made is the most important of your life," McGurney said. "Sadly, many do not choose to receive the free gift of salvation when they are confronted with the Knowledge."

Hanson shook his head and cleared his throat. "How can they not? How can you turn Him down?"

McGurney thought for a moment. "Fear. A sense of un-worthiness. A belief that they are too far gone to be loved un-conditionally."

Hanson nodded. "I guess that was me."

"The key word is *was*," Zak said.

Hanson swallowed and smiled. "I'm not going back to that place. No—never again. When He looked at me I felt so—so *vulnerable*. I mean, it was like He saw right into my heart. I felt dirty at first. Like He was looking at all the bad stuff and re-alizing how much of a mess-up I am—*was*. But then—but then He smiled at me. I saw it in His eyes—the love—the incredible love. And then He whispered to my heart. He called my name and—and I just *knew* I would never be the same again."

"Redemption," Paul McGurney said with a smile. "Grace."

A look of comprehension played on Hanson's face.

"Hey—it makes sense now. The old hymn—"Amazing Grace." How does it go? 'I once was lost but now I'm found. Was blind but now I see.' Man, do I see!"

Margaret felt the warmth of moment, the sheer joy the angels must feel as another prodigal came Home. She could barely contain her own emotions.

"Yes, Jason," Paul McGurney said with a nod. "You once were lost and now you have been purchased by the blood of Jesus Christ. You have a new name, a new beginning. The old has passed and the new has come."

Hanson beamed as tears trickled down his cheeks. "I—I need to thank you, Mr. McGurney. I need to thank you for allowing me to—uh—step through your window."

Paul McGurney laughed. "You don't have to thank me, son. I did nothing but what I have been commissioned to do. Thank the One Who gave you life and anew heart."

Jason Hanson nodded and swallowed.

All was well; the world was right for a brief snatch of time.

Chapter fifty-six

*S*omething was wrong.

Horse-face could feel the turn in the air, could sense the change as a ball of lead in the pit of his stomach. As he hovered over Paul McGurney's dilapidated porch, he knew beyond a shadow of a doubt that something has gone horrifically wrong. And whenever he felt like this, it could only mean one thing.

The Knowledge is at work.

All of a sudden, a searing pain erupted in Horse-face's chest. It sliced his insides, burned like a brand on his black heart. With a muffled groan, he was thrown from the air and bounced off the top porch step. All around him, demons fell from the air as if stricken by the plague. Fly-face nearly thumped on top of him as another jolt of electric pain sizzled his insides.

"The Knowledge! It's the Knowledge!" Fly-face said, his disgusting face contorted in agony.

A few feet away and slumped over the porch's railing, Mosquito-face spoke Horse-face's worst fear.

"It's the fat one! The Knowledge took the fat one!"

Horse-face roared in agonized rage.

"No! He was to be our tool! He was to be used for the master's purpose!"

Mosquito-face cursed and doubled over in pain. "What else could it be? All the others already claim the Knowledge! It has to be the fat one called Hanson!"

Horse-face new his counterpart was right. As revolting as it was, the one called Jason Hanson had chosen his side. And the Holy Spirit had just shown up.

Another slice of agony ripped through Horse-face's chest, and for a moment he wondered if he would fall over dead. He'd known demons who had been slain in the Presence of the Knowledge, and he hoped today was not the day for his time to come.

"We must flee!" Horse-face yelled when the pain became too great to bear. "We must regroup at a safe distance!"

Without any more prodding, the swarm of terrorized demons limped off the porch and struggled to find their wings. The Knowledge was too much. The Presence too great.

The Knowledge had won this round.

Chapter fifty-seven

*T*he Stranger nears the destination.

The worthless brat slung over the killer's shoulder will be properly stowed—if she isn't ripped apart, of course—and the assassin will transport to Infinity to kill the one called Todd. And the Stranger is very interested in the one called Todd; maybe even more interested in gutting him than the wretched Paul McGurney.

The murderer traverses the elegant sections of Babylon as darkness falls over the city. Ahead is the palace, where King Darius is most certainly being attended to as he prepares himself for slumber. But the palace is not the assassin's destination. The killer must weave through the luxurious and lethargic richness of the city in order to arrive at the predetermined destination. The assassin is headed for nothing more than a hole in the ground.

The Stranger steals a glance at the girl. She is completely inert, helpless to ward off any impending attack She could easily be mistaken for dead. The Stranger finds it almost miraculous that a townsperson or public official hasn't accosted the killer concerning the issue. The Stanger has predetermined that whoever would dare interrupt the mission would end up dead. The master's plan is far too important to be tampered with.

The girl is as lifeless as ever. The assassin realizes that, *should the serum continue its mastery over the girl's motor functions, she will not survive the night. Forget stowing in her in the ancients; she will be nothing more than torn flesh and shredded clothing within the next ten minutes. This is going to be a violent death, even by the Stranger's standards.*

The assassin is running now. The destination is straight ahead. There is no time to waste. Being thwarted by the old woman was bad enough. Things must stick to the plan with no deviation. The one called Todd must be eradicated while he is still separated from the rest. It is best to cut off the snake's head before hacking away at its body.

A slight shiver shakes the assassin. The master hates the snake analogy, and no mention of snakes is allowed in the master's presence. He had cloaked himself in snakeskin millennia ago and had successfully destroyed Eden, but not without a price. For where he had once struck the heel of man, ultimately, the master's head will be crushed. It's the snake analogy—a prophesy already fulfilled and awaiting its completion—that chills the master to his core.

The Stranger is now just outside the city. All is black as the death that will most certainly come to the one called Andrea. The destination is less than one hundred yards away, and as the Stranger approaches, the killer sees it is "guarded" by two disinterested, blatantly-drunk soldiers. The Stranger is disgusted that ones such as these should be allowed to stand guard over such an awesome means of execution. King Darius is to be blamed just as much as the carousing soldiers. The master would kill these sloths on the spot for taking their responsibility so lightly. Look what the master did to the Opposition...

The assassin slows to a walk and is grateful for the black mask which veils al the killer's facial features. The Stranger makes no move to conceal the girl from sight. The guards will be dealt with accordingly. The assassin will not even have to bother to disguise the situation.

200

One of the guards, a stubby oaf reeking of wine, steps forward and unsheathes his sword.

"Stop! Who goes there?"

The Stranger smiles beneath the mask. The assassin's fingertips tingle. The killer makes no move to slow down.

"Stop! Who goes there?" the guard repeats.

The guard thrusts his sword at the Stranger and glances to his counterpart. The other soldier, a lanky wisp of a teenager who also smells of spirits, unsheathes his own sword and thrusts it in the Stranger's direction. The Stranger continues to advance, having no intention of stopping.

"I said stop! You are on the king's property!" the stubby soldier yells again. The Stranger is now five feet away, the girl dangling from the killer's shoulder like a freshly-butchered chicken.

"Back away and you won't get hurt," the Stranger says calmly, even though the promise is a lie.

"Are you mad? Stop, under penalty of death--" the stubby soldier begins to shout. But it is too late for him. In one swift movement, the Stranger's knife is out and the hypodermic needle is thrust into the soldier's jugular. The soldier crumples like a rag doll, his muscles instantly paralyzed just as the girl's are. In the same instant, the Stranger side-kicks the lanky soldier in the stomach and the soldier doubles over, giving the Stranger enough time to refill the syringe from a vial on the assassin's belt. Without breaking a sweat, the Stranger yanks the tall soldier by his hair to his feet and plunges the needle deep into the drunkard's neck. The boy soldier tries to choke out a word, but it is muffled by the sound of his body hitting the dirt. Both soldiers are now incapacitated, and the Stranger is free to dispose of the girl

"I warned you."

The Strangers looks down on the two inert soldiers. The assassin knows killing them would have been just as easy. But the killer doesn't want to cause pandemonium when the sun comes up. Two dead soldiers would create an uproar, and a small army would be called upon to find out what had happened to the two unfortunate men. Should anything go wrong with the girl, the Stranger would have to fight through the king's army just to get her back, and that is not a chance the assassin is willing to take. The serum option allows the muscle paralysis a whole night to wear off, and, even if the soldiers see everything that is about to transpire, they must recount it through a drunken haze. Their story will be unreliable at best, the Stranger's presence waved off as an inebriated aberration. And in the morning, should everything go right with the girl, no one will know anything transpired at all.

The Stranger laughs into the darkness. It is all too easy.

"We are here," the Stranger says to the girl. "This is where you find out if you live or die." The Stranger laughs again and moves to the destination. "But let's be honest, here. You are going to die."

The destination is nothing more than a large pit covered by five planks of wood, an unceremonious decorum for one of the Stranger's most favorite means of execution. This pit is alive and savage. It is what is waiting at the bottom of the pit that makes the destination so deadly. This method of execution makes a simple knife stroke across the neck seem humane.

The Stranger drops the girl to the ground and carefully removes the five planks. The assassin hears a restless rustling from the bottom of the pit and smells the unmistakable odor of death. They are ripe today. Ready to devour a sorry soul.

When the killer is through removing the planks, the assassin picks up the girl and holds her over the pit by her armpits. With one hand the Stranger grabs a wad of her hair and snaps her head from her chest so the assassin can look her in the eye. The killer laughs again, a sneer of triumph on the Stranger's face.

"Welcome to the lion's den," the Stranger rasps. "When I let go of you, your body will fall ten feet and smash against the bottom of this pit. You might want to pray to your cruel God that

202

you die from the fall. Because, should you live, your body will be torn apart by five very big and very hungry lions. I hear they haven't been fed for a week." The Stranger laughs again, relishing the moment.

"You know, this never would have happened had you not dabbled in things you can't possibly understand! Where is your God? Will He save you from this pit?" The Stranger pauses, dramatically proving the point. "You see? You are alone. Your bones will be broken, your skin will be torn and ripped, and there is no one to save you."

The Stranger laughs once more at the master's victory. One down, five to go.

"Take this moment to despair in the knowledge that your God has turned His back on you. He might have risen from the dead, but He is a selfish, cruel God Who must be praised by His peons to feel validated. And in the end—nothing. So much for a loving Savior."

The Stranger pauses, allowing the words to sink in.

The time has come.

"Goodbye, Andrea!"

The Stranger lets go and Andrea disappears into the lion's den.

Chapter fifty-eight

*A*ndrea was in freefall. Her brain screamed at her to animate her limbs, to flail around if only to brace herself for the jarring impact that was sure to come at the pit's bottom. But she was incapable of locomotion, completely resigned to falling into the smelly darkness with no means to deaden the impact that would surely shatter her bones.

Three seconds was all it took for Andrea to freefall to the bottom of the hellish pit. Three seconds of gravity yanking her to her death, three seconds left in a life that would be extinguished years too soon. Three seconds of lightning-flash memories and more profound thoughts than she would have ever thought imaginable. Three seconds of regrets and failures and hopes and dreams and loves and laughs and sorrow and joy. Three seconds, Andrea realized, could feel like an eternity.

She had no idea how far she was falling, but she sensed the ground, knew it was there to annihilate her. What is more, she smelled the lions. Their feral odor, their stinking excrement, their lust for flesh. The Stranger had not been bluffing. There truly were wild beasts waiting to devour her.

Andrea's mind flashed through all that had brought her to this point, all that would make her a martyr at the hand of sheer evil. How different she had been just last summer! How lost without knowing it! How frail and diseased by her own shortcomings! Over the past year, life had been much more fulfilling and promising, even if a portion of it was spent dodging the Opposition's advances. The change she felt and saw in herself, the change she saw in her brother and cousins, was remarkable. The Knowledge was and is not tame, and having your heart set to a burn for Truth is like a lit match in a dry forest. So much had changed in her family, so much beauty from ashes. Her mother had begun to loosen the chains of guilt and shame that being a single mother whose husband walked out brought. Her uncle now drove the family to church every Sunday and was involved in an early morning Bible study. So much was different in a matter of a year, so many wrongs rectified because of Jesus Christ that Andrea knew her death was worth it. She was not dying in vain. She was dying because Christ died for her first and rearranged her situation and the lives of others. Her death was for His ultimate glory.

The moment before she hit the pit's bottom, Andrea's eyes welled with tears. But she wasn't mourning her own death; these weren't tears of sorrow. These were tears of joy. She was going Home.

The impact came, but Andrea didn't feel it. She had already beaten death because death was beaten for her. As the blackness overtook her, she rejoiced that the next time she would open her eyes she would be in Paradise.

Chapter fifty-nine

"We need a plan," Jordan said, sitting back in Paul McGurney's big leather couch.

"Weren't you the one who said we should wait for the Stranger to bring Andrea back?" Zak asked. "I mean, I'm not against a plan. But why the change of heart?"

Jordan shook his head and swallowed hard.

Yeah, why the change of heart?

"Jordan?" Margaret gently asked. "Is there something wrong?"

Jordan sharply exhaled. "I don't know. It's just—I feel like something's different. Something's changed. I think—I think Andrea might be in trouble."

"You feel that?" Jason Hanson asked, sitting forward in his chair. "What do you mean? I need to learn how all this works."

Paul McGurney folded his hands atop his belly. "Jordan has been gifted with intuition and discernment. The Spirit whispers to him and Jordan is quick to listen."

"Incredible," Hanson breathed.

"I think I was wrong," Jordan said, looking to Paul McGurney. "I think we need to chance the window."

Margaret touched Jordan's knee. "Jordan? Are you sure? This could be dangerous."

Jordan swallowed hard and looked his grandmother in the eye. "I think she's in trouble. And I think—I think it will be dangerous."

"But wait just a little minute," Hanson said, holding up two big bear paws. "You key in a location and that window will take you there?" He glanced to Paul McGurney's portal-window and back to Jordan. Jordan looked at McGurney.

"As I said before, dear ones, I am but a messenger. I have no authority but that which is granted me. I do not control the window."

"But you think we should go, Jordan?" Zak asked. Jordan could tell his cousin would jump through the window right now if he got the go-ahead.

Jordan's heart pounded. How was it that he had become the decision-maker? Maybe it would have been best for him to keep his mouth shut until he was certain. But what was certainty? If he waited for absolute certainty, Andrea could be dead.

If she's not already…

Jordan swallowed again. "Not just yet. Let's wait a little while longer."

Zak could take it no more. He stood up and threw his hands into the air.

"Dude! This isn't a game! This is my sister we're talking about! *My sister!* I can't sit back and let that monster kill her!"

Hanson touched Zak's elbow. "Maybe we should just calm down a bit--"

"Calm down? *Calm down?* Maybe we should *get a move on* instead of just sitting around and talking about it!" Zak backed away from the couch and stood beside Paul McGurneys chair.

"Zak, please, son--" McGurney started.

Zak looked to Paul McGurney and Jordan's heart broke when he saw the desperation in Zak's eyes.

"Please—please, Mr. McGurney. Let's go—let's find Andrea."

Jordan watched McGurney's deep blue eyes study the air above Zak's head. Jordan could tell the old man had not yet been given the authority to make a decision. He was a messenger, after all. He heard from God and, at the appointed time, gave direction and insight. And Jordan's sinking heart confirmed that now was not the time. Yet Zak was forcing the issue, and Jordan could tell it was breaking the old man's heart.

"I'm sorry, Zak. I cannot say whether it is right to go after Andrea. We must be vigilant and persistent with our prayers and then we may have an answer."

Zak shook his head and ran his fingers through his hair. "But we don't have that long! I'm sorry—I—I can't wait that long." He started to back away from the sitting area. A wave of panic swept over Jordan.

"Zak, why don't you come sit down and have a drink," Margaret said, rising from her chair.

Zak's jaw clenched and Jordan knew Zak had made a decision. Jordan also knew he must stop Zak from doing what he was about to do.

"I can't sit down, Grandma. I can't do that anymore. I love my sister too much. I have to find her." He turned began to walk toward the window.

Jordan was on his feet, as was Jason Hanson.

No—please don't do this!

"Come on, buddy," Hanson called, taking a step to follow Zak. "This isn't right."

"None of us knows what's right," Zak said, advancing to the window.

Jordan didn't waste time walking. He took off in a sprint after his cousin.

"Zak—it's not time!" A piece of shattered banister tripped him up and sent him sprawling onto the floor. As he hit the ground, he knew he was powerless to stop his cousin from doing the insane.

208

"Zak, please!" Jordan heard his grandmother's voice behind him.

"I'm sorry, Grandma. But I have to get her back." Zak stepped up to the window as Jordan helplessly watched from the floor. He saw his cousin clench his jaw once, twice. Zak swallowed hard and took a deep breath.

"I'll bring her home." He swallowed once more and stepped into the window. Jordan heard his grandmother gasp behind him, heard Jason Hanson take his last heavy step. The leather from Paul McGurney's big chair creaked once, and then everything went still. A shocked silence filled Paul McGurney's big house.

No—come back, Zak. Come back through the window.

But he knew it was no use wishing Zak back. He was gone. He had made the decision to chance the window and the ancients and there was no turning back.

Jordan dropped his head to the floor and felt tears sting the corners of his eyes.

What is going on?

Chapter sixty

*A*ndrea was dead. Or at least she thought she was. All was black and her breath came in short spurts. She could feel nothing, and she couldn't seem to raise her head. But she sensed something, some imminent danger so close her brain screamed of its horror. But she could not remember. There was something blocking her memory, something lodged in the gears of her recall. It felt as if she were waking up after being gone a long time, like an entire section of the filmstrip of her life had been cut out and thrown onto the editing floor. There was a gap, black and confusing, and Andrea's brain couldn't bridge it no matter how hard she tried.

A rustle beside her made the screaming in the back of her mind strobe like a warning siren. She was not alone in the blackness. Someone was here with her. She tried to raise her head, but her neck muscles wouldn't cooperate.

What is going on?

She tried to open her mouth to address whoever lurked in the blackness, but found her lips to be sealed shut and her vocal chords debilitated.

No!

Panic seized her as she heard another rustle from the darkness. This time, a low growling sound accompanied the movement.

Please! Get me out of here!

The smell hit her nostrils and she thought she might vomit. Putrid and wet, the odor of animal dung and the metallic smell of blood filled the blackness, and Andrea knew she was no longer dealing with a *someone* but a *something.*

And then it all came back to her in a flood of terrifying images. Her abduction. The shot of serum that numbed all feeling. The firefight at Paul McGurney's house. Being carried through the streets of Babylon. The Stranger. She remembered it all and wished she could fall back into the filmstrip's gap. The void was much better than her reality; death was a welcome escape from the hell she found herself in. It was a hell of enveloping blackness and ten-foot-falls into a den of hungry lions. She would be ripped apart in a matter of minutes.

How did I survive the fall?

Andrea prayed the lions would shred her before the serum wore off and she would realize the extent of her injuries. Her bones were no doubt shattered, her blood spilled out upon the ground. For all she knew she could be dying from blood loss. But she knew she would not be so lucky. There were hungry lions lurking in the darkness, and they smelled her blood. It would only be a matter of time before they made to devour her.

Jesus—please get me out of here!

She heard another rustle, another growl. The smell was horrendous, hot and heavy like raw meat. It seemed to be on top of her—right over her face.

Please—please get me out!

All of a sudden, two yellow eyes appeared from the blackness, no more than an inch from Andrea's own. The lion let out a thunderous roar that was answered by what seemed to be ten— one hundred—one thousand lions. The sound was deafening in the closed space, an ovation of death. Andrea tried to scream, tried to call for help, but her body failed her. In the end, she was alone in the den of lions.

Dear God—make it quick!

The lion growled, and Andrea knew her death was upon her.

Chapter sixty-one

*T*he vortex of time washes over the Stranger. It is a balm that soothes the assassin after a victorious mission. There is nothing better than victory. The blasted Knowledge had taken much ground when the Opposition had failed, but the Stranger is evening the playing field by dividing the brats one by one. The one called Andrea is properly stashed in the ancients, and the Stranger is headed to present-day Ohio to destroy the pack leader called Todd. With the oldest and the youngest properly dead, the rest will fall like dominoes. Their hope will be decimated, their resolve will be gone. The Stranger chuckles as the centuries fly by.

Finding a portal to the present had been easy. No doubt the master had allowed one to materialize after the success of the Stranger's mission. The Stranger had been drawn to a merchant's tent and found it to be a portal to the present. It was really that simple. The master never ceases to amaze the Stranger. And now the master is preparing the way for another kill.

The Stranger smiles. The one called Todd will be dead before he knows what hit him.

Chapter sixty-two

"Say that again—he *went after* Andrea?" Todd was on his feet, pacing his living room and wishing he had an extra hand with which to pull out his hair.

"That's exactly what I said," Jordan replied from Colorado. Todd heard the panic in his brother's voice and desperately wanted to be there to try to make things right. His family was disintegrating around him; first Andrea had been taken captive by the Stranger, and now Zak had foolishly traveled to the ancients by himself to get her back. Todd felt so helpless in Ohio he could scream.

"Are you guys going after him? What does Mr. McGurney say?"

"He just keeps shaking his head and saying it wasn't time," Jordan said. "I don't like this, Todd. Zak could be anywhere."

Todd kicked the sofa. He had forgotten that the portal window could travel to anywhere and anywhen. Zak's chance of ending up where and when Andrea was was nearly impossible. Add the fact that Mr. McGurney kept saying it wasn't yet time to go after Andrea, and Zak was in a world of hurt.

"I don't know what to tell you, Jordan. I wish I was there."

"I still have Grandma, Hanson and Mr. McGurney," Jordan said.

Todd froze. "Hanson? Who's Hanson? Jordan, you have to be careful! Hanson could be the--"

"He's not the Stranger, Todd. Trust me. I'll tell you all about Hanson sometime, but right now we need to think about Andrea and Zak. Todd—I think you need to tell Mom and Dad and Aunt Patty."

"I'm already ahead of you on that one. Mom and Dad should be home in a little bit, and I already called Aunt Patty and told her she needed to come by the house after she got off work. I told Mom already, though."

"And?"

"She didn't believe me at first, but I think she might now."

Jordan sighed. "We don't have time for this, Todd! I'm going to hang up with you and call the three of them and tell them to leave work immediately. We don't have time to wait for them to believe."

"I can't believe it got this bad, Jordan," Todd said, feeling tears pool in the corners of his eyes. "I can't believe this."

Jordan didn't speak for a moment. Todd heard him sniffle and he knew Jordan was crying, too.

"Believe it, Todd. It got really bad really fast. We need all hands on deck, here. We need everybody we can. I think we're going to have to fight our way out of this one."

Todd swallowed hard. He felt as if he were on a ship that was about to go down and was powerless to stop it. He clenched his jaw and warred with the tears that wanted to stream down his face.

"Then we fight, Jordan."

Jordan sniffled again and said nothing.

"We'll be to Colorado soon. Don't do anything rash until we get there."

"Todd? Be safe, OK? We don't exactly have tabs on the Stranger right now."

"If he showed up right now I think I'd rip him apart, one good

215

arm and all."

A silence settled between them, but it spoke louder than any of their words had.

"Call Mom and Dad and Aunt Patty. Tell them," Todd said softly. "And be safe."

Chapter sixty-three

Zak realized his mistake as soon as he felt the void of time envelop him. He had no business trekking to the ancients alone and unarmed. And, to make matters worse, he had no idea how to get back to the present.

I shouldn't have been so rash!

Call it a character flaw or something to work on, but in stressful situations, Zak tended to lose his head. He had been getting better at keeping his cool and thinking things through, but when no one had been able to step forward to make a sound decision regarding rescuing Andrea in the ancients, his old self had taken over. His old self emerged when he dropped his guard and allowed instincts and emotions to rule his decisions instead of prayerful consideration.

I wish I would have stayed with the others…

Zak's surroundings began to come into focus, and the first thing he felt was the bite of icy wind. His hair was whipped by the stuff, and a mist of equally icy water sprayed his face.

Oh, no.

The ground pitched back and forth, and before the rest of his surroundings even came into focus, Zak knew he was on a boat.

The Stranger took Andrea to sea?

Another horrible realization washed over him.

This might be all wrong. This might not be where the Stranger took Andrea!

Zak ran his hands through his now damp hair and felt the isolation stab him in the gut. He was alone. No one was here to save him should he fall into trouble. He had made a dreadful mistake. Hadn't Paul McGurney said something about not knowing where the window portal led until it was revealed to him?

I jumped the gun...

His surroundings came into complete focus and Zak saw he most certainly was on a boat in the middle of a choppy sea. His stomach roiled when he thought back to Todd's encounter on the Sea of Galilee. Sure, Todd had ended up seeing Jesus walking on the water, but the ordeal had been terrifying. The familiar burn in Zak's heart whenever Jesus was near was not present. Zak knew this was bad. Turning in a complete circle, Zak's heart dropped when he saw no land on the horizon.

I wish I wasn't alone!

A boom of thunder made him jump. Looking up, Zak realized his situation was about to get much worse. Overhead, one of the blackest skies Zak had ever seen stretched for miles. A lick of lightning, bright and close, made his mind flash to Devil's Playground the previous summer. Ever since the ordeal on the mountain, Zak had been petrified of lightning.

I'm not safe! I need to get below deck!

The wind was picking up, and for the first time Zak saw crewmembers desperately scrambling to prepare the boat for the siege of a storm. Their dress gave no clues as to where and when Zak might be, as their clothes were primitive and handmade like all the others' were in the places he had been. No one had seen him yet, and Zak wondered whether he was visible at all to the ancient sailors. Another boom of thunder followed by an extraordinary flash of lightning made Zak realize he had other things to worry about

I need to find shelter!

The boat pitched to the right and Zak was thrown from his feet. His left knee hit the wood deck hard, and for a moment he was in too much pain to gather himself to his feet.

I never should have come!

As he waited for the pain to stop flaring in his knee, Zak knew beyond a shadow of a doubt that this was not where he'd find Andrea. Although he couldn't confirm his suspicions, he sensed it nonetheless. He was on his own.

Zak struggled to his feet as the boat danced beneath him. This storm was going to be a whopper, and Zak knew he had better find some shelter or at least something to hold onto or he would be at the mercy of the waves. Another heavy crack of thunder and a dangerous bolt of lightning made his mind race with panic. Steadying himself as best he could, he hurriedly made his way to where a pile of cargo was stashed and tied down under a canvas covering. Falling once and banging his throbbing knee again, Zak felt the terror grip him like vise.

I'm going to die here! I'm never going to get back home!

The wind picked up and swirled about the boat with a shrill whistle. Heavy raindrops began to pelt the deck, and Zak almost face-planted again before reaching the cargo.

Almost there...

The boat canted to the right again and Zak lost his balance. Grasping at the cargo covering, he tossed up a prayer of thankfulness when his hand found purchase and he was able to pull himself into a small slot beside the cargo.

I need to get out of here! This isn't where I'm supposed to be!

Zak took a moment to collect his thoughts. Swiping his wet hair back, he swallowed hard as the canvas was bombarded by machinegun rain.

What should I do? It's not like I have a choice but to stay right where I am.

Zak felt the boat being assaulted by the waves. He scrunched

219

himself into the fetal position and rested the back of his head against a wooden crate. It had all come to this, then. This is how he would die; curled into a ball underneath a flimsy shelter while a storm threatened to take him and the boat under.

This can't be it! After all we've been through—after all we've experienced—this is how it ends for me?

A huge blast of thunder cannoned and even through clenched eyelids Zak could see the lightning. The boat was buffeted and slapped by the waves in such a way that Zak knew the inevitable was coming. And he didn't have to wait long.

All of a sudden the ties that held the canvas covering in place broke free. The frayed ropes flapped in the wind like demented snakes, and the cargo was thrown to the left and to the right. A large basket of coconuts fell onto Zak's stomach, knocking his wind away. He gasped for breath as the rain fell hard. The boat hit another powerful wave, and, for a moment, Zak was airborne.

No! No—please!

He landed hard against the boat's side, realizing nothing separated him from the churning water but a few wooden boards. Fighting to regain his breath, he rolled onto his stomach and tried to get to his feet. He couldn't have made a worse decision. As he pushed himself onto his knees and then onto his feet, the boat was rocked by another wave. Zak was thrown back against the side of the boat, the wood biting into his back and making him cry out into the shrill wind. For a moment, Zak leaned against the boat's side, paralyzed by the pain. He looked out across the boat's deck and saw that the rest of the crewmembers were holding on for dear life. When he saw them clinging to whatever sturdy objects they could, Zak panicked.

I have to get away from the side! I have to find something to—

The boat slammed against another wave and Zak found himself airborne again. His mind flashed with the notion that something wasn't right; he should be slamming against the deck as he had the first time. It was when he hit the churning water and caught one last glimpse of the boat that he knew death had found him.

Zak instinctively took a breath and felt his lungs burn with the icy seawater. The moment before the blackness overtook him, he realized his mistake for coming to the ancients alone had been a fatal one.

Zak sunk below the waves and was lost in the black sea.

Chapter sixty-four

"Todd's not making it up, Mom! *I'm* not making it up!" Jordan shouted into his cell phone. He paced the rug in front of Paul McGurney's leather couch and swiped his hand through his hair.

"Just calm down, honey," Jordan's mother said on the other end of the line. "Now, tell me what happened again."

"Mom. Please. Listen to me," Jordan began, trying to stay calm. Why was this so hard to understand? Andrea had been kidnapped and now Zak had foolishly ventured into the ancients alone. "I'm telling you that Andrea's been abducted by a crazy killer who took her back in time. Zak followed them, and now he's gone, too."

"And they both went through a window?"

"Yes, Mom! I know it sounds wacked out, but it's true. And we need you guys to get here ASAP! You might not be safe!"

His mother went silent on the other line. Jordan knew he had gotten to her. She was his first call in the progression of three. He had to make her believe so his father would believe. If Jordan were his mother, it'd be extremely hard to blow off two sons who had told her the same thing concerning Andrea, no matter how outlandish it sounded. And now Zak was gone. He couldn't imagine what was going through his mother's head.

"Jordan?" Donna Lawrence said softly. "Call your father. Tell him what you told me. I'm going to search online for airfare. We'll be out there as soon as possible."

Thank you! Thank you!

"Mom, I'm serious about you guys not being safe. Leave work and get home

with Todd. The Stranger's out there somewhere."

He heard his mother's breath catch, and Jordan wished he could give her a hug. This was a lot of bad information in one dose.

"OK, Jordan. I love you. I may not understand everything, but I believe you. Please, be safe."

"I'll try, Mom. I love you, too."

"Can you put your grandma on? I'd like to talk to her real quick."

Jordan passed his cell phone to his grandmother, who had been listening to the entire conversation from the couch.

"It'll all be OK, Jordan," Margaret said as she took the phone. "It will all be OK."

I hope you're right. I want to believe—but it's so hard!

Chapter sixty-five

*T*he Stranger stalks the forest on the outskirts of Infinity.
This mission is to come to Ohio and obliterate the one
called Todd before the worthless brat has a chance
to connect with the other Knowledge-bearers in Colorado. The
Stranger knows Infinity well. This forest has been the assassin's
stalking ground before. The Stranger also knows that when you
meet a victim on his own playing field, the victim is more confident and willing to fight. The Opposition found that one out the
hard way.

The Stranger will wait until night provides the stealth cloak
needed for the mission to proceed. The assassin knows the
Opposition failed in one other regard; he did not try to eliminate
the brats' family in order to make things easier for himself. The
Stranger will not make this mistake. The assassin is unfazed at
the thought of more dead bodies. A dead body is nothing to be
afraid of or lose tears over. Besides, dead bodies only become
that way when they get in the way of the mission at hand. And the
one called Todd's parents are in the way.

The Stranger stops walking and sits against a tree. The
assassin is deep enough into the forest that detection from the
nearby park or highway is impossible. The Stranger removes the
heavy mask which conceals the assassin's face. This is the first

time in as long the Stranger can remember that the Stranger has been able to remove the mask while on a mission. The breeze feels good against the Stranger's face, and the assassin chuckles. If only the children knew what the Stranger's face looks like! The concealment makes it so much worse for them. From the Stranger's perspective, people often fear what they cannot see. The mask is as powerful a weapon as the Stranger possesses.

The Stranger thinks of the small brat, the one called Andrea. The serum will be wearing off by now, and the lions are very hungry. The assassin wonders if the small child will even put up a fight or just allow herself to be consumed by the lions. That is another thing the Stranger doesn't understand about people. Most people are willing to just roll over and die without a fight. Even Christians buy into the notion that when trials come and things get hard it is better to succumb to the struggles than to fight their way out. The Stranger recalls a verse from the wretched Scriptures that says the thief comes to steal, kill and destroy. Well, the Stranger is the thief and the stealing, killing and destroying are underway. But if Christians would only consider the rest of the verse, the Stranger knows the killing missions would become much tougher. The rest of the verse makes the Stranger cringe, for it states that I, Jesus, come to give abundant life. The Stranger shudders. There are two very different parts to that particular verse. Death and life. Terror and peace. A life of being stalked and a life of stalking. If Christians truly knew the power they possessed...

The Stranger doesn't want to think of such things anymore. Besides, the brats are too stupid to realize their power. They are too focused on being terrified to realize they possess an authority that could call ten thousand angels to their aid. The Fiends are at work on the brats, and that will be enough to keep them thinking they are going to die at any moment. Right now, the Stranger must focus on the mission at hand. The Stranger will eliminate Todd and his family and then make a beeline to Colorado to finish the job. The master will be so proud. Where the Opposition had been unable, the Stranger will come through. Too many things are going the Stranger's way for failure to be an option. There is killing to be done, and much of it.

Chapter sixty-six

*T*he lion growled, and Andrea thought she might pass out. In many ways she thought that would be better. Let the lions devour her while she was dead to the world.

The lion pawed at her, one of its razor claws tearing the sleeve of her pajama top. Andrea's brain sent off flares when she felt the claw rake the flesh of her arm.

Oh, no! No—I can feel it! The serum is wearing off!

Another lion circled the darkness above Andrea's head. She felt the wind the lion made tickle her hair and cool her forehead. She started to panic.

Of all times for the serum to wear off! No, please! I don't want to feel this!

The lion above her head roared and pawed at her hair. Some of it became tangled in the lion's claws and ripped out of her scalp. She screamed.

The sound of her own voice startled her. She hadn't expected anything to come out of her vocal chords, and when it did, she wasn't ready for it. The lion on top of her apparently wasn't expecting it either, for it flinched at her scream and swiped a paw at her face. One of the lion's claws bit into the side of her nose and tore the flesh off with sickening ease.

They are just going to play with me for awhile! Oh—I can't take it! Please, God, make it quick!

An enormous flare of pain exploded in Andrea's left shoulder. Another of the same kind ignited in her left knee. Andrea screamed as loud as she could. The pain was so intense, so severe. It was unlike anything she had experienced before.

It's from the fall—the serum is wearing off and now I'm feeling the pain from the fall!

Another lion came out of the thick blackness and started to lap up something on the ground beside her wounded knee. Its tongue made a disgusting slurping sound in the enclosed space, and Andrea didn't have to be a rocket scientist to know what the lion was lapping up.

It's my blood. The lion is lapping up my blood.

Andrea was in so much pain she thought she might die of it rather than at the sharp teeth and claws of the lions. Her left hip flared in searing pain, and she now knew her left side had taken the brunt of the fall before her momentum had rolled her onto her back.

How many bones did I break? My hip has to be shattered!

The lion at her knee continued to lap up her blood. Andrea heard another tongue begin to slap against the hard ground, and then another. She didn't want to think how much blood she had actually lost—*was* losing. The thought of it made her lightheaded.

Dear God, take me now!

Andrea tried moving her right arm and realized she had locomotion. The sudden movement made one of the lions swipe at her wounded leg, the claws slicing her pajama pants and flesh like warm butter. She cried out and felt a scratchy tongue begin to greedily lick the wound.

Her right arm now rested on her stomach, there to ward off any lion that wanted to attack her face. She tested her left arm and realized quickly that it was useless to her. A hot streak of

228

pain sizzled from her shoulder to her fingertips, and Andrea knew her shoulder was out of socket. She whimpered and thought of Todd lying at third base, his arm grotesquely out to his side, his shoulder completely dislodged and useless. That was her now. Except she was surrounded by lions that lapped at her blood and tore her flesh.

One of the lions grew restless with lapping up her blood and decided to test the taste of her flesh. Andrea felt sharp teeth lining up on her left calf. When the lion clamped down and punctured her skin, she screamed. The lion wasn't fazed by her blood-curdling shriek, and proceeded to rip off a chunk of her flesh. Andrea swatted the air with her right arm as the tears streamed from her eyes.

Oh, dear Jesus! Oh, God help me!

Through the screaming pain, Andrea wondered how much muscle the lion had taken from her. The bite felt deep, the blood no doubt flowing in rivers. She felt the lion's sandpaper tongue on the deep wound and knew he would bite again. Another tongue joined, and Andrea heard a scuffle in the darkness. The lions were fighting each other for the next bite.

Please—let me die now! Please, I'm ready!

A scraping sound from above made Andrea tense. The lions stopped pawing and licking her and looked toward the sound. A slice of moonlight broke the darkness of the den and, for the first time, Andrea raised her head and counted the lions. Ten lions surrounded her with two other females lying in the corner, apparently disinterested in human meat. Andrea's stomach turned when she saw that six out of the ten lions had red mouths, her own blood smeared onto their noses and fur. Another scraping sound from above made one of the lions growl.

Someone is here! I'll get out of here!

A flare of pain made Andrea drop her head. Her shoulder was throbbing, her knee and hip pulsed with her every heartbeat. But it was the wound on her calf where the flesh had been ripped away that really hurt. She groaned in agony as the planks overhead were being removed, allowing moonlight to pierce the darkness. The stars overhead were little comfort, though. Her calf was on fire, and she knew she had to take a look at the damage.

Andrea lifted her head and her right hand trembled. Looking would make it worse, she knew. Looking would only cause the pain to become more severe. But she had to know what her leg looked like, had to know what the lion had done. She moved her leg a little so she could see the whole wound, and a ripple of pain made her wince.

Just look—you have to look.

Andrea looked at her leg and saw she was missing a six-inch portion of her skin. What was worse, her muscle was exposed, some of it shredded and torn like a chopped-up chicken breast. Blood was puddled under the wound, and it continued to flow out of her torn flesh at an alarming rate. Andrea felt her stomach gurgle, and she turned her head and vomited onto the ground. The pain was horrendous! Her leg was destroyed!

Tears streamed down her cheeks as the fifth and final plank was removed. More light fell into the den, but she didn't care. Her only concern was the pain. She opened her mouth and screamed as loud as she could, hoping whoever was on the surface would hear her and save her.

"Help me! Help me, please!"

Her own voice frightened her. It sounded like someone whose desperation and will to live was at its end.

Andrea heard voices from above, and she continued to scream.

"Help me! There're killing me! Please!"

A head peered into the den, its facial features unreadable in the darkness.

"Is someone down there?"

If Andrea hadn't already been crying, she would have wept at the sound of the voice. Here was her safety! Here was her help!

230

Andrea composed herself the best she could and swatted at a lion that began to lap up her vomit.

"Yes! Please! Get me out of here!"

Another head appeared in the opening and called to her.

"Are you hurt?"

"Yes! The lions—they're *eating me*!"

The two heads turned to each other, and, to Andrea's horror, began to laugh.

"Then it serves you right!" one of the heads called. "You aren't in the lion's den for nothing!"

The other head stopped laughing. "And you're about to get company!" The two heads disappeared from sight.

Andrea went ballistic. "No! Please! You don't understand! I was kidnapped! I shouldn't be here at all!" She clenched her eyes shut and beat the ground with her good hand.

No! No! No! Why is this happening?! Why are they not saving me?!

A loud thump to her left jolted her. The lions backed away and growled. Andrea turned to the sound and was horrified to see another person had been dropped into the den of lions.

Now it was too much. Now she broke completely. She yelled and screamed and beat the ground with her hand. She thrashed and kicked and allowed the searing pain to overtake her. What did it matter anymore? What did it matter if she was in pain? She was going to die anyway. How could human beings do this to each other?

The lions circled her once more, some going over to investigate the new food source that had been dropped from above. The new person was too far away for Andrea to clearly see, but she knew whoever it was had not moved. The fall must have knocked the person out.

The men on the surface were closing the opening again, and the light was extinguished faster than it had come. This time, a large stone was rolled over the opening, and a sense of utter hopelessness washed over her.

I wish I could see the others one last time…

But she didn't have time to complete her thought. A lion sniffed the wound on her calf and clamped down with its jaws of death.

Andrea passed out from the pain.

Chapter sixty-seven

Margaret stood up from the floor and heard her knees pop in protest. From his big leather chair, Paul McGurney smiled.

"My knees aren't as young as they used to be," Margaret said, straightening her legs and stretching her calves.

"Maybe not as young, but much more powerful," McGurney said with a glint in his eye.

Margaret completely agreed with the old man's assessment. One year ago she would never have found herself seeking God on her knees, not to mention praying itself. But she had grown so much over the past nine months. It was as if she were a new-born who had to first learn to crawl and then to walk. The things she was learning and experiencing in her prayer life and through her worship sessions were amazing. And one thing she learned quickly was that she had a heart for prayer. When she earnestly sought God's hand, she hit the floor, old knees or not. And that is what she had been doing for over three hours on Andrea's and Zak's behalf.

"Has God laid an answer on your heart?" Jordan asked, standing up from the couch where he had been seeking God in his own prayer time.

Margaret shook her head. "I'm afraid not, Jordan."

Jordan rubbed the bridge of his nose with his fingers. "Me, neither."

Jason Hanson spoke from the loveseat. "Uh—I know I'm new at all this stuff, but—but something Mr. McGurney said to me when I first got here has been slamming around in my brain for quite awhile."

Margaret saw Jordan perk up. "And? What is it?"

Hanson looked at Paul McGurney, who sat with his hands folded over his belly, a knowing smile on his face.

"Well—it looks like Mr. McGurney already knows what I'm gonna say."

Paul McGurney chuckled. "I have a hunch, son. I, too, have been seeking the Lord's wisdom. And He has spoken a phrase in reference of you."

Hanson nodded. "Yeah—yeah, maybe. I guess—I mean I could be wrong--"

"Say it!" Margaret and Jordan shouted in unison.

Hanson swallowed and scratched the back of his head. "Um, OK. You know how Mr. McGurney said I was a bridge? Well—I think I'm supposed to go through the window to get Zak and Andrea back."

Margaret sucked in a breath and looked at Paul McGurney. Could they risk another body through the window when the Stranger could be anywhere?

McGurney chuckled. "I was hoping you'd say that."

Jordan held up his hands. "Wait, wait, wait. So Jason here is supposed to go through the window alone? Isn't that what we told Zak *not* to do?"

McGurney nodded. "It is precisely what we told Zak not to do."

Margaret watched her grandson look at everyone in the room as though he was missing something.

"So—why is Jason going by himself?"

The old man smiled. "Because now is the appointed time.

Three hours ago it was not."

Jordan threw up his hands. "I wish I understood God's timing."

Paul McGurney laughed. "Don't we all, son. Don't we all."

The reference to time triggered something in Margaret's mind.

"Speaking of time, Jordan, didn't you and Zak tell me that the portal to the ancients doesn't play by the laws of the clock?"

Jordan scrunched his nose. "What do you mean?"

"I mean, didn't you tell me that time passes quicker in the ancients than it does in the present?"

Jordan nodded. "Yeah, sometimes. The portal doesn't always play by the rules. Sometimes the same time elapses in both worlds, and sometimes it doesn't. Sometimes it actually slows down, believe it or not."

Hanson picked up Margaret's line of thought. "So, what you're saying is that when I show up in the ancients, I could be hours or days behind Andrea and Zak? Or I could even show up before they get there?"

Jordan nodded.

Hanson shook his head. "Talk about changing time zones!"

"Basically, Jason, you are going in blind," Margaret said. She looked to Paul McGurney. "No pun intended."

McGurney held up a timeless hand. "I follow."

Hanson stood up. "Well, I guess I'm wasting time here. I better get through the window, huh?"

Paul McGurney slowly stood from his big chair. "But first, dear one, let us lay hands on you and pray for your strength and safety."

"I'm all for that," Hanson said. He looked at Margaret. "Oh, by the way. I know it's not the most opportune time to tell you this, but your cabin needs to be rewired. The wiring might be older than Mr. McGurney, here."

Margaret laughed, as did the others. It felt good to laugh.

Laughing was much better than crying.

The three remaining Colorado dwellers laid hands on Jason Hanson, and he left through the window portal to join the world of the ancients.

Chapter sixty-eight

Zak rolled onto his stomach and vomited what seemed to be a gallon of water. His lungs burned, and he felt weak all over.

What happened?

Zak clenched his eyes shut as a searing pain tore through his skull. A migraine like he'd never experienced erupted from his brain's core and wrapped its fiery tentacles around the back of his head and down his neck. He turned his head and retched again.

Where am I? What happened?

It came back to him in an instant. Going through the window. The violent storm. Being tossed from the boat. Sinking into the turbulent sea…

Sinking into the sea!?

Zak opened his eyes and gritted his teeth against the pulsing pain. Blackness stared back at him, and for a terrifying moment, Zak thought he had died. A putrid smell hit his nostrils, and Zak gagged and tried to keep his stomach from spilling forth once again. The odor was nasty, dead fish and other decomposing substances. The smell was thick and heavy, the air humid and damp as if it were trapped in a concrete box.

What—where am I?

Zak raised himself to his knees despite the torrent of pain sizzling in his head. When he moved, he heard the unmistakable splash of water. For the first time, Zak realized he was kneeling in some watery substance. Putting a hand into the water, Zak felt nameless particles bounce off his skin. His stomach threatened to empty again.

I need to get out of here—wherever here is!

All of a sudden, a flash of light erupted overhead. An incredible noise accompanied the new light, like an industrial air hose at full power. Zak tensed when he felt the watery substance puddled beneath him being lifted into the air. To his surprise, the water was expelled from the new hole in the ceiling, shot out like a cannon with an incredibly loud rushing sound. Zak was thrown from his knees onto his back as an intense rush of hot hair whooshed through the enclosed space. The sound was deafening, and Zak threw his hands to his ears and covered them as the hole in the ceiling closed again and the water that had not been shot out rained back down upon him.

What is going on?

The light had illuminated his surroundings for a brief moment, and Zak had seen nothing but slimy walls and floating sea plants. He wondered if he might be deep in some watery cave.

If the water's coming in, it has to go out…

Zak raised himself to his knees and then to his feet, fighting to ignore the flares of pain that exploded in his brain. His shoes felt like balls of lead, as they were soaked through with seawater. He contemplated taking them off before realizing doing so would be a dumb idea.

I don't want to step on a sharp rock or something worse.

Zak took a tentative step and water swished underfoot. The surrounding blackness seemed infinite, and Zak felt a lump of fear lodge in his throat.

I don't even know where I'm going! I have no idea which way is the right way!

Zak paused and slicked his wet hair back on his head. How

had he even gotten here? The storm had been so violent, the water so turbulent, that his chances of survival had to have been nonexistent. But somehow, someway, he was still alive. But the enormity of being alive hit him like a punch in the gut.

What does it matter if I'm alive? I'm alone and in the dark. I could be walking into something far worse than the storm and I don't even know it.

Zak took another step forward and found the blackness to be more than disorienting. He clenched his eyes shut and opened them again.

How am I going to know if I'm going the right way?

Despite his qualms, Zak took another step forward. He had to move, had to find a light. Sitting in the wet darkness wouldn't get him back to his family. Or save Andrea from the clutches of the Stranger, should he be in the right time and place. He seriously doubted the latter; he had stubbornly chanced the window when the time had not yet been ripe. What had he been thinking? He took another step forward.

"I wouldn't go that way."

Zak nearly fainted from terror. The voice came out of the blackness so unexpectedly that Zak fell to his knees. The realization that he wasn't alone in the blackness petrified him.

Zak swallowed, and, against his better judgment, spoke into the darkness.

"H-hello? Who's there?"

"Someone who's in the same boat you are," the male voice answered. To Zak's surprise, the speaker chuckled. "I guess we aren't in the boat anymore, are we?"

Zak felt some of his fear evaporate. The speaker had chuckled, and his voice hadn't been menacing. In fact, his voice has been calm and kind.

"Then where are we?" Zak asked, standing up again.

"I wouldn't move around much if I were you," the voice said. "You're too close to the stomach the way it is."

What?!

"I don't understand," Zak said. "What do you mean, 'the stomach.'?"

The voice laughed. "You don't have any idea where you are, do you?"

"N-no. Please—tell me how to get out of here."

"If I knew, I wouldn't be sitting here in the dark," the voice said. Zak heard water slosh about five feet to his right. The person was closer than he had first thought.

"But you do know, right?" Zak turned to where he thought the person might be and spoke into the darkness. His heart was thundering so loudly he wondered if the faceless speaker could hear it.

The man chuckled again. "Oh, I know, alright. But let me introduce myself, first. My name's Jonah."

Zak's stomach dropped to his feet. He'd heard this story before. And he knew exactly where he was.

Oh, please, God—no!

Chapter sixty-nine

*T*he silence was so profound it was almost deafening.

Say something—someone speak!

Todd looked around his living room and saw three pale faces staring back at him. Not staring back at him, really, but through him into some frightening imagination of what could be transpiring with Zak and Andrea. His Aunt Patty was the worst. She sat in the loveseat and shivered with terror. Her mascara ran down her face in inky rivulets, and from time to time Todd's mother would pass her a box of tissues. And why wouldn't she be obliterated by the news? Both her children were in the ancients, one in definite peril at the hands of the Stranger, and one alone as can be with no clues as to his whereabouts.

Somebody break the silence!

Todd had received a text from Jordan telling him that Jason Hanson had voluntarily gone through the portal window. Jordan had written something about Hanson being a bridge, but Todd couldn't care less about the specifics. At the most, Todd thought Hanson's passage through the window screamed of desperation, and he had texted Jordan back as much. Jordan had written back that he would explain later, and Todd had to be OK with that, because he had bigger fish to fry in Infinity. Jordan had called all the adults and relayed the news, and now they sat in the

Lawrences' living room deliberating about what they should do next. Todd thought the next course of action was fairly obvious: get to Colorado, and fast.

"So, when are we leaving?" Todd asked, his patience finally up. "I mean, we're past the point of you guys not believing us. Grandma even confirmed it."

"The earliest flight I can find is for six o'clock tomorrow morning," Todd's mother said, snapping out of her trance-like state. "Out of Toledo."

"Can't we ask someone who has a small airplane? What about Norris Tannenbaum from church?" Todd was desperate to get into the air. Driving would get them there slower than flying, at this point, even if they were to ignore speed limits.

"Norris flew his plane to Kentucky yesterday," Bill Lawrence said from his spot in the recliner. "He has family down there."

"There has to be some other way!" Todd said, looking frantically looking about the room. "They're in trouble in Colorado!"

"We have no other option but to wait for the flight tomorrow morning," Donna Lawrence said. "Patty, are you going to be OK? Do you want to lie down?"

Todd watched his Aunt Patty struggle to respond. It broke his heart to see his aunt so emotionally broken.

"I'm fine. My babies are going to have to be strong until we get there."

"We should pray," Todd's father said, leaning forward in his recliner. "We should pray that the electrician finds Andrea and Zak and brings them home."

With that, the foursome fell into a deep prayer session. Even though Todd's mother had not yet taken the steps to become a Christian, she prayed fervently for God's protection and hand to be upon the children. While Todd waited for his turn to pray aloud, he prayed in his spirit for God to perform a miracle.

Jesus—we need You now! We need Your hedge of protection to surround Zak and Andrea and all the rest of us. We need Your

242

peace and Your power, Your knowledge and wisdom. Go before us and follow behind us. Take our fear away with the sweep of Your mighty hand. You are God, and we are not. We love You, and we thank You for what You are going to do. We praise Your name and await Your move. Amen.

Chapter seventy

*T*he three vile Fiends were in transit. After the humiliating defeat at Paul McGurney's house on the hill, the Fiends found themselves dispatched back to Infinity, Ohio, by a very angry and very menacing Father of Lies. As they swooped into Northwest Ohio, the Fiends remembered their defeat the last time they had ventured here. The one called Todd had proved to be too much for them, as the blasted boy had taken authority in Christ and dispelled them. But now the tides had turned. Todd would be distracted by the chaos in Colorado and he and his wretched family would be vulnerable to attack. Horse-face smirked at this.

Christians are so dense! If only they would realize that distraction was one of the master's favorite weapons, they would be more potent and powerful!

Fly-face looked to Horse-face and asked the same question he'd asked at the onset of the journey.

"So, what is our objective here? We were thwarted once before, and I don't want to feel that kind of pain again."

Horse-face scowled at him. "I've told you all this before! The Stranger is planning an attack on the Lawrence house and we must pave the way."

"I can't wait to pay that little brat back," Mosquito-face said with a snarl. "He deserves what's coming to him."

"They're already distracted," Horse-face said. "It's our job to make sure they stay that way."

Mosquito-face laughed. "The master never tires of that one, does he?"

Horse-face allowed himself a smile. "Why fix something that isn't broken? These Knowledge-bearers have one-track minds. They see only what's in front of them, and they miss the bigger picture."

"Time to build some walls," Fly-face said with a raspy laugh. "The more walls they build the less they can see through the windows."

The three Fiends reached Infinity as darkness fell over the town.

Chapter seventy-one

*A*ndrea felt the sizzling pain the moment she came to. Her whole body seemed ripped in two, torn apart by ferocious feline teeth. Her calf felt shredded, and her bones felt out of joint and fractured. Her shoulder throbbed, her hip felt shattered and her kneecap felt cracked in two. The pain was so intense, so immediate, that Andrea wished she could fall back into blissful sleep.

Andrea moaned and swallowed. A low rumbling sound filled her ears, and for a fleeting moment Andrea wondered if a motor was running nearby. Realizing the absurdity of the thought made her almost chuckle.

"There, there, child. It will be all right."

Andrea's eyes flew open at the sound of the voice. To her astonishment, she found herself looking up into the face of a young man. Through the darkness, Andrea could just make out the features of his thin, yet kind face. The man was smiling at her.

This is the guy who was dropped in here with me! How did he not break every bone in his body! And who is he?

Andrea opened her mouth to speak but found she could not form words. The inside of her mouth was dry as sand, and she swallowed in an attempt to moisten it even a little.

I'm so thirsty...

"Shh, you don't have to speak," the young man said, the smile still on his youthful, hairless face. "I'm Daniel. I guess you can say I'm your den mate."

Daniel?

The name struck a chord with Andrea, but she couldn't place it. Despite Daniel's advising her not to speak, Andrea swallowed again and found her words. The low rumbling sound seemed to fill the lion's den.

Lions! Where are they?!

"D-Daniel?"

The young man brought his face closer to hers so that now she could see him more clearly.

"Yes?"

"Th-the lions. Wh-where--" but Andrea could not finish. Speaking required too much strength, and she could all but feel the energy seeping out of her body. She must have lost a lot of blood. The thought set off warning sirens at the back of her brain.

Daniel chuckled. "The lions? They're still here."

The we're still doomed! They'll rip us apart!

Andrea's heart beat on overdrive. Every heartbeat sent a current of pain throughout her body. She wondered how long she could last. She had lost an enormous amount of blood, her level of thirst was extraordinary, and the lions were still in the den. To say the scales weren't balanced her favor would be the understatement of the century.

"Th-they're still here?" Andrea managed.

Daniel nodded. He gently lifted Andrea's head from the ground as the low rumbling sound seemed to intensify. "Here, let me show you."

Daniel gently tilted Andrea up so she could peer into the darkness. The first thing she noticed was that he had wrapped a piece of material around her calf, probably from his own clothing, to stop her bleeding. It was what she saw next that nearly sent her back into her faint.

No way! How did he do that?

"How did you…?" But Andrea could not complete her question. The sight before her was too surreal to waste words on. For surrounding Andrea and Daniel in a crescent moon semi-circle lay the ten lions. These huge cats—these wild savages—these kings and queens of the jungle—were now as tame and as gentle as kitty cats. They looked at the two humans through yellow eyes not of hunger and brutality, but of curiosity and playfulness. How had Daniel done all this? The low rumbling continued to fill the den.

What is that sound? Are we still in trouble?

And then it hit Andrea. The low rumbling sound she heard was ten ferocious beasts *purring*. If it wouldn't have sent shrieks of pain throughout her body, Andrea would have laughed. *Purring*! The lions were *purring*!"

"It's amazing, isn't it?" Daniel said, gently lowering Andrea's head back into his lap. "They seem like kittens."

"H-how did you do that?" Andrea asked, looking up at her hero.

Daniel shook his head. "It wasn't me. I had nothing to do with it. I cried out to God and He shut the lions' mouths."

Andrea didn't need any help believing Daniel's claim. The things she had seen and experienced over the last year were enough to give Daniel's testimony validity. But even though she had seen and experienced God's move before, she still had trouble finding her breath. The thought of God taming the lions was amazing. But Andrea had another question.

"Why are you even in here? Are you a criminal or something?"

Daniel shook his head. "I'm no criminal. That is, unless you count praying to my God a crime. I'm in here because I refused to pray to any other god but the One True God, despite a decree issued by King Darius stating that for thirty days no one was allowed to pray to anyone other than him." Daniel shook his head again. "You see, it was a trap. There are some people who don't like the way I've risen to my position. The king wanted to set me over the entire kingdom, and some of the other officials and administrators didn't like it. So, to make a long story short, they came to the king with the decree I mentioned, knowing full well that I would not abide by it. My God—the God Who shut the mouths of these lions—is the God of gods. When a king issues a decree, it is binding. So, these officials and administrators arrested me on the grounds of praying to God instead of to the king. The punishment was the lions' den, and here I am."

Andrea's thirst was great, and she struggled to find words.

"B-but that's not fair."

Daniel chuckled. "That's what I thought. But it is what it is. I wouldn't have it any other way. I would gladly be devoured by the lions for the sake of my God."

Andrea swallowed, trying to find blessed moisture. "But you're not dead. And, obviously, you're not hurt. How did you make it through that fall without breaking anything?"

Daniel chuckled again. "Oh, I'm bruised, believe me. I think I might have a few broken ribs. But other than that, I'm unharmed."

"And—and you came over to me and wrapped something around my leg?"

"The lions were all over you," Daniel said. "That's when I cried out to God, and He shut the mouths of the lions. By that time, the pain had become too much for you, and you had fallen asleep. I tore a strip of cloth from my tunic and wrapped it around your leg."

"Thank you," Andrea breathed, feeling her energy draining from her body. She was *so* thirsty and *so* tired. For some reason, she knew that if she were to succumb to the sleepiness, this time she would not awake. She had to keep her eyes open, had to fight off the tiredness.

"You are seriously injured," Daniel said, all trace of mirth in his voice gone. "We have to get you to a physician as quickly as possible."

"How are we going to get out of here?" Andrea asked, her throat constricting against the words.

Daniel didn't answer right away. Finally, he sighed. "I don't know, child. We must seek the Lord. We were both thrown down here to die. I don't know when they will roll the stone away."

Andrea's eyelids were heavy. "Why the stone?"

Daniel repositioned Andrea's head and looked up. "The stone bears the king's seal. If anyone tries to remove the stone without his express order, they will most likely be dealt with in a similar way."

"So, you're saying we could be down here awhile?"

"God willing, no. We must pray for a quick deliverance. You need a physician in the worst way."

Andrea was horrified to find that her eyes wouldn't produce tears. The realization hit her like a blow to the gut.

I'm going to dehydrate! All my fluids are gone!

Daniel sensed her fear. "Before we seek the Lord for His delivering hand, why don't you tell me how you happened to be hurled into the den of lions. We need to keep you talking."

Andrea took a deep, painful breath and told him the entire story. Daniel listened as she warred with encroaching sleep. She knew if she would close her eyes, she would never open them again.

Chapter seventy-two

"You mean to tell me we're in the belly *of a whale*?" Zak shook his head in the darkness. His heartbeat sounded to him like successive cannon blasts, the blood pulsing in his temples and fingertips as adrenaline coursed through his veins. The pain in his skull wanted to rip him in half, but Zak wasn't focused on the pain. He now hung on the next sentence of the man named Jonah.

The man answered from the oppressive darkness. "Not the *belly* of a whale. But we're headed in that direction, should the whale—or big fish—or whatever it is decide it's time for another feeding."

Zak's brain had trouble making the right connections. Was it even possible to live inside a large fish? And what had that light been?

Jonah seemed to read his mind. "If God grants us favor, the blowhole might open again so we can gauge our surroundings."

The blowhole!? What is this, the Discovery Channel*?*

Zak struggled to find words. This plight was not at all what he had expected. Sure, waking up this morning had brought with it the expectation that something out of the ordinary was going to occur. He and the others were, after all, in the thick of a nasty battle against the forces of darkenss. But this? This was preposterous! Even after a year of strange and mysterious and amazing things, this one took the cake in terms of its sheer absurdity. He was *in a fish,* for crying out loud!

"I can't believe this, I just can't believe this!" was all Zak could manage. He heard Jonah chuckle.

"Well, believe it. I, for one, should have expected something like this to happen."

Zak thought maybe he needed to clean his ears. Had he heard the man right? How in the world could anyone *expect* to be swallowed by a fish?

"Uh—I mean, I've read your story and all, but maybe refresh me on the particulars, again," Zak said. "Why in *the world* would you expect to get swallowed by a bg fish or a whale or whatever this thing is we're trapped in?"

Zak's question was met with a moment of silence. Finally, Jonah responded with a quizzical tone.

"What do you mean you've read my story?"

Dumb move, Zak! How would he know he has a special spot in the Bible chronicling this particular event?

"Uh—I mean, I've heard of you. If I told you how, you wouldn't believe me."

Weak cover.

Jonah didn't say anything for another long moment, and Zak thought the man was going to press him for answers. To Zak's surprise, Jonah didn't press. In fact, his voice took on a dejected tone.

"It's that bad, huh? I've become infamous in such a short time? I knew I should have listened in the first place. That's why I'm here."

Zak shifted to his right knee and water sloshed beneath him.

"Listened? What do you mean?"

Jonah chuckled. "Sometimes we're so set on doing our own thing we think it is better than God's plan. I'm afraid that's what happened to me."

252

Zak shuddered as strand of seaweed brushed past his hand. He quickly picked it out of the water and flung it to the side.

"So, you didn't listen to what God was telling you?"

Zak heard Jonah shift his weight, the water sloshing beneath him. "God told me to go to Nineveh to preach to the wicked people of the city. But what did I do? I ran. I boarded the first ship to Tarshish. I don't know what I was thinking, but I was actually trying to run away from God!"

"So—that's why we're inside a whale?"

"It's why I'm inside a whale. I don't know your story—hey, and what is your name, by the way?"

Zak realized he had never told Jonah his name. "Zak Reynolds. I'm from—a long ways away."

"So, we're both a ways from where we are supposed to be?" Jonah asked.

Zak felt his face burn. How foolish he had been to think he could travel through the portal window before the appointed time. With a sinking heart, Zak realized that, like Jonah, he was right where he should be: in the mouth of a stinking fish in the middle of a nameless sea.

"I guess you can say that," Zak said. "Did you get knocked overboard, too? I was hiding under the cargo and it came un-hooked from the deck. Before I knew it, I was in the sea. And then I kinda—well—I blacked out."

"I didn't get knocked overboard," Jonah said. "The crew threw me from the ship."

"What? Why would they do that?" Zak was floored. How could the crew have been so cruel? The storm had been violent. Zak knew it was miraculous that he was even alive at all. Why had the crewmembers thrown Jonah into the sea?

"They threw me overboard because I told them to," Jonah said.

Zak thought he must have heard the man wrong. "You what?"

Jonah sighed. "I knew right away the storm was my fault. I was running from God, after all. Sometimes when we run, God will try anything to get us to come back. He sent a storm that shook the boat and scared the crewmembers to death. So, I told them the storm was my fault, to throw me overboard and the waves would stop."

"That's incredible," Zak breathed.

"Well, they didn't want to throw me over. In fact, they first tried to row back to shore. When the waves got worse, they knew they had to get rid of me or die. They said a quick prayer to God for mercy and then tossed me into the sea. And that's how I ended up here."

"Did you see the whale?" Zak asked. "Because I blacked out while I was sinking below the waves."

"I did the same," Jonah said. "But I came to just before the fish opened his mouth and took you in. I only saw you for a brief moment, and that is how I knew where the beast's throat is. We don't want to go anywhere near it."

"We have to get out of here!" Zak said, a panic seizing him. "We can't survive inside a whale's mouth!"

Zak felt the fear grip his throat. It was his fault he was in this predicament. He had foolishly acted in a rash way, and now he was paying for it. Paul McGurney had said it wasn't yet time to go through the portal window, and what had Zak done? He'd gone through anyway. Like Jonah, Zak had acted on a selfish impulse, and now he was paying the price.

I get it, God. I'm sorry for getting ahead of You!

Zak felt the tears start to flow, and he sniffled into the darkness.

"I know it seems bad, Zak," Jonah said. "But we must repent and ask for God's deliverance."

Zak was about to say something, but could not get it out. At that moment, the whale opened its mouth and light streamed in. Zak felt a sudden surge of hope.

254

I have to get out! I have to make it to that light!

Zak stood and started moving toward the whale's open mouth. He glanced to his right and caught a glimpse of Jonah struggling to get to his feet.

We're going to get out! I'm going to make it back to Colorado!

But then the rush of water came. Zak realized too late that the whale's opening of its mouth was both a blessing and a curse. The blessing was that it provided an escape route. The curse was that escape was impossible. For when the whale opened its mouth, a surge of seawater rushed in, knocking Zak off his feet and onto his back. Zak swallowed a mouthful of water and struggled to get air. He felt Jonah smash into his side, and he knew then what was happening. And there was no way he could stop it.

Desperately flailing his arms in search of anything to grab onto, he was shot by the water's forceful stream to the whale's throat, where he and Jonah's body momentarily clogged the opening.

No! No! Please!

Water surged around his head, and all of a sudden he no longer felt Jonah's body pressed against his own.

No! Please, God! No—

But it was all over in a flash. The water's pressure was too much, and Zak felt himself fall into the opening.

Chapter seventy-three

*T*odd's nerves were frayed like sliced wires. He couldn't think straight, couldn't sit still for more than a few minutes at a time. Six o'clock tomorrow morning seemed so far away, so abstract. Too many things could happen before then, so many terrible things that just thinking about them made him nauseous. Both of his cousins were in the ancients, and Jordan and his grandmother were unsafe in Colorado. Todd knew Paul McGurney's house on the hill would be the safest place for them to be, but he even wondered if that was true anymore since the old man's home had been infiltrated by the Stranger.

What can I do? How can I help?

Todd reached into his pocket and grabbed his cell phone. His parents sat in a constant daze of worry, and his Aunt Patty was all but nonresponsive. The family had prayed together, but the prayers hadn't taken the edge of panic away.

I feel so helpless…

Todd made his way to his bedroom and shut the door behind him. Thumbing up Jen's number, he plopped onto his bed and waited for his girlfriend to answer.

"Hey, Todd!" Jen chirped after three rings.

"Uh—hey," Todd said, trying his best to mask his nerves.

Jen wasted no time in figuring out there was a problem.

"Todd? What's the matter? Are you OK?"

Todd sighed. Where to start?

"Uh—actually, Jen, I'm not. Something—something bad has happened, and now my family is flying to Divide in the morning."

"You're coming to Colorado? Todd—what's wrong?"

The concern in her voice broke Todd's heart. He felt warm tears puddle at the corners of his eyes.

Should I tell her? Should I risk her safety and wellbeing by telling her the whole story?

"It's a long story, Jen. I don't know if--"

Jen's voice took on a firm tone. "Todd Lawrence, you tell me what's going on. I care about you too much not to know. If you don't tell me, I'll worry myself sick tonight."

Todd licked his lips and ran his good hand through his hair.

It's too much to tell her over the phone. But seeing her face-to-face in Colorado could be dangerous. She could be walking right into the Stranger's arms if she tries to come to Divide to see me.

"It's too long and too messy to tell on the phone. I'm sorry. It's just—I needed to hear your voice."

"I suppose you're flying into Denver. What time does your flight get in?"

Todd hesitated. He knew what she was going to say after he told her.

"We're scheduled to arrive in Denver at eight forty-two. But I don't think you should--"

"I'll have my uncle drive me to the airport and I'll ride back to Divide with you."

"No, Jen, I don't think that's a good idea--"

Jen wouldn't hear otherwise. "It's an hour and a half to Denver from Colorado Springs. My uncle has an office downtown, and I'm sure he wouldn't mind stopping by for awhile. He can drive back to Colorado Springs on his own, and I'll ride back

257

to Divide with you and your parents. Besides, you need someone who knows the area to help navigate."

Todd sighed. Her idea did seem like a good one. But he didn't want to put her in harm's way.

But I want to see her...

"OK. That should work," Todd said.

"And you'll tell me everything tomorrow morning?" Jen asked.

"I promise," Todd said. "Now's just not the best time."

"Then I'll see you in the morning. And, Todd? I hope you're OK."

"Yeah, me, too," Todd said.

But he knew he wasn't OK. Too many things were up against him, and OK seemed a million miles away.

§ § §

The Fiends hovered above the one called Todd's head and whispered violence and fear into his ear. They were glad to have another shot at the brat after what he had done to them the last time they were here. What made their second coming all the more pleasurable was having three more adults to whisper lies to. The idiots in the living room were like putty in Fiends' hands, easy to manipulate and petrify because they were so afraid.

"Fear is so powerful," Horse-face said as he buzzed around the one called Todd's head. "Once they're afraid, they're stripped of their power."

Mosquito-face laughed. "Humans are so stupid. They only see what's right in front of them."

"And they miss what lurks in the darkness!" Fly-face said, throwing back his head and laughing.

"Where's your authority now?" Horse-face taunted the unsuspecting Todd. "You're weak! You're worthless! You're helpless! You're a bad Christian!"

And the three Fiends assaulted Todd well into darkness. Their mission was complete. Now the Stranger must complete the next phase.

Death was in the air.

Chapter seventy-four

*D*arkness has overtaken Infinity.

The Stranger is on the move, stealthily weaving through backyard shrubbery and avoiding the motion-sensing lights the people of Infinity attach to their decks and roofs. These people think the lights protect them from danger, but they have no idea that if danger wants to come a-knockin', the lights are nothing more than mere decorations. But the Stranger is not interested in these ignorant people. The Stranger wants the one called Todd and his wretched family. And tonight there is no playing games. Death will come to all who inhabit the house.

The Stranger is a block away from the one called Todd's house. The plan is set, and it is a good plan. Foolproof, really. And it involves the two things the Stranger loves the most: excruciating pain and sure death.

The Stranger sees the house, and the assassin's pulse quickens. The Fiends have been doing their work, and now the family should be primed for murder. In a few short minutes, the game gets really serious. And after the one called Todd and his family are dead, it is a beeline to Colorado to take out the five remaining Knowledge-bearers. The fat Hanson is one of them now, but he is young in his faith. His death will be quick and easy. It is the old bag and the two remaining boys who might put up a fight. And *then there's that blasted Paul McGurney...*

But the Stranger must focus on the task at hand. No use thinking about future kills when there are present ones to accomplish. And accomplishing the kills is paramount. The master won't stand for any more thwarting of his mission. If the Stranger doesn't perform, the assassin might end up like the Opposition.

The Stranger pushes all other thoughts away. The assassin has arrived at the one called Todd's house. The windows are dark, the house is still. Just the way the Stranger likes it. The assassin knows the layout of the house, knows who sleeps in each bedroom. It is all falling into place. Just the killing remains.

The Stranger doesn't hesitate. Walking around to the back door, the Stranger picks the lock and is standing in the one called Todd's kitchen.

Chapter seventy-five

Margaret couldn't stand the waiting. Night was falling over the Colorado Rockies, and the hope she had in her heart that everything was going to work for the good was wavering. First, Andrea had been snatched away by a nameless Stranger. Next, Zak had foolishly rushed into the ancients. Most troubling, Jason Hanson, the supposed bridge to bring them back, had been gone for hours. That fact didn't sit well with Margaret, and now desperation was setting in. It was too much for her heart to bear.

"Jen Valentine just sent me a text," Jordan said from his position on Paul McGurney's large sofa.

"Who?" Margaret asked, shaken from her thoughts. She had been futilely trying to clean up the mess the shootout had made, but now she leaned her broom against McGurney's grand cherry table and set the dustpan on the floor. Wiping her hands on her pants, she joined Jordan on the couch. Paul McGurney sat sipping a glass of iced tea in his oversized recliner.

"Todd's girlfriend. She's in Colorado Springs this summer. Anyway, she's going to meet us at the airport so she can ride back to Divide with Todd."

Margaret sighed. "It's not safe; did you tell her that?"

Jordan shook his head. "She apparently knows something

is going on. She said Todd has to tell her something important tomorrow. I just hope he knows what he's doing in letting her come here."

Margaret nodded and looked at Paul McGurney. She had been contemplating asking the old man about a thought that had been brewing in her mind for quite some time, but her stubbornness and independence threatened to keep it in.

Get off it, Margaret Jo! I'm sure he'd be more than happy to let us stay the night here. Besides, your independence and foolishness would put Jordan in harm's way.

Margaret sighed again and decided to ask the old man if she and Jordan could stay the night. It would only make sense, and she had been thinking about asking him even before Andrea had been snatched from her cabin. Besides, driving home in the dark sounded less than appealing, especially when the Stranger could be waiting in ambush.

"Mr. McGurney? Do you think it'd be too much to ask for Jordan and me to stay the night?" Despite the obvious need for it, Margaret felt ashamed for asking. Living on her own in the Colorado wilderness for the past decade had taught her to be resourceful and independent. She hated having to ask favors of others.

Paul McGurney laughed, his blue eyes sparkling. "Of course, Margaret. I wouldn't have it any other way. In fact, I think we might begin to consider my house your permanent residence until all this is sorted out."

Margaret felt a weight release from her. In reality, this is what she had been thinking for quite some time. How good it was to hear Paul McGurney confirm her gut instincts! It was also great to hear him laugh. There certainly hadn't been too much laughter over the past three or four hours.

"Thank you," Margaret said, reaching over and touching the old man's hand.

"It is my pleasure, dear one. Tomorrow you can get what you need from your cabin, and then drive your family straight here.

263

We need to be together in such perilous times."

"Do you think Jason has found Andrea or Zak yet?" Jordan asked. Margaret's heart nearly broke in half at the sound if her grandson's voice. He sounded so scared—so young!

Paul McGurney took a deep breath and let it out. "I don't know, Jordan. In the book of Habakkuk it talks about the revelation waiting for the appointed time. Well, child, I believe this is the waiting hour. Although I cannot see through the eyes of God, I know His heart, for His Spirit lives in me, as He lives in you. The heart of God is gracious and compassionate. He is slow to anger, and rich in abundant love. I say all this because I know it is hard to wait. I, too, am fearful for Andrea and Zak and Jason. But I also know that whatever happens, God will be glorified. Remember, Jordan, the apostle Paul said to live is Christ and to die is gain. He also said to suffer is Christ. Any way you look at it, child, we win. So, rest in the comfort of His presence, knowing He will never leave you in your time of need, nor will He abandon your family in their hour of peril."

Margaret looked at her grandson and saw the tears were freely flowing.

"I want to be strong, Mr. McGurney. I want to believe what you said—that whatever the outcome God will be glorified. I just don't see how God can allow such suffering for His glory."

Margaret felt tears pool in her own eyes. Her grandson had just articulated the very thing that had been plaguing her own heart. If God was the Creator of life and all good things, then why did He allow His children to suffer?

Paul McGurney nodded. "It is difficult, I know. The ways of God are beyond our understanding. But rest in the fact that it is all for His glory and renown. A tree is stripped of its leaves and beaten by the wind through the winter months. But in the spring, lush green leaves and new fruit begin to grow on what was once dead. You see, Jordan, it's all about death and life. To understand life, we must first understand death. The tree had to die to produce new life just, as Christ had to die for You to live. Likewise, you had to die to yourself in order to live in Christ. Suffering plays a large role in the grand scheme of things. You suffer for Christ so that His name is renowned. His name is renowned and brings forth new life. Do you see, Jordan? It is all about Christ. When we profess His name, when we bear His cross and all that comes with it, we suffer. And that suffering either refines us or kills us; but, in the end, it allows us to live."

Margaret nodded, despite her heavy heart. The old man was right. All they were experiencing, all the pain and tears and terror, was for the glory of Christ. She didn't have to like it now, but she could see its truth in the bigger picture. She swiped at her eyes and looked at Jordan.

Jordan's tears had stopped and his eyes were red and puffy. Margaret reached to the coffee table and retrieved a tissue, which she gave to Jordan.

"I'd rather it be me," Jordan said, wiping his eyes and nose. "I'd rather be the one suffering. It shouldn't be Andrea and Zak."

Paul McGurney's vacant blue eyes studied the space above Jordan's head.

"Child, you are suffering. Oftentimes it is more difficult being on this end of the suffering."

Margaret was struck by Paul McGurney's statement. It was so true. The torture of uncertainty and helplessness was, at times, unbearable.

Jesus—helps us through this dark hour.

Margaret cleared her throat. "I think we should pray again."

Paul McGurney smiled. "I think that is a splendid idea."

Jordan nodded. "Yeah. I don't know why, but I feel like we should really be praying hard for Todd and the others back home."

Without further conversation, the three interceded for all the suffering.

Chapter seventy-six

*A*ndrea knew she was dying. All her strength had left her, all her muscles ceased to perform their ordered tasks. She had stopped trying to raise her head a little over an hour ago. Or was it two hours? Ten minutes? Time seemed to swirl in her head, playing tricks on her. She had lost so much blood. Now, she was parched, her body shriveling in on itself, and there was nothing she could do about it.

"Stay with me," Daniel said, patting Andrea's shoulder. "I need you to stay awake."

He knows it's bad. If I close my eyes, I'm dead.

Andrea tried to form words, but the effort was too great.

Jesus—either save me now or take me Home.

Home. Heaven. The glory of God revealed. Andrea thirsted more for this than for water. What would it feel like to fall asleep in this life and wake up in another? Would Jesus be there to greet her? Would He give her a tour of heaven? Take her to meet His Father? Would she be able to see the others from heaven?

The others…

If Andrea could have produced tears, they would have streamed down her face as her foggy brain thought about the others—her family—her co-heirs in Christ. As Daniel stroked her shoulder and hummed an unfamiliar tune, Andrea knew she was not done yet. She had a purpose for living that needed to be fulfilled. As much as she wanted to close her eyes and awake in Paradise, Andrea knew it was not her time to die. She must live and get back to the ones she loved.

But, Jesus—I love You, too..

YOU CAN LOVE ME AND LIVE.

What? But don't you want me to be with You? To come Home?

I AM PREPARING A PLACE FOR YOU. IT IS NOT YET YOUR TIME. YOU MUST LIVE IN ME BEFORE YOU CAN LIVE WITH ME.

But I'm so weak...

DO NOT LOSE HEART, DEAR CHILD. YOUR DELIVERENCE IS COMING. BELIEVE. TRUST. I AM WITH YOU ALWAYS. AND I LOVE YOU MORE THAN YOU CAN BEAR TO KNOW.

And I love you...

"Stay with me, child. Keep fighting." Daniel's words broke her from the conversation her heart had been having with Jesus. She wanted to go back to it, wanted to remain in it forever, but Jesus had said she must live.

I must live in Him before I can live with Him...

A rush of adrenaline coursed through Andrea's veins, and a new wave of strength swept over her body. She raised her head from Daniel's lap.

"No, no---conserve your strength," Daniel said, trying to push her head back down. "You mustn't move too much."

Andrea swallowed hard and shakily brought her hand to Daniel's. Gently brushing it aside, she summoned all her remaining strength and pushed herself into a sitting position. Her hip screamed at her, the wound on her calf pulsed in immense pain, her shoulder roared in agony. But Andrea didn't care. She had been promised a deliverer. She gritted her teeth against the searing pain and swallowed again.

"W-we're getting out of here," Andrea said. It came out in a whisper, all she could muster, but she was grateful for even that. She looked around the darkened den and saw the lions watching her every move. Their purring filled her ears again and, for a moment, Andrea forgot they were ferocious beasts. Now, they looked like housecats sitting contentedly by the coffee table.

"I have been praying that God would open the den," Daniel said. "You have, too, apparently."

Andrea gingerly turned her head to look at Daniel. "S-something like that. I'm Andrea, by the way."

Andrea could see Daniel smile in the darkness. "Andrea. It's good to finally have my denmate's name." His boyish face dropped the smile. "But you are seriously injured. You need to conserve your strength."

"We're getting out of here," Andrea said as though it had already come to pass. "You are probably going to have to carry me to a doctor once we are delivered from here."

Daniel's eyes widened. "Delivered? Are you planning on someone coming?"

Andrea thought about it a moment. Jesus had promised her in her heart that help was on the way. There was only one way she could answer Daniel.

"Yes. Someone's coming. I don't know whom, but I know we are getting out of here."

"Incredible," Daniel breathed. "Just as I prayed. Our God is good."

Andrea looked at the lions, heard their purring fill the enclosed space. She smiled.

"All the time."

🐌🐌🐌

The pain threatened to take her under as she waited for deliverance. Another length of time had passed, whether an hour or fifteen minutes Andrea had no idea. But the passage of time had been enough to suck more precious energy from her body. Doubts began to swim through her mind about what Jesus had spoken to her heart. Maybe she had mistaken His voice for her own. Maybe she had been in some sort of deathbed trance and she had imagined the whole thing.

No. It was real. HE is real.

Andrea's strength had left again, and Daniel held her head in his lap. To keep her awake he had been telling her stories of his life—of being taken captive by the king of Babylon and of his God-given ability to interpret dreams. Daniel's stories were fascinating, and they had kept the greater part of Andrea's mind from the pain, but the tiredness was setting in with a vengeance. Her eyelids felt as though they were attached to balls of lead, and a strange heaviness had set in over her body. From the back forty of her mind, Andrea wondered if the heaviness was the shroud of death.

He promised me I would be delivered. He shut the lions' mouths for Daniel. If He can do that, He can certainly get us out of here.

A scraping sound from above snapped Andrea from her foggy thoughts.

"D-did you hear that?"

Daniel looked down on her with wide eyes. "I did! There is movement above us!"

Another scraping sound filled the enclosed space, and a beam of light sliced through the darkness. If she had had the ability to make tears, Andrea would have wept.

"Someone is moving the stone!" Daniel said.

Andrea felt her heart accelerate. So, it was true! She was being delivered from the den of lions! Once again, God was moving a stone and setting her free. The first one had saved her soul. This one would save her life.

More light streamed into the den, and Andrea had to squint

her eyes so the glorious light wouldn't blind her. In that moment, Andrea realized she would never again take light for granted.

"Praise God!" Daniel said, his face beaming with a smile. Andrea saw his features for the first time, a mop of curly black hair atop a lean face accentuated with boyish dimples. If Andrea was honest, Daniel was quite good looking.

"The first thing we'll do is get you to a physician," Daniel said, looking up as chipped rock and loose gravel rained upon their heads.

"I—I need to get back through the window," Andrea said.

"What? Through what window?"

Andrea felt a lion brush against her leg, felt the vibrations of its purr.

"It's a long story—hard to explain, really. I just—I need to find a way to get back to my home."

Daniel squinted in thought. "We can arrange a camel for you."

If she had had the strength, Andrea would have laughed. "Uh—I don't think a camel will get me to where I need to go."

A sweep of panic overtook her.

How do I get home? I might get delivered from the lion's den, but I was never promised a trip back home!

Voices overhead made Andrea look up. Another scraping sound filled the den, and all of a sudden, a wave of morning light streamed into the once darkened abyss.

"I don't believe it! I *do not* believe it!" a man's throaty voice rang out.

"It has never happened this way before, my king," another man's voice answered the first, a fearful tremble in his voice.

"Move out of the way. I want to address the prisoner," the first voice said.

"As you wish, sire," answered the second voice.

Andrea saw a head appear at the den's opening.

"Hello, down there—*two*? There are *two of you*."

270

"I'll take this," Daniel said with a grin. "I'm going to have to place your head on the ground for a moment so I can address the king."

"The king?" Andrea asked as Daniel gently lowered her head to the den floor.

"Yes. King Darius. Remember the story I told you about how I ended up here?"

Andrea thought for a moment, remembered Daniel's story. "Right, the guy who issued the decree."

"Yes. This is he." Daniel stood to his feet and looked to the den's opening.

"Answer me, down there!" Darius shouted. "How is it that there are two of you in there? And how did you both manage to stay alive? Has your God been able to rescue you from the lions?"

Daniel laughed. "May the king live forever! My God, the one and only true God, sent an angel to shut the mouths of the lions! He did this because I was found innocent in the eyes of God!"

"Praise the God of Abraham, Isaac and Jacob!" Darius shouted back in a stunned voice. "And the other one with you?"

Daniel looked down to Andrea and the smile left his face.

"Please, King Darius. This child's name is Andrea and she is in dire need of a physician. If it pleases you, help us out of here so that she might live."

"A physician? Certainly, certainly. She will have the finest physician in all of Babylon. I will have my servants send down a rope." Andrea heard Darius shout for one of his servants to fetch a rope. Daniel looked at Andrea, saw her critical condition, and shouted back to Darius.

"The child is too weak to climb a rope. Will you send down a cot so she will experience minimal discomfort?"

Darius's head popped back into the den's opening. "A cot? Certainly." He yelled to his servants again and they presumably left to fulfill his order.

Daniel looked down on her and his smile returned.

"We will get you out of here, first. Everything is in God's hands now."

Andrea managed to smile back. "Th-thank you for all you did for me in here."

Daniel waved her off. "Please, don't thank me. Thank God for His deliverance. He is good and He fulfills his promises."

Andrea couldn't agree more. Even though she was battered and torn open, she had been promised deliverance and deliverance had come.

Now I just have to get home…

A few minutes passed, and Andrea was reminded again of the pain that scorched throughout her body. She had broken bones, no doubt. Her shoulder was separated, and her kneecap might be shattered. What was more, her calf was torn to shreds, and when she peeked at her leg, she saw the makeshift tourniquet Daniel had applied was soaked through with stunningly dark blood. She tried to move the leg and stopped when incredible jolts of pain shot through her body.

Won't do that again…

But what was worse than the pain, Andrea realized, was the dehydration. Her mouth was as dry as construction paper, her tongue swollen and threatening to stick to the roof of her mouth. She had lost so much blood, so many fluids, that in the back of her mind she knew her chance of survival was dwindling. And what of the lion bites? Was she infected with some feral disease in addition to all the rest of her ailments?

Andrea was knocked out of her dismal thoughts when a cot attached to ropes smacked against the ground. Andrea would have to ride the thing to the top of the den.

"Place the child on the cot," Darius shouted down. "Quickly, Daniel! I want to get you both out of there. I have a new decree to write! On this day, the God of Israel has shown Himself to be the one true God!"

Daniel looked at Andrea.

"Are you ready?"

Andrea managed to smile. "I've never been more ready to get out of a place in my life."

The lions continued their purring as Andrea, and then Daniel, was hoisted to the top of the den.

Chapter seventy-seven

*T*he Stranger watches the one called Todd sleep. The wretched boy is deep in slumber, ignorant of the fact that with one swift motion his life can be extinguished. One fluid slice with the assassin's menacing knife and the brat will be gone forever. It is a thought that makes the Stranger's blood surge with adrenaline. Taking out the little girl was once thing, but killing the leader of the pack of brats is another. This kill will have a ripple effect that will bring the children and their bag-of-bones grandmother to their knees.

The assassin glances around the bedroom and views Todd's belongings. These are the things that make this worthless brat who he is. Athletic trophies and posters of singers and professional athletes line the walls. A thick Bible rests on the boy's bed stand, and, on a wild impulse, the Stranger almost raises the knife and stabs it through the heart of the mocking book. This book is the Truth—or so the Knowledge-bearers claim. This Truth—capital "T"—has the ability to set souls free. The Stranger is trembling with rage. A verse from the book of Truth is running through the assassin's mind, one so simple in its scope yet so weighty in its punch that even the Stranger has ears to hear it.

'It is for freedom that Christ has set us free.'

The verse is so simple, so direct and to the point, that it petri-

fies the Stranger. It is the verse that makes the Stranger's master weak in the knees, the one that makes him tremulous in equal parts rage and terror. This verse, and the act associated with it, brought the master pain, took from him what was rightfully his. Freedom hadn't come without a cost, and Jesus had paid it at the cross. After that, the master's hand had become stacked against him. After that, the world had changed. And for the Stranger, it had changed for the worse.

The Stranger's pulse is racing. The assassin shakes the thoughts and remembers the kill. This kill is everything. This kill is the beginning of the end for the worthless brats. And the best part about this kill? It will be accomplished unhindered and in the secret darkness.

The Stranger's entrance to the one called Todd's bedroom had been easier than the assassin had imagined it would be. How stupid could these people be to believe mere door locks would keep out the creatures of the night? The Stranger had simply picked the backdoor lock, had walked through the kitchen and into the hallway that led to the Knowledge-bearer's bedroom. So easy—so incredibly easy!

The Stranger lifts the heavily serrated knife to the boy's face. It hovers over Todd's head for a moment before coming to rest inches above the vital arteries in the boy's neck. In a millisecond, the worthless maggot's life will end.

The one called Todd stirs in his sleep. The boy's movement disgusts the Stranger. The fact that this pathetic excuse for a human being is still alive is despicable. How could the Opposition have not succeeded in exterminating this roach? He is nothing but a child, after all. What makes this Todd so important, anyway? What could the Creator God see in this punk kid?

The Stranger can wait no longer. Todd's breathing is disgusting to the assassin. This boy deserves nothing less than instant death.

The Stranger moves the knife to the boy's neck. The angry

275

blade is mere millimeters from Todd's flesh. The Stranger can see the worthless brat's pulse under his skin. The Stranger will start the cut at the wretched pulsing. And the blood will flow and the assassin will be off to do the same to Todd's parents.

The Stranger begins to apply pressure, and the boy's eyes snap open as the knife blade bites through his flesh. This is it! This is the moment the Stranger has been waiting for!

A sudden noise behind the assassin—the creak of a floorboard-- stalls the knife. The Stranger spins around just in time to dodge the lamp base that is hurdling toward the assassin's face. The Stranger's reflexes are quick, but not quick enough. The lamp base misses the assassin's nose and cheek but crashes into the Stranger's temple with the night-waking sound of crashing glass.

The Stranger sees blips of swimming yellow light, and stumbles onto the one called Todd's bed. There is screaming and blood on the sheets, but in the chaos of the moment, the Stranger doesn't know where either is coming from. The assassin slashes with the angry knife and tries to regain composure. Underneath the Stranger's seat, the wretched punk called Todd is struggling to get free. The boy has only one good arm, but the Stranger knows the brat's strength. He is an athlete, strong and with a survivor's stamina. If the boy gains his freedom, the Stranger could be a cornered raccoon.

The Stranger's eyes refocus after the devastating blow. The assassin has just enough time to see the one called Todd's father raise a wooden baseball bat. The boy's mother is behind the father, and she is sobbing into her hands. The Stranger knows the woman will prove to be the assassin's way out.

"Stand up!" the father shouts, the ball bat above his head. The Stranger sneers and then quickly darts to the other side of the bed. The one called Todd is bleeding from his neck. It is nothing but a flesh wound, as the Stranger was interrupted by the lamp base before the deadly blade could bite home. But the blood is enough to stun Todd. Like any seasoned assassin, the Stranger uses the moment to gain the upper hand.

"I said, stand up! Get away from the bed!" Todd's father shouts.

The Stranger laughs and presses against the wall, grabbing the shaken Todd in the process. The assassin has the knife at the boy's neck in less than a second, the boy's good arm pinned behind his back.

"Get back!" the Stranger shouts to the father. The mother sobs in the background, calling her worthless son's name. "Drop the bat or you watch him die!"

Todd tries to dart from the Stranger's grasp and the Stranger rewards him with a long slice of the ugly knife down the boy's good shoulder. Blood seeps from the wound beneath the boy's sliced T-shirt, and his mother shrieks.

"You move again and I'll make you wish you were never born!" The Stranger hisses into Todd's ear. The assassin looks at the father again. "I thought I told you to drop the bat!"

"Dad—don't!" the one called Todd shouts. The Stranger drags the angry knife over the boy's shoulder again. Blood bubbles from the fresh wound and Todd screams in agony.

"Keep quiet! No one asked you to speak!" The Stranger is done messing around. The assassin pulls the hair on the back of Todd's head and exposes the flesh of his neck. The Stranger addresses the father again.

"I'm not telling you again! Drop the bat or your son dies!"

The father doesn't try to be a hero. He throws up his right hand and slowly lowers the bat with his left. "OK—OK—the bat's on the ground. Now, let Todd go."

The Stranger laughs at the father's stupidity. "You're a fool! I haven't come all this way to let this brat live! I will kill him first and your wife next!"

The father's nostrils flare and the wife shrieks again. The Stranger relishes the moment. Mental and emotional anguish is *just as good as physical pain.*

The boy's shoulder is bleeding profusely. Blood is running from the gashes onto the sheets below. The Stranger realizes that the mission is already thwarted, and the assassin is livid at the thought. The Stranger knows this pathetic family can't live to see the morning, or the master will have the assassin's head on a platter.

"Please—why are you doing this?" the mother asks through tears.

The Stranger laughs. "I'm doing this because the boy and the father meddled in the Knowledge. When you play around with something you don't understand, it can come back to bite you."

"But—I don't--" the woman sputters. The Stranger laughs again.

"And you! You are a spineless, whimpering woman who hasn't yet accepted the Knowledge in a personal way. You are wise. But for the foolishness of the boy and the father, you will die. You will be collateral damage."

"Just take me," the one called Todd says. The Stranger yanks the boy's hair and a ripping sound is heard from the boy's scalp.

"Todd—no!" the father says, taking a step forward.

"Back, fool!" the Stranger yells, glaring through the slits in the black mask.

"Take me—please. I'm the one you want," Todd says again.

"I want you all dead," the Stranger says, pulling Todd's head again.

"But—but you'd really like to kill me," Todd says. The boy's voice is coming out strong and confident. The Stranger is un-nerved by the one called Todd's resolve.

"You are right. And I will kill you, you worthless brat!" the Stranger yells.

"Then take me out of here and kill me," Todd says. "Think about it. You have no way out of here when it's three against one. The best you can hope for is a standoff the rest of the night."

"Todd, what are you saying?" the mother asks, tears streaming down her face.

"It's OK, Mom," Todd answers. "It's OK."

"It's not OK!" the Stranger sneers. "If I take you out of here I am going to kill you and come back for the rest! You are really proving your stupidity, here!"

"But if you don't take me out of here immediately, things could get very bad for you."

The Stranger realizes the boy is right. The assassin is literally between a wall and a hard place. The only way out is to take the boy as a hostage.

The Stranger looks at the father and mother. "I am going to take your son and you are going to let me pass. If you make so much as a move to rescue him, he dies on the spot."

"You are not taking him!" the father roars. The Stranger slashes Todd's shoulder again. The boy's agony is heard in his screams.

"You don't have a choice, old man! Either I take him out of here or you watch him die! Which do you prefer?"

"Dad—I'll be OK," Todd says.

The father now has tears in his eyes. The Stranger loves the anguish of the moment.

"I know what I'm doing, I promise," Todd says.

"That's where you're wrong," the Stranger answers. "You are a fool for giving up your life for these two bumbling idiots."

"It's happened this way before," Todd says. The Stranger realizes the meaning behind the boy's words and the assassin rakes the knife over Todd's shoulder again.

"So, you want to be Christ for them, is that it? You want to 'take up your cross' and all that goes with it? I have news for you, boy! Christ was a fool! He died for people who couldn't care less about Him!"

"He died for you," Todd answers. The Stranger yanks his hair and more follicles rip out of the boy's scalp.

"That's my point! Christ thinks He did me a favor when He really died for nothing! I don't want Him! I despise His followers and I want them all dead! He died for a lost cause!"

The Stranger's chest is heaving. How dare this brat challenge the assassin?

"There's no such thing as a lost cause," Todd says softly.

The Stranger has had enough. "If you don't shut your mouth, you are going to die!" The Stranger looks at the parents. "Clear the way. We are leaving through the bedroom door."

"Todd—no! You can't!" the woman shrieks again.

The Stranger snarls. "Oh, but I can and I am going to. Get out of the way!"

"I love you, Mom," Todd says. "Dad—I love you, too. Everything is going to be OK."

The father looks like a beaten dog. He is helpless to save his son. The Stranger realizes the mission is not a complete and utter failure after all.

"Move out of the way! Now! And remember what I said about trying to be a hero!" The Stranger inches off the bed as the parents move to opposite sides of the bedroom.

"There. That's good. Just like that."

The Stranger moves into the center of the room, the knife firmly pressed to the boy's throat. The Stranger backs to the door, never losing sight of the parents.

"After we exit the room, you will not move a muscle for ten full minutes, do you understand?" the Stranger asks the stupid parents. They only nod, defeat heavy in their eyes.

"Good. And I'll know if you move. Believe me. I have my ways of finding things out." The Stranger now stands in the bedroom doorway. "It's been a pleasure. I'll be back to kill both of you."

With that, the Stranger backs out of the room with the boy. The Stranger grabs the boy's shoes before exiting the room. There is a new plan. One the assassin is formulating right now. The brat *will need his shoes later. There is no time to waste on bare feet. The Stranger looks to the parent one last time and sneers*

"I'll take good care of him. You can be sure of it. I'll see you sniveling cowards soon.

The Stranger exits the room with the boy and the two make their way through the still house. Everything is quiet, as though heaven and hell are watching in hushed apprehension.

All the assassin can hear as the two exit the house is the anguish of the parents. It is a beautiful sound.

Chapter seventy-eight

*T*he Fiends hovered over the scene playing out before them, and realized the victory was theirs as much as the Stranger's. They had been sent to spear the Lawrence family with thoughts of doubt and fear and trepidation. And they had succeeded. Now the one called Todd was in the Stranger's clutches, and the boy would surely die.

"The master will be pleased," Horse-face said as he flew above the devastated parents. "We must report to him and receive further instructions."

Mosquito-face swooped between the parents, who stood motionless as the Stranger had instructed them. "But what about these two? Don't we have them where we want them? Shouldn't we inflict more pain?"

"We have them on the ropes; now's our chance to destroy everything they've ever believed in," Fly-face said as he whispered terror into the mother's ear.

"We have orders," Horse-face snarled. "Besides, these two blubbering idiots are hopping a plane to Colorado tomorrow morning. I would think our next mission will take us back to the Rockies to obliterate the spirits of the remnant."

"Where do you think the Stranger is taking the one called Todd?" Mosquito-face asked as he stuck his proboscis into the neck of the father and injected a dose of doubt.

Horse-face laughed. "I'd say the one called Todd is as good as dead. But, if I had a guess, I think the Stranger will choose a fitting ending for the leader of the children."

"A fitting ending always means pain," Fly-face said with a sneer.

"That's what the Stranger does best. It is what the Opposition failed to do," Horse-face said.

Mosquito-face removed his proboscis from the neck of the father. "I'm ready to destroy the rest of them. Let's report back to the master and see what he has in mind."

"Darkness will reign," Horse-face said as he flapped his heavy wings. "And when the master has dominion, the hearts of the faithful will rot."

The three Fiends took to flight, relishing the mission's success and eagerly anticipating the coming darkness.

The ends of the Earth

Chapter seventy-nine

Zak hated the darkness. What was more, he hated not knowing whether he would live or die. The whale had swallowed him, had taken him down into its abysmal stomach, and now Todd sat in digestive juices and wondered if the acidic nature of the substance would eat away at his skin.

I can't believe I got myself into this...

Zak had had a lot of time to think. The darkness afforded one time to search the nooks and crannies of one's heart to see what was really there. They always say hindsight is twenty-twenty, and Zak was experiencing the kick-yourself-for-acting-on-im-pulse-rather-than-listening-to-voices-of-reason feeling right now. Jonah, too, had gone silent; and in the blackness of the whale's stomach, Zak realized how alike the two really were. Jonah had been running from God because he had thought his ways were better, and Zak had acted on impulse because he had thought his method for retrieving Andrea was better. The sobering thought that he might die for his mistake sat on his chest like the weighti-est anvil.

Zak felt the whale's stomach acids bubbling against the bare flesh of his arms. He was bellybutton-deep in the stuff, his entire lower half submerged in the thick fluid. He raised his arm out of the brew and heard the residual liquid drip back into the acid below.

There are consequences for actions. Everything has a consequence.

Zak had been thinking about consequences for some time. He contemplated the nature of God, and how God doesn't always bale Christians out of situations that were of their own making. Zak believed wholeheartedly that God was good, compassionate and abounding in unconditional love. He also knew that God was a father. And fathers disciplined their children, not to harm them, but to teach them. Zak realized that many Christians had the notion that God was nothing more than a golden parachute used to get out of sticky situations. Sometimes you had to sit in stomach acid to get the point. Sure, God was a deliverer, but He also gave His children free will. And free will meant living with the consequences of your actions, whether good or bad. Zak remembered reading a verse located somewhere in the New Testament that said Christians had the freedom to do anything, but not everything was beneficial. In the darkness of the whale's stomach, Zak realized he had made a decision out of the free will God had given him, and it had not been a beneficial one. Was God going to deliver him from the whale's stomach? Perhaps. Zak wouldn't put it past God to work in such a way. Would Zak's actions bring forth his death? Perhaps. And if Zak's actions led to his death, did that make God less compassionate? No, because it was Zak's choice to go through the window in the first place.

I have control over what I do. It's nobody's fault but mine.

Zak heard Jonah moving in the darkness.

"Hey. How're you doing over there?"

"I've been better," Jonah answered.

"I know what you mean," Zak said, feeling tears well in the corners of his eyes. He fought them back, determined not to cry.

"I am just thinking about the people of Nineveh. How was God going to use me there? I think I missed out on an amazing

286

opportunity, Zak. I can't believe I ran from God. I have let Him down. I have let the poor people of Nineveh down," Jonah said. Zak could hear the anguish in the man's voice, and it broke his heart. Here was a man whom God had called to speak to a nation of sinners, and Jonah had missed the boat, no pun intended. Zak wondered, most certainly as Jonah was now wondering, whether the man would ever get the chance to fulfill the call he'd dodged the last time.

What about me? Will I get a chance to make things right?

"I just wonder if—if I'll get a chance to go back. Not just to Nineveh, but to life in general."

Zak shuddered at Jonah's words. He knew exactly what the man meant. All he had to do was read between the lines just a little.

"Where did you say you come from again?" Jonah asked.

"I didn't," Zak said, feeling a smile creep onto his face.

This is going to be interesting.

"Well, where do you come from?"

Zak laughed. The sound of his laughter in the darkness made him perk up a little.

"You wouldn't believe me if I told you."

Jonah didn't miss a beat. "Try me."

Zak hesitated. The next sentence he said would change his relationship with Jonah forever. The man would either think Zak was a total nut job or probe him for details about the future.

"I—uh—I came from—from the future."

Zak's words were met with momentary silence. Finally, Jonah spoke, fascination creeping into his voice.

"The future? Tell me your story, Zak."

"I—uh—I don't know where to begin. In order for you to believe anything I'm about to tell you, you kind of need the whole story. And it's kinda long."

This time Jonah laughed. "I think time is something we have plenty of."

As Zak told Jonah his story, the two kindred spirits bonded in the darkness, and Zak felt his level of hope rising.

Chapter eighty

"He's taken Todd," Jordan said, feeling the blood pulse in his temples. All of a sudden Paul McGurney's lavish home began to spin, and Jordan had to sit down to make it stop. His grandmother was over to the sofa in a matter of a second.

"What, Jordan? What happened?"

Jordan didn't have words, or maybe he had words but didn't know how to articulate them. He had just received the awful call from his sobbing mother, and he willed the terrible news to be untrue. But he knew what had happened had been as real as his grandmother's hand on his knee. The Stranger had taken Todd, and now Todd was as good as dead.

"The Stranger—he—he took Todd. He--" But Jordan couldn't finish. He felt his stomach lurch and cold beads of sweat break out on his forehead.

"Calm down, just calm down," Margaret said, rubbing his knee. But Jordan saw that his grandmother was anything but calm. Her hand was trembling, and her voice caught in her throat.

"They are scattered to the ends of the earth," Paul McGurney said quietly.

"What do we do now? How do we get them back?" Jordan heard his grandmother ask the old man. Jordan looked up and saw Paul McGurney's blue eyes sparkle with tears.

"I'm afraid I don't have the answer," McGurney said. "We

can only pray for God to intervene."

"Are your parents and your Aunt Patty still coming tomorrow?" Margaret asked Jordan.

"They don't have a choice, really," Jordan said through his sobs. "What good can they do from Ohio?"

"What good can they do here?" Margaret asked.

Paul McGurney shifted in his seat. "It is good they are coming. The family needs to be together in times such as this."

"What family?" Jordan asked. "The Stranger's taking us out one by one! Stop and think for a second—we're next!"

"The Stranger has been traveling through time without obstruction. His master must be setting the assassin's course," McGurney said.

"He could pop up anywhere," Margaret said, looking at the big window. "How are we ever going to feel safe?"

"I can't believe he's got Todd," Jordan said, the absurdity of the situation still thick in his mind. "I have to call Jen. She was going to ride back with him to Divide. She's gonna freak out."

"She'll probably still want to come," Margaret said. "Insist she should stay back. She doesn't need to get involved in all this."

"My brother's taken," Jordan said, pulling out his cell phone. His hand shook so badly he couldn't open the phone. "I—I don't know what to think anymore."

"Things are most certainly at a boiling point," Paul McGurney said. "After you make your phone call, we should seek the Lord in prayer. It is best that we cover those who are in the clutches of evil with a heavy dose of prayer. We must continue to seek God. We must continue to trust that in some way, somehow, His glory will be the end result of all this madness."

Jordan took a deep breath. He didn't want to make the phone call, but he knew he had to.

Jesus—I don't know how much more I can take!

Chapter eighty-one

"I've got the perfect end in mind for you," the Stranger said as the surroundings began to lose their fuzzy edges. The wounds on Todd's shoulder throbbed, the blood flowing freely down his arm in alarming rivulets. The angry knife was still at his neck, the Stranger's breath sizzling the tiny hairs that rested there.

"You are going to like where I'm taking you," the Stranger's metallic voice said. "It'll give you a warm and fuzzy feeling."

"I doubt it," Todd said, determined not to give the Stranger any ounce of fear. The assassin only laughed and assumed a tighter grip on Todd's hair.

The Stranger had walked Todd out of his home and into the blackness of the Infinity night. At that point, Todd had wondered where the assassin could possible take him. Would the Stranger execute him on the spot or take him to a remote location like the thick woods that served as the city limits and do the deed amongst the oaks and maples and scurrying creatures of night? When the Stranger had walked him to the end of the street and simply stepped into the intersection of Vine and Pleasant, the time- traveling portal had opened and the two were swept into its vortex. Todd had wondered how the Stranger had commanded the portal to be at his disposal when and where he needed it. Probably the

Stranger's master had something to do with it. The Prince of Darkness seemed to have a hand in everything these days.

"I bet you think we're headed back in time, don't you?" the Stranger said with a sneer. "You'll be surprised to know that we're going to Divide, Colorado, to end all of this."

Todd was actually surprised, but he didn't wish the Stranger to know so. Why Colorado? Why would the Stranger be taking him back to Paul McGurney's house? To use him as bait? To mock the others by making them watch him die? This scenario didn't make sense for two reasons. First, the Stranger could have accomplished the former by killing Todd in front of his parents. Second, taking Todd to McGurney's house left the Stranger at a disadvantage. If things went bad for the assassin, it would be four against one, bad odds even though two of the four were over seventy years old. Todd didn't think the Stranger was stupid enough to do either. Another thought swept through his mind, making the hairs on the back of his neck stand on end.

Jen!

The possibility that the Stranger had abducted and stashed his girlfriend somewhere in the wilderness enraged him. How could the Stranger even know she existed? Had he bugged Todd's cell phone and computer? Todd allowed the thought to run its course before mentally shaking it off. No. There was no way the Stranger had been that resourceful without Todd's knowing it. The assassin had no idea Jen and Todd were an item, and Todd would do everything in his power to keep it that way.

The surroundings came into focus, but the clarity of the picture didn't help. Blackness surrounded the abductor and his prey, and Todd could instantly tell by the sound of the wind in the trees and the calls of nocturnal animals that they had were standing in the Colorado wilderness in the dead of night.

"We're here, Todd. Back in good old Colorado. Should we pay a visit to your girlfriend while we're here?" He walked Todd forward through the blinding darkness, the last remnants of snow crunching under their feet.

What!? He knows!! How does he know!!

Todd flinched in response to the Stranger's revelation, but found the assassin held him in a vise grip.

"Didn't think I knew about her, did you? What's her name again? Oh, that's right. Jen Valentine, 414 Spengler Street, Colorado Springs, Colorado. I wonder if she feels safe on a night like tonight? What do you think, Todd?"

"I think you're a heartless monster," Todd said, showing no emotion. In reality, his insides screamed for him to break free and to rip off the assassin's black mask and to claw the man's face with his fingernails. Why would he bring up Jen unless he had taken her? Todd's heart sank into his stomach when he realized the truth.

He wouldn't. He wouldn't bring her up unless he had her somewhere.

"You're acting brave, but I know I hit a nerve," the Stranger mocked. "Did you underestimate me, Todd? I'm not the Opposition, you know. I've done my homework."

The Stranger continued to walk Todd through the blinding darkness. Todd's mind reeled at the possibilities of what—and who—he would find whenever they arrived at the intended destination.

"I'll put your little heart at ease for now," the Stranger said. "It's just you and me tonight. I'm going to kill you, make no mistake about it. But your death with have a dual purpose, two birds with one stone, if you will. I'll kill Jen for fun after this whole mess is over. Maybe her uncle, too. What do you say?"

So, he doesn't have Jen...

"We're almost there, Todd. You've been a good boy so far. I'd hate to have to kill you before we get to our destination, so don't try anything heroic. Oh, and speaking of heroic, I thought your dad would at least have put up a fight when I said I was taking you. He must be weaker than his sons."

"You'll get what's coming to you," Todd said evenly. "You won't get away with this."

The Stranger laughed. "I love it when my victims get cocky. It makes their deaths so much more enjoyable."

Chapter eighty-two

*A*ndrea was in and out of consciousness. The world swam around her in distorted pictures and video clips, and she had trouble determining what was reality and what was from her scrambled mind. This much she was able to deduce: she and Daniel had been hauled out of the lion's den and she had been swept away to the King Darius' palace, where a physician had attended to her injuries. The physician had used water to cleanse her shredded calf, and Andrea had almost passed out from the searing pain of it. She had been given water and had greedily drunk in a chaliceful. But the water had refused to stay down, and Andrea had found herself retching it back onto the floor. After that, everything had become bits and pieces of reality. Deep in her mind, Andrea knew she was dehydrated and that she had lost way too much blood, but she couldn't find the words to articulate her concerns. Whoever was attending to her obviously didn't have access to modern medicine, and Andrea worried that whatever he was prescribing her was doing more harm than good. What she really needed was an IV and a doctor to set her bones and to surgically repair her torn calf.

She heard Daniel's voice beside her, although it seemed distant and faint, as though he were speaking from the opposite end of a tunnel. Her vision was blurry, but she could make out his distorted figure sitting beside her cot.

"Stay awake, Andrea. The physician says you must stay awake."

But I'm so sleepy...

"King Darius is commissioning an escort to take you back to your hometown, wherever your hometown happens to be."

You don't understand. No procession of camels can get me back to Colorado.

Andrea heard someone enter the room. Her bleary vision afforded her only a smeared and distorted picture of the figure who walked to the side of her cot and stood beside Daniel.

"I'm afraid I've done all I can for the girl," a male voice said. "It is up to the gods to make her well again."

"It is up to the one true God to decide Andrea's future," Daniel said in a correctional tone. Andrea heard Daniel stand and move a few feet from her cot. The other man, presumably the physician, walked with Daniel. Andrea heard the two conversing in whispers.

"How bad is she?"

There was silence as the physician thought a moment before answering Daniel in a matching whisper.

"I am of the opinion that she will be dead in a matter of hours. Why don't you get some rest, son. You look like you are about to fall over from exhaustion."

"I won't leave her," Daniel answered. "My God is about to perform a miracle. You just watch."

Andrea heard the physician chuckle. "And a miracle it would be. The girl is practically dead right now."

"I don't appreciate your smug attitude," Daniel said. "If you don't mind, I'd like you to leave us now. I must seek the Lord for His will in the matter."

"As you wish, sir. I'll keep some of the servants on standby should they need to—uh—remove the body from the premises."

"Leave us at once," Daniel answered, an edge to his voice.

296

Andrea heard the physician exit the room and Daniel return to her cot.

Even the doctor thinks I'm going to die...

"I am going to seek the Lord on your behalf, Andrea. If our God can deliver us from a den of hungry lions, surely He can heal your wounds."

Andrea swallowed and tried to form words. She cleared her throat twice before her voice managed to squeak through her cracked lips.

"Th-thank you for staying with me."

Although she couldn't see him, she knew Daniel was smiling.

"I will be here no matter how long it takes. Take my hand, dear one. We are going to petition the Lord God."

Andrea felt Daniel take her hand and she did her best to grip his tight. She knew she must not close her eyes for fear she might never open them again, so she listened to Daniel pray with her eyes open, convinced that God saw her plight and would understand. She prayed along with Daniel in her heart. The young man's words flowed like warm honey.

"Great God of the universe, mover and shaker of the waves and sea, painter of the heavens, creator of the land, hear us now in our hour of need. You saw fit to deliver us from the den of lions, and you shut the mouths of the beasts before they could consume us. We give thanks for Your mercy and Your sovereign ways we cannot begin to understand. And now we come before You asking You to perform another miracle. Your child, Andrea, needs Your healing touch. She needs You to bind her wounds and to restore her health. She needs Your cover and protection in her time of distress. God, she needs Your healing. We petition You on this morning You have made, and we ask You to build a bridge to health and healing for Andrea. We worship and exalt You, Most Holy God."

What interesting choice of wording. "Build a bridge" to

health and healing...

Andrea listened and prayed in her spirit while Daniel poured his heart out to God on her behalf.

It was midmorning when the visitor appeared.

Chapter eighty-three

*T*he Fiends were once again in transit, and they zoomed over the Kansas prairies en route to Colorado. The night was dark, the blackness hung heavy and thick like a lead blanket over the land. This was evil's kind of night. This was when creatures of the black liked to come out to play.

The master had been very specific in regard to the Fiends' next mission. The Knowledge-bearers were divided and would be at their weakest points. Now was the time to attack the hardest. The Fiends were to go to Colorado and cause further division and discord between the grandmother and the one called Jordan. If those two could be separated and the old man could be neutralized, the rest of the Plan would fall like dominos. The Stranger's job was becoming easier by the minute, and it was Fiends' duty to make the assassin's job even easier.

Chapter eighty-four

The Stranger has never been more excited for a kill. The one called Todd will be the assassin's reward for a victorious mission. Of course, the mission had not gone as planned, but, in the end, it couldn't have ended any better. A thwarted mission turned into a successful one is not the norm, and for the one called Todd to have fallen into the Stranger's clutches so easily has been incredible. The punk kid's parents will be easy kills, the stupid aunt an equally nonthreatening prey. The master will be pleased with how things have shaken out, and even more pleased when the Stranger eliminates the one called Todd.

The Stranger leads the punk kid through the thick Colorado wilderness, the assassin's vicious knife still to the boy's neck. The boy is dripping blood onto the melting snow below, but the Stranger is not concerned. With the first few hours of morning sunlight, all traces of the snow will be gone, and so will Todd's blood. Todd himself will be dead long before the sun rises over the Colorado Rockies, killed in a way that will bring a fitting end to his worthless life.

"Why don't you just finish me off right here," the one called Todd says as the assassin leads him into a thatch of thick trees.

"I didn't ask for your opinion," the Stranger growls in re-

sponse.

"What if the others show up? What then? It will be four against one. You'll be outnumbered."

The Stranger laughs and it sounds like nuts and bolts thrown into a garbage disposal. "And what of it? Your brother Jordan poses no threat to me. He's a weak, sniveling child. And McGurney and your wrinkled bag of a grandma? Let's just say my knife really enjoys elderly flesh."

"Listen--I'm willing to trade my life for theirs. Why not just kill me and leave the others alone?"

"This isn't a negotiating table, you worthless maggot! I'm going to kill you and then kill the rest of the lot. You have no say in my actions. The Plan is in motion, and you and the other Knowledge-bearers will die in accordance with the Plan. Begging and pleading won't save your life or the lives of the others, so I'd just shut your trap and let me go about my master's business."

"I'm not begging," the boy says evenly. "And your master's business is a fool's parade."

The Stranger is immediately incensed to violence. In one swift motion, the assassin removes the knife from the boy's neck and rakes it across his already seeping wounds. The boy cries out in agony, and the Stranger snarls.

"My master's business is what is bringing the world to its knees! Have you looked around lately? The world is in shambles, society is in chaos. Who do you think is responsible for all the broken families? Who do you think orchestrates murder, lusts of the flesh and apathy for the Knowledge? My master feeds on the fears and urges of the nature inside all humans and exposes the weaknesses of the flesh. When the spirit dies, so does the body. You must know that from your Bible!"

The one called Todd is panting from the fresh wound inflicted by the assassin's knife. The Stranger firmly thrusts the knife back into place above the vital organs of the boy's neck and continues to lead the boy to his final resting place.

"But--you lose," Todd says, inhaling a spurt of air through his clenched teeth to ward off the pain. "No matter what you do here and now, you lose in the end."

"You're a fool!" the Stranger growls. The assassin contemplates slicing more of the boy's flesh but decides against it. The Stranger wants the boy as whole as possible in order to savor the brat's death. A terribly maimed Todd will not be as satisfying as a coherent, fighting one.

"No, I think you're a fool," Todd says softly. "What are you gaining by killing Christians?"

"I'm gaining a place of honor and respect in my master's kingdom!"

"But his kingdom is only temporary," Todd answers. "It's going to crumble when Jes--"

"Don't you dare say His name, boy!" The Stranger hisses. "And what is it to you? My life is my own, my destiny my own making."

"Maybe so. But the apostle Paul killed Christians before he saw the Light of Christ. Have you ever thought of that? You don't have to keep doing what you are doing."

The Stranger's vision strobes with yellow light. How dare the boy preach at a time like this? How dare the boy liken the Stranger to the apostle Paul? The apostle Paul--when he had been known as Saul--had been a feared assassin. The man had made a job out of killing Knowledg-bearers. But then Saul had changed sides, changing his name to Paul and placing the master's bull's eye on his back. The master had eventually killed that renegade Knowledge-bearer, but not before the traitor had converted thousands of the master's own to Christianity while he was still alive. And then the traitor's letters had become sacred books of the Bible, so that even after Paul's death, his divinely-inspired words spoke louder than ever. By now the backstabbing idiot had converted millions--if not billions--over the course of history to the Knowledge. The wretched apostle was one of the *master's greatest defeats, simply because the master had claimed Paul as his own and the Knowledge had snatched him away. The Stranger has had enough chit-chat. The boy has struck a nerve in the assassin with his apostle Paul comment, and the Stranger wants no more of it.*

"We're done talking," the Stranger says as a tree branch slaps Todd in the face. "You'll keep your mouth shut until we reach the destination."

"Or what?" the boy responds, "you'll kill me?"

The assassin can contain the rage no longer. The boy must be taught a lesson, regardless of how the Stranger feels about maiming the brat. The assassin cannot have the worthless punk talking back to him. The boy will pay for his cocky attitude.

"You should have kept your mouth shut!"

Shoving the boy to the ground, the assassin is atop Todd in a less than a second. The boy is facedown in the snow, his surgically-repaired shoulder absorbing the brunt of his fall. His other arm is above his head, his hand open atop the snow. The Stranger wastes no time. Raising the knife to shoulder level, the assassin viciously thrusts the razor point into the back of Todd's hand. The knife divides flesh and bone and jams into the hard ground beneath the boy's palm, pinning Todd to the ground. The boy screams in agony.

"That's what you get, you fool! Keep your mouth shut next time!"

The Stranger stands and leaves the knife in place. The boy's screams echo throughout the Colorado wilderness as his legs kick and thrash as the knife doesn't come loose. The Stranger laughs.

"I bet you wish you could move your other shoulder right about now. You look ridiculous--like an insect pinned to a child's science project." The Stranger spits on the boy. "That's all you Knowledge-bearers are: insects who need to be exterminated."

The Stranger stoops and watches Todd struggle for a while

longer, allowing the rage to trickle back into calm. An assassin must keep composed at all times. A killer cannot allow the prey to gain the upper hand.

"Have you learned your lesson?" The Stranger asks. Todd doesn't respond and the Stranger laughs. "I think you have. But if you speak one more time, there'll be more of this kind of pain. Believe me, you don't want to push it. I know methods of torture that will make your skin crawl."

The Stranger grabs the knife and yanks it from the ground, but not before giving it a half-twist. The boy's screams reverberate off the trees, and the Stranger takes a moment to soak in the thrill that torture brings before pulling the boy to his feet and resuming the walk to the destination.

Chapter eighty-five

*A*ndrea continued to slip into the black. Her breath came in short spurts, and she labored for every gulp of oxygen she took. Her vision was blearier than ever, and once or twice she thought she saw phantoms floating above her cot.

I must be hallucinating...

Daniel remained by her side, diligently faithful in making sure she didn't close her eyes and let death overtake her. He talked and Andrea listened, telling her about his early life and his life in captivity and his three friends with really long and hard to pronounce names. Andrea couldn't be more grateful to Daniel, and Andrea knew that, in other circumstances, Daniel would be a true friend she could trust and rely upon. But these weren't other circumstances. She was at death's doorstep with foot over the threshold, just waiting for Jesus to call her to come Home.

It's not so bad. Why can't I just sleep? What could be better than waking to Jesus and eternal bliss?

Andrea felt her spirit smiling at the thought. Jesus had delivered her from the lion's den, and now He would deliver her from pain and agony unto Himself. Isn't that what He meant? If so, than it would be a perfect ending to a terrible ordeal. And the she would be at peace...

A shuffle of feet snapped her from her thoughts.

"I'm sorry sir, but there is a visitor who says he is here to retrieve the girl."

Andrea heard Daniel stand.

What? A visitor?

"Who is he?" Daniel asked. "Is he from Andrea's hometown?"

The servant sounded nervous. "Please, sir, I do not know all the details. The man insists he is to retrieve the girl."

All of a sudden, Andrea's mind set off warning flares.

No! No--Daniel, please--you can't let him take me! You can't let the Stranger take me!

"How do I know this isn't the man who threw her into the den of lions?" Daniel asked. "Please, fetch me a sword. And bring the man to me."

"As you wish, sir." Andrea heard the shuffling of the servant's feet as he hurriedly went on his way to fulfill Daniel's command. Daniel returned to Andrea's cot.

"I will protect you, dear one. If this man has evil on his mind, I will run him through with my blade."

Andrea took comfort in Daniel's words, but her mind still screamed warning sirens.

Be careful! He's strong! He's a killer!

Andrea heard the servant return and quickly cross the room to Daniel.

"Here you are, sir. It is the best sword in the armory. If it is your wish, I will admit the visitor."

"Thank you. Please, post two guards outside the door. If the man has evil intentions and I should fall, save the girl at all costs."

"Right, sir. I will do as you say. I will escort the visitor to this chamber and post two guards at the door."

"Thank you."

The servant left the room in haste, and Andrea knew the rest

306

of her short life hung on the next few moments. Dying in peace was one thing, but dying at the hands of the Stranger was another. Andrea hoped and prayed Daniel could ward him off. She wanted nothing less than to fall into the assassin's clutches in the eleventh hour of her life.

Jesus, keep us safe!

"Here they come," Daniel said as Andrea heard footsteps approach the room. "I will protect you, child."

"Sir, the visitor," the servant said, a tremor in his voice. The servant hurried out of the room, and Andrea knew this was it. She wished she could raise herself so she could see the door, but her muscles were far too weak. She would have to be a silent, helpless listener to whatever went down.

"You've come to retrieve the girl, I hear," Daniel said, a razor's edge to his voice. "Are you from Andrea's hometown?"

"Uh, not exactly," the voice answered. "I'm from Divide, Colorado, and she's from Ohio."

Andrea's brain flashed flares again. But these weren't warning flares, these were flares that screamed recognition.

I know that voice! I've heard it before!

Daniel wasn't budging. "I've never heard of those towns. Why is it you have come?"

"I've come to take the girl back to her grandmother. Please, mister, put the sword down. I've had enough weapons aimed at me in the last week to last a lifetime."

And then Andrea knew.

Jason Hanson?! The electrician?! What in the WORLD was he doing here!?

"I will not lower my sword until I know you do not have evil motives. This girl has been seriously injured, and she was thrown into the den of lions by an evil man."

"A den of lions?" Jason Hanson said. "I'll break his neck! Where did the Stranger go?"

What is going on?

"So, you are not the man--this Stranger who threw Andrea in to the den of lions?" Daniel asked, his voice softening just a little.

"No! Of course not! I'm just an electrician. I'm new to all of this--stuff--but I'm not so new that I don't know evil when I hear about it. It was the Stranger who stole Andrea from her--er--time--and brought her here."

"And where is this Stranger now?" Daniel asked.

"Your guess is as good as mine, buddy. But he could be back any moment. Please, I need to take Andrea back to her grandmother. She needs serious medical attention."

How is this possible? What is going on?

But Andrea knew better than to question it. Jason Hanson had come to take her back to Divide, and now she had to communicate to Daniel that Jason should be allowed to fulfill his mission.

Andrea tried to speak, but her voice came out in nothing more than a murmur.

"What is it you are trying to say, Andrea?" Daniel asked, stooping over her cot. His face was bleary and distorted.

I'm saying that it's OK! Jason can take me with him!

Andrea swallowed and tried again. "Iths--iths OK," she breathed. The energy it took to say the words was incredible. She didn't know whether she could do it again, so she hoped Daniel and Jason had been able to decipher her affirmative statement.

Daniel stood to full height. "Andrea has given her blessing for you to take her."

Yes! Yes!

"And I'll do just that," Jason Hanson said. "If you don't mind, sir, I need to be quick about it. Look at her. She needs to get to an emergency room, *pronto*."

"You have my blessing as well," Daniel said. He stooped over Andrea once more and took her hand in his. "May God grant you life, dear one. It has been my pleasure making your

308

acquaintance."

Andrea couldn't answer Daniel, but she mustered all her remaining strength and squeezed his hand.

"You may take her," Daniel said to Jason Hanson. Andrea saw the big electrician stoop over her bed.

"We're going to have to be real gentle about it," Hanson said. And then Andrea felt herself being lifted off the cot.

That was when she knew her bridge had come.

Chapter eighty-six

"That is quite the story," Jonah said, "one I wouldn't believe if not for the situation we are in."

"I used to think all of this stuff wasn't possible, either, but now, how can I not believe?" Zak spoke into the darkness in Jonah's general direction. His legs had become stiff during the telling of his story, so he stood and let the whale's digestive juice fall from his jeans and shirt back into itself.

"You know, it really stinks in here," Zak said, trying not to breath through his nose. "Kind of like dead fish and other foul things."

Jonah laughed. "What I wouldn't give for a breath of fresh air."

Zak sat back down in the belly-deep liquid and tried not to think about the effect the goopy substance was having on his skin. He and Jonah had been talking for an indeterminable length of time. Talking was all they could do in the darkness of the whale's belly. They couldn't see each other, but Zak had a good idea how far away from him Jonah was. The humidity of the stomach was fierce, the wet heat causing Zak to feel like he would never get dry.

If I ever get out of here...

Zak had told Jonah his story, starting at the beginning before all the adventures started and ending with being swallowed by the whale. He had left out the portions he felt he should keep to himself. As much as Zak wanted to tell Jonah about Jesus, Zak felt in his heart that he shouldn't. Jonah was awaiting the Messiah's arrival, and Zak didn't want to unduly influence Jonah's teachings by telling him all about Jesus and what He was like. Zak felt as if he would be messing with history, and he wanted no part in doing that. He also avoided telling Jonah that he had read his story in the Bible. Zak had slipped earlier, telling Jonah just that, but Jonah had not pressed the issue. Besides, Zak had forgotten how the story of the Jonah in the belly of a great fish ended. Zak seriously hoped it ended on a good note. But even if the story ended well for Jonah, that didn't mean it would end well for Zak.

I want to be with the others...

Whenever Zak thought about Andrea, it tore him apart. Not knowing what had become of her was torturous. And he knew that he had done the same to Todd and Jordan. By going the window on his own accord, Zak had inflicted the same pain on the boys as he experienced with Andrea.

Zak was amazed at how one action could lead to such large consequences. Sin worked like that, he knew. The sin of one could lead to the downfall of many. All he had to do was look at his father's example. His dad had walked out on the family when Zak had been in middle school and it had created a string of pain and poor decisions in Zak's life. If there was something Zak was learning from his experience in the belly of a whale, it was that people's choices--good or bad--had far-reaching effects.

"So, what now?" Zak asked Jonah.

"We pray hard. And then we pray harder. We ask for forgiveness and we pray some more," Jonah said.

"Do you think we can pray ourselves out of this mess?" Zak asked.

Jonah was silent for a moment. Finally, he spoke in a near whisper.

"I think our prayers shouldn't focus on us as much as on what God can use through our experience. We are the ones who got ourselves into this situation. Our choices landed us inside the belly of a whale. We should ask forgiveness and ask God to use our circumstances for His glory, whatever the outcome."

Zak sighed. "That's a dangerous prayer. When we say 'whatever the outcome,' we might be sentencing ourselves to death."

"It's all about faith, Zak. Are we willing to die so that His glory might be revealed throughout the nations of the earth?"

Zak thought for a moment, searching his heart for the true answer to Jonah's question.

"I think so," Zak said, "now more than ever."

"Then let us pray."

Chapter eighty-seven

Jordan snapped the phone shut. Jen Valentine wasn't answering. She was most likely asleep, as the vast majority of Colorado was. Jordan sent Jen a quick text and prayed she would see it before she made the trip to Denver in the morning.

"I can't sit here any longer," Jordan said, rising from Paul McGurney's leather sofa. "I just need to know that one thing is going our way. Just one."

His grandmother reached over and rubbed his shoulder. "Maybe you should try to get some sleep. You look exhausted."

"There's no way I'm going to be able to sleep," Jordan said. "Not with all this craziness going on."

"It is best you try, dear one," Paul McGurney said from his chair. "I think you both would do well to get some rest. If anything happens while you are sleeping, I will awaken you at once."

Jordan looked at his grandmother and sighed. "I don't know if I can, but I'll try."

"Good. You can have the sofa. The loveseat over there will be sufficient for me."

His grandmother moved from the couch to the loveseat and Jordan sprawled out on the sofa. When he laid his head on the sofa's cushioned armrest and kicked off his shoes and threw his feet onto the couch, Jordan realized how tired he truly was. He felt guilty for letting himself drift to sleep, and Paul McGurney must have sensed so.

"It's all right, child. Sleep. Find peace and allow it to overtake you."

And then Paul McGurney did something he'd never done before. The old man started to sing. McGurney's voice was baritone and soothing, and he softly sang a song Jordan didn't recognize but knew was ancient. The words weren't in English, but Jordan felt the overwhelming peace in them and found himself floating on the sea of their tranquility. Before Jordan knew it, he was asleep.

Chapter eighty-eight

*T*odd's hand was on fire. He could feel the blood oozing from the wound, and in between his fingers. The bones and ligaments and muscles beneath his ripped flesh felt torn and frayed and, for once, Todd was grateful for the blackness of the night and its ability to conceal the horrific wound from his sight. The last thing he wanted was to hold his hand in front of his face and see the sun shine through the nasty hole the Stranger's knife had made.

The Stranger had picked up the pace since the stabbing. The two had covered quite a bit of ground, and Todd was beginning to wonder where the Stranger could be taking him. Todd doubted the Stranger would be foolish enough to take him to Paul McGurney's house, so that left a plethora of possibilities. Was the Stranger going to march him to Devil's Playground? Was the assassin going to kill him somewhere in the thick of the forest as a sacrifice of sorts? Todd's words had ignited a profound anger in the Stranger. When Todd had compared the assassin to the apostle Paul, the Stranger had blown a gasket. By the Stranger's reaction, Todd was certain the assassin had had those thoughts before. The Stranger was pure evil, yes. But weren't all human beings wallowing in the sin that would lead them to eternal death? Without Christ, there was no hope for survival.

People could only live in the vileness of their sins and keep feeding on the things that would surely kill them. And that's where the Stranger was. The Stranger had chosen a master other than Chirst, and evil doesn't like to be reminded of its evilness.

Todd's shoulder felt raw in the places the Stranger had raked his knife over it, but his shoulder pain was overshadowed by the throbbing agony of his hand. He wondered if he was losing too much blood. He felt the blood running down the back and front of his arm from the shoulder wounds, and the gaping wound on his hand seemed to be a faucet of the stuff. Would Todd reach the predetermined destination alive? Did it really matter?

Todd knew he had to fight the Stranger for all he was worth. If the Stranger took his life, he would be unable to keep the monster from consuming the others. The assassin had no interest in the trade of Todd's life for the lives of the others, so going down without a fight wasn't an option. But how could Todd fight with one arm in a sling and the other shredded pulpy to the point of uselessness? Todd determined one thing as the Stranger pressed him on through the darkness: he would scratch and claw and fight to the death before he let the Stranger take the others. The Stranger had already taken so much from him; his two cousins were lost in the ancients, and his brother and family were being hunted like wounded prey. Todd would not go down without a fight. And if he had to, he would kill the Stranger.

"We're almost there," the Stranger hissed, sick excitement thick in his voice. "Once we step out from behind these trees, you will see your final resting place."

Todd didn't answer, but his heart cannoned in his chest cavity. The Stranger pushed him forward, and Todd could see silver moonlight streaming through a cluster of trees up ahead. A few more feet and the two would be out of the forest.

"And here we are" the Stranger said as he shoved Todd through the last remaining trees. Todd fell forward and instinctively put his wounded hand out the break his fall. His shredded hand absorbed the weight of his body, but with a searing pain so profound Todd almost passed out. Hurriedly getting to his knees, Todd looked at his hand in the new moonlight and saw it was as bad as he had thought. And now it was additionally caked with dirt and pine needles from his fall. His flesh hung about the wound like ribbons, and Todd felt his stomach lurch when he saw a sharp fragment of white protruding from the flesh.

"Quit worrying about your stupid hand and take a look at your tomb!" the Stranger growled, grabbing Todd's hair and yanking his head up. When Todd saw where the Stranger had taken him, he felt the blood drain from his face.

He's taken me to my grandma's cabin…

The Stranger laughed as Todd saw the quaint cabin illuminated with its own slice of the moon. The cabin looked so quiet, so peaceful. Here was a place of rest, a pocket of his childhood that had been so innocent and right. And now it would be the site of the greatest battle of Todd's life.

The Stranger yanked him to his feet, the assassin's iron grip ripping Todd's hair out at the roots.

"It's a fitting ending, isn't it?" the Stranger sneered. "It all started here, and now it will end here."

The Stranger shoved him forward again, but this time Todd retained his balance.

"Start walking. Grandma's not home to save you. This is my house now."

Todd felt the first tears pooling in the corners of his eyes. He gritted his teeth and was determined to fight them. There was no need to become a blubbering idiot. That's exactly what the Stranger wanted, anyway. Todd would face whatever came next with a lion's courage and a pounding heart.

"Isn't this great?" the Stranger laughed as the two crunched across the stone driveway. "Are you ready to die, Todd?"

Once again, Todd didn't respond. The two reached the front door, and Todd stopped.

Now what?

"No need to knock," the Stranger said. With one powerful kick of his heavy boot, the Stranger broke the lock and the door swung open. The familiar smells of the cabin wafted to Todd's nostrils, and the jagged knife scars and obscene words and phrases came into focus as the Stranger flipped on the kitchen light. The Stranger saw Todd's horror at the sight of the destroyed kitchen.

"You like my handiwork, I see. Believe me, I had fun. Desecration is kind of my thing."

Todd didn't respond, and the Stranger laughed in triumph.

"You're a pathetic little maggot. I don't see why the master finds you so important. I've killed brats like you in my sleep."

Todd swallowed and waited from the Stranger's next move. When the Stranger saw that Todd was not going to respond, the assassin mocked him.

"So you're pulling a Jesus. All of a sudden you're silent. I bet you're expecting me to ask you some stupid question like 'what is truth?'" The Stranger moved his face to within inches of Todd's, the assassin's black mask brushing Todd's cheek, his hot breath burning Todd's lips and nose. The killer's dark brown eyes glared into Todd's, his pupils black, angry bullet holes.

"Let me tell you something, you filthy brat! Jesus tried the silent treatment and look where it got Him! And *you're* no Jesus! So if you think you're proving some point by being all brave, you're wrong. Jesus was weak, and you are weaker. Jesus was a peasant moocher and you are a slug not worthy to wash the dust off His sandals. Before I kill you, I want you to know how much I hate you--how much I *loathe* you-- and your God and your arrogant righteoussness! Your Jesus says that no one comes to the Father but through Him, but I'm not interested. I have my own god, and he's the one who rules the world right now. And Lucifer is all I need."

"Right now," Todd whispered.

"What did you say, you insolent brat?"

318

"I said 'right now.' Your god might have dominion now, but his future set in stone. He's a goner."

The Stranger spit on Todd's face and raked the knife over his shoulder again. New blood spattered to the ground, and the Stranger grabbed Todd's forearm as Todd panted in agony.

"You reap what you sow, maggot! After you," the Stranger said. He shoved Todd through the doorway and Todd face-planted onto the kitchen floor, his shredded hand screaming with the impact.

At that moment Todd knew he had to act and act quickly. His life clock was ticking, and Todd needed to formulate a plan before it expired.

The Stranger came up beside him and kicked him in the stomach. The blow was vicious, and for a few horrific seconds, Todd thought the Stranger had shattered all his ribs. Todd's wind left him, and he gasped for breath.

"Now you can't fight," the Stranger said. The assassin grabbed Todd's hair as Todd gasped for oxygen and began to drag him into the living room. Todd pawed at the floor with his pulpy hand. When Todd saw the bloody smear it left, his heart sank.

I'm going to die here!

Chapter eighty-nine

*A*ndrea felt herself being carried through the streets of Babylon. Her mind played tricks on her, and her vision smeared and distorted the townspeople who scurried about their morning activities. Everything was cloudy, her brain a foggy mess of reality and fantasy. Had she really been nearly devoured by a lion? Had she really been comforted by a compassionate young man named Daniel? Had she really been snatched from King Darius' palace by Jason Hanson the electrician? All of these thought knocked together in her hazy mind like bumper cars. And now what was to become of her? All she wanted to do was sleep...

"We'll get you back home," Jason Hanson said. His winded breath came from above her, and Andrea realized he was cradling her in his large arms. Her muddled thoughts struggled to find coherency.

What home? Infinity...Colorado...Heaven?

"I've been all over looking for you! Some of the things I've seen--incredible! You know the story about Lazarus? The one where Jesus raises him from the dead? Yeah--I saw that!"

Lazarus...Jesus.....

"Come on, now! Stay with me! Stay awake, now! We're gonna get you to a doctor! We just have to find a portal."

Find a portal…a window…find a way back home…

"You wouldn't believe how big Sampson is! Good night is he huge! Come on, Andrea--open your eyes! Stay with me, now! We're gonna get you back to your grandma before you know it"

Grandma Kessler's house is burning down…Grandma's house is burning down…the Stranger…blood….Todd…burning… Jordan sleeping…Grandma Kessler's house is burning down… Devil's Playground…the Opposition…burning…

"I never know how these things work! One minute I'm watching Sampson bust up some people with a donkey's jaw-bone, the next I'm next to a weeping Mary and Martha. I just--Jesus--please give me a portal! Show me the way to get Andrea home!"

Burning…The Stranger…the cabin…closing in…Todd…

Chapter ninety

*T*he cabin seemed to be closing in on Todd. The four walls and ceiling were a prison cell that would encapsulate Todd until his demise, and his window of opportunity to act before it was too late was fading.

I have to think! I have to be the last one standing when this is all said and done! But how?

The Stranger dragged the still gasping Todd into the living room. Todd's scalp burned as the Stranger's vise grip ripped the hair out by the roots. Todd's shoulder and hand were a pulpy, bloody mess; and as the Stranger dragged him into the living room, the scarred and defiled wood floor began to look like a crime scene.

"I've been waiting for this moment since the Opposition died and I was put in command of this mission," the Stranger breathed as he slammed Todd against the living room rug. The assassin let go of Todd's hair and delivered another vicious kick to his stomach. The blow rolled Todd onto his back, and he found himself staring up at the Stranger's looming black figure.

"I don't make mistakes, Todd," the Stranger continued in his deep, robotic voice. "I get the job done." The assassin grabbed Todd by the hair again and yanked him to his feet. Todd screamed in agony and this only made the Stranger tighten his grip. The assassin threw him by his hair onto the sofa, and Todd knocked his knee hard against the sofa's base.

"Get up, child of God! Stand up and fight back!"

The Stranger lunged at Todd and grabbed his surgically repaired shoulder. With one swift motion, the assassin brought Todd's arm down across his knee, and Todd heard the sickening pop before he felt the incredible pain explode in his shoulder and elbow. In one move, the Stranger had undone all the doctors had accomplished on Todd's right arm. Todd screamed as the pain moved like a tidal wave throughout his fractured bones.

"See! You're weak! Just like your Jesus! Come on, brat! Come and get me!"

He's going to kill me if I just stand here!

The Stranger wasted no time. Grabbing Todd's shredded hand, he drew Todd to himself and delivered a devastating knee kick into Todd's stomach. The blow obliterated Todd's wind and sent him sprawling against the couch.

He's going to kill me! I'm dead unless I do something!

Todd sputtered and coughed as the Stranger stood over him and gloated.

"Should I have you flogged? Should I make a thorn crown for your worthless head?"

Think...I have to act...

"Answer me, boy!" The Stranger made a move toward the couch and Todd reacted on instinct. Rolling to his right, Todd thrust his left leg in the Stranger's direction with as much force as he could muster. Todd's kick landed below the assassin's solar plexus, the blow catching the Stranger by surprise. The assassin stumbled backwards, and Todd sprang to his feet.

For the first time Todd had a moment to size up his opponent. The Stranger was surprisingly slight of frame, standing no more than five feet, eight inches tall, probably a full three inches shorter than Todd. Cloaked in black from head to foot, the Stranger was no Opposition, who had relied on brute strength that, at times, had made him clumsy. The Stranger was lithe and agile, more like a ninja to the Opposition's Incredible Hulk. The Stranger's speed would be his strength, and Todd found himself wishing he was facing off against the Opposition instead of the slight-of-frame killer before him.

"I see you found your feistiness," the Stranger said with a snarl. "I like that. It'll be more fun to watch you bleed this way." The Stranger's arm reached back and his combat knife was in the air before Todd could react. All of a sudden, a sharp, searing pain sprouted in Todd's right foot and shot up his calf. When Todd looked down and saw the assassin's angry knife protruding from his shoe, Todd instinctively tried to move his foot away from the blade. His foot wouldn't budge, and another jolt of agony swept up Todd's leg as his brain registered what had just happened. In a flash, the assassin had thrown the knife through Todd's foot and pinned him to his grandmother's cabin floor.

The Stranger was upon him before Todd could react. With one fluid motion, the assassin yanked the knife from Todd's foot, a ribbon of beaded blood trailing the blade, and swept it across the front of Todd's body. The white undershirt Todd was wearing fell away from his chest and shoulders as the assassin laughed in demonic ecstasy. Todd felt the blade's bite on his chest and belly only after the Stranger had stepped back to observe his handy work. Looking down, Todd saw the assassin had carved a crude X into his flesh. The blood was just beginning to run from the new wounds, and Todd felt a wave of nausea sweep over him as the combined forces of the pain inflicted upon his body threatened to overtake him.

"What's the matter, brat? I thought you were playing Jesus. Now you are pierced through your hand and foot like your beloved Christ!" the Stranger's brown eyes were wild and manic. "And I've marked you as my own. You know the saying, X marks the spot!"

He's going to kill you, Todd! You have to do something!

324

But the pain was too great for Todd to do anything. The Stranger had successfully maimed him, and Todd had no ability to fight back, even though everything inside of him screamed for him to do so. The dread sat upon him like a lead blanket. This was it; he would die here, and there was nothing he could do about it. And if he died here, the Stranger would surely take the others as well.

Blood flowed freely from all of Todd's wounds and he felt his strength ebbing away. The Stranger looked on and laughed as he wiped Todd's blood off his knife onto Margaret's armchair.

"You realize it's all over, don't you?" the Stranger taunted. "You lose. You're done. I win."

Todd didn't say anything. He couldn't; he knew what the assassin was saying was true.

Just make it quick...

"We're done messing around," the Stranger said. "It's time to kill you so I can kill the others. You're not worth wasting my energy. I misjudged your resolve. You truly are nothing but a weakling. Just like your Jesus." The Stranger sheathed his menacing knife and wasted no time with inaction. The assassin lunged at the staggering Todd, and the last thing Todd saw was the Stranger's fist about to slam into his temple. After that, everything was full black.

Chapter ninety-one

Margaret wouldn't have been able to sleep even if she had wanted to. The whole situation was too much to process, too much to absorb at once, so that her nerves felt like frayed wires. Across from her, Paul McGurney was deep in prayer, his lips moving silently as he petitioned God from his plush recliner. To her left, Jordan slept on the sofa, his head resting on the cushioned armrest, his foot twitching every once in a while, as happens when one reaches a deep sleep. Margaret sighed and tilted her head back and began to search the ceiling for answers. But that was the problem. Answers were as elusive as the Stranger, and becoming even more elusive with every minute that passed. Three of her grandchildren were gone, two snatched by a crazed assassin and one lost heaven knew where. Margaret knew she couldn't take any more. When she had called her daughter to confirm what Jordan had said about the Stranger's abducting Todd, Donna had been an absolute mess, as any mother would be in the same situation. Margaret had felt her heart being ripped out as she had listened to her daughter sob, and she had tried to placate Donna by telling her everything would be OK. But would it? Would everything *really* be OK? *Could* everything be OK? Margaret didn't know anymore, and she had felt like a liar telling her daughter that all would be fine in the end. What if it wasn't? What if her grandchildren were slaughtered at the hands of the angry assassin? Would faith be enough to pull her through the storms that would surely rage inside of her? Could she actually believe that the same Jesus who had saved her soul by dying a vicious death on the cross would allow her three grandchildren to be murdered by pure evil?

Margaret felt the tears falling down her cheeks.

Why not me? Why did the Stranger have to take my grandbabies? Why couldn't he have taken me?

Margaret heard Paul McGurney stir in the leather chair and she quickly brushed the tears from her eyes. With a sniffle, she looked across to the old man and saw that his blue eyes studied the air above her head.

"How are you holding up, dear one?" Paul McGurney said softly.

Margaret glanced at the sofa where Jordan was peacefully sleeping.

"I'm not. I'm a mess," Margaret answered, feeling the tears come again.

"As I can imagine. You are a grandmother and your love for the children runs deep."

Margaret let a few tears slip down her cheeks. "I just feel guilty, you know? I just wish the Stranger would have taken me instead."

Paul McGurney nodded and folded his hands over his belly. "It is normal to feel guilt when others suffer. Especially when you feel like your hands are tied."

"That's exactly how I feel," Margaret answered. "I feel like I'm sitting here doing nothing while my grandchildren are being--" She couldn't say the last part aloud. Hearing it would somehow make it more real, and Margaret couldn't bear to ingest more reality of this kind.

McGurney nodded. "Yes. I, too, have felt helpless here. It was not yet the season for revelation."

Margaret's ears honed in on one word the old man had spoken. "Was? Did you say it *was* not time for revelation? Do you know something, Mr. McGurney?"

Paul McGurney took a deep breath and exhaled slowly. "I have been praying earnestly for a revelation, some word from the Father that I could impart to you. I believe He has spoken just now."

Margaret leaned forward in the loveseat. "And? What is it?"

McGurney's vacant eyes looked in the direction of the large portal window and then back to Margaret. "Our bridge will be returning shortly. Jason Hanson will arrive back from his journey, and we must be ready for whatever his arrival means."

Margaret's heartbeat accelerated. "What does that mean? I don't know if I like the sound of that."

McGurney shook his head. "That is all I know. Its meaning I cannot decipher."

Margaret ran her fingers through her hair. "I need more. I need a lot more. I sometimes feel as if God is playing a game with us. Like--like I'm supposed to decipher a secret code or something in order to save my grandchildren."

McGurney nodded. "Life itself is a secret code. Its mystery is what keeps us seeking the Lord for His good and perfect will. But rest assured, dear one, that God is not dangling a carrot in front of you. His ways, although good and perfect, cannot be measured by our human minds. We are not made to fully understand the mind of God. We are made to seek His will in order that we might be privy to His mind. I, too, become frustrated at times. I want my needs to be met in the ways I see fit. But my ways are not always God's ways. Many times God has revealed to me that if I had gotten my way in a given situation, it would have led to my ruin. All too often we try to tame the Creator by putting Him in a box of our design. We must remember that God does not fit inside manmade boxes, nor do His ways prove faulty. He is God, and we are not. Is that always easy to digest? Of course not. But I am convinced, just as the apostle Paul was, that nothing can separate us from the love of God. And if God loves us as much as we claim He does, then why do we doubt His motives?"

Margaret nodded and sighed. "I agree, I really do. Sometimes I wish I had more to cling to than Christian rhetoric."

McGurney chuckled. "I know, Margaret. But keep faith. God will be glorified no matter what the outcome. We must wait and see how He decides to move."

"And the first thing we have to do is wait for Hanson to come back through the window," Margaret said, glancing at the portal. "If you'll excuse me, Mr. McGurney, I have some serious praying to do."

The old man chuckled again. "I was just thinking the same thing."

❥❥❥

Margaret had not realized she had drifted to sleep until she heard a commotion coming from the direction of Paul McGurney's portal window. Her eyes snapped open and her pulse spiked as she turned to see what the noise had been.

What's going on?

"Margaret--ma'am--we need to get--" Jason Hanson's voice rang through McGurney's large house.

Margaret nearly wept with joy when she heard the big man's voice. That is until he stepped out of a shadow and Margaret saw whom he was carrying.

This can't be happening! Andrea--is she--?

"Oh--oh, no!"

"What is it, Margaret?" Paul McGurney asked, fumbling with his cane. The old man tried to raise himself from his leather recliner, but failed to muster the necessary strength on his first try.

But Margaret hadn't heard the old man. All her focus was

attached to the lifeless child in Jason Hanson's arms.

Andrea! Oh, Jesus--no!

A million thoughts crashed through Margaret's mind, none of them good. How could she have let this happen? Was Andrea dead? Where had the Stranger taken her?

Jason Hanson hurried across the shotgun-scarred room, and Margaret met him halfway. The big man was panting, his face bright red, with beaded sweat streaming from his brow and cheeks. His eyes were wild with panic, and the moment Margaret reached him, she knew it was bad.

"I'm sorry, Margaret! I got to her as quick as I could!" Hanson said.

Margaret was in total shock as she reached out a hand and touched her granddaughter's arm. Andrea's skin was still warm, but Margaret was horrified to see Andrea's skin turning an ashy gray.

"What--what happened?" Margaret managed. She saw the makeshift tourniquet wrapped around Andrea's leg. It was soaked through with shockingly crimson blood. Andrea's shoulder hung awkwardly from her body, and Margaret could see the girl's left knee was in bad shape as well. Margaret's world spun, McGurney's big house swirling about her as the realization of the situation began to set in.

"Is the child all right?" Paul McGurney asked as he hobbled to Margaret's side.

"She was thrown into a den of lions," Hanson began. Margaret gasped, and McGurney put a steadying hand on her shoulder.

"She was thrown into a den of lions, and the lions--well--you can imagine. She's lost a lot of blood and some of her bones are broken and out of place. I might have made it worse by the way I carried her, but I didn't know what else to do. I knew I had to get her back here as fast as I could."

"You've done well," Paul McGurney said. He turned to the trembling Margaret. "Now, Margaret, listen to me. You must get this child to the emergency room. There is no time to waste. Her life depends on your haste."

Margaret felt herself begin to lose it. The sobs rocked her, and her tremors shook her to the core. Paul McGurney squeezed her shoulder and looked into her eyes with his blue, vacant ones. He spoke in a stern adamancy Margaret had never heard before.

"Margaret, dear one. You need to get this child to a doctor. There is no time to waste."

McGurney's words snapped Margaret into action. She had to get Andrea to an emergency room as fast as possible. From the looks of things, her granddaughter was at the footsteps of Heaven the way it was.

"There's an ER in Divide, but it's small and not equipped to handle this sort of thing," Margaret said, already taking the keys to her Jeep from her pocket. "I'll have to get her to Colorado Springs fast."

Margaret felt a hand on her back, and she turned to see a wide-eyed Jordan staring at his broken cousin.

"Grandma--wh--what?" Jordan stammered.

"I'll explain on the way to the ER," Margaret said. She pointed to the door. "Jason, I'm going to need you to put her in the backseat. Jordan, you get in the back with her and hold her head in your lap. You'll need to call your parents and your Aunt Patty on the way." Margaret looked at Paul McGurney. "Are you coming with us?"

The old man shook his head. "I must stay. There are things to attend to here, I can feel it."

Margaret didn't take the time to analyze the old man's statement. "OK, let's go! Fast!"

And, with that, Margaret, Jordan and Jason Hanson left to take Andrea to the emergency room. As she pulled her Jeep onto the wilderness road, Margaret prayed she wasn't too late.

Chapter ninety-two

*Z*ak was beginning to seriously wonder whether he would ever see the light of day again. The soupy stomach juices he sat in made his arms and legs itch, and the conversation between Zak and Jonah had whittled into silence hours ago. Darkness and dread ruled Zak's existence, and he felt the humidity of the enclosed space pressing in on him.

What if this is it? What if I never get out?

Zak realized that since he and Jonah had been swallowed, his emotions had been strapped into the first car of one really fast and perilous rollercoaster. Deliverance had been the hope in the beginning. God would provide a way out, why wouldn't He? But when God hadn't immediately reached into the belly of the big fish and plucked the two stowaways from the nasty juices, Zak's heart had sunk into depression. Where was He? Why wasn't God saving Him? Wasn't He a God of hope and compassion and unconditional love?

Zak realized he had been down this road of thought before, and immediately dismissed the notion of putting God on trial. It was Zak's fault he was in a whale's stomach, not God's. It was Zak's fault he had foolishly jumped into the ancients without waiting for the appointed time. Zak could not blame God. But Zak could blame Zak.

I wonder how the others are doing? What about Andrea?

Zak's stomach churned at the thought of his sister. A ball bearing lodged in his esophagus as his mind poured through all the vicious and cruel things the Stranger could have done to her. The most chilling thought of all gripped the back of Zak's neck like a cold tentacle.

He might have killed her. He might have taken her to the ancients and finished her off. And I'm here inside a whale, helpless to do anything about it.

And then a more horrific thought exploded in Zak's brain.

What if it's my fault? What if I was supposed to save her, but I jumped the gun and now she's--she's dead? Because of ME!

The humidity slammed against Zak's temples, and his head pulsed with the ache of impending doom. The realization that he could have inadvertently killed his sister was too much for Zak, and he felt his chest rise with the first of a series of explosive sobs.

If she's dead--if it's my fault--I don't want to be the one left living! I would rather die here than have to live without my sister! Zak couldn't contain the sobs that rocked him to his core. He let them out in a groan that reverberated throughout the whale's stomach and back to his ears. When Zak heard his own desperation, something within him snapped. His resolve was broken, his will to live destroyed.

"Zak--what is it? Are you hurt?" Jonah called from the darkness. Zak heard the young man swishing around in the stomach juices, but couldn't answer him because of the sobs that exploded in his chest.

"Zak--answer me!" Jonah said, the concern in his voice mounting.

How could I have been so stupid!? How could I have been so selfish!?

Zak gulped in air to answer Jonah, and when he did, his reply only devastated him further. From deep inside of him came the truth of the situation, and it thundered inside the whale's stomach.

"I killed my sister! I killed my sister!"

Chapter ninety-three

The first thing Todd realized was the searing pain that tore at his upper body. The pain sizzled in criss-cross cuts over his shoulder and exploded down his upper arm. Its electric current pulsed in his left hand and flared and expanded over his chest.

The second thing Todd realized was that he couldn't move his arms or his legs. He felt pinched into himself, as though he were wrapped in bailing wire.

Why can't I move?

The third thing Todd realized was that his head felt about twenty pounds heavier than it should. The back of his skull cannoned in pain in rhythm with his heartbeat, and Todd squinted his eyes in order to allow his surroundings to come into focus.

Where am I? What happened?

"I thought you'd never come to," a robotic voice said. Todd turned his head to the right and saw the man dressed in black sitting on his grandmother's love seat. It all came back in a flash.

The Stranger--I'm in Grandma's cabin--he's going to kill me!

"You looked surprised to see me," the Stranger said, rising to his feet. "I think I hit you a little too hard. You were out longer than I intended. If I were one to apologize, I would tell you I am

sorry. But since I'm not, I'll just say you should have ducked."
The Stranager put his hands on his hips and stood looking down
at Todd from the center of the room.

"There was no way I was going to kill you while you were
under. Not a chance. I want you alive so you can feel everything."

Todd tried to move his legs, but found he couldn't move them
even a milimeter. With horror, he realized for the first time that
he was tied to his grandmother's sofa.

"I wouldn't bother trying to kick and thrash," the Stranger
said, crossing the room. "Those chains are brand new. Your
stupid Grandma uses them to get down the mountain in the
snow." The Stranger extended his gloved hand. "And those
locks--they're the strongest on the market. You won't be going
anywhere without bolt cutters."

Todd raised his head as much as he could and looked down
over his body. He was wrapped in chains from chest to feet,
two heavy-duty padlocks making sure he would not so much as
flinch. Todd felt a lump of fear lodge in his throat.

This is really it, then. I'm going to die here.

"Do you know what the best part of this whole thing is?" the
Stranger asked. "I can see the fear in your eyes. I can smell
death on your skin. You know beyond a shadow of a doubt that
I am going to kill you and there is nothing you or your God can
do about it." The Stranger ruffled Todd's hair as though Todd
was a child.

Todd was surprised to hear himself respond. It took effort
with the pain thundering at the base of his skull. "You might kill
me, but there's no way you're getting away with this."

The Stranger laughed. "How cliché! Really? That's the best
you can do? Come on, Todd. You're supposed to be the big and
bad one. All you can come up with is a cheesy B-movie line?"

Todd swallowed hard and felt the warm blood ooze between
the chain links. His body was cut and torn, his right shoulder

separated and hanging from its socket like detached tree branch. There was no way he would survive the night.

"So this is it?" Todd asked. "You're going to tie me to the couch and, what? Starve me to death? Leave me here for the mice? What's with the long drawn-out death scene? Talk about cliché."

"You're still cocky. I like that. It will make this all the more enjoyable." The Stranger stooped and picked something up from behind the couch's armrest. Todd heard the slosh of liquid against plastic, and when the Stranger returned to the center of the room, Todd smelled the contents of the assassin's red container.

"Lucky for me your grandma had a full tank of gas waiting for me in the garage," the Stranger said. "You don't have to be a rocket scientist to see where this is going from here, Todd." The Stranger stepped back an unscrewed the gas cap. The sharp odor of gasoline filled the room.

"This is your end, you worthless maggot. A fitting end, don't you think? Here you thought your Jesus had saved you from the flames. But guess what, Todd? He's not going to save you from the kind of hell I'm about to bring."

The Stranger turned his back to Todd and walked to the kitchen. Without wasting any more time, the assassin doused his grandmother's scarred cabinets and countertops with gasoline.

"You see, Todd," the Stranger said as he moved into the bedroom Todd, Jordan and Zak had shared the previous summer. "I'm bringing the brimstone. I'm going to give you signs and wonders and billows of smoke." Todd heard the gasoline splashing all over the bedroom's innards. Sweat trickled down Todd's forehead despite the cold temperature of the room. How could this be happening? How could this be the end?

The Stranger stepped out of the bedroom and proceeded to douse the living room with gasoline, leaving a seven-foot arc around Todd dry of the stuff. He moved into Andrea's bedroom and splashed the tiny room with gas. Todd heard the Stranger toss the can aside and walk back into the living room.

"You knew it would end this way, didn't you?" the Stranger said, stepping into the middle of the living room. He pulled a simple book of matches from a pouch in his belt. "You knew all along that I am far superior to you and that idiot Paul McGurney. Deep down, you knew I was going to kill you and your family. It was only a matter of time."

The assassin opened the book of matches and picked out one solitary match.

"And now's the time, Todd. Now's when I win and you lose. When I strike this match, your surroundings will burst into flame. But you won't, not right away. I've left enough space around you free from gasoline so that you can enjoy the show. There will be heat, there will be smoke, and then, you will burn."

"You might kill me but you're only delaying the inevitable. You lose in the end," Todd said evenly. His heart beat on overdrive, but he willed himself to remain calm and composed. If he was going to go out, he would go out with dignity.

The Stranger laughed. "Your words have no effect on me. They come from a worthless speck of nothing that God doesn't see fit to save."

"He already has," Todd said.

The assassin wasn't fazed. "Whatever. It's a good thing my clothes are flame retardant. Unfortunately for you, your flesh is not."

Sweat poured from Todd's brow as he tried to take deep breaths. The heavy chains didn't allow him to suck in the air he so craved. Todd knew he had to come to grips with dying here and now. Barring a miraculous intervention, Todd would perish on his grandmother's couch inside his grandmother's cabin. And what about the others? What would happen to them once Todd was out of the picture? Todd had always felt he could protect them. Even from Infinity, Todd had felt Zak and Jordan relying on him for strength and direction. But now what? What would happen once Todd was gone?

Todd studied the assassin in black and wondered how depressed and self-loathing one had to be to stoop to killing for love of evil. In that moment, Todd felt an immense pity for the Stranger. A wave of sadness washed over Todd as he realized the Stranger had made his decision, as Todd had his, and that the assassin's eternity was stapled to a losing cause. At least when Todd drew his last breath he would awake in Heaven.

Jesus, I love you!

The Stranger moved the match to matchbook's back. With one swift motion, Todd's life would be extinguished. Todd's breath became short staccato bursts of air.

Jesus--I love you! Please, make it quick.

"Remember, Todd," the Stranger said, "my master always wins. This is no exception. Too bad your Jesus is weak. Goodbye, maggot!"

And with that, the Stranger struck the match and threw it into the boys' bedroom behind him. The room was immediately engulfed in flames with a whoosh Todd had only heard in movies. The Stranger's demonic laugh filled the living room as flames shot through the bedroom door and into the kitchen. The fire spread quickly into Andrea's bedroom, and Todd felt the immense heat as the cabin lit up with eerie orange light. The whole cabin was engulfed in a matter of seconds. The only spot not touched by the flame was where the Stranger was standing before Todd.

"Good luck, maggot!" the Stranger yelled over the deafening spread of the flames. And with that, the assassin ran into the kitchen and through the growing flames, escaping into the black night to wreak havoc on the others.

Lamps crashed and glass broke as the flames consumed whatever was in their path. Todd heard the cabinets crackle under the fire's lick, heard the screeching beep of the smoke alarms that warned of danger. Everything was fair game for the flames, and Todd watched as his grandmother's whole life was eaten by the greedy fire.

Todd didn't even try to struggle against his chains. He was bound fast, and he knew thrashing about would be futile. The Stranger had come to kill him, and the assassin would fulfill his mission. Todd closed his eyes and began to pray, not for his own deliverance, but for the deliverance of the others from the hands of evil.

Jesus, please be with them! Rescue them from the clutches of darkness. Let them not weep over my death, but rejoice that I am going to be with You for eternity.

The flames were unbearably hot as they inched closer to the couch. Todd knew that when they did finally reach the sofa they would consume the chair and his body in a matter of seconds, as the sofa's cushioning was highly flammable. But Todd didn't care. The prospect of eternal life with Jesus far outweighed the momentary pains he had endured. The apostle Paul was right; to live is Christ and to die is gain.

The Stranger is wrong. I win because Christ won first.

And with that thought in the forefront of his mind and the flames inching closer to the sofa, Todd closed his eyes and waited for death to bring him new life.

Chapter ninety-four

*T*he Fiends hovered over the car that carried the one called Andrea to the emergency room in Colorado Springs. The girl was very close to death; a slight corruptive breeze could push her over the edge. And that was all the Fiends could hope for.

"There is news out of Divide," a moth-faced Fiend said as he flew quickly to catch up with Horse-face.

"What is it?" Horse-face asked, looking to Mosquito-face, who was trying to whisper words of discord and fear through the car's glass windows.

"I have been sent to tell you that the eldest boy, the one called Todd, has been neutralized," Moth-face said.

"You mean he's dead?" Fly-face asked.

"Yes. The Stranger has set the grandmother's cabin ablaze. The one called Todd is chained to a sofa inside. He is surely dead," Moth-face reported.

Horse-face whooped. "Yes! One down, one lost in the ancients, and one on the brink of death!"

"Now we must work on the one called Jordan," Fly-face said. "He must know the Stranger's pain."

"All in good time," Mosquito-face said, looking through the car window. "He is afraid--petrified. He is holding the girl's head and trying to remain calm. But I can tell he is crumbling on the inside. Just let me work on him a little more. His hope will vanish and the Stranger will win the day."

"Thanks for your report," Horse-face said to Moth-face. "Now, go back to where you came from and report that the girl will be dead in a matter of minutes. There is no way she is going to live through this."

"Yes, sir," Moth-face said, flying off into the wilderness. Horse-face turned to Mosquito-face and Fly-face. "Our work has not been in vain. But we must stay focused. This girl is going to die and we must be there to throw the old woman and the one called Jordan into fits."

"I love causing chaos," Mosquito-face said with a raspy laugh. "It feels great to kick them when they're down."

Chapter ninety-five

*J*ordan snapped his cell phone shut as his grandmother's Jeep took the mountainous roads out of Divide at breakneck speeds. His parents were in complete and utter shock, his mother so numb she couldn't form words and had to hand the phone over to Jordan's father. Aunt Patty was already with Bill and Donna Lawrence at the Lawrence's house, called over as soon as Todd had been abducted by the Stranger. When she had heard the extent of her daughter's injuries, she had let out the most haunting groan Jordan had ever heard. The adults were powerless in Ohio. They could do nothing but wait for their flight to Colorado. Jordan couldn't begin to imagine what they must be thinking and feeling right about now, because he knew what *he* was thinking and feeling as he held his cousin's head in his lap in the back seat of his grandmother's Jeep.

She's not going to make it to the hospital. She's going to die right here in my arms.

"How's she doing?" Jason Hanson asked from the passenger seat.

Jordan looked up at him through weary eyes. "Her breathing has slowed way down. It feels like--like she's slipping away."

Margaret gasped from the driver's seat and punched the accelerator. The roads were still slick from the recent snow storm, but Jordan knew now was not the time to be playing it safe. They had to get to the hospital faster than humanly possible in order to save Andrea.

"How long until we're there?" Jordan asked as nothing but rockface on both sides of the car zoomed by.

"Twelve miles," Margaret said. "Can she hold on for twelve more miles?"

You're asking me? What do I know? I want to say yes, but her breathing is so irregular, and she's lost so much blood...

"She's going to have to," Jordan said. "Can you go any faster?"

"These roads are too curvy to go above sixty," Margaret said. She hit the steering wheel with the heels of her palms. "That Stranger! If I ever get my hands on him I'll--"

"Keep talking to her," Hanson said. "She needs to know we're here."

Jordan looked down at his torn and broken cousin. His breath caught in his throat as he tried to push all the terrible thoughts and images of what could be out of his mind. He willed himself to remain composed. Instead of crying, he would pray for her.

"Jason, turn around in your seat."

"What?"

"Just turn around enough so that you can touch Andrea's shoulder. We're going to pray for her. We are going to lay hands on her and petition God for His healing touch with a full expectation that He will come through." Jordan didn't know where his words were coming from, but they continued to spill from his mouth. He closed his eyes, and touched Andrea's forehead.

"Father, we come to You right now not knowing what to say or how to pray for Andrea. The Bible says that when we don't have words, the Spirit intercedes with groans on our behalf. Jesus--we are groaning. We need You to work miracles. We need You to send Your healing down and touch Andrea right now in a mighty way. Lord, we've felt You move before, and we need You to do it again. We love Andrea. It is hard for us to understand that You love her more, but You do. You knitted her together in her mother's womb, and she is fearfully and wonderfully made in Your image. She is Your creation and Your Spirit resides in her heart. Please, Jesus, heal her. Touch her and make her whole. Don't let her slip away, but bring her back to the land of the living…"

Jordan prayed for Andrea in such a way until his grandmother's Jeep screeched into the emergency room's parking lot. He didn't know where the words were coming from, but it didn't matter. The Spirit was interceding, and Andrea's life was in His hands.

Chapter ninety-six

*T*he Stranger is on the move. There is no time to revel in such a massive victory; an assassin shouldn't waste time gloating and basking in a kill. But destroying the varmint Todd is a huge victory, one the master will commend the Stranger for. As the assassin quick-steps through the Colorado wilderness, the implication of Todd's death sinks in. The boy is the leader of the bratty children, the glue that holds them together. When he went up in flames, so did the ties that bound the children together. They will now crumble one by one. Even the old bag and McGurney will be brought down a peg by the nasty edge of the assassin's vicious knife. Things couldn't be going any better.

The Stranger knows the forest surrounding the old woman's cabin will most likely burn. When the propane tank on the west side of the garage blows, so goes the thick brush ten feet from it. Before it's all said and done, a massive forest fire will wreak havoc on the mountainside, all because that worthless brat stuck his nose where it didn't belong.

The Stranger laughs out loud. Let it burn. Let it all burn. The children must know who wins in the end. They must see the master's wrath can equal that of the children's God. The master might not be compassionate, but he most surely rains destruction upon all his detractors.

The Stranger has reached the fork in the road leading to the wretched Paul McGurnrey's house. Fresh tire tracks run over the light snow still sticking to the earth. The assassin looks to the road leading down the mountain. The old woman apparently up and left for some reason without even stopping at her cabin. The Stranger knows something big has happened but can't begin to guess what.

The assassin looks down the road leading to McGurney's house and then to the road leading down the mountain. Now it is decision time. Should the assassin follow the woman's tire tracks and ambush her on her way back up the mountain? Or should the Stranger continue to Paul McGurney's house and eliminate whoever decided to stay behind?

The Stranger doesn't pause to ponder long. The assassin knows the old woman would never let the ones called Zak and Jordan out of her sight. Not after the Stranger has stolen two of her beloved brats from right under her nose. No--if the woman took the two remaining maggots down the mountain, that could only mean Paul McGurney is in the mansion alone...

The Stranger takes off on a dead sprint down the road leading to McGurney's house. The assassin's veins course with renewed adrenaline at the prospect of another high-profile kill.

Two noteworthy kills in the same hour. The master will be pleased.

Chapter ninety-seven

Margaret slammed the Jeep's door and began running to emergency room's glass doors.

"Carry her in, Jason! I'm going to tell them we're here!" she called as the automatic doors parted and she bustled into the emergency room's lobby. The sterile smell of hospital immediately assaulted Margaret's nostrils, and for a moment her mind flashed to when her husband had slipped away quietly in his sleep after a long battle with pneumonia inside a hospital room that smelled just like this. Margaret pushed the thought from her mind. There was no time to mourn the dead; she had her granddaughter's life to save.

Margaret ran to the oval receptionist's desk, breathless and fearful that she was taking too long in getting Andrea help. Behind her, the glass doors opened and Jason Hanson came in carrying Andrea, Jordan trailing him looking pale and uncertain.

"Do you have an emergency?" the sharp-nosed, thin-boned receptionist asked.

"Why else would I be here?" Margaret snapped. Realizing her tone was uncalled for and that calm needed to rule the situation, she put her palms up. "Look, I'm sorry for biting your head off. But I have a grandaughter's who's--"

The receptionist's eyes flashed to Jason Hanson coming up

behind Margaret. They widened when she saw the lifeless girl in his arms.

"Please--hurry!" Jordan pleaded with the receptionist.

"OK--OK--everything's going to be OK. I'm paging for a gurney right now," the receptionist pushed a button and looked up again. "What happened to her, ma'am?"

Margaret and Jason exchanged glances.

They are never going to believe me! But--it's the truth.

Jason Hanson answered before Margaret. "She took a tumble into--into a lion's den."

The receptionist's eyes went saucer-wide. "She fell into a mountain lion's den?"

Hanson looked at Margaret and continued. "Something like that. Anyway, the lions did a number on her leg here. She's lost a lot of blood, and she has a few broken and separated bones. She's been--been slipping away. Please--where's the doctor? We need to hurry!"

Just then an orderly bustled into the lobby with a gurney.

"This the girl?" the stocky orderly asked.

"Yes! Please--she's dying!" Margaret shouted.

"She's in good hands, here," the orderly said, nodding to Hanson. "If you'll please put her on the gurney, we'll get to work."

"Mountain lion bites and broken bones," the receptionist said to the orderly.

"She was attacked by a mountain lion?" the orderly asked as Hanson laid Andrea on the gurney.

"Something like that," Hanson mumbled.

"OK, follow me," the orderly said as he began to wheel Andrea toward a set of double doors. Margaret made to follow, but the receptionist stood from her desk and touched Margaret's shoulder.

"Uh--ma'am. If you would, please, read through these and fill in the necessary blanks." She handed Margaret a clipboard with a small mound of assorted-colored paper clipped to it.

"But my granddaughter--" Margaret began to protest.

"It will only take a minute. Please, ma'am, have a seat," the receptionist said, pointing to a chair sitting before a coffee table littered with tattered and outdated magazines.

"Andrea doesn't have a minute!" Margaret said as she stomped to the chair.

Jesus--please help her to hold on!

Chapter ninety-eight

*T*he Stranger sprints up the hill leading to Paul McGurney's house, lusting for more blood on an already perfect night. The assassin has already seen that the old woman's Jeep is indeed gone. If Paul McGurney is inside his mansion, he is alone.

As the Stranger reaches the top of the hill, the assassin realizes that with this kill, the children are finished. After the Stranger kills McGurney, the old mansion will be torched so the old grandma and Zak and Jordan cannot find sanctuary here. The old woman's cabin is burning to the ground right now, and the children and the old woman will have no fortress to run to.

But they won't know that.

They will drive back up the mountain and find their two compounds destroyed, and the assassin will pick them off quickly and easily. The Plan is almost finished. The master is close to ultimate victory.

The Stranger is up the hill and onto the dilapidated porch. Only a novice assassin would get tripped up by the loose boards and gaping holes, and the Stranger is no novice. With two large steps, the Stranger reaches the mahogany door. There will be no knocking. The Stranger has come to murder. Unsheathing the vicious knife, the Stranger kicks the door with a heavy combat *boot. The lock immediately falls away and the door swings into the mansion.*

The Stranger steps into Paul McGurney's home and takes in the destroyed floor and other reminders of the battle the battle that was fought here. The Stranger isn't concerned with the past. Whatever happened before doesn't matter. This will be the last battle, and the assassin will be the victor.

"Where are you, old man?" the Stranger shouts into the big house. Dim light casts round shadows on the walls. At the back of the big room, a fire in the fireplace makes some of the shadows dance.

"Where are you, you old kook?" the Stranger shouts again, kicking over the suit of armor to the right of the door. "I'm back! Come out, you weakling!"

The Stranger sees movement from the back of the large room, and the assassin's eyes dart to the seating area.

"So, you've come back, I see," Paul McGurney says, standing from his big leather chair.

"You can't see anything, you worthless rat! Your God didn't see fit to give you something as simple as sight! How kind of Him!"

"I don't need sight to see evil," Paul McGurney says calmly.

The assassin wastes no time in crossing the room. The Stranger is to the sitting area in a matter of seconds. All that separates the assassin from the old man is fifteen feet and a leather couch.

"Where are the others?" the Stranger growls.

"They are not your concern," Paul McGurney says evenly.

The Stranger laughs. "You and I both know they are."

"I am alone here," McGurney says, reaching for his cane.

The Stranger's eyes flash to the old man's age-spotted hand as it grasps the cane's head.

"You being alone makes it easier for me to kill you. No cane will save you, old man."

"Weapons do not save," McGurney says.

"Stop with the Jesus rhetoric," the Stranger snarls. "The oldest brat tried the same thing. And then I killed him."

An explosion sounds in the distance, a thundering boom that can only mean one thing. The old woman's propane tank has exploded and the cabin has been obliterated, burnt to the ground in a glorious inferno. Paul McGurney flinches, and the assassin is invigorated by the old man's painful comprehension.

"What have you done?" Paul McGurney asks. The old man's blue eyes water over as they search the air above the Stranger's head.

"Let's just say it got too hot for Todd to handle." The Stranger plunges the knife into the back of the leather couch. "I killed him, old man! The brat burned alive in the old woman's cabin! What you just heard was the grand finale."

"You are a monster," McGurney says, his jaw clenching.

The Stranger laughs. "No, you fool. You and your little fan club of Jesus fanatics are the monsters! You spout rhetoric about righteousness and loving one another and giving to the poor, but look around, old man! If half of you Christians--no--if one-third of you Christians-- practiced even a marginal portion of what you preach, then my master wouldn't stand a chance! But you all are the same! You go to your churches on Sundays and tear each other down on weekdays! You are all hypocrites! Every last one of you! At least I know where I stand! At least I am true to my cause!"

The old man swallows, a tear falling down his aged cheek.

"My tears are as much for you, Stranger, as they are for the child you've just killed," Paul McGurney says. "You are blinded by your perceptions of Who Christ is. It will ultimately lead to your doom."

The Stranger rips the knife from the back of the couch.

"Enough of this! I've come to fulfill my master's purpose, not to debate theology! I've killed Todd, I've sent Andrea to certain death and now you will be next!"

The old man looks at the ground for a moment and then back to the Stranger. McGurney's blue eyes are a placid lake, his face set in resolve. If the Stranger didn't know better, it is almost as if the old man is welcoming death.

"Do what you came here for," McGurney says in a whisper.

The Stranger wastes no time. With a roar of victory, the assassin leaps the couch and raises the knife.

The old man never attempts to move.

Chapter ninety-nine

*J*ordan sat with his grandmother and Jason Hanson in a too-white waiting room. A television was mounted high in the corner of the wall, *The Weather Channel* rehashing the day's highs and lows on a low volume setting. Hanson nibbled at his fingernails and nervously flipped through a two-month-old *Sports Illustrated* while Margaret's knee bounced up and down in a rapid cadence that made Jordan all the more antsy.

What is going on in there? Is she OK?

The doctors had rushed Andrea into emergency surgery after unraveling the makeshift tourniquet wrapped around her leg and finding shredded muscle and torn ligaments. But Andrea's leg and broken bones were the least of the doctor's worries. What the doctors were most worried about was the amazing amount of blood she had lost. Not only was Andrea severely dehydrated, but Hanson had recounted to the doctors Daniel's story of the puddles of blood Andrea had lost in the lion's den. The urgency of the situation intensified immediately. As the orderlies had wheeled her back into surgery, Jordan had thought Andrea looked like nothing more than a shell, a husk of a person who was knocking hard on death's door.

I can't take the waiting...

Margaret stopped the rapid bouncing of her knee and spoke the first words in over an hour.

"Jason, honey. It's four thirty in the morning. Do you need to call anyone to let them know you're here?"

Hanson closed his magazine and tossed it back onto a chipped coffee table.

"I'm not married, and tomorrow's my day off. Nobody's gonna miss me if I stay here."

"You know you don't have to be here if you don't want to," Margaret said. "You really just met us and--"

Hanson held up a big palm. "I want to be here, Ms. Kessler. We might not have known each other very long, but--but I feel like I'm part of this whole--*thing*--whatever it is."

"Well, just know Jordan and I are forever grateful to you for going to the ancients and bringing Andrea back," Margaret said, looking to the double doors that led to the operating room. Jordan felt a lump form in his throat. His grandmother's apprehension only made his worse.

"I just wish I could have gotten there sooner," Hanson said, more to himself than to Jordan's grandmother.

The waiting room fell silent as Jordan watched a nurse bustle by, her white sneakers lightly padding the shiny white floor.

How could anyone work in such a place of pain and uncertainty?

"When this is all over, I am moving to Infinity," Margaret said after a time. "I don't think I'll ever be able to view Colorado the same after--after all this."

"It will all be OK, Ms. Kessler. Andrea will pull through. She seems like a fighter," Hanson said, reaching a big arm around Margaret's shoulder.

Margaret chuckled sadly. "Yeah, she's got spunk. She's always been the feisty one."

Jordan couldn't argue with that. Andrea was rough and tumble, a tomboy athlete who loved competition and didn't mind a little pain.

"Let's hope she'll rely on her feistiness," Margaret said.

All of a sudden, the double doors opened and a tall, fifty-something doctor walked out. He was still in his scrubs, his sharp, tanned facial features and silver hair striking against the oppressive white of the waiting room. But when Jordan saw the man's dark eyes, he knew something was wrong.

His eyes are sad...his eyes are looking everywhere but at us.

Margaret rushed from her seat and intercepted the doctor before he could reach the middle of the room. Jordan trailed behind, knowing full well that when he reached the doctor the man would impart some awful truth that would forever change Jordan's life. Jordan felt Hanson's hand on his shoulder as he caught up to his grandmother.

"How is she?" Margaret asked, breathless. "How is Andrea?"

The doctor looked to Margaret and then to Jordan, his eyes heavy with an unnamed burden.

"Ms. Kessler--let's sit," the doctor said, pointing to the waiting room chairs.

Margaret waved him off.

"I don't want to sit, doctor! I want to know if my granddaughter is going to be OK!"

The doctor licked his thin lips, and Jordan's stomach hit the floor. The room began to spin, his insides roiling.

"Ms. Kessler, I'm afraid I have some bad news," the doctor said, swallowing.

"What! What is it! Tell me already!" Margaret shouted, gripping the doctor's shoulders. But Jordan saw in his grandmother's eyes that she already knew. Whatever the doctor said next would only confirm what she knew in her heart.

The doctor inhaled and exhaled. "Ms. Kessler--I'm afraid we've lost her."

And with those seven words, Jordan's life was forever changed.

Author Acknowledgments

There are so many people who have helped shape and form *The McGurney Chronicles*. You all have been instrumental in bringing the story to life. I'd like to first thank the Knowledge Who never lets go, even in the direst of circumstances. This book is for You and for Your glory. To my beautiful wife, Cindy: I love you more each day. I'm so blessed to love you, and even more blessed that you love me back. You are amazing beyond words. I love you so much! To Mary Mueller: your friendship and mentorship mean the world to me. You have made me a better writer, and I am blessed to call you a friend. To Will Riley Hinton and the rest of my writer's group: you all have had a huge impact on my life and on this manuscript. You guys rock, thanks! To Pastor Kent Norr: thanks for allowing me to use your sermon notes for a pivotal chapter of this book. I can't imagine the story without them. You are a blessing to my family. Thanks. To Skip Coryell: you gave me a shot and I cannot thank you enough. You are a great man, father and friend. I can't wait to read the next Coryell creation. To my friends and family: you all are inspirations. Thanks for loving me, and thanks for praying for me and believing in me. I love you all. Finally, to my students: you are the reason I write. May you hear the Voice in these books.

Josh Clark is an English teacher in Ohio. He enjoys writing for young adult readers, and is currently working on his next project.

Visit www.authorjoshclark.com for more about Josh and his current and future works.

Be Sure to Watch for...

The McGurney Chronicles:

Book V:

Ten Thousand Strong

Coming Soon!

Turn the page for a
special sneak preview!

Chapter One

Jordan was too numb to cry. The sterile waiting room seemed to choke him, the cords on the grim-faced doctor's surgical mask, now hanging tired against the sharp-eyed physician's stubbly neck, seemed to reach out to him like demonic, smirking worms.

We got her! They seemed to gloat. *We got her, and you're next!*

Jordan tried to swallow but found his throat clamped shut, a wad of unspeakable agony closing off his esophagus.

"Son? Do you need to sit down?"

Jordan felt a large hand on his shoulder, but he didn't know if it was Jason Hanson's or the doctor's. And he didn't care. His cousin was dead. His cousin, once a vivacious, spunky go-getter with big brown eyes and a smile that could make even the dimmest room brighten, was now covered by a cold hospital sheet in a cold operating room. Andrea Reynolds would never smile again.

"Jordan? Why don't we sit down."

Another hand gently rested on the back of his neck, and this time Jordan was sure it was Jason Hanson's. The doctor's hand wouldn't be dry and calloused from hours of manipulating wires and gripping and squeezing the tools of an electrician's trade.

"Let's go sit down," Hanson repeated. Jordan heard his grandmother suck in a mouthful of air as a sob rocked her wiry body.

Jordan allowed himself to be led to the cluster of too-uniform hospital chairs. As he sat down he wondered how much tragedy their cushions had soaked up, how many tears had stained their cappuccino-colored upholstery. His own eyes were filmed with tears, and when he looked up through them he saw the tall doctor's bleary figure standing over him.

"I'm sorry, son. Was she you sister?"

Jordan clenched his eyes shut and tried to snap back to reality. The heavy tears that had pooled inside his lids now spilled down his cheeks in thick globules.

She wasn't my sister by blood, but she was my sister by Blood.

Jordan's throat finally allowed him to swallow, and when he answered the doctor his voice sounded miles away.

"Something like that."

My sister in Christ.

The doctor looked puzzled for a moment, but then raised his thin lips into a sympathetic smile. Jordan briefly wondered if the physician had really read between the lines of his statement or had decided not to bother a grieving relative with another question.

"Are--are you sure, doctor?" Margaret Kessler asked through her sobs.

Jordan saw a muscle in the doctor's jaw line twitch. The man swallowed and nodded, his lips forming a tight line.

"I'm afraid so, ma'am. She lost so much blood. It was a miracle she even lived to make it to the emergency room."

Jordan's head buzzed with the doctor's words. This wasn't supposed to be happening. Andrea wasn't supposed to be dead. This was all a bad dream he would snap awake from. It was too horrible to be real.

But it is real. All of it.

Jordan took a deep breath. He felt Jason Hanson's big hand on his back and he was glad for it.

"When can we see her?" Margaret asked, struggling to reign in her frayed emotions.

The doctor nodded and smiled a half smile. "You can see her in a bit. Allow us ten minutes or so to prepare her body. I'll come get you when we're through."

Prepare her body...she's not Andrea anymore. She's a body.

The doctor turned and walked back through a set of double doors. Jordan felt the tears coming again, and as Jason Hanson's big hand stroked his back, he allowed them to overtake him.

Why, God? Why not me? Why Andrea?

𐅫 𐅫 𐅫

The movers and shakers of hell itself sat around the massive oak table in the war room, although a more fitting name for the dismal concrete enclosure was war *bunker*. The darkness in the cramped space seemed to breathe, and the walls crawled with repulsive insects and gnarled vines and putrid plant life.

The highest-ranking Fiends sat rigid and silent as the Master outlined the next phase in the plan. Cloaked in a sulfurous black cloud, the Prince of Darkness assessed his conglomerate of demons with his smoldering eyes. Every Fiend at the table knew those eyes and their ability to instill fear with a mere glance. Now, they searched the faces of the officials, and each Fiend felt the chill of the valley of the shadow of death creep over them.

"One child is dead," the Master seethed. "The girl has been eliminated. Though she herself is saved by the Knowledge, she no longer pollutes the world with the stench of her message."

The gathered Fiend officials didn't know whether to applaud or let the Master continue speaking. They all knew that one false move could sentence them to the dungeons. The Prince of Darkness had executed such a sentence for far less.

"I have also received a report that the oldest boy, Todd, has been killed at the hands of our assassin whose identity is known only to me."

At this, celebratory murmurs broke out. Killing the girl called Andrea was one thing, but taking out Todd was another. The eldest of the young adult Knowledge-bearers, Todd was their leader and strategist. With him out of the picture and Andrea eliminated, only two of the Redeemed remained.

The Master continued to pace the room, the asphyxiating cloud hovering with his every step.

"The one called Zak is currently in the belly of a large fish somewhere in the ancients. If he meets his demise, only one Knowledge-bearer remains."

A worm-faced general had the incredible nerve to ask Lucifer a question.

"And what of the old woman? And that blasted time-traveler, Paul McGurney?"

The Master stopped dead in his tracks. For a moment the Fiend officials thought the general who had asked the question would be vaporized where he sat. Instead, the Master only exhaled.

"The old woman is with the one called Jordan. They are mourning the loss of the girl. The fat Jason Hanson--the newest convert to the Knowledge--is with them. All efforts must be made to kill these three immediately."

The Master chuckled, a guttural sound that sent shivers to the Fiend officials.

"As for Paul McGurney…"

Made in the USA
Charleston, SC
02 December 2011